How to Destroy your Husband

By Jess Kitching

KINGSLEY
PUBLISHERS

First published in South Africa by Kingsley Publishers, 2022
Copyright © Jess Kitching, 2022

The right of Jess Kitching to be identified as author of
this work has been asserted.

Kingsley Publishers
Pretoria, South Africa
www.kingsleypublishers.com

A catalogue copy of this book will be available from the
National Library of South Africa
Paperback ISBN: 978-0-6397-0362-6
eBook ISBN: 978-0-6397-0363-3

Also by Jess Kitching

The Girl She Was Before

For Poppy –

Writing books is amazing but getting to be your auntie is even better. Just maybe wait until you're a little older to read this one…

The *End*

The clock over his shoulder tells me it's ten to three.

Ten to three, a time that used to be as inconsequential to me as any other but now could be the time of my death.

A bubble of laughter builds in me at the absurdity of the sudden importance of this moment. It fights to break free, but the way Jamie's hand crushes my windpipe tells me no sound will escape my lips even if I try allowing it to pass.

Who would have thought we would end up here? Here, on the day of our wedding, with the most beautiful dress I'll ever own now crumpled beyond recognition.

Here, with Jamie's hands around my throat, my life in his hands. This man I loved, now a stranger, and not just because of the murderous intent in his eyes.

How did it get to this?

How did we get to this?

For that there is only one answer.

The First *Beginning*

I first stopped believing in love five years ago thanks to yet another bad breakup, only this one wasn't mine. Over a Chinese takeaway one Saturday night, my best friend Lily wasn't presented with the engagement ring she'd been expecting, but instead received a bumbling apology from her teenage sweetheart Andy as he left her to 'discover' himself in Thailand.

Dumped, after everything, just like that.

Andy didn't even have the decency to clear his stuff out of the apartment they'd shared for the last two years. It would have been 'too painful', apparently. Instead, he asked Lily to box everything up and send it to his mum's house, a task he didn't stop to think might be 'too painful' for her as well.

After smashing his aftershave collection into a million indecipherable pieces and burning his beloved pit-stained football shirts, Lily called us from the foetal position on her bedroom floor. Half an hour later and armed with multiple bottles of cheap white wine, my best friends and I were sat beside her.

Obviously, the news shocked Lily the most, but Alisha, Laney and I were a close second. We'd known Andy since we were awkward year sevens battling acne and clueless about who we wanted to be when we grew up. Andy was our friend. He bought the first round of drinks on a night out and showed us flowers weren't only gifted when coinciding with an apology. He provided advice better than an agony aunt ever could. He was, in short, our idea of a good man, and one half of the only 'real' couple we knew. The kind of couple who hosted dinner parties and had matching kitchenware. The kind of couple you looked at and thought, 'Oh, so *that's* what all the films and songs are about'.

But when Andy turned out to be the villain of the story and not the romantic lead, it dawned on us that everything we thought we knew about love was, in fact, wrong.

"Eight years of my life I gave him!" Lily ugly cried, snot dripping from her upper lip. "I even went to the same university as him because he said he couldn't stand to be apart from me. Can't stand to be apart from me, huh? Thailand isn't exactly around the corner!"

"He's an idiot. They all are," Alisha sighed. With D-cup breasts, a bum that practically invented the peach emoji and an award-winning PR firm she built from scratch, Alisha was who most girls dreamed of being when they grew up.

However, according to the men she dated, she was also a vain, ruthless bitch… but only once they realised she earned triple what they did.

"Do you know what Andy said to me? He said he doesn't fancy me anymore. He said I don't make enough effort, but it's hard to want to dress up when the person you're with jabs your stomach and asks when you're due!" Lily pinched the roll of flesh above the waistband of her pyjamas to emphasise her point.

Despite being beautiful both inside and out, Lily was forever following the latest celebrity endorsed diet regime to try shrink herself to twiglike proportions. She had a smile that lit up a room and hair the exact shade of blonde many spent hundreds trying to emulate, but whenever Lily looked in the mirror, all she saw were flaws. The fact that Andy used her body image issues against her in their breakup poured lighter fuel on the already raging fire inside us all.

"He seriously said that? He was hardly Mr Perfect himself!" Laney cried.

"I know, but he was perfect to me," Lily said, then she threw her head back to release a gut-wrenching wail.

Alarm flickered across Laney's face. She opened her mouth to speak but with a subtle shake of the head, Alisha silenced her. In that silence, Lily cried. She cried with a rawness none of us could bear or imagine.

The three of us exchanged helpless looks over the top of Lily's head as it became glaringly obvious how out of our depth we were. This was a real, serious, grown-up heartbreak, the kind that defined a portion of someone's life. How could we help with that? Laney was going out every weekend as if she was still a student, Alisha was on a dating ban so she could focus on growing her business, and I was three months into dating a man I only heard from when he had no one else to hang out with. Never in the history of the world had there been a group of people so ill-prepared to fix the sudden disappearance of a lifetime of plans and the breaking of years' worth of promises.

Four glasses of wine in and Lily's tears were no longer cascading waterfalls, but sad, singular drops trailing miserably down her cheeks. "I just don't get it. Where did it all go wrong? What did I do to deserve this?"

"You did nothing," I soothed, but Lily shook her head.

"I give up! You can do anything and everything for them, be anything and everything they say they want, and it's still not enough. Do you know how many of Andy's socks I must have picked up off the floor during our relationship? Hundreds! I was like his personal cleaner, and he still left me."

"Andy didn't know how lucky he had it. In fact, they rarely ever do," Laney said, picking at her chipped black nail polish. "I mean, how many times do you hear about middle-aged men leaving their wives for someone younger because their wife doesn't look like she did when she was twenty-one? It's like women aren't allowed to age. Push out the children, remember the birthdays, book the appointments, sure! But get a few wrinkles or find a grey hair? No way!"

"Exactly!" Lily hiccupped. "The standards are too high. They're impossible to meet! You're supposed to have the body of a supermodel but still order a takeaway on a Friday night."

"And you've got to be edgy enough to stand out in a crowd, but not so edgy that their friends think you're weird," Laney added, rolling her heavily eyelinered eyes. "If one more person says to me, 'you're great, but you're just so... different' like it's a bad thing, I might scream."

"Don't forget money. You can't earn more than them because that's emasculating, but if you earn too little, you're not someone they can see a future with. You know, because someone who can't pay for half the meal isn't 'wife material'." Alisha air quoted the phrase with a bitter sigh.

"Wife material," I scoffed. "What even is that? Florals on one side to show their mother, leather bondage on the reverse?"

Laney and Alisha tittered, but Lily was too upset to even raise a smile. "See? It's hopeless!"

At this, Alisha put her arm around Lily's shoulders. "Lil, it's going to be okay! I know it doesn't feel like it now, but it will be. We've been through this before and we'll go through it again but one day, when it's our wedding day, we will look back and laugh. You'll have the man of your dreams, a man who thinks Thailand is overrated and knows where the clitoris is, and Andy will just be the name of someone you think you know but can't remember where from."

Lily's blue eyes glittered with hope. "You promise?"

"I promise. We all do, don't we?"

"Of course," Laney agreed, but my words stayed lodged in my throat, not budging even when Alisha raised her eyebrows to prompt me to nod along.

In that moment, I felt my spirit leave my body. It floated above the tragic scene, looking down at the four of us sat in an exhausted heap on the floor, wine soaking into the carpet and spinning ourselves a make-believe story with the same yarn we were gifted as little girls. 'One day your prince will come, but until then you're going to have to put up with peasants with commitment issues and a minor binge drinking problem'...

it was bullshit!

I couldn't shake the feeling that we were doing Lily a huge disservice. Her future had been torn from her in the most brutal way, yet there we were, feeding her vague lines about being fixed by someone she'd yet to meet. We were bad friends for sending that message, even though every rom-com we'd ever watched had trained us to respond to a breakup in such a way.

In fact, when I thought about it, we'd been trained to respond to every part of a courtship-to-relationship timeline like that. Spewing half-baked sentiments about fate and soulmates as if they excused the appalling treatment we'd endure on the path to finding 'The One'.

I found myself wondering how many nights we had wasted over the years worrying if a man who played video games as frequently as a teenager loved us.

How many conversations had we had trying to decipher the meaning behind cryptic texts from our latest romantic prospect? Ones that were vague enough to keep us as someone they were 'seeing' but not harsh enough to make us realise we deserved better.

How many tears had we wiped from our eyes because of men who cringed at the mention of a period but expected us to smile after a cum shot to the chin?

I didn't need a calculator to work out the answer was too many.

As soon as this realisation hit, something inside me changed. I was never going to be the heartbroken girl again. My self-worth was never going to be pushed to the side so I could have someone to cuddle up to at night. I wouldn't suppress my annoyance when plans were cancelled at the last minute in favour of going to the pub with moronic mates. Never again would I pretend a supermarket bought gift voucher purchased on the way home from work was a good enough birthday present from a romantic partner. Forget *that*. That Cassie was dead.

Like a caged animal, I waited for the next one to come along and try it, just try it.

I didn't give up on dating altogether. I was open to the idea of meeting someone – I just expected my opponent to match my energy.

I played my part like society told me I was meant to. My stray hairs were torn out with wax strips and I spent too much money on skincare products that promised to make me beautiful. I stayed up late flirting on various dating apps and worrying if the photos I used on my profile gave the 'right' impression, but still I was repeatedly reminded of the truth Andy had shown us – love was a myth, one we were stupid for believing in.

I flitted from bad date to bad date, a merry-go-round of terrible experiences I wouldn't wish on my worst enemy, until eventually, spirit sucked dry, I snapped.

"I give up!" I declared one night over pizzas at Lily's. "I have a new rule – one date, one chance. If it's not flowing, then it's not happening. There shall be no second chances for 'it was alright' nights or mediocre conversation from me anymore."

"Good for you," Alisha agreed. "There's so much more to life than chasing romance, anyway."

"Spoken like a true career woman," Lily laughed. "Dating is meant to be fun! Don't take it so seriously."

"I'm with Lily on this one. Besides, don't you think the whole 'one chance' part is a bit harsh? I mean, what if they're having a bad day when you meet?" Laney replied through a mouthful of pepperoni.

"Laney, your last date was with someone who told you they'd been wearing the same t-shirt for the last three days, and you still met them again. If anything, I think we're not harsh enough."

The debate about my new standard continued all night, but the more dates I went on, the more evidence I had to prove the standard was wise to keep.

I mean, why would I want to spend another evening with Imran who listed what he believed to be his ex's physical flaws within the first hour we met? Or Peter who was vocal about the fact that he expected whichever lucky lady he married to give up work and take care of their children, no discussion on the matter? Or Hudson who was open to the point of being proud that he'd cheated on every girlfriend he'd ever had?

My conversations online weren't much better than the ones I had in person. I lost count of the amount of abuse I received on dating apps when I said I wasn't interested, never quite understanding how I could go from *'hey gorgeous'* in one message to *'you're an ugly bitch anyway'* in the next.

The longer my single status went on for, the more people seemed to think they had a right to comment on it, as if my lack of a romantic partner meant there was a fundamental flaw with my life.

My mum fretted with every friend she had that my dad passing away when I was five had scarred me for life. She never once stopped to think being alone was a choice I was happy with, one that didn't stem from the childhood trauma of watching her cry herself to sleep in an empty double bed for months on end.

Every aged relative mentioned my biological clock until it became a ticking timebomb narrating the 'lonely girl' label those relatives placed on me. It didn't matter that I wasn't emotionally or financially ready for children, or that I wasn't lonely. I was in my late twenties, single and childfree, therefore pity oozed from them every time we met. It was almost surreal, feeling whole but being questioned as if I wasn't.

"When are you going to settle down?"

"Have you met The One yet?"

"Well, you'd better get a move on... time's ticking for a woman your age!"

Everywhere I looked, all I saw were signs shouting that happiness meant being on the arm of someone else. The way you could buy hundreds of cards congratulating someone on their engagement, wedding, or pregnancy, but only a few lacklustre designs were available for celebrating a promotion or individual success. Cinema tickets were cheaper... if you came with another person. It was outrageous, but no one else seemed angry about it but me.

The more I looked at the world through this lens, the more cynical I became.

I watched as Alisha met Simon. Simon who wore retro cardigans because he misguidedly thought he could pull the look off. Simon who read TripAdvisor reviews like they were passages from The Bible. Simon who was punching not one or two leagues above his own but who was with a woman from a totally different sport.

I watched Alisha insist she was happy, that she had met 'The One', all the while wondering if what she meant was 'I've met The One Who Won't Leave Me'.

I watched as Lily flirted her way through flings with men and women who promised they would heal her broken heart, only to walk away a few weeks later once they'd got what they wanted.

I watched Lily claim she was happy, that Andy had done her a favour by allowing her to experience sexual liberation, all the while wondering if that was the case, then why was Lily still stalking Andy's social media? Especially now he was married to an American with a flawless tan and teeth so white they hurt your eyes.

I watched as Laney met Anton, fell head over heels and ditched her all-black ensembles and bright hair dye for cutesy tea-dresses and muted pink lipstick. Then, eight months later, I watched Anton walk out the door and back into the arms of his ex-girlfriend.

I watched, I waited, I simmered.

Then one night, out of the blue, I met Jamie.

Dating websites and hook-up apps would have you believe organic meetings don't happen anymore, but Jamie and I bucked that trend. The minute our eyes met across the heaving dancefloor, 80s party tunes blasting from the speakers and cheap vodka flowing through my veins,

I knew he was going to mean something in my life. Call it fate, call it intuition, call it a good old-fashioned crush, but I just knew.

After his drunken friend hollered across the bar at me for the third time, Jamie approached me. His body was so close I could feel the heat radiating from him, but he kept a respectful distance between us. He never once put his hand on my waist the way some men do when they think loud music in bars gives them permission to touch you without consent or consequence.

"Sorry about my friend," he shouted over the music, the low pitch of his voice sending a flutter through my stomach. "I'd say he's not usually like this, but he's an embarrassment most of the time. I should ditch him, shouldn't I?"

Maybe it was the vodka talking, or maybe it was because I felt alive in his presence, but I hit the ground running. "You should thank him. If it wasn't for him, you wouldn't have had a reason to talk to me."

Jamie's twinkling eyes locked on mine. A current of electricity passed between us, one so strong I was surprised the power to the bar didn't short circuit. "You wanted me to talk to you?"

I bit my lip and gave a confessional nod. The next thing I knew, Jamie was buying me a drink.

Leaving Lily and Alisha at the bar, we sat together in a faded booth beside the dancefloor and fell into easy conversation about everything and nothing. After years of bland exchanges, I was finally sat opposite someone who wasn't afraid to share their deepest secrets in and amongst lighter titbits of information like their favourite food.

The sticky table in front of us and the sea of people on the dancefloor faded into insignificance until all I could see, hear, feel, and think of was the man sat beside me. The man who had a small scar on his left hand from a childhood bike accident and a laugh that made fireworks burst inside my chest. The man who was at once both a stranger and someone it felt like I'd known forever.

One by one, all the secret, closed off parts of me began to unlock. The weight of the cynicism I'd carried for so many years drifted away, and I softened into the moment until, quite abruptly, the lights in the bar came on to announce closing time.

Reality was jarring, unwelcome even. I remember blinking and wondering how it could possibly be time for the bar to close when Jamie and I had only just sat down?

But when I checked the time on my phone, it confessed that Jamie and I had been talking for the last three hours. The fizzing feeling I'd felt since I first saw him intensified, and I gulped in the acceptance that maybe I'd been wrong to shut down the idea of love quite so firmly.

Jamie's hand wrapped around mine as we manoeuvred towards the exit. I held on tight, dreading the moment I would have to let it go.

Bitter, frosty air assaulted me the instant we stepped outside, but my body barely had time to tremble before Jamie wrapped his coat around my shoulders. The gesture caught me off guard. I couldn't remember the last time someone had given me a strip of gum, never mind their coat on a freezing night. I looked into Jamie's big, brown eyes and melted, and in that puddle of my being, every doubt I ever felt simply evaporated.

"I don't want to leave you," Jamie confessed as we waited for our respective taxis.

"So don't," I replied, and that was it – that was the moment everything changed.

Overnight my fury disappeared. I didn't need to fight back or overrule whatever narrative was being forced upon me because I had a man who didn't want me to play a role other than his equal.

I had a man I couldn't imagine a future without. A man who donated a chunk of his salary to charity, who recycled, who volunteered at a homeless shelter on Christmas Eve. A man who was a teacher too, who understood the pressures of the job so did all he could to make my load easier to carry. A man who went for beers with my stepdad and took my mum shopping when her car broke down. I went on holiday to places like Paris and Rome and saw why everyone said they were romantic cities instead of scoffing at the sentiment. I received thoughtful gifts on my birthday and at Christmas and sometimes just because. My life was good.

No, it was *more* than good. I had a partner who liked my friends and friends who liked my partner back. I woke up to kisses that gave me butterflies almost three years down the line. My future felt like it was filled with endless possibility.

I gave into the happiness. I trusted it. I let myself get comfortable with the idea that this was to be my life – blissful, happy, loved. I noticed how much brighter the world seems when you're in love, how easy it is to get out of bed on a morning. My colleague Shari even called me a walking advert for romance, a badge I wore with pride.

With no clouds of fury blocking my vision, I noticed how Laney's sense of self was stronger than ever after her breakup with Anton.

I noticed how single Lily laughed more than she ever had when she was with Andy.

I noticed how Simon treated Alisha like a queen and gave into the idea that the two of them were happy together after all.

Smitten, I dived headfirst into love. That was the problem. That's where it all went wrong.

That's how I've found myself trying to digest the fact that even though I am to be married in less than one month's time, my teaching assistant Debbie's phone is in my hand and I'm staring dumbly at a photo of Jamie and his colleague Tara kissing.

1.

"Cassie? Cass, are you okay?" Debbie's voice sounds far away, as if she's calling me from the lawn while I'm underwater in a swimming pool. I blink, reality and my classroom flooding back into focus with an audible 'whoosh'.

"Hmm?"

"The photo. I know it's a shock for you, but I had to tell you. You're so amazing, I couldn't stand the idea of you marrying the wrong man! He doesn't deserve you. He... I... well, I can't believe him. One minute I was getting into a taxi, the next I was looking out of the window at the pair of them with their tongues down each other's throat! And on a street corner for all to see, can you believe it?"

I wince because no Debbie, I can't believe it. Not even with the proof right here in front of me.

While I try to process what I'm looking at and what it means for my life, Debbie continues to talk. Her relentless babble rattles around my skull, but her words don't sink in. They bounce off my skin and land at my feet like confetti.

Confetti.

I groan at the word and all its connotations.

Debbie stops speaking, her uncharacteristic silence jarring. She looks at me through her greying fringe, her eyes big and sad. "Cass, say something. You're worrying me. You're not mad at me for telling you, are you?"

"Mad at you? No, I couldn't possibly be mad at you!" I hear the soothing words leave my mouth, but I don't remember ordering them to. In fact, I can't remember anything other than that photo, their intertwined bodies, Jamie's lips on someone else's...

Forcing down a shudder, I look at my desk and notice a pile of exercise books laid out before me. I jolt as if seeing them for the first time. What was I doing before life took a baseball bat to my chest?

Debbie's soft voice interrupts my thoughts. "Do you need some water?"

"I'm fine," I reply, but we both know that's a lie.

Debbie sighs and shifts closer to me, and for the first time I notice the pity swimming in her eyes. She's never looked at me like that before. No one has, not even when my dad died.

I press back into my chair as if creating space between us can shield me from the victimhood I'm being drawn into, but it's no use. Debbie's potent sympathy drowns me.

She clears her throat. "When I was younger, before I married Phil, I was with someone called Tony. We were only together for about five months, but I thought he was the love of my life. Then one day I found out he'd been dating someone else too. She was called Philippa. We'd been friends when we were at school. She knew I was with Tony, but she still dated him. Let me tell you, Cass, it broke my heart."

I study Debbie, wondering why she is introducing me to more tales of misery.

"It was the worst pain, the worst shock, the worst humiliation imaginable. At points I didn't think I'd survive it, but I did. I'm not telling you this to take away from how you're feeling, but to let you know I'm here for you. I'm here for you and I know exactly how horrible this feels."

I can't take my eyes off Debbie, this woman with silver stars printed on her cardigan and a glinting wedding ring on her finger. This woman telling me she knows how I feel, a sentence that's so absurd it makes me want to laugh. How can Debbie have experienced the same pain that's currently tearing me apart? How can she have survived it and lived to tell the tale?

"You're not alone, Cass. I know right now you'll feel like you are, but that's how all victims of cheating feel at first."

Debbie's comments singe my skin. She says the word 'victim' so casually. Worse still, she says it as if it applies to me, but that can't be right. Last night I was messaging Jamie's mum about collecting photos from Jamie's childhood to display at the wedding. There's a stack of messages from our venue queued on my phone, waiting for a response. My left hand is weighed down by a diamond. Victim of cheating? No, those words don't apply to me.

But as Debbie takes another step towards my desk, her thighs so close they're almost grazing it, it dawns on me that no matter how much I try to dodge those words and all that they imply, they *do* apply to me. Debbie says they do. This photo says they do.

Jilted lover, heartbroken ex, betrayed victim… that's me. Thanks to that photo, thanks to Jamie, that's me.

Inside my chest, something splinters. Something I fear will never fully heal.

"My point is, Cass, that this moment, however awful it is, is just a drop in the ocean of your life. Cheating is a vile act done by vile people. It gets to you like nothing else. That hurt… well, it makes you want to destroy the person who did it to you. But you're better than that, better than him. Good things will happen again. Look at me - I'm married to Phil now and have three wonderful children. I'll be a grandma soon! What happened with Tony was a blip in my timeline, something that's now barely even a sentence in the story of my life, let alone a paragraph."

I nod because I don't know how else to respond. Am I supposed to say congratulations for finding Phil? Well done for creating a happy ending for yourself?

Or be honest and say thank you for trying to help but Jamie's betrayal doesn't feel like a sentence or paragraph in my story, but a whole library. There would be rows of anthologies on who we were meant to be and a stand displaying every broken promise ever made. Then the most painful section at the back, shrouded in darkness and lined with cobwebs - an area dedicated specifically to the victim of love I fought so hard to not become.

For the first time since seeing the photo, my eyes prickle with tears.

"Do you want to talk about it?" Debbie asks.

I almost choke on the suggestion. Smiling a gummy smile, I shake my head and lock my words inside me. They stick in my throat, unprocessed and feral, but at least I don't have to hear them out loud.

"Cass, you don't have to be brave in front of me."

"I'm not being brave. I'm... I'm..."

Debbie's face twists as she watches me struggle. "It's a lot to take in, I know. Maybe I should stay with you for a bit? We can talk about this and work out a plan for how you'll leave him."

"No, you go home. Phil will be wondering where you are."

"Phil can wait," Debbie says, putting her hand on top of mine.

Instinctively, I pull back.

Debbie's reaction is as instinctive as mine. She blinks, bruised. "You are mad at me, aren't you?"

I don't know how to tell her that no, I'm not mad, I'm just having to bite my cheeks to stop myself from screaming. That I don't want her pity, that her hand on top of mine makes me feel like a victim when I want to be anything but one.

But I can't say any of those things because saying them makes this real, and I don't want it to be real. I want to be in my classroom marking the day's work and thinking about what I'll have for dinner tonight, not wondering how the hell I'm meant to start my life over again.

Starting over again... my insides howl at the thought.

"Debbie, I'm fine and we're fine. I'm glad you told me. I just need to focus for a minute, you know? Let my brain settle. I think seeing how badly the children understood fractions today might do me some good!" I joke, my pathetic attempt at humour sounding as hollow as I feel.

Debbie hesitates, but she knows me well enough to not push it. Despite everything in her mothering nature telling her to pull me into a hug, she accepts my wishes and grabs her handbag from the classroom cupboard.

"I'll keep my phone on all night, okay?" Debbie says. "If you need to call me, you can."

"Thank you, that's really kind. I'll keep it in mind," I reply, even though I know I won't be calling Debbie tonight. Still, I appreciate the offer.

Before Debbie leaves the classroom, I call her name. She stops in the doorway.

"Can you send me the photo? Send it then delete it, please."

"Of course."

"And not a word of this to anyone, okay? Not until I figure out what to do."

"Cass, I'd never say anything to anyone about this. I'll take it to my grave, you know that," Debbie replies breathlessly. I know I've hurt her by insinuating she would be anything but discreet, but I don't have it in me to make her feel better. Phil can do that when she gets home, the good husband he is. Right now, it's taking all my energy to not trash the classroom in a raging fit of disbelief.

"Great. Thanks, Debbie, I appreciate it. I'll see you tomorrow."

I don't look at her as I grab the first exercise book from the pile in front of me. Logan Carter's Maths book. The dream student who always presents his work with beautiful precision. A great book to start with when ugliness is all I can see.

Debbie hovers at the door, but as I pick up a pen, she leaves. I smile at her final abandonment. As long as a teacher is marking, they're okay, right? As long as the ticks are green and the children's writing gets neater, it doesn't matter that two-thirds of the staff are on antidepressants or the verge of burnout.

I open Logan's book, thumbing the frayed corner and half hoping I get a papercut to prove I can still feel something other than the absolute numbness of shock. With a sigh that rattles my bones, I read Logan's first answer.

$2/3 = \frac{1}{4}$

Wrong.

He's got it wrong.

I scan the rest of his answers and find that, despite possessing presentation skills that suggest Logan is far cleverer than he should be in year two, not one of his answers is correct.

My grip on my pen tightens. I look at Logan's work, his pencil markings so neat they could have been typed, and a rush of energy surges through my body so strong it makes me nauseous. I bite my cheeks, but every time I see those obnoxious incorrect answers, a sickly swelling balloons inside my throat.

I snap.

In one brutal motion, I rip the page from Logan's book and claw at it. My veins come alive, twisting and slithering around my body. "It's not hard, Logan," I want to shout. "A fractions wall is on the Maths board! Copy it if you must, I don't care, just get it right!"

When it's too small to tear anymore, I launch the disintegrated page into the air then sit back in my chair, panting. Tiny scraps of what was once Logan's work flutter around me. The scene is mesmerising, beautiful almost, like being caught in falling snow.

Out of the corner of my eye, I catch sight of my shining, emerald cut engagement ring and let out a shaky breath. "I'll be nice to Logan tomorrow," I promise myself. "It's not his fault he couldn't do it. Sometimes, no matter how hard we try, we get things wrong. Logan's not the only one."

2.

My legs stay put, two reluctant, fleshy lumps. I need to go inside, but they refuse to take me. There's a whole unknown that exists in my apartment, one they're happy to avoid. I've already stayed at work as late as possible and took the long route home, but now there is nowhere else I can go and no more time I can waste. As impossible as it feels, I must face him.

But I know as soon as I see Jamie, it will be over. The second he flashes me that handsome, lazy smile and asks, 'How was your day?' as if it's the most normal day in the world, we will break. The tie between us will sever like the slicing of an umbilical cord and my intestines will spill onto the floor.

Sure, survival instinct will kick in. I'll scoop my insides up and shove them back into my body, but there will be something I miss, an organ that skids under the fridge or a splatter of blood I'll never quite scrub from the tiles.

Would Jamie notice?

Would he care?

I let out a sigh and unlock my phone. Ignoring a text from my mum, I stare at the photo Debbie sent me. Jamie and Tara, entangled in a moment of passion. I don't need to see it again – it's etched into my memory forever – but my eyes still scrutinise every pixel until they burn.

I would recognise those broad shoulders in a crowd of millions.

I bought that fitted, charcoal coat for his birthday.

I have been smothered by that tantalising, all-consuming embrace, the same one now encasing her.

I drop my phone onto my lap and stare at the grey garage wall ahead.

It's really him. It's really him kissing another woman.

I press my eyelids shut with my fingers, forcing away the tears that threaten to fall. "Come on, Cass, come on," I whisper, my new, desperate mantra.

Behind me, the metal shutter rattles as it rises to let someone else into the garage. I take it as my cue to leave. To not be the woman crying in her car and instead be the woman about to close what she naively thought was going to be the greatest chapter of her life.

Before leaving my car, I check my reflection in the rear-view mirror. I've looked better, less lined forehead and knotted hair, but looking anything other than a shaky two out of ten right now would be a miracle. Smoothing down my curls, I tuck my hair behind my ears and lick my well-gnawed lips. With one last glance at the photo, I'm ready.

I stride through the garage, holding my head high to shut down the hum of nerves threatening to undermine me. I press the button for the lift, and it arrives in seconds. Stepping into the juddery box, I push level four. The button illuminates, the doors close and then I'm on my way. I lean against the back wall, wishing I was going anywhere but home.

When the lift doors slide open, I don't allow my resolve a second to waver. Marching past the wilted plant in the communal hallway, I reach our apartment. The silver 407 nailed to the front door glints under the artificial lighting, daring me to come inside.

Swallowing hard, I put the key in the lock and turn it. One foot crosses the threshold, then the other. The door shuts behind me, falling louder than I intend it to.

"Hey!" Jamie's voice comes from the kitchen, semi-shouting to be heard over the top of the indie playlist he blasts while he cooks. My body stiffens at the sound of his voice. I drop my handbag to the floor then pad purposefully towards the kitchen.

26

As I walk through our cosy apartment, glimpses of artefacts from our shared life leap into my field of vision. A thriller novel Jamie got me for Christmas. The perfect grey corner sofa we spent over a month searching for. The fluffy rug we've had sex on those times we're too in the moment to make it to the bedroom. I pass it all with a wail bubbling in my throat.

The kitchen looms closer and my senses tingle on high alert. The beat from the speakers, the brightness of the lights, it's all so overwhelming, but I force myself to keep going. Every movement I make must be meaningful. Every step, no matter how much they feel like walking barefoot on broken glass, is one closer to the ugly truth.

I turn from the living room into the kitchen and there he is… Jamie.

His back is to me, a floral towel thrown over his left shoulder. He's wearing his grey joggers. They make his bum look good - I always tell him that when he wears them. His white t-shirt is splattered with red sauce. Typical. He's such a messy cook. He cooks, I clean, that's the way it works with us. It works well. We work well.

At least I thought we did, anyway.

On the hob, Bolognese bubbles in a pan. The sight of food shouldn't shred a soul, but tonight it does just that. Jamie knows Italian food is my comfort food. He knows I've had a long day. He's made it to cheer me up. He's thought of me. He's cheating on me, but he's thought of me.

A sudden spike of pain ricochets through my chest and I bite my cheeks to stop myself from howling so hard I draw blood.

Sensing my presence, Jamie turns around. Pink cheeked from the heat of the kitchen, he holds out two glasses of white wine. "Welcome home! I thought you could use one of these after a long day."

I take the glass with the most wine in it, the chill of the liquid against my skin anchoring me in reality, then I force myself to look at Jamie. The familiarity of his face brings with it an entirely new agony. Those dark eyes, his plump lips, the stubble that scratches when we kiss… I will myself to stay upright, to not succumb to the urge to collapse at his feet and scream until my throat tears.

"Cheers," Jamie says. He clinks his glass against mine and takes a sip.

I go to speak but no sound comes out, so I press the wineglass to my lips and take a gulp. As soon as the wine hits my tongue, everything I don't want to say out loud threatens to pour out of me like an irrepressible stream of vomit. I keep the glass at my mouth, scared of what will happen if I don't have it there to stop me, and drink until it's nearly empty.

"You must have needed that!" Jamie enthuses, kissing me on the cheek. My skin burns from the touch of his lips, but I'm too stunned to react. He tops up my glass and walks back to the hob to inspect dinner.

Then I hear them - the words I knew were coming. Words that are usually so innocent, only this time they are the ones that mark the final, splintering end.

"So, how was your day?"

3.

I swear I hear my heart split in two. It's so loud, so painful. I clutch the kitchen counter to hold myself upright.

He said it.

He *said* it.

He dares to ask how my day was as if he cares, all the while he is on street corners, kissing someone else.

In this moment, I know it is over. We are done. There is no going back from this.

Thoughts of happier times swim in my mind, memories that were once full of colour but now appear greyscale. I remember our first kiss and how our mouths tasted of sugar donuts and promise. I remember our holidays, stinging sunburn, poorly mixed cocktails, sweaty sex, and lazy cuddles afterwards. I remember our first fight, when Jamie was on the verge of tears and the sight of him so upset made me rush to his side and forget why I was angry in the first place. I remember Saturday mornings, waking up with a yawn to a cup of coffee and a cuddle.

I remember falling in love and completely, utterly, no questions asked giving myself to this man.

I remember it all, and all of it hurts.

My fingers twitch, wanting nothing more than to dig into Jamie's chest and pull out his heart. To throw it into the Bolognese, cook it then force him to eat every morsel until he chokes.

"Earth to Cass?" Jamie says, waving a sauce covered wooden spoon in front of my face.

I jump, sloshing wine onto the counter.

"Jeez, Cass, you must have had one hell of a day! Come here." Jamie slips his arms around my waist. With the familiar warmth of his body against mine, I fall into him. It's so easy to do. Our bodies are a jigsaw, slotting together like a perfect match because we *are* a perfect match.

Aren't we?

I long to feel home and safe in Jamie's arms, but the feeling never comes. Everything has changed. I wriggle free, tugging at my neckline and trying to find air.

"Are you okay?"

"I don't feel well," I manage to reply. "I'm too warm."

"Here." Jamie opens the window and I collapse onto a wooden stool by the breakfast bar. "Should I swap that for water?" he asks, nodding at my wine.

I shake my head and down the rest of the glass. Jamie watches me, his eyebrows knitted together in loving concern. If I didn't know better, I'd believe he really cared.

But I do know better, don't I?

The photo of Jamie and Tara leaps to the forefront of my mind, demanding attention. I hold my head in my hands to push it away, but it goes nowhere.

"Cass, you're scaring me now. Are you sure you're okay? Has something happened?"

I mull over his question.

"Why, yes dear, you could say something has happened. Today I saw a photo. That sounds so innocent, doesn't it? Like something your grandma would show you over a cup of tea, only this photo was anything but innocent. It showed me that people who cheat will do it out in the open for anyone to see because they really do not care about the people they're hurting. It told me that the man I love, the man I want to spend the rest of my life with, who looked my mum in the eye and told her he would never hurt me, is in fact a barefaced liar. But worst of all it told me that I'd been enchanted by a pretty web of lies I once swore to stop believing altogether. So yes dear, you could say something happened today."

The acidic rant is on the tip of my tongue, ready to spit in Jamie's direction. All I have to do is open my mouth. My verbal lashings will strike, then it will be over for Jamie like it is for me.

All I have to do is speak.

Then I hear them, echoing in my brain like a ghostly whisper. Debbie's words from the classroom… 'it makes you want to destroy the person who did it to you', and the swirling turmoil of humiliation, disbelief and devastation that's been tormenting me contorts and moulds into one singular, searing emotion – rage. It flows through me, igniting every cell in my body until I feel more alive than ever before.

I am not going to be Jamie's victim. I refuse.

Tonight there won't be a screaming match where I tell Jamie what I've found out and play all my cards at once. I'm not going to listen to his excuses and watch him wipe away tears that deep down we both know he doesn't mean.

No, tonight is just the beginning, the beginning of something much bigger.

My gaze settles on the calendar stuck to our fridge, lingering on our wedding date, underlined twice and circled in red.

An exciting countdown.

The perfect opportunity.

A smile twitches on my lips. My tired eyes meet Jamie's alert ones. "It's been a long day, that's all. You know how it is," I hear myself say.

"Oh, Cass, I'm sorry," Jamie pouts. He strokes my cheek before turning to check on dinner. I watch him, this man who has turned my world upside down, and suddenly feel at peace.

Everything is so clear now, what I must do and who I must become.

I won't settle for just a photo - I want to see everything. I want to know how long it's been going on for, where they've been meeting, who knows, who suspects. I want to discover everything there is to know about Tara, the woman half responsible for taking a wrecking ball to my life. I want to swim in the sea of Jamie's deception, taste the bitter lies I have swallowed as sweet truths.

Then, when I know it all, I am going to show Jamie how wrong he was to cast me as a fool. In front of everyone he knows and loves and on what is supposed to be the happiest day of his life, I will ruin him.

All I need to do is make it to that day. Living alongside Jamie as if all is well and pretending to Debbie I'm unsure whether to leave will be tough but it will be worth it. As soon as I witness the moment Jamie's life falls apart, it will all be worth it.

As I force a smile, I seal my fate. I just hope Jamie is ready to be played at his own game.

4.

Jamie goes for a run after dinner. While crawling under a pile of blankets and watching sad films on repeat calls to me, there's no time to breakdown when answers must be hunted for.

A quick internet search tells me there are apps that can track your partner's whereabouts and spyware you can add to phones to intercept messages, but I'm not a secret service agent. I'm a normal woman who up until this afternoon thought she led a normal life. Hacking and cyber-spying isn't in my DNA. Besides, I don't have access to Jamie's phone, so turning detective in my home it is.

Exactly what I'm looking for, though, I don't know. Lipstick on his collar? A scrunched receipt from a seedy hotel? I've no idea, but whatever it is, I'm determined to find it.

I scan the living room, taking in the pale wood furniture and minimalist styling, and decide there's nowhere to hide anything in here. It's too communal, too risky.

Even though I think the same about our bedroom, I trawl through it just in case. I ransack the pockets of everything in Jamie's wardrobe, open the empty suitcases under our bed and rifle through his bedside cabinet. Nothing unusual comes up, but that only makes me more determined to sniff out his deceit.

Pushing open the door to our second bedroom, I survey the scene. The room contains a sofa bed, a wardrobe, and a desk, but that's where its functionality ends. It's where we store our towels and bedding and contain our mounds of school supplies, Jamie's golf clubs and clothes we no longer wear. Generally, it's a room we close the door to and ignore until someone asks if they can stay overnight.

If Jamie was going to hide evidence of his relationship with Tara anywhere in our apartment, it would be in here.

I go to the desk and yank open the drawer we stuff our life admin paperwork in. If pop culture has taught me anything, it's that there's always a 'paper trail' with affairs, although these days I'm not sure how much actual paper will be in that trail.

Still, the drawer is worth a try. Pulling everything out onto the floor, I realise how long it's been since either of us sorted through the mail we receive. I flick through student loan repayment reminders, takeaway leaflets, and our annual phone statements, finding nothing incriminating.

But then I spot a letter from the bank addressed to Jamie.

Fumbling to pull the contents from the envelope, my desperation punishes me as the paper slices the tip of my thumb. I hiss at the sudden zap of pain and wrench the letter free. With my bleeding thumb pressed inside my mouth, I read what it has to say.

My stomach plummets as I realise it's a letter confirming a credit card has been taken out in Jamie's name.

But that can't be right. Jamie doesn't have a credit card. He did when he was younger, but three months into our relationship he sheepishly confessed he had got into masses of debt when he was at university. It was so bad that his parents had to bail him out. After that, he swore to never use a credit card again. In fact, he's so anti-credit card he once convinced Laney to cut hers up.

Besides, Jamie doesn't need a credit card. His financial planning is borderline obsessive. At the end of every month, he goes through our accounts, double-checking we're on track with our savings goals and on top of payments. Those skills are the reason we can afford to save for a house and pay for a wedding at the same time.

No, the Jamie I know would never have, or need, a credit card.

But clearly I don't know Jamie because he does have one. The proof is in my trembling hand.

A balloon of panic swells in my chest. Are we in financial trouble? I can't remember the last time I checked our accounts. I know the basic structure of what we have set up – individual accounts our wages are paid into, a shared everyday account for bills and rent, then a joint savings account – but I let Jamie take the lead with it all. He enjoys it at the end of the month when he can proudly walk into the room and tell me we've saved five percent more this month compared to the last.

It's not very feminist of me to give him control of our financials, I know, but the truth is that since finding full-time employment, I've never really worried about money. I know what my wage is and what I can and can't afford. Strict saving has never been my style, nor has extravagant spending.

But what if my lax attitude towards money has made me ignorant to the fact that we aren't as financially secure as I thought?

Frantically, I pull my phone from my pocket and log into my online banking app. A loading icon whirls on the screen, so slow it's like it's mocking me.

When it finally logs in, I click on the account summary. My muscles relax when I read that both my individual account and our savings account have a higher balance than I'd have predicted. I might not have picked up on Jamie's affair but at least I haven't turned a blind eye to him robbing me senseless too.

While I'm on the app, I check the shared accounts for anomalies. I open the latest statement from our everyday account and scan the list of transactions. Bills, groceries, petrol, date nights… everything is normal.

The statement from our savings account contains no surprises either. We both add the same amount each month on payday and have only taken money out to finance things for the wedding.

I slump in on myself, my excitement at finding a lead with the credit card letter short-lived. The shared accounts are a dead end. What I need to see are Jamie's personal accounts, but I can't because this isn't his banking app. I can't access Jamie's accounts either. The only way to do that is via his phone, a phone I don't know the passcode for or have thumbprint access to.

Bitten by frustration, I scream into my knuckles. I'm so close, I can feel it, but there's something stopping me reaching out and grabbing what I need to. I know he's cheating. I know he has a secret credit card. I know there is more to this than I can see right now, but the dots aren't connecting.

Stuffing the papers back into the drawer, I force it shut then continue rifling through the rest of our junk. I rake through DVDs we should get rid of, a staff handbook from a school Jamie doesn't work at anymore and thank you cards from the children we enjoyed teaching the most. The stream of clutter is endless, but it tells me nothing other than we should think about having a clear out more frequently.

Thirsty for more, I go to the wardrobe and fling open the double doors. I check the pockets of every item hung in there only to end up empty-handed.

"Come on," I mutter furiously. There must be something here, there *must* be.

Then I see them.

Stacked on top of each other at the bottom of the wardrobe - our memory boxes.

When we first moved in together, Jamie and I both brought an abundance of childhood belongings with us. We agreed to condense them all into one box each. Our second weekend in the apartment, we spent a whole day in our pyjamas laughing at each other's terrible artwork, tragic haircuts, and creepy toys. It's one of my most favourite memories, and the reminder of it is a blow to the back of my skull.

Sinking to my knees, I pull my memory box from the wardrobe and remove the lid. Instantly, I regret it.

Ted, the inventively named teddy bear my dad gifted me on the day I was born, sits at the top. Missing one eye and more threadbare than fluffy, he's a little worse for wear. I hold him close, breathing in his musty scent.

There was a time in my life where holding Ted would make everything bad disappear, but right now he's doing nothing to heal the aching in my chest, no matter how hard I squeeze him. I look back to my memory box, a photo of me sitting on my dad's shoulders the first thing I see. Emotion swells in my chest and I push the box away.

With a wobbling chin, I drag my watery eyes to Jamie's memory box, and just like that, the past attacks me.

I remember howling at Jamie's sporting participants award and his tale of playing football so badly his coach said Jamie might make a good water boy one day, but not a footballer. I remember listening to Jamie recount the meaning behind each of his childhood toys and feeling like I was unlocking some secret part of him that people rarely ever saw. I remember finding an old holiday photo buried at the bottom of the box, the image of Jamie's freckled, sunburnt skin and goofy grin perfectly capturing pre-teen awkwardness. The boy in the photograph was so far removed from the man before me it almost seemed like the photo had been planted as a joke.

"Please tell me our children won't look like this?!" I cried, holding the photo in the air as if I'd won a prize.

Jamie grabbed the photo, his cheeks crimson. "Where did you find this?"

"It was with the rest of your stuff."

Jamie groaned. "I hoped you'd never see me like that. In fact, I hoped no one would ever see me like that again."

"It's not that bad," I giggled, reaching for the picture and laughing harder as I studied it once more. "You really were an exceptional looking child, weren't you?"

"You mean you don't think I was cute?"

"Not even a little bit."

With an outraged shout, Jamie grabbed me by my waist and pulled me on top of him. "That's harsh, Miss Edwards. It's a good job I grew up to be so handsome, isn't it?"

I was about to respond with a feisty retort when Jamie silenced me with a kiss, something that always annoyed me in films but made me swoon when it happened to me.

My stomach knots at the memory. We were so in love, so happy... weren't we?

My memories can't be that out of sync. What I felt, what I saw, what I lived must have been true. Jamie asked me to marry him - you don't do that if you don't love someone, do you? Surely I didn't give up everything I believed in for someone who didn't care for me back?

My grip on my memory box tightens as I desperately cling onto my wavering strength, but my brain doesn't care how much I'm holding on. It fires a barrage of gut-wrenching questions my way until I can't do it anymore. I can't open Jamie's memory box and be reminded of a time when it felt like the future was ours for the taking. I can't search for clues that will show me the end when, if I'm honest, I don't want anything to end.

Crushing Ted inside my memory box, I put the lid back on and stuff it inside the wardrobe. I press the doors shut as if closing them will keep the pain at bay, but nothing can hold back the past. Memories ravage me until the torment of remembering rips me in two and I can't suppress it anymore.

So, alone on the floor of our second bedroom, I sit and I howl for the life and the love I have lost.

5.

Some people are glamorous when they cry. They can shed their tears, dab them away with a crisp, white tissue and still look immaculate.

I am not one of those people. If anything, I am the opposite of one of those people, so when Jamie comes home – not very sweaty for someone who has been for a run, I note - he sees my upset straight away. "Cass! What's wrong?"

I lift my gaze to look at him. Everything about Jamie tells me he cares; from the way he holds my hand like it's precious to the way worry lines have appeared on his forehead. My bottom lip quivers.

"Cass, you're worrying me now. What is it? Are you still feeling unwell?"

Unable to find the words to conceal the enormity of what's actually wrong, I find myself saying, "It's the wedding."

"Okay, the wedding. Tell me more, maybe I can help?"

With a lie out there for me to follow, I swallow my tears. "I'm stressed with it, that's all. It's less than a month away and I have so many questions, like will we get everything ready on time? Is it going to be the day we imagine? Can we afford it?"

Jamie's face softens. "Well, that one I can help with. Of course we can afford it. We wouldn't have booked it if we couldn't."

"I know but it's been more expensive than we first thought, especially because we had to postpone it thanks to Covid."

"I know but honestly, Cass, there's nothing to worry about. You know I go through our accounts at the end of every month. Trust me, we're doing great."

"How come you never talk to me about it?"

"You don't ask."

"Well, I want to keep up with our finances more. Maybe I should start now. Show me how much money we've got." I reach for Jamie's phone, but he doesn't hand it to me.

"Why don't you check on your phone? That way you can see how much is in your personal account too."

"My phone's charging in the bedroom," I lie, hoping Jamie doesn't notice the bulky outline of my phone in my pocket. "Show me on yours."

Jamie nods and unlocks his phone with his thumbprint. The position of his hands makes it difficult for me to see the screen properly, but I see he has a queue of notifications waiting. Somehow, I suppress the urge to wrench the phone out of his grip to see who they're from.

He shifts in his seat, moving his phone so the screen is out of my eyeline.

"I can't see," I say, craning my neck to steal a glance at his banking homepage. "Jamie, I can't see!"

"Here," Jamie replies, turning his phone around. He's already opened the statement for our savings account, bypassing his homepage before I could peek at the balance of his personal account or secret credit card. "We've sent off the final payments for most things and we still have loads in there. We're doing great, see?"

I do see, but our joint accounts aren't what I wanted to check in the first place. "Do you think we should be saving more?"

"More? Cass, we've pretty much paid off an entire wedding for over eighty people and still got thousands in savings. We're doing better than most people we know, except maybe Alisha. Although I hate to break it to you, but unless we leave teaching altogether, we'll never match her level of income." Jamie grins at his joke, squeezing my legs as if prompting me to laugh.

My lips twitch in acknowledgement, the closest thing to a smile I can muster when the truth I so desperately crave is right in front of me, but still in Jamie's control. "Maybe if you show me your account then we could see if we can save more," I push.

"Honestly, we don't need to save more."

"But maybe we *could* is the point I'm making. If you just show me your account -"

"Why do you need to see my account?" Jamie cuts in, narrowing his eyes.

My cheeks flush. "I don't *need* to, Jamie, I'm asking to. It's joint finances, you know."

"Joint finances as in we have a shared account for bills and rent, then a shared savings account. The rest is ours to do what we want with, that's the arrangement. That's always been the arrangement."

"I know, but as your soon-to-be wife I didn't think seeing your bank account would be such a big deal."

"And as your soon-to-be-husband, I thought we agreed to respect each other's need for our own money," Jamie challenges. "You're acting weird. We have enough money to pay for a wedding and a start to saving for our first home, you've seen that. What more do you want?"

I want to shout 'the truth' in his defensive face, but I can't, even if the furious words are bubbling in my throat. I drop my shoulders. "I'm sorry. It's just stressful organising it all, you know?"

"That's not my fault," Jamie snaps before softening. "I'm sorry, I didn't mean that. Look, I know it's hard. Wedding planning was always going to be tough, right? But you don't have to take it out on me. I'm on your side! Is there anything I can do to help?"

Afraid of what I'll say if I open my mouth, I shake my head.

"How about asking your bridesmaids for some assistance? Isn't that their job?"

"I can't ask Alisha – you know how busy she is - and Laney's taste is so different to mine it would be like explaining a recipe to someone who doesn't know how to turn an oven on. Plus, Lily's a bit sensitive about weddings after Andy. I don't have anyone to help me."

Jamie's features twist. "Cass, you have me. I'll always be here for you. Plus, I'm sure our mums would be happy to step in if needed."

Remembering how our mums had opposingly different ideas for where the wedding should be held, never mind about all the other choices that are made along the way, I pull a face.

Jamie laughs. "Okay, bad idea. But seriously, Cass, we can get you some help. I don't care who it is or even if they want paying - anything to stop you crying."

I reach for Jamie's hand. "Thank you."

Fiancée soothed, Jamie pulls me towards him. At the sight of his puckered lips drawing closer to mine, my stomach clenches and for one terrifying moment I think I'm about to throw up.

Before I get the chance to move away, Jamie's mouth presses onto mine.

The shock blows my soul open, but my body's response is even more surprising than his kiss. A hunger takes over me, wanting, needing the intimacy of physical connection. Jamie's lips claim me, and my own lips respond automatically, still under the illusion it's their job to kiss this man.

Jamie takes my response as an invitation, drawing me closer and pressing my body against his.

This time, searing panic rises in me. From the urgency of his kiss, it's clear where Jamie wants this to go. Sex is a loving route we have taken so many times together, but that was before. Kissing him so he doesn't sense something is off is one thing, but sex? That's a whole new level, and one I am not willing to plummet to, no matter what my body's muscle memory says.

Just as I'm about to recoil, Jamie's phone leaps into life.

The unexpected sound breaks us apart. He checks who's calling and grimaces. "I'd best get this," he says, rising to his feet. "I'm going to prep lunch for tomorrow. Put your feet up and relax, okay? I'll make something for both of us."

Jamie pecks me on the forehead and answers the phone, asking whoever is on the other end of the line how they're doing. My stunned lips stay parted as I watch him disappear into the kitchen. My shellshocked body wants a second to process what happened, but I refuse to berate myself for kissing him when tuning into Jamie's movements is more important right now.

I hear him rattling about in the kitchen, opening cupboards and firing the hob to life, then the sound of soft indie music filters through the air. My shoulders tense. Jamie always listens to music when he cooks. 'It helps me focus,' he said when we first moved in together, but now my skin prickles with uncertainty. Surrounded by sound, Jamie's muffled voice barely carries to the living room. What if all this time Jamie was using guitar riffs to cover up his conversations with Tara?

I push myself to stand and head to the kitchen doorway, my heart hammering as I listen in on his call.

"I know, it's been a tough day for me too," I hear him say before he turns the extractor fan on. It whirs into life, drowning out his voice.

On any other day, I'd be too blinded by the sweetness of Jamie prepping my lunch to suspect he was hiding in another room to cover up his conversation, but this isn't any other day. This is the start of the time of truth. Knowing that, I push open the door and enter the kitchen.

Jamie smiles when he sees me then turns his attention back to the chicken he's cooking. "I agree, it's totally out of order. Did you say that to her?"

He laughs at something the other person says as I reach for a glass from the cupboard. The joyous sound grates against the tension I radiate with.

"Sounds like that was something she needed to hear, although I can't believe you said it. Good for you."

I fill my glass with water and take a long drink, my gaze fixed on my target.

The conversation sounds normal enough. It could be with anyone, a

43

co-worker or even a friend or family member calling to rant about their day, but I don't trust that's all there is to it. Tara works at the same school as Jamie, they have the same colleagues - why wouldn't she call him to talk about her day? Work chat could be a clever ruse, Jamie's ploy to talk to his mistress whenever he wants. The thrill of talking with me in the room could be something they get off on. They could laugh about it when they're tangled together. Dumb Cassie. Deluded Cassie. Cassie the fool.

Bitterness swims in my mouth. I take another gulp of water, but the acrid taste remains.

"I'm going to have to call you back. I'm right in the middle of something."

I lean against the sink, watching Jamie say goodbye and hang up. He places his phone facedown on the kitchen counter, a habit I never noticed before but now can't stop spotting. "You didn't have to cut your call short because of me," I say.

"It's not because of you. I need two hands for cooking," Jamie grins, waving both palms at me.

I smile back tightly. "Who was it?"

"Jonah. He had an issue with his teaching assistant this afternoon and doesn't know how to handle it. He spoke to her, but it wasn't the most diplomatic way to approach the subject. You'd think after twelve years of teaching Jonah would know how to talk to people but he's useless. He's going to need coaching through this one."

"He's lucky he has you to help him."

"What can I say, I'm a good guy."

As Jamie focuses on prepping tomorrow's lunch, I raise my glass to my lips and wonder if he's lying to me now. He doesn't look or sound like he is, but I didn't think he was lying before, so what good is my judgement? He's hiding his bank accounts from me. Is it really such a stretch to think he'd be hiding calls too?

Our joint life flickers through my mind, each moment morphing and shifting before me until I don't know what I'm looking at. When Jamie's home late, is he really staying back to mark books? When he says he's going for a run, is he seeing Tara instead? Whenever I go out with my mum or my friends, does he invite her to the apartment? Do they revel in the freedom of tainting our space by claiming it as theirs, drinking our drinks, eating our food, rolling around in our bedsheets?

I grip the kitchen counter until visions of Jamie and Tara in the bed I am to sleep in tonight fade away.

Is this to be my life until the wedding day, I wonder. A paranoid, anxiety-ridden wreck?

The thought makes me fold in on myself. The deception, the uncertainty - it's already too much. I need to make a move on the truth soon or I'm going to explode.

I glance at Jamie's phone. Everything I need to know, every detail of their affair, in one place, just waiting to be uncovered. I don't know his passcode, I don't have thumbprint access, but I do have determination. Sheer, unwavering determination.

Whatever it takes, I need to get into that phone.

6.

Exhaustion crusts my eyes, but I ignore the temptation to snooze my alarm and head into work early. With home no longer somewhere I can trust, my classroom is all I have. It's a sombre admission, but as I take a seat at my desk, having nowhere else to go doesn't feel so bad. At least my classroom isn't filled with furniture purchased in preparation for buying our 'forever' home or tokens and artefacts saved from years of memories.

Unpicking the web of lies that twenty-four hours ago I didn't know existed isn't going to be easy, but I've got to start somewhere. Where else but social media? After all, nowhere provides a more detailed insight into people's lives than the stuff they share online thinking others care enough to want to see it.

Even though I've met Tara a few times at Meadow Park Primary events I tagged along to as Jamie's plus one, we aren't connected on social media. It makes sense – why would you want to see photos of the man you're secretly shagging having a good time with a woman whose heart you're partly responsible for breaking? Being in the same bar for end of year drinks is manageable, but online friendship? Too far, thank you.

As I reach for my phone, the first time I met Tara comes into focus in my mind. The event was nothing special, just dinner and drinks at a local restaurant, but it was one of the first times I'd been invited into Jamie's world. I was so proud to be introduced to his colleagues as his girlfriend, devouring every story of how great a teacher he was until my heart was fit to burst.

Halfway through dinner, I went to the bathroom and discovered I'd been caught out by my period arriving a day earlier than expected.

"Fuck," I cursed, blotting at my bloodstained underwear with a piece of tissue.

"Are you okay?" asked a voice from the other side of the door.

Heat tickled my cheeks at being overheard talking to myself. "I'm fine, thanks," I responded, stuffing tissue in my underwear and praying it would stop the blood from leaking onto my dress.

When I emerged from the cubicle, I found I knew who the voice belonged to. Tara, the other year four teacher at Jamie's school. She was at the sink applying a pale pink lipstick. Our eyes met in the mirror, and we shared a smile.

"Having fun?" she asked.

"It's lovely! Everyone's so nice."

"Yeah, we're lucky at Meadow Park. Not all schools have such a strong staff team."

A silence crept in as I washed my hands, one I felt the need to fill. "Sorry for the swearing. My period's started earlier than I thought," I confessed.

"Oh, I hate it when that happens! Here, let me see if I have anything."

"You don't have to –" I began, but I'd barely finished my sentence before Tara pulled a sanitary pad from her handbag and thrust it towards me.

"Take it," she smiled, and I did.

I left the restaurant thinking how sweet Tara was. I even told Jamie he was lucky to work with someone like her, a fact that makes me shudder considering what I've found out.

Shaking off the past, I search Jamie's name on Facebook so I can find Tara in his friend list. As the only Tara he knows, she's easy to find. Pursing my lips, I click on her profile, ready to learn more.

Tara's profile picture is a photo of her stood on top of a hill under an impossibly blue sky. The cynic in me rolls its eyes at the blatant editing, but the rational part of me concedes it's an impressive picture. Posed and polished, but perfect.

In the photo, Tara's wearing tiny shorts that showcase impressively toned legs. Damp hair frames her face and the glowing flush of her makeup free skin highlights her natural beauty. A wide, unashamed grin spreads across her face like she has accomplished something other than fucking my fiancé.

I scroll through as much of Tara's profile as I can. With it being mandatory for teachers' social media accounts to be so locked down you practically need a degree in hacking to access them, I can't see much. I know it's to stop parents seeing that, shock horror, teachers have a life outside the classroom, but I still hate those privacy settings for blocking me from snooping.

However, with Jamie being a mutual friend, anything relating to the two of them is visible to me. I'm grateful to discover that there's a long history of public communication between the pair, even if reading it is crushing.

From lesson ideas to in-jokes about teaching to clips from comedy shows, their giggling exchanges have long been published for the world to see. The last time one of them shared something on the other's wall was November, but I guess that makes sense. Sharing memes is fine, but it's probably best to tone it down when you're having an affair, right?

Scrolling further, I suck my teeth as a photo of Jamie and Tara at a Meadow Park Primary party fills my screen. Partners weren't invited this time, or so Jamie said, but now I wonder if that's true.

I try not to torment myself with that thought and instead let the photo before me do the torturing.

In the picture, Jamie and Tara are both wearing quirky party hats, his red, hers yellow. She's poured into a sequin dress while he's looking suave in the navy shirt he bought for the occasion. Their arms are wrapped around each other, skin touching skin, smiles that are all eyes and teeth.

I wonder if this was when it started. Did the light from the DJ booth hit her sequins and dazzle him? Did her newly highlighted hair catch his attention? Did she flutter her eyelashes so much that he couldn't stop staring at her eyes, eyes that were just blue to him before but on closer inspection were all the colours of the ocean? Was that the moment they decided to become more than co-workers, to lie, to betray me?

Or had it already happened by then? Is this innocent photo a decoy and usually their ones together were nudes, mid-sex, and revelling in the deception?

Had Jamie gone to her to vent after a hard day? Had she listened in a way he felt I didn't? Had she hugged him, making him realise how soft her touch was, how exciting it was to be held by someone new? Had their romance burned slowly before it became too bright and too hot for them to ignore? Had they had sex on a classroom desk?

I press my hand over my mouth and swallow the vomit threatening to force its way out, then flick from the photo to Tara's 'About Me' section.

Tara Cartwright, twenty-six, graduated with a degree in primary education. She has a sister who is a curvier, older version of her and a mum who looks like she spent the Eighties attached to a sun bed.

Then I see it.

Tara Cartwright *is in a relationship with* **Nico Bianchi**

I blink twice, but the letters don't unscramble and transform into something else.

I didn't know Tara was with someone. She never brought a partner to any of the events I went to with Jamie. There was no reason to think mine wasn't the only heart being broken in all this, but there it is, in black and white – the true depths of their betrayal.

Suddenly, I feel sicker than ever.

With shaking hands, I load Nico's profile, relieved to learn that I couldn't have found a better place to snoop. Nico's security settings are so lax I almost message him to say anyone could steal his identity, but for now his blasé attitude to privacy is perfect for my needs.

First, I study his profile picture. Tall and tanned with stubble that's especially neat, Nico clearly takes care of himself. His eyes are set too far apart and his lips too thin to be conventionally good looking, but there's no denying he's attractive. The petty bitch in me thinks he's a little too handsome for Tara, and, if you believe looks matter, definitely too handsome to be cheated on.

A quick stalk of his profile tells me he's an engineer and the youngest of five boys. He plays football for a local amateur team. His mum adores him, and he adores her back. She tags him in photos every time he goes to her house which, judging from the timestamps on the pictures, is often. I try not to imagine how devastated she will be when she finds out what Tara's been doing behind her son's back.

Swallowing my wobbling emotions, I push thoughts of Nico's pain to one side and scour his profile for posts about Tara.

There are a lot of them. The pair enjoy meals and cocktails in the city often. Every momentous occasion in their relationship, even the anniversary of their first date, is marked with a special post. They are adventure junkies who love to travel, a bond that was cemented when they met two years ago in Rome.

"How romantic," I scoff.

I dig deeper, scroll further, learn more. Tara and Nico completed a four-week tour of Europe last summer, which explains the I'm-queen-of-the-world-on-a-hill-and-yes-I-will-fuck-your-fiancé photo on Tara's profile. No ring yet, but an impressive, modern house they bought together a few months ago. In every picture, Nico looks at Tara like he is consumed by his love for her. In every photo, she beams back as if she is worthy of that love.

Splintering at the devotion in his eyes and the deception in hers, I set my phone down on the desk and let out a long, unsteady breath.

Things have become so much bigger than I first thought. Two hearts are on the line here. Two people deserving of the truth. Two people needing to reset the balance after it was unfairly tipped against them.

Anger simmers in my chest. Goosebumps line my limbs even though it's not cold. A scream builds in my throat, one I'm tempted to let burst free when a movement in the doorway startles me.

"Debbie," I exhale.

She does her best to hide it, but it's clear from the way her eyebrows almost touch her hairline when she enters the classroom that Debbie is surprised to see me at my desk. Not only physically present but looking good too. Heartbreak masked underneath layers of makeup and wrapped up in my favourite outfit, no one would suspect a torrent of agony sits beneath the surface.

"Morning, Cass." Debbie unzips her coat slowly, staring at me the whole time. "Are you sure you should be in work right now?"

"Why wouldn't I be here?"

"Well, I mean, you've just left your fiancé."

I flinch at her words. "I haven't left him. I haven't even spoken to him about it."

Debbie's horror at my admission slices me open. "Cass! Your relationship can't overcome what he's done."

I close my eyes, drained by the pretence that I don't know what to do and I've only just started the performance. "Please, Debbie, don't."

"I'm not having a go at you, sweetheart. I'm trying to stop you making a mistake. However tempting forgiving him might seem, it's not the answer. Staying won't fix things. Pretending this didn't happen won't make you forget it did."

Hearing Debbie trying to convince me to leave as if she believes I'm someone who wouldn't kicks me in my gut. "I'm not going to forgive him or stay. I'm just trying to process everything before I make my next step."

"What's there to process, Cass? You've seen the photo. You know he's cheating."

"But it's not enough. I want to see everything, to know everything, so that when I confront him there won't be a single part of me left that loves him."

"Oh, Cass," Debbie sighs, a devastation to her voice that spears me. "It breaks my heart to see you like this. You need to leave him, sweetheart. There's nothing left to do but walk away."

Her words enter my brain, but they don't process. Walk away? It sounds so weak. Jamie promised me the world and more. For him to break those promises and face no consequence? Everything about that is wrong to me.

But I don't let Debbie know that. Instead, I nod. "You're right, Debbie. It's just it's not easy, you know?"

"If it were easy, there'd be far fewer people stuck in bad relationships," Debbie surmises. "Look, we're a few weeks away from the end of term -"

"I'm supposed to be getting married then," I say, choking on the sadness coating those words.

"I know, sweetheart, but instead of giving your future to someone who doesn't deserve it, you're going to take that time to rest and rebuild. You're going to heal, be with friends. Hell, you can even move in with me and Phil if you need to."

I can't help but smile. "You're too kind, Debbie."

"I'm only as kind as you deserve, Cass. Please walk away. You can do it and you'll be fine when you do." Debbie gives my shoulder a squeeze then straightens up. "Now, we can't have you crying when the children arrive, and they'll be here in a few minutes. So tell me, what's the plan for today?"

My body exhales now we're no longer on the topic of Jamie, his infidelity, and my fake indecision at knowing what to do next. I talk Debbie through the day, then check the clock on the wall.

"It's time."

Marching through the bright cloakroom to the outside door, I peep through the glass. My class are already there, waiting patiently for their day to begin. They look so small in their serious coats and fresh uniforms, these tiny humans with their whole lives ahead of them. My chest twinges and suddenly I'm overwhelmed by the urge to cry.

Blinking away my tears, I transform into Miss Edwards. Preppy, bubbly, full of fun and knowledge Miss Edwards. The persona slips seamlessly over my skin, and I open the door to invite the day in.

"Miss Edwards, did you see how fast I was running?!"

"Miss Edwards, I drew a picture for you last night! It's in my bookbag."

Miss Edwards, Miss Edwards, Miss Edwards... never before has my name carried such meaning. I almost want to say it out loud to prove it's who I am. My identity outside the one Jamie has carved for me. A teacher, a professional, a person devoid of the heartache of her personal life.

As I usher my students into the classroom, a wave of contentment sweeps over me. These children need me. To them, I matter. Despite everything making me think otherwise, I matter. That's something Jamie can never take away from me, no matter what he does.

7.

The day passes in an uneventful blur, with home time arriving in the blink of an eye. Waving the last student goodbye, I head back into the classroom and grab a stack of English books that need marking.

"You did well today. How are you holding up?" Debbie asks.

"I'm good," I reply. Debbie catches my eye and I smile. "Honestly, Debbie, I'm good."

"Good enough to go home and leave Jamie?"

I drop the stack of books I'm holding onto my desk. "Debbie, come on."

"What? I'm just trying to give you a friendly nudge in the right direction."

"I appreciate you looking out for me but there's a lot more to this than screaming and walking out. We live together, our finances are combined, we've booked a wedding. I can't leave yet, but I will."

"Do you promise?"

The lie clogs my throat, but I know that even if it suffocates me, I have to say it. "I promise. I need you to trust me when I say that."

Debbie squeezes my hand. "I trust you, Cass, and I'll try to stop fussing. I just worry about you, then the mother in me takes over. This morning I was even tempted to bring you lunch."

I laugh for the first time since finding out about Jamie and Tara. "My order for next time is a cheese sandwich."

"Got it," Debbie replies with a wink, then she eyes the mound of books waiting to be marked. "Are you sure you should do that tonight?"

"You're fussing again, Debbie," I joke. She holds her hands in the air, feigning innocence, and I smile. "I need to be here. I need to focus on something other than wanting to ruin Jamie's life."

"Now I know you're more sensible than to do something silly like that."

I let Debbie's words skim over me because no, Debbie, I am not more sensible than that.

"Still, I bet it's a fun fantasy," Debbie says, nudging my ribs. "Go on, how would you ruin him?"

Visions of different ways of hurting Jamie burst into my mind. From extreme acts of violence to small, stupid vengeances. But then I see it, my moment of glory – me on our wedding day, stood in front of all our guests, watching Jamie's face fall as he realises everyone knows exactly who he is and what he has done.

Fighting back a smirk, I answer. "I'd find out everything then tear his world apart, bit by bit."

"That's the way to do it, I suppose. Information first, then revenge. You don't want to think you've planned something great then be sideswiped by more bad news." Debbie looks around then leans closer, inviting me into a conspirator's huddle. "You know, I used to daydream about ruining Tony all the time."

"Really? I wouldn't have you down as the vengeful type. What did you imagine doing?"

A mischievousness takes over Debbie's features. "He had a motorbike he was obsessed with. One day I saw it parked outside the supermarket. I came this close to scratching it with my key." Debbie holds her thumb and finger millimetres apart, and I laugh.

"Debbie, you rebel."

"Trust me, in my fantasies I did more than scratch his bike – I stole it and gave it to a learner driver. Someone clumsy, someone who'd really mess it up as they practised."

I laugh harder. "What else?"

"Oh, I don't know, it was so long ago! I guess the key to any revenge plot is to go after the things they care about the most. For Tony, his bike was one thing, then his local pub. He went every Friday night, and most Saturday afternoons. I'd have got him banned from there, I suppose."

"Yes, Debbie!"

"It's a good job I didn't go through with any of it, though. If I'd keyed Tony's bike, I'd have been arrested. I'd have a criminal record, then I'd have never been allowed to work in a school."

"You'd have had to do it in secret so you didn't get caught."

Debbie leans further towards me, so close I can smell the coffee she had in the afternoon on her breath. "This is terrible, but I always imagined framing Philippa for it. It was a double whammy, getting revenge on him for cheating and her for dating someone she knew was with someone else." Debbie shakes her head. "I tell you, talking about this is like talking about another life! I'm so glad I didn't go through with it."

"Even though it was tempting?"

"Even though it was *very* tempting," Debbie agrees, then her expression shifts. "You'll get through this, Cass, and you'll do it without turning into a vengeance seeking menace along the way. Men like Jamie aren't worth ruining your life over. Now, I'd best go home so I can crack on with some jobs before Phil gets home. Call me if you need me, okay?"

As Debbie rises to stand, my lips flick in acknowledgement, but I don't say anything. I can't, not when my mind is so busy ticking over with ideas. Not only ideas of how to humiliate Jamie, but how to get away with it too.

Like Debbie says, it's not worth ruining my life over. I've already been hurt enough by this. Besides, surely if I'm the one to humiliate Jamie at the wedding, all sympathy for me dies? I'd become the 'crazy ex', arguably a worse stereotype to have forced upon you than 'cheating victim'. After all, I could have walked away instead of dragging his friends and family along to such a public spectacle.

But what if I'm not the one who drops the bombshell? What if everyone thinks I'm as shocked as they are?

Suddenly knowing it's Tara that Jamie's cheating with doesn't seem like such a bad thing after all. I mean, she deserves a taste of pain too. She has a partner she's lying to, someone else who deserves to discover the truth. Maybe I don't have to stoop to Jamie's level and be the bad guy. Maybe Tara can take that title for me.

As my imagination runs wild, I can't fight my happiness. It's like Debbie said - what's better than the double whammy of getting revenge on both the people who have hurt you?

8.

While Debbie's words and the possibilities they've inspired dance in my brain, I know there's little I can do to action any ideas I have right now. I'm still clueless as to the extent of Jamie and Tara's relationship. Before I can do anything, I need information. Information only Jamie has access to.

With that in mind, I flee the school building to make my next move on the truth – finding a way, any way, to get into Jamie's phone.

My fingertips tingle as I drive towards my destination. For the first time since seeing the photo of Jamie and Tara, I'm doing something other than flailing in disbelief and it feels good.

Spotting a sign for Newington Pharmacy in the distance, I park up and head inside. A bell above the door chimes to mark my entrance. The figure behind the counter looks up and I freeze as their familiar features register in my mind.

"Cassie! What a lovely surprise."

I can't bring myself to fake happiness at bumping into Alisha's mum at the best of times, never mind today. Gill is nice enough, in small doses. She's one of those people who asks too many questions and thinks every answer has a hidden meaning. With everything going on right now, I fear all it will take is one poorly worded response and Gill will see straight through me.

Gill leaves her position behind the counter to hug me. Her sweet perfume fills my lungs, her long, black hair tickling my cheek. "It's good to see you!"

I muster as much enthusiasm as my weary body can manage. "It's good to see you too! I didn't know you worked at this pharmacy?"

"Oh, I don't but you know how it is. Staff shortages, cover needed here, there and everywhere, so let's send Gill, she'll pick up the slack." Gill waves her hand dismissively. "How are you, anyway? Excited for the wedding?"

I strain a smile, my eyes bulging and every tooth on show. "Can't wait!"

Gill skims over my response, her thin lips pursing as she studies me. "Are you getting enough sleep? Are you trying to lose weight? You look thin – too thin for your body shape. I hope you're doing it the healthy way?"

"I'm fine, just a little stressed. You know how it is."

"You girls and your stress. Alisha's the same, always running off to meetings, always on the phone, always working until stupid o'clock. It's not good for your health, you know."

"I guess when you make as much money as Alisha, you can buy good health," I joke.

"Good health isn't something that can be bought, Cassie. As a teacher, you of all people should know that. I hope a poor work-life balance is not what you're passing onto the next generation. I don't know, you career women," Gill sighs.

I'm about to snap at Gill that she should lay off women working hard and focus her fussing efforts on her son Anwar who's twenty-nine and working eight hours a week in a dive bar when an elderly man enters the pharmacy.

Gill squeezes my arm. "I'll serve this gentleman, then I'll be with you."

"Oh, it's no bother. I might even go elsewhere –"

"Nonsense! What's so private you can't buy it in front of me? Unless…" Gill's eyes travel down to my stomach. Instinctively, I wrap my arms around myself.

59

"Not that! Definitely not that."

"It wouldn't be the worst thing to happen, dear. You're not getting any younger. Anyway, back in a second."

As Gill bustles away, my foot moves a fraction towards the door, but I stop myself. If I leave now, Gill will tell Alisha she saw me and that I was acting strange. Before I know it, I'll be on an intervention phone call or receiving gift baskets filled with baby clothes.

With a sigh, I accept my fate and trudge around the pharmacy until I locate medication to enhance sleep. I scan the packages. Words like 'natural remedy' and 'drift off' spring from the boxes. While most people would think that sounds wonderful, it's not enough for me. I want dead to the world, knock you out, unconscious pills. I want the photos printed on the boxes to be of people sprawled out, drooling, and lost to their subconscious, not resting peacefully with a cloud for a pillow.

Suddenly, Gill appears at my side. "Sorry about that. Now, what can I help you with?" She sees what I'm looking at and tuts. "I knew you weren't sleeping. One look at you and I knew, didn't I tell you? It's like I say to Alisha - you can't fool me. I've a trained eye, and you look terrible."

My hands ball into fists, but my expression remains serene. "I'm sure I'll look better once I reset my sleeping pattern."

"Why, are things not okay at home?"

"Things are fine, there's just a lot happening at the moment."

"I swear, you young ones think you're the only people to be stressed. You didn't invent it, you know." Gill shakes her head as she scans the shelf. "Well, some of these are herbal blends, a bit on the weaker side –"

"Strong. I want strong."

"I can't give you strong without a prescription."

"Well, the strongest you've got then."

Gill eyes me sceptically but for once says nothing. After a moment's deliberation, she reaches out and plucks a box from the shelf. "These are usually what I suggest for people who want a good, solid chunk of rest, like someone who has a long-haul flight they want to sleep through. One of those will put you out of action for a few hours but it will be a nice, peaceful sleep."

"What if I take two?"

"You'd feel pretty sluggish the next day, let's put it that way."

"What about three?"

Gill's lips purse. "Three would be lunacy." Nodding, I reach for the box, but Gill pulls her hand back. "Are you sure everything's okay?"

"Of course. I'm just tired, that's all."

With one last dubious look, Gill takes the box to the till and scans the barcode. "Take these one at a time. I mean it, Cassandra, you want to sleep, not be knocked out. One is enough, okay? Don't make me worry about you."

I force a laugh and tap my card to pay. "There's nothing to worry about, I promise. You know me – I love a lie in!"

"Well, here's hoping when I see you walking down the aisle, you're rested. Either that or you have a good concealer for those eye bags."

Grabbing the pills and gritting my teeth, I wave goodbye to Gill and leave the pharmacy. The whip of cold air stings my cheeks, but the chill outside feels better than being on the receiving end of Gill's verbal jabs.

As I walk to my car, the pills and all their possibility weigh heavy in my hand. I slide into the driver's seat and scan the information on the back of the box. It promises fast results and a calming sleep. It promises everything I need.

I push Gill's words of warning from my mind as I set off driving. After all, why would I need to listen to them? These pills aren't for me in the first place.

9.

I intend on heading straight home, but I find myself travelling in the opposite direction to my apartment. I don't know where I'm going until I stop in a carpark on the edge of the city, one Jamie uses when we go on date nights. Why I stop here, I don't know, but as soon as I'm parked I realise that going home is the last thing I want to do. When I do, I'll become someone I never thought I would be.

Abandoning my car, I mooch about the city, blending into crowds grabbing on-sale bargains and perfect homeware for their perfect lives as if I belong in this world of couples and families and intact hearts. I trudge behind a giggling group of university students and suddenly the pills weigh heavy in my handbag. They're a sign of how messed up things are, and one I no longer want to carry.

The sky darkens to welcome in the night as I sit on a chipped bench and pull out my phone. My group chat with my friends is alive with talk of a new bar offering a bottomless brunch deal. Laney's shared a screenshot of the advertisement, a pale pink social media post featuring a group of glamorous, smiling women clinking glasses of Prosecco.

I try imagining myself at that table but it's impossible. Weekend plans with friends are so far removed from my life right now. I'm going to break the law tonight. I'm going to drug someone until they're unconscious… knowing that, how can I possibly type a cheery response about my availability and what outfit I'd wear?

Ignoring the messages and my impending criminality, I check Nico's social media for updates. Tara's posted a link to a spring market at a country estate named Motham Hall on Nico's wall. He's commented saying they can go on Saturday before their lunch reservation at one. I screenshot their exchange then continue scrolling until my vision glazes over.

When social media can no longer distract me, I watch the world around me. Commuters rush to beat the traffic and couples meet up after work, no doubt to go for romantic meals at trendy restaurants before heading back to their magazine-worthy homes to have passionate sex. I watch lips brush cheeks, hands caress waists. I watch everything that was once mine but no longer is.

Misery sits beside me, making itself at home until my phone ringing drags me from its company. Jamie's name appears on the screen, and for the first time I notice three texts from him queued in my notifications.

"Is everything okay? It's almost six thirty and you're not back from work yet."

"Sorry, I thought I'd messaged to say I went for a drink with Shari," I lie.

"That's nice. Are you staying out?"

An almost unfairly happy, good-looking couple choose that moment to slink past me. The woman tosses a cascade of glossy red hair over her shoulder and snuggles into her partner of choice, and my heart turns to stone.

"No, I'll come home now."

"Are you sure? Stay out if you want to, I don't mind."

"No, it's alright. I'll be home soon."

"Alright, I'll have dinner waiting for you when you get in."

"You're the best," I reply as I hang up. I take one last look at the epitome of young love and walk away.

When I arrive back at the apartment, Jamie greets me at the doorway. "As promised, dinner is ready."

"My hero," I say, offering him a kiss. "I'll be with you in a second."

I make a performance of hanging my coat up and watch Jamie leave. When he's gone, I slide the pills into my pocket then follow the sound of gentle music. I find Jamie stood tall and proud by the dining table. A plate of curry waits for me, perched alongside lit candles and a vase of fresh flowers.

"Surprise," he grins.

"You got me lilies," I reply, biting my cheeks to stop myself from bursting into tears.

"Of course. They're your favourite."

"I know, but you didn't have to."

"Well, you deserve them. In fact, lilies are the least you deserve." Jamie moves to pull out my chair for me, but I stop him.

"I'll get a bottle of wine from the fridge. We can make this a proper date night."

"You sit, I'll get it," Jamie says, but I put my hands on his chest to stop him.

"It's the least I can do after you've cooked dinner. Start eating, I'll be back in a second."

Jamie does as he's told, and I slip into the kitchen. With the scent of lilies still tickling my nose, I hide the sleeping pills in a box of low-fat crackers. Thanks to their sugar-free, fun-free taste, I know Jamie will never look in there.

Grabbing a chilled bottle of wine, I go back to the dining table.

Sitting opposite Jamie at dinner, I study him. He's attractive, there's no denying that. When Alisha and Lily caught us chatting the night we met, they gave me a sly thumbs up, but even without their approval I knew he was handsome.

But Jamie isn't perfect. He looks like someone you might see on your local rugby team or in a group of laddish men at a pub. He's broad, stocky, and stubbled. He doesn't dress particularly well. If anything, he looks like he runs blindfolded through the nearest men's clothing store and puts on whatever items he grabs first. He isn't overly tall or imposing, but he looks protective, capable, and strong. He's humble and thoughtful and… well, normal.

I wonder if that's how he's got away with it. Has his decent demeanour fooled me into thinking his personality matched his appearance? Is it what Tara's fallen for too?

Jamie catches me staring at him. "Everything okay?"

"It's been a long day, that's all."

"Tell me about it. Work has taken it out of me this week! You know how it is - marking, marking, marking."

"I think you forgot to mention marking," I quip.

Jamie grins. "I'm so lucky you're a teacher too and you get it."

"We get each other," I reply tightly.

After dinner, Jamie and I settle down to watch the latest true crime TV series everyone at work is raving about. He holds his arm out for me to curl underneath and I oblige, but I keep my body stiff. As familiar as the loving position is, I need to reinforce the knowledge that nothing about this Friday night, from the love in Jamie's voice to the fact that he lit candles at the dinner table, is how it seems. I must fight against every instinct telling me I need this man and in his arms is where I belong.

Halfway through the second episode, Jamie yawns, a dramatic wail bursting from him.

"You are tired! Let me up, I'll make you a tea," I say, squeezing his thigh as I stand.

In the kitchen and out of sight, I put the kettle on and take the pills from the box of crackers. There's a tremble to my hands as if they can't believe what I'm about to do, but I force them into action. The silver foil of the packaging strains as I press it, then it splinters and a little white pill pops free. It lands on the counter, waiting to be put to use.

My brain chooses this moment to broadcast Gill's words of warning about the pills, and suddenly I feel sick. What if Jamie has an allergic reaction to them? What if he doesn't wake up? I'd go from being a woman on the hunt for answers to a woman who murdered her partner.

As the trembling in my hands intensifies, I open the kitchen window to invite some air into the room, catching sight of my reflection in the glass as I do so. My breath catches in the back of my throat. I've never seen myself look so pale, so knotted with anxiety. I look like a woman possessed.

Horrified, I go to put the pills back in the box, but then I hear Jamie's phone ping with a notification.

My intestines wither. I lower my gaze away from my reflection and stare at the pill on the countertop. Gnawing my lip, I pop another two pills from the foil and drop all three into Jamie's tea. I wait for them to dissolve before taking the steaming mug to him.

"Thanks, Cass. If I'd not asked you to marry me already, I would right now."

Laughing, I hand Jamie his drink and watch out of the corner of my eye as he takes a gulp. Every few minutes, he drinks until eventually he drains the mug. When he goes to set it down on the coffee tables, he misses.

"Careful," I say, picking the mug up from the floor. The remnants of tea leave three splashes on the carpet. I scuff over the stains with my toe and listen to Jamie's slow, sleepy breathing.

"Sorry," he whispers before his head flops back. Almost instantly, he beings to snore.

"Jamie?" I call. I lift his arm, now a deadweight, into the air and drop it. Even the jerking movement doesn't make him stir. I clap in his face. "Jamie!" I shout, but he doesn't respond. He doesn't even flinch. "Jamie?" I ask again, my voice croaky this time, but there's still no response.

My mouth dries as I reach for Jamie's neck, pressing my fingers into his flesh to search for his pulse. My knees almost give way as I feel it beneath my fingers. He's not dead. Dead to the world, maybe, but not dead.

With Jamie passed out, it's time. Time to hunt for answers.

Adrenaline surges through me as I reach for his phone. Every hair on my body stands to attention, waiting for Jamie to jerk awake and shout, "What are you doing?".

But I need to do this. I need to read their affectionate pet names and see how they gloss over my existence. I need to find out where Jamie takes Tara and check if they're the same places he takes me.

With no time to waste, I grab Jamie's hand and hold his thumbprint to the sensor on his phone. His print is recognised, access granted.

My heart is in my throat as I scour Jamie's home screen. He has over twelve and a half thousand unopened emails, a sight that makes me grimace. I can't stand notifications, never mind that many of them, but I pull myself together. I'm not here to check Jamie's phone operating etiquette. I'm here to find out what really goes on underneath his loving pretence.

With trembling hands, I open his message inbox, but nothing could prepare me for what I find.

10.

Empty.

The entire folder is empty.

There are no texts about hook-up locations, no '*I miss you*' declarations, no promises Jamie will leave me for Tara.

But more than that, there are no texts to or from anyone else, not even me. No '*don't forget to pick up milk on the way home*' reminders or '*have a good day*' wishes. There isn't even the text Jamie sent me earlier this evening saying, '*drive safely*'.

My brows furrow, the blankness of what I see feeling like a trick I can't quite understand. I exit the inbox then reopen it as if doing so will make Jamie's text history appear, but of course it doesn't. I manoeuvre to his call list only to find another empty screen staring back at me.

Everything on Jamie's phone has been erased.

I look at my sleeping fiancé, a man so guilty he deletes messages and calls to and from everyone, including me. "Who are you?" I whisper.

Dragging my eyes from Jamie, I focus back on the phone. Messages aren't the only place I want to investigate.

I open his banking app and the login screen loads before me. I take hold of Jamie's hand to use his thumbprint to gain access but then he chokes on a snore.

I drop his hand like it's on fire, my breath caught in the back of my throat.

Time suspends as Jamie snuffles and grunts, his eyelids flickering like he's on the edge of waking up, but then, after a loud snort, heavy snoring continues.

I wait for him to stir again, but when Jamie's breathing remains rhythmical and his sleep deep, I reach for his hand once more. Pressing his thumb to the sensor, Jamie's banking app logs in.

Four accounts appear before me – our joint everyday account, our savings account, Jamie's personal account and Jamie's credit card. My stomach falls to the floor as I read the balance of the credit card.

-£8,675.57.

I read the number twice, willing the figures to rearrange and the minus symbol to disappear, but it doesn't. If anything, the number seems to grow bigger and bolder, the harsh black pixels mocking me and my naivety, asking if what I've found is what I wanted to see.

I gulp. How could this account belong to the man who sighs with such disappointment if we break our monthly spending limit? It doesn't make sense. The Jamie I know would never do this, never have a balance so far in the negative.

Trembling, I click on the transaction list and a history of extravagant spending appears before me. Multiple payments to fancy restaurants and trendy cocktail bars, ones we never visit. A costly trip to a sex shop, even though no new toys have been introduced in our bedroom. Shopping sprees at designer stores, but no expensive clothes are in Jamie's wardrobe. Hundreds spent in lingerie shops over the last two months, although I've never been presented with a new racy underwear set.

My intestines set. For Tara, for their relationship, Jamie's willing to do everything, even if that means spending money he doesn't have in the process. I burn with the injustice of it all, then I see another punch to the gut expense. The weekend in February Jamie told me he was visiting his friend Pete in Edinburgh is the same weekend a bill for The Harrington Hotel was charged to his card.

I'd suggested going to The Harrington Hotel for our anniversary. Jamie said it was too expensive with the wedding coming up, but clearly it's not too much money to spend on Tara. She must be worth it.

My bottom lip quivers. It's bad enough knowing Jamie's cheating but getting into debt to give Tara the things he never gave me somehow makes it even worse.

I skim over the transaction list again, letting each expense cut just that little bit deeper. I note how the only constant, other than the relentless spending, is the little to no attempt Jamie makes to repay his debt. He makes purchase after purchase, stacking them on top of each other, the total rising and rising, the spending continuing and continuing. I don't know how he does his monthly financial audit without bursting into tears. Reading the amount owed makes me break out in a cold sweat and it's not even my debt.

Sickened but hungry for more, I flick from his credit card balance to his personal account. Part of me flushes with relief to see this account isn't in negative numbers but when I scan the list of transactions my relief doesn't last for long.

Jamie made four purchases at different coffee shops in the city this week, but Jamie doesn't work in the city. Besides, I don't know a single teacher who has time in their day to go for a coffee. It makes no sense that he could make those transactions.

I keep scrolling, getting more and more confused by what I see.

Last week Jamie visited another three coffee shops, two of those in the next city over. He also took Tara to another expensive restaurant the day of his staff meeting. Bella, the new Italian I've been suggesting we go to for weeks. Again, that restaurant is in the city.

Then I notice something else.

It was payday last week. Jamie put his share of money into our joint accounts, but no money had gone into his bank. Looking at Jamie's statement, it's like he hadn't been paid at all.

A foreboding sensation creeps up on me, one I can't stifle no matter how hard I try.

Scrolling past more coffee shop expenditure and bills from upmarket restaurants, I learn that the only money that's gone into Jamie's account in months is a deposit of fifteen thousand pounds from his parents, Anne and Martin. Money I know nothing about.

I flick faster through his spending history, trying to find when Jamie last received a wage. My eyes pop when I see it was in December.

"Fuck," I exhale because I don't know what else to say. I lift my gaze from the phone to Jamie and watch him sleep. He looks so peaceful, so innocent, but he isn't. He's guilty of so many things, cheating seemingly just one of them.

I gulp as I stare at the stranger before me.

Who is this man I had wanted to spend the rest of my life with? Who is he and where does he go every day when he tells me he's at work?

11.

My coffee cools on the kitchen counter, the number for Meadow Park Primary lit up on the screen before me. My finger twitches to press call so I can ask them what the hell happened with Jamie's job, but I can't. It's Saturday. There will be no one there. My sad, empty questions would be recorded by an answering machine, ready to be played into a stale office on Monday morning.

I tell myself I can wait, that Monday isn't so far away, clinging to those words even though not a single part of me believes them. Despair takes over, starting at the edges of my vision before seeping in until it takes over everything.

I'm staring at the wall opposite when Jamie stumbles into the kitchen still wearing the clothes he came home from 'work' in the day before. "I fell asleep on the sofa?" he asks.

I nod. "I tried to wake you, but you were out of it."

"That's not like me."

"You said it yourself, you've had a long week," I shrug, not allowing myself to add the 'but doing what, no one knows' that's on the tip of my tongue.

"I guess so, but I'm sorry you had to sleep alone."

"Oh, I don't mind. I quite enjoyed the extra room," I reply, my first honest comment of the day.

Jamie's arms snake around my waist. "Well don't get too used to it. You've got a lifetime of stealing the duvet from me ahead of you." I let out a laugh and wriggle free of his grip. Jamie frowns. "What's wrong?"

"Nothing, we just need to get ready."

"Ready for what?"

I sigh. "The spring market? I told you about it last night. You said we could go this morning."

"I did?"

"Right before you fell asleep, you told me we could go and see if there was anything we could get for the wedding," I lie, folding my arms across my chest.

"Of course," Jamie nods as if remembering a conversation that never actually happened. "You get ready. I'll grab a coffee and wake up."

I leave the room, knowing just how much Jamie will need that coffee after ingesting three sleeping pills the night before.

In the car on the way to the market, I ask Jamie about work. He tells me about a disastrous history lesson, what the subject of this week's staff meeting had been and makes jokes about one of the mums who has a crush on him. He tells me specific facts and detailed anecdotes and all the while I look at him as if I'm seeing him for the first time.

He tells a good story, I'll give him that. If I didn't already know it was a lie, I'd be adamant he was telling the truth, but I've seen his bank statement. If he's not being paid by Meadow Park then he's not working there, it's as simple as that.

A flaming rage of loathing supercharges my body. I focus my attention out of the window and count the number of red cars we pass. Anything to distract myself from the itching in my fingers as my hands beg to wrap themselves around Jamie's thick neck and squeeze until no more lies can escape his lips.

Ten minutes later, we join a queue of cars snaking their way up the hill towards Motham Hall.

"Looks like everyone's had the same idea as you this weekend," Jamie says.

"What can I say, I'm a trendsetter."

After sitting in traffic for an almost insufferable amount of time, we finally make it through the wrought iron gates of the venue. Driving through the beautifully manicured grounds, I'm reminded of the time Anne suggested we check out Motham Hall as a potential setting to host our wedding.

"It's a fantastic venue. Just think, my son getting married somewhere like Motham Hall! What a day that would be," she marvelled, so we requested a brochure. The pricelist made us laugh out loud – three times what we could afford – but fantasising about a wedding here had been a blissful daydream, one that now cuts to remember.

We find a parking space and I hop out of the car before Jamie can spot the tears in my eyes. As we join the crowds and make our way through the market, he links my arm. "So, what exactly are we looking for?"

"Anything that catches our eye."

"That narrows it down," Jamie grins.

Smiling, I scan the crowd. Children beg for handstitched toys and women try on knitted scarves while their husbands look on in bored approval. The air is thick with the scent of freshly baked goods and cooking spices. People are everywhere, bustling past each other and cooing, 'Oh, isn't this pretty?'.

Then I spot her. Four stalls ahead and handing over a note in exchange for a box of gluten free brownies.

My stomach flips.

Her pale blonde hair is long and loose, her smile natural. She has minimal makeup on yet still looks glowing, the way only someone blessed with naturally good skin can. Nico beside her is a little bored but he's smiling, his arm loose around her slender waist.

My legs move before I can stop them.

"Tara? Tara, is that you?" I exclaim, doing my best to sound happy to see her. If I could give myself an Oscar for my acting, I would. I at least deserve a high five for not knocking the box of brownies out of her hand.

Tara spots me and her eyes flick to Jamie. She jolts in shock but catches herself well. "Jamie, Cassie, what a surprise!" She pats Nico on the arm to alert him to our presence. "Nico, this is Jamie and his partner Cassie. Jamie who was my year group partner last year, remember?"

Nico's eyes widen in recognition. "Jamie, of course!"

"Nice to meet you, mate," Jamie says, reaching out and shaking Nico's hand. "Tara remains to this day the best year group partner I've ever had."

As Tara bows her head to hide her blushes, I do my best to not balk at Jamie's audacity and instead focus on the tension Tara radiates with. Her two worlds colliding like this can't be comfortable, and I feel a somewhat gleeful pride at orchestrating this meet up.

"Fancy bumping into you here," I say, my honeyed voice dripping with insincerity. "We're actually on the lookout for last-minute wedding bits."

I watch Tara's lips clamp together in a tight, curved line. Jamie beside me says nothing, acting as if this interaction is the most normal thing in the world.

"You're getting married? Congratulations!" Nico says.

"Thank you! Less than one month to go now, isn't that right?"

Jamie squeezes me. "It is. I can't wait."

"One month! That's got to be stressful, right?" Nico asks.

"Oh, you've no idea," I sigh. "I don't have a moment to myself! What with wedding planning and teaching and trying to find the perfect-but-a-bargain honeymoon - I need an organisation fairy!" I look at Tara as if I've only just realised she's there. "Tara, this might sound strange, but I can't help feeling that running into you today might actually be fate."

"Fate?" she echoes.

"Jamie was always telling me how brilliant you were when the two of you worked together and wedding stuff is getting on top of me like you wouldn't believe! I know we don't know each other well, but this idea has sprung to my mind, and I'd kick myself if I didn't ask. Would you mind helping me out with the last few bits of planning?"

There's a beat of silence before Tara speaks. "Sorry, what?"

I feel Jamie's eyes on me, but I don't look at him. "I promise it won't be anything big, just sorting favours and double-checking my lists – you know teachers and their lists! I'd need to meet you twice, three times tops, and I can pay you for your time."

"Cass, that's a lot to ask when Tara's working full-time," Jamie says.

"I know, I know, you must think I'm so rude!" I wail, reaching out and grabbing Tara by the hand. Her skin is cold against mine and I swallow the urge to bend her fingers back until she yelps. "I'm sorry, it's just – woman to woman here – I'm struggling. My friends are great, but they don't have that teacher's touch, you know? It would mean the world if you could spare some time to help me."

Tara shifts on the spot, looking from me to Jamie and back again. Her mouth opens and closes a few times before she paints a toothy half smile on her face. "Sure, why not?"

"Really? You'll do it?"

"I mean, if it would help then yes."

"Oh Tara, thank you so much!" I cry, throwing my arms around her. "I promise you'll both have the best seat at the wedding!"

Tara laughs awkwardly. "Oh, you don't have to invite us."

"Nonsense! If you weren't helping, I don't think I'd even make it to the big day. So please, come. We'd love to have you there."

"Can we add people to the guestlist at this point in time?" Jamie asks, his forehead creasing.

"Why not? We're the ones paying for it. You'll be there, won't you?"

"Well, maybe -" Tara begins, but Nico cuts her off.

"Not maybe – we'll be there. Who knows, we might pick up some tips for the future."

As Tara blushes once more, it takes everything in me not to tell Nico the truth right here, right now. "I really hope it's an informative day for you," I say to him, and I truly mean it.

"Anyway, I think it's time we left these two alone before you have them organise our honeymoon," Jamie jokes, wrapping his hand around mine.

"Now that would be the dream! Any amazing last-minute deals you spot, you know where to send them. It was lovely to run into you both. Tara, I'll add you on Facebook and arrange our first meet up!"

"Sounds good," Tara replies, her tone stilted. Nico waves goodbye and the pair walk away, hand in hand.

"He seems nice," I comment, turning to find Jamie staring at me like I've sprouted two heads. "What?"

"You're asking Tara to help with our wedding?"

"Why not?"

"For starters, you don't even know her."

"So? You always told me how brilliant she was when she was your year group partner and I've told you it's all too much for me. If I remember rightly, getting help with the wedding was your idea. Why shouldn't I ask her?"

"Don't you think it's a bit weird having a stranger helping to plan the most important day of your life? Especially one who wasn't even coming to the wedding in the first place."

"She's coming now," I shrug, slipping my arm through Jamie's. "Relax. You always said she was your friend, so it's not like I've asked a stranger. I'll buy her some wine to say thank you then spend the next few weeks not on the verge of screaming every five minutes. This is a good thing! Why isn't it making you happy?"

Jamie studies me with an indecipherable expression then shakes his head. "You, Cassandra Edwards, are mad but if you're happy, then I'm happy."

I beam at him. I am happy. Ecstatic, even. Today went exactly as planned. How could I not be happy about that?

12.

As soon as I'm back in the car, I add Tara on Facebook. When she accepts my request an hour later, I message her to arrange meeting up. We lock in plans for next Saturday, then I spend the rest of the day trawling through her profile. The more I learn about her, the more the hollow outline of 'the other woman' is filled in.

Two boyfriends during her time at university, a few 'fling' years and then she met Nico. Her best friend is called Mina and they go for bottomless brunch together once a month. She shares an annoying number of quotes about travel. She has a small, pink birthmark by her left eyebrow. She's passionate about high quality education for all, and last year ran a marathon fundraising to buy toys for refugee children.

Every post that builds a bigger picture of Tara, especially the ones that don't depict her as a monster, twists my soul. I don't want to hear how kind she is or see how many friends she has. I don't want her to be anything but the target of my hatred and the scapegoat for Jamie's public humiliation.

When I go to the bathroom after dinner, I notice my hand is fixed in a claw-like shape from gripping my phone so furiously. I flex my stiff fingers and splash my face with cold water, a pathetic attempt at self-soothing. I'm too furious at Tara's wholesome perfection, too rigid with anger, too aware that outside the bathroom stands a man who lies to me every chance he gets.

I need a distraction. Thankfully, I get one.

As adult women with demanding careers and a range of social engagements to juggle, finding a night where Alisha, Laney, Lily, and myself are all free is a rarity. When we do find such an occasion, we lock it in tight. Bails are only allowed for relatives on deathbeds, hospital stays or the end of the world. Even if that wasn't our rule, I'd cancel everything on my calendar for a night with my friends right now.

Jamie drives me to Alisha's house. We talk about work, the wedding, and what we want to watch on TV next. We talk about everything but the truth.

"Have a good time," he says as I gather my things. "I'll pick you up at eleven."

"Thanks. Enjoy your evening on the sofa."

"Oh, I will. I have a date with the rugby highlights!"

My laugh comes out strangled as my mind runs wild with ideas of other plans Jamie may have. Blowing him a kiss, I climb out of the car and walk down Alisha's driveway.

I've been to Alisha's house many times but I'm always as awestruck when I see it as I had been the first time I visited. With five bedrooms, four bathrooms, a double garage, and a garden five times the size of my entire apartment, it's the home of dreams. No one deserves it more than Alisha.

I press the doorbell and listen as it chimes throughout the house.

"I'll get it!" Simon shouts from somewhere inside. A few seconds later, the hazy outline of his figure draws closer through the frosted glass. "Cassie!" he cheers when he throws open the door.

The smell of spiced candles ushers me inside. Simon takes my coat and hangs it up, then we walk towards the kitchen where I find Alisha and Lily picking their way through an assortment of snacks laid out on the countertop.

"You made it on time," Alisha smiles.

"Of course," I reply, handing her a bottle of wine. "I'm guessing Laney isn't here yet?"

"Would she be Laney if she were ever on time?"

"No, but she'd be a lot easier to track down." I joke, grabbing a carrot stick. I'm reaching for another when Simon speaks.

"Cass, did those tablets help you?"

I freeze at the question. "What?"

Simon looks around the room, realising the inappropriateness of what he asked. "Sorry, I didn't think you might not want to talk about this in front of people. Alisha told me Gill said you've been struggling with sleep so popped into the pharmacy for some sleeping pills. My heart goes out to you. I went through a patch of insomnia myself at university. I hope you're getting the rest you need."

The carrot suddenly tastes rotten in my mouth, and I struggle to swallow it. "Oh, I'm fine. Just a bit of stress keeping me awake."

"Well, if you need any sleeping tips, let me know. I've mastered the art of rest now, so I'm happy to help."

Alisha reaches for Simon. "Simon's so dedicated to his night routine I'm almost jealous of it."

"No more dedicated than I am to you," Simon grins. He bends his neck to kiss Alisha. I look away, half embarrassed to witness their affection, half bitter it's something I no longer have in my life.

"Get a room, you two. There are other people here, you know. People who don't want to watch you play tonsil tennis," Lily cries, throwing a piece of cucumber at them.

Alisha and Simon laugh and break apart. Alisha wipes her lip gloss from his lips, and Simon looks like all his Christmases have come at once.

"I guess that's my cue to leave. If you need me, I'll be in my study."

"Enjoy," Alisha calls after Simon.

"What's Simon working on?" Lily asks when he's left the room.

"He's illustrating a children's book. It's a new author so the pay is a little less than he hoped, but the storyline is so beautiful he just had to take the job."

Part of my brain hisses that, having been out of a commissioned role for the last few months, Simon should be grateful for any work at all. The speed at which the poisonous thought springs to my mind makes me shrivel. I bathe in the shame of pulling Simon into the role of money-sucking leech so I can take the shine off Alisha's fairy tale to make myself feel better mine is over.

"You'll have to let me know when it's published so I can buy a copy for my classroom," I enthuse, hoping my over-the-top niceness resets my karma.

Alisha, Lily, and I chat while we wait for Laney. Alisha tells us about her latest client acquisition, and I recite my latest, 'Yes, children really do say the wildest things' story. By the time Laney arrives, I've almost fooled myself that everything is normal.

"What time do you call this?" Lily demands as Laney bustles into the kitchen in a whirlwind of stressed energy.

"I know, I know, I'm useless!"

"I think this might be a Laney record," I quip. "You're almost forty minutes late."

"I was once an hour late to a date," Laney says, grabbing a handful of crackers and shoving them in her mouth. "By the time I got there, he was gone."

"Are you sure you didn't get stood up?" Alisha asks.

Laney's face falls and I laugh, a laugh so pure it has me wondering if maybe everything will be alright after all.

Once our wineglasses are refilled, we carry the snacks into Alisha's living room and sink into her plush sofas. Conversation carries on in the same vein as it did in the kitchen before swooping to the wedding.

"So, are you all set for the big day?" Alisha asks.

I groan, the relaxing effect of wine letting my 'everything is *fine*' guard slip. "Do we have to talk about the wedding?"

"Aren't brides usually dying to talk about their big day?" Laney asks.

"I was and I wasn't even engaged to Andy," Lily jokes. "Cass must be playing it cool."

A blush climbs up my neck as my friends' eyes fix on me. "It feels like it's all I ever talk about these days."

"Well, you've not gone Bridezilla on us yet so it must be going well," Laney says. "Although there's still time…"

Lily replies on my behalf. "Not that much time. It's less than a month away, can you believe it?"

Laney's eyes bulge. "It's that soon?!"

Alisha shakes her head. "Laney, I love you but if we got to the aisle and you weren't there because you'd overslept, I wouldn't be surprised."

"Look, I'm not saying that *will* happen but as long as Cassie shows up, that's all that matters."

"That's right - no runaway bride allowed!" Lily grins, wagging her finger at me in warning.

My body stiffens, a frozen smile paralysing my lips, not that my friends seem to notice.

"Can you imagine spending all that time and effort planning a wedding only to run away on the day," Alisha grimaces.

"Don't even think of it, Cass. Your gift wasn't cheap, and I don't have the receipt to return it," Laney laughs.

"Please, we've nothing to worry about with Cass and Jamie. They're not me and Andy, their wedding will happen," Lily jokes.

My toes curl and I find myself wishing Debbie was here, a ludicrous thought if ever there was one. Debbie doesn't know my friends, she couldn't possibly be here, but as the one person who knows the truth, she could save me from this conversation.

A line is being drawn around me and the people in my life, I realise. One that grows deeper with every word spoken until it becomes an uncrossable gulf. My friends can breeze their way through the next few weeks, but I can't. I'm immersed in the trenches of a battlefield while everyone else is blissfully unaware a war is even going on. Even Debbie, the one ally I have, doesn't know everything and never can. If she knew I was planning to use my wedding day to humiliate Jamie, she'd only try stop me.

I'm alone. Completely and utterly alone. Jamie's seen to that.

"Everything okay?" Alisha asks when she notices how quiet I am.

I push myself to nod. "Yeah, I'm just debating a top up."

"Now that's a plan!" Laney says, leaving the room to get more wine. I watch her go, knowing she could bring all the wine in Alisha's kitchen, but it still wouldn't be enough to numb the river of agony flowing through me.

I sit on the periphery of my friends, chipping into the conversation when I can muster the energy to, until my phone lights up with a message from Jamie.

I'm outside x

Anger bubbles in my gut as I look at the time. Jamie's arrived fifteen minutes before he said he'd pick me up. That's fifteen minutes less time with my friends, and fifteen minutes more with him.

"I'd better go," I sigh. I breathe in my friends as we hug goodbye then I trail towards Jamie's car.

"Hey beautiful," he says when I slide into the passenger seat. He leans towards me, his lips puckered for a kiss. Our lips are about to connect when I notice Jamie's no longer dressed in the t-shirt he dropped me off in.

I pull away. "You're wearing different clothes."

Jamie looks down at his pale blue shirt. "Jonah asked if I wanted to go to the pub, so I met him for a few drinks."

His words sideswipe me, and I scramble for composure. "You've been out? I thought you were having a quiet night in?"

"I was, but I thought Jonah could do with a friend after his troubles at work. Don't worry, I'll catch up on the rugby highlights another time,"

Jamie jokes then he pulls me in for a kiss. When our lips meet, I sniff him for perfume or the lingering scent of sex, but the only smell I notice is his heady aftershave.

Disappointment flattens me. It's not like I want to inhale Tara on my fiancé, but right now I'd take any evidence of their illicit meetings I can find.

We break apart and Jamie sets off. When we get back to the apartment, I pretend I'm wine-drunk tired and climb into bed. Sleep comes for me eventually, but not before forcing me to listen to Jamie's gentle snores and stew about how he can rest peacefully despite all the lies he has told. Lies it's clear I'm only just scratching the surface of.

13.

The next morning, reality and wedding planning awaits like an unwanted invitation from a distant relative.

I spend my day writing cards for table places. Once upon a time, I'd thought it was a wonderful idea to write a personalised message inside for each guest, but that was before I found out my relationship was a sham. Now writing gushing messages feels like the definition of cruel.

I scan the names of our wedding guests. Every person listed will find out what Jamie has done. After that, everything they see me as now will be gone. Cassie Edwards will be a name said with a sad grimace in a sympathetic tone.

The injustice of it all tightens inside my chest. My hand jerks to tear the list apart but a shadow falling across the page stops me from doing so.

"Wow, Danny Millard! He'll be showing off at the wedding, won't he?" Jamie says over my shoulder. "The night we met he shouted at you across the bar, do you remember?"

My lips stretch into an instinctive smile at the memory of the night we met. "Of course. You came over to apologise for your loutish friend."

"And to get your number, of course," Jamie adds with a playful wink. "We'll have to call him Cupid, he'll love that. That can be the message in his card."

"Great idea," I enthuse. I write a Cupid-based joke in Danny's card, using all my strength to not write *'thanks for ruining my life'* instead.

It's not only Danny's card that gives me a headache. Every soppy message I write makes me want to scream. I grip the pen tighter, scratch the nib deeper into the thick, white card, faking it until my cheeks ache and my spirit splits.

By the time Monday rolls around, I'm hollow. My weariness must show on my face because as soon as I walk into the school building, Shari grimaces at the sight of me. "Is wedding planning really that stressful?"

"You've no idea," I reply.

"Remind me to never get married," she jokes. I don't even have the energy to pretend to laugh.

When I get to my classroom, I quickly set up for the day then check the time. With ten minutes until Debbie's due to arrive, I've enough time to make what could be the most important call of my life.

I open my search for Meadow Park Primary's phone number. Even though I know I'm not going to be blindsided by this call like I was with the photo of Jamie and Tara, my hands still tremble, but I just need to hear the words aloud.

Biting my lip, I press dial. After three rings, someone picks up.

"Hello, this is Julie Brenner from Meadow Park Primary School. How may I help you?"

"Hi, Julie. I'm trying to contact a teacher at your school. He said to reach out to him for advice about taking on the responsibility of being a subject leader, but I lost his number so I'm not sure how to contact him." My words come out in a frantic jumble and I wince, wondering if I've given too much of a backstory to sound believable.

"That's not a problem, although I can't give you any information other than confirm if he works here or not. Data protection, you see. But I can pass on a message if you need me to. Who are you looking for?"

"That's great, thank you. His name is Jamie Patrick."

I swear I hear a sharp intake of breath on the end of the line.

"I'm sorry but there must be some mistake. Mr Patrick doesn't work here anymore," Julie replies, her voice notably stiffer than before.

My throat closes. "Really? He told me the other week that he did."

"Well, I can assure you that is not the case. Mr Patrick left before Christmas. Mr Afzal has taken over his class and his subject leadership role. All this information is available on our website, where really you should have looked before calling."

"I'm sorry, I didn't even think to check the website. Can I ask, why did Mr Patrick leave?"

"I'm not at liberty to say, and in all honesty I'm not sure why you need to know that. Is there anything else I can help you with?"

"No, that's everything," I manage to reply before Julie hangs up without saying goodbye. I sit back in my chair, trying to catch my breath.

Jamie hasn't worked since December.

December.

How? How have I not noticed he doesn't have a job anymore? Where does he go every day? What is he doing? Where does his money come from?

I think back to the bank transfer from Jamie's parents listed on his account, but even that doesn't make sense. If Anne and Martin had lent us money, surely they would have told me?

Unless… unless they didn't know what the money was really for.

I groan at the thought of Jamie not only conning me, but his parents too.

I shake my head to scramble what I've heard into making sense but even with the truth still ringing in my ears, nothing about this situation makes sense. Teaching is Jamie's life. It's as much a part of his identity as it is mine. He'd never give teaching up, ever. I might not know him as well as I thought, but I do know that.

The only explanation is that Jamie can't have left Meadow Park through choice. Something must have gone wrong. Something had to have pushed him out.

A sinking sensation takes over me, warning that Jamie isn't done with his life-shattering bombshells just yet. I hold my head in my hands to suppress the animalistic wail climbing up my throat.

"Cass?"

I jump at the sound of Debbie's voice. Our eyes meet. As soon as she sees the tears brewing in mine, Debbie rushes towards me, but I hold my hand up to stop her.

"Please, Debbie, don't. If you hug me, I'll start crying and once I start, I don't think I'll be able to stop."

Debbie lowers her arms. "Do you... do you want to talk about it?"

I shake my head.

"How about we run through today's lessons?"

I nod. Lessons I can do. With lessons, there's a plan for me to follow. The resources are already prepped and made. Nothing can go disastrously wrong. In this classroom, I know my role. In this classroom, I'm in control.

If only I could say that about everything else in my life.

14.

At home time, I lean against the frame of the outside door and watch the children leave. Their innocence and joy shine bright as they chatter to their parents and carers about what they learned today.

When do we lose that innocence, I wonder? What change happens that makes us want to lie, to cheat, to hurt the people who love us?

A fierce wave of protectiveness washes over me as one of my students turns to give me one last wave goodbye. I return the gesture and they skip away, going home to their life of cartoons and bedtime stories.

With a sigh, I close the door and rest my forehead against the cool glass of the windowpane. My breath fogs before me and I fight the childish urge to draw in the mist.

"Do you want to talk about what happened this morning?"

Lifting my head from the glass, I face Debbie. The worry she exudes almost knocks me to my feet.

I could lie, I realise. Lie like Jamie. Tell Debbie it's fine, just a headache, nothing else. Protect Debbie from worrying about me more while keeping these hurts and humiliations on the inside. Instead, I say, "Jamie lost his job at Christmas."

Debbie blinks, wrongfooted.

"Jamie lost his job at Christmas," I repeat. I wrap my tongue around the words until their spiked truth makes me bleed, but that's okay. The cuts make the words real.

"I don't understand," Debbie replies.

"Me neither."

I move past Debbie and take a seat at my desk. Tipping my head back, I stare at the ceiling. There's a questionable brown stain in the middle of it. I've been told it was from a science experiment gone wrong, but who knows if that's true. Who knows what's true anymore?

"How did he lose his job?" Debbie asks, approaching me.

"I don't know. I didn't even know he'd lost it until this weekend."

"Didn't he tell you before?"

"He didn't tell me at all. He doesn't know I know."

Debbie sinks onto a classroom desk. "Cass, if he can lie about that…"

"He can lie about anything, I know."

"So leave him."

"I will, when the time is right."

"Cassie, the time *is* right. Look at what you've found out! Where does this end?"

A vision of the moment Jamie's identity as a 'good guy' lies smouldering at my feet appears before me. I soak it in then sit up straight. "It'll be okay, Debbie. Nothing about my plan has changed. I'm going to find out the truth - all of it - then confront him and leave."

"I don't like your plan, Cassie. Your plan sounds like playing with fire."

"I'm not going to get burned. I won't allow it."

Debbie sighs but she doesn't push it. She rises to a stand. "Every night before you go to bed, I want you to text me and let me know you're okay. I mean it - every night. I don't trust him."

My lips flick. "That makes two of us."

Debbie doesn't return my smile. She squeezes my shoulder before she leaves, then I'm left alone with only the lingering stench of her worry for company.

With Debbie gone, the silence in my classroom is booming, so I visit Shari. We mark books together, but when it hits five, she leaves to meet her girlfriend for dinner.

"Go home if you've finished, Cass. This place will take your soul if you let it!" she shouts over her shoulder as she walks away. Little does she know that my soul has already been plundered by the man who promised to protect it forever.

When I can stay at work no more, I haul myself to my feet and drive home. I find Jamie lounged on the sofa, not a care in the world.

"You look tired, Cass. Tough day?"

"The worst."

"Why don't I run you a bath then start dinner?"

My tense muscles perk up at this suggestion, even though I imagine trying to relax them would be like trying to carve marble with a toothpick, but I shake my head. "That's sweet, but why don't we make dinner together instead? I could do with talking to someone who isn't a child asking me about when they should use a question mark."

"Ah, punctuation, every teacher's favourite frustration! Cooking together sounds perfect." Jamie throws his arm over my shoulder and walks me to the kitchen. He slides a box of mushrooms and a chopping board towards me, and we stand side by side, prepping dinner.

It's not long before the air around us thickens with his lies.

"McKenzie had a fight with Felix again today," he says. "It's their third one this term."

"Wow! What are you going to do about it?"

"I've already spoken to both parents, but they're no use. They don't like each other which is probably why McKenzie and Felix are fighting in the first place. McKenzie's mum even smirked when she heard McKenzie had called Felix a 'fucking twat'."

My eyebrows raise. "I don't think I knew what the 'f word' was until I was a teenager."

"Tell me about it. Children these days are more clued up on sex and drugs than I am."

"It's scary," I comment. Jamie nods in agreement, but I'm not talking

91

about the feral children he supposedly teaches – I'm talking about the ease in which he creates elaborate fictional narratives and the calm, convincing manner he tells me about them.

After dinner, with Jamie in the shower, I check the laptop bag he carries to 'work' every day for clues about what he's really up to. Inside the bag is a laptop, but it's not the battered, school regulation one he's had for the last few years. It's a smooth, sleek, expensive model. For a man with no income, he sure doesn't mind treating himself to the finer things in life.

Riffling through the rest of the bag, the only things I find are a laptop charger and a blank notebook, but it hasn't always been blank. The perforated remnants of torn out pages confess it has been used several times before. Used for what, though, I have no idea.

Whatever Jamie is doing every day looks like work, I surmise, but not the work he tells me about, or work he gets paid for.

I'm staring at the inanimate objects, waiting for them to confess their secrets, when the shower stops running. I stuff Jamie's laptop back inside the bag, scramble to my feet and dash into the living room.

By the time Jamie flops onto the sofa a few minutes later, damp haired and yawning, I'm under a blanket watching an episode of reality TV.

"Not this again," he groans.

"Here," I say, tossing him the remote. "Put what you want on. I've got work to do anyway."

While Jamie half watches rugby, half taps away on his phone, no doubt talking to Tara, I sit at the dining table with my laptop. From my position, I can see everything Jamie does and he can see me, but importantly he can't see what's on my screen.

I search for Meadow Park Primary's website and, sure enough, Jamie's name is no longer on the staff list. Reading it in black and white makes my skin burn. Questions bubble behind my lips. It's all well and good knowing Jamie doesn't work at the school anymore, but I need to find out *why* he left.

For a moment, I wonder if Jamie's lack of employment has anything to do with Tara, but when I scour the rest of the staff list, I learn she is still at the school. Miss Cartwright, Year Four teacher and Head of Art.

Whatever happened was bad enough for Jamie to lose his job, but not Tara. While that rules out the idea of them being caught having sex in a classroom, it doesn't tell me much.

I search for Meadow Park Primary on social media and find the school's Facebook page. Scrolling through old posts about nonuniform days, class events and school trips, I uncover no mention of Mr Patrick leaving or the reason why.

I chew my lip. From experience, whenever a teacher leaves a school, an announcement is shared alongside a thank you message from the staff and students. The only time I've ever known that not to happen was... well, when someone left under a dark cloud.

Clenching my jaw, I check to see if any comments on posts from December give clues about what happened, but all I read are responses like '*Harley loved this trip*' or '*how cute is this photo?!*'.

I bite back a sigh at the uselessness of it all. I'm close to answers, I know I am, but they feel further away than ever.

I flick back through Meadow Park's page and scan the comments across multiple posts. One person replies more than anyone else. A woman called Patricia Campbell. Knowing what I do about schools, I know the loudest mouth on the social media page is usually the woman who knows everything about everyone.

I load Patricia Campbell's profile. She has black hair with thick blonde roots poking through and severe eyebrows. Her go-to pose is either an aggressive pout or an angry stare into the camera. She posts frequently, either about her children, being an independent woman, the cost of living and how no one these days can be trusted.

I smile. I know the Patricia types well. They frequent my school gates too. Strong women who can be lovely... if you're on their side.

If I want to find out what happened with Jamie, Patricia is the woman to ask.

But I can't ask as myself. There can be no trace leading back to me, not if I'm going to pretend I didn't know about the affair. I can't pretend to be Tara, either. She works at Meadow Park – what's stopping Patricia going to her after school and bringing up the conversation? The thought makes me shudder.

No, contacting Patricia needs to be done by someone new. Someone who can disappear as easily as they appear.

I study Patricia's profile and imagine the kind of person she would want to befriend, then get to work. Opening another tab, I generate a new email address then head back to Facebook and create a new account. Using a photo of Jamie's nephews Ethan and Joel as my profile picture and a quote about overcoming cheating as my cover photo, I bring to life Abby Dunne, a woman moving to the area with her children and on the hunt for good schools.

I write my first status – '*new home, new start, new profile*' – then set about adding as many people from the Meadow Park Primary page as I can. For good measure, I click through a few of their profiles and add their friends too.

I continue sharing quotes and post two more photos of Ethan and Joel, all the while friend requests trickle in from people who have no idea who Abby Dunne is, but for some reason want to befriend her.

Within half an hour, I have 42 friends, one of whom is Patricia Campbell. My skin tingles as I type a message to her.

Hey Patricia! Hope you don't mind the random add. I've recently moved to the area after splitting up with my partner and I'm thinking of sending my boys to Meadow Park Primary. I thought you might be able to tell me if it's a good school or not. I saw your comments on their page and thought you looked nice so might be able to help x

I chew my lip as the 'read' sign pops up under my message almost immediately. The speed doesn't surprise me. It's easy to predict Patricia is the kind of person who's always on their phone, but when her reply isn't as instantaneous as her ability to open my message, I panic. Was I too polite? Did I ask for too much? Is 'Abby Dunne' someone Patricia Campbell would want to help?

My nails embed themselves in my palms, my eyes only tearing from the screen when Jamie's phone lights up. He glances at the notification and grins before replying, then he puts his phone down and continues to watch rugby.

Witnessing his joy at Tara's message should bother me, but I can barely muster the energy to care. I'm too focused on the flashing dots on my screen which mean one thing... Patricia Campbell is typing a response.

Awe no worris babe! I knw Meadow Park well – u cum 2 the xpert!x

The teacher in me cringes at Patricia's spelling, but the part of me that's desperate for answers exhales at her friendliness. Flexing my fingers, I reply.

Thanks so much – you're the best! Hopefully all the other mums are as nice as you x

Ha! They r not but ur in gud hands wiv me! Y dn't we meet 4 a coffee? U can ask away thn!x

My eyebrows raise at Patricia's suggestion. I thought I was going to have to butter her up more before she would meet, but Patricia is more open than I imagined. That bodes well for me, given the questions I want to ask.

Sounds great – how about Friday? X

Fri no gud. Can we do Mon @ 1 – I luv a gud lie in ha!x

Disappointment claws at me. The idea of surviving another weekend not knowing about Jamie's occupational issues seems impossible, but I can't push Patricia. She's the only hope I have, a depressing statement if ever there was one.

Monday sounds good to me!x

Patricia suggests we meet at a café I've never heard of, and I confirm our plans. Fizzing with excitement, I open Abby Dunne's profile and share a quote about the kindness of strangers. Seconds later, Patricia comments with a series of love heart emojis.

I sit back in my chair, satisfied.

Patricia is firmly on team Abby Dunne, therefore on team Cassie Edwards. With her on side, I'm exactly where I need to be – one step closer to the truth.

15.

Despite my initial positivity, it takes no longer than an hour for me to realise that keeping Patricia Campbell amused is a full-time job. By the end of the first day of befriending her, Patricia has tagged me in four videos, sent three motivational quotes and spammed me with countless messages complaining about her children. It seems like every time I check my phone, I have a notification, or twelve, from her. It's exhausting, but I remind myself as soon as Monday comes around, it will be worth it. Patricia is my one link to the truth. Without her, I have nothing.

As the days go by, I realise how true that statement is.

Every spare minute I have, I hunt for Jamie's other life. The only thing I learn is how good he is at covering his tracks.

I've checked the website of every school in a fifty-mile radius to see if Jamie's name is on their staff list. It never is.

I've scoured social media pages of countless bars and restaurants to see if Jamie and Tara are in the background of any photos. They never are.

I've tried peeking over Jamie's shoulder every time he receives a message, but he always angles his phone so I can't see the screen. The closest I got was catching a glimpse of three kisses at the end of a text, but his phone was turned away before I could see who it was from.

In an act of ultimate desperation, I even call hotels in the local area to ask if a man named Jamie Patrick recently stayed there. The answer is the same every time – they aren't allowed to tell me the names of past guests.

"But he's cheating on me!" I shout down the line to one bewildered receptionist.

With no new evidence in sight, everything carries on the same. We come home to each other every evening. We sleep together at night. We live as we always have.

With the truth so well wrapped up, sometimes, in my most pain-filled moments, I almost convince myself it's all a mistake. My life as I know it can't be over, my heart can't be broken, because everything seems fine. Everywhere I look there's no proof anything is wrong.

No proof other than the photo of Jamie and Tara. I stare at it until my eyes sting. It's the only thing I possess that reminds me I'm not crazy. It keeps the fiery desire to right their wrongs burning bright and at the top of my to-do list.

I spend hours lost in fantasies of our wedding day, Jamie's face falling as his life splinters beyond repair. Tara turning to Nico to explain but he's already walking away. Me, the victim, yes, but the one having the last laugh.

But you can't host a wedding day to mask a revenge plot without planning one, so my role of excited bride-to-be must still be played.

Even though it kills me, on Wednesday night I set about charming my fiancé. I make Mexican food, Jamie's favourite. Mexico, our dream honeymoon destination. Mexico and all its connotations, forever ruined for me.

As the scent of spices fills the air, I sit and wait for my darling to return home and devour his dinner, but Jamie doesn't saunter into the apartment at the usual time.

He's still not walked through the door when the enchiladas are ready at six thirty. I text him, but there's no reply. When the cheese on top blackens, I take the food out of the oven, slamming the dish on the side so furiously I check to see if I've cracked it.

Half an hour later, there's still no sign of Jamie and no response to my text. I check his social media accounts and they confess that he hasn't been online since lunchtime.

Three missed calls later and I'm pacing the apartment. I run my hands through my tangled curls, trying to decide what to do. Is finding out all the gritty details of how deep their betrayal goes worth this, or instead should I just pile up Jamie's clothes, throw them out of the window and save myself the pain of prolonging the inevitable? Should I forget getting even and get angry instead?

At eight thirty, I open a bottle of wine, half impressed, half horrified it's taken me this long to turn to alcohol. The cool liquid runs down my throat but does little to extinguish the fire raging inside me.

Two glasses of wine later and I'm more furious than ever, which is why when Jamie strolls in after nine, I fly into the hallway, a tipsy ball of rage.

"Where the hell have you been?!"

"Woah, Cass!" Jamie says, holding his hands up.

"Don't 'woah Cass' me – it's ten past nine!"

"I know how to tell the time," Jamie replies, his eyebrows furrowing.

"Oh, so you can tell the time but can't tell your fiancée you aren't coming home?"

"What are you talking about?" Jamie sighs, his tone a toxic mixture of tiredness and irritation. He shrugs off his coat and hangs it up without looking at me. "I went for drinks with Ricky and Pete. I told you about it the other week."

I fold my arms across my chest. "No, you didn't."

"Yes, I did," Jamie replies, walking past me.

Watching him breeze through the apartment sets off a roaring in my skull. "Jamie, I'd remember you telling me you were going out!"

"Well, clearly you don't," Jamie snaps. He points to the dining table. "You were sat there on your laptop, and I was on the sofa. I told you Ricky had messaged saying Pete was coming down from Edinburgh and suggested we go for a drink. You said, 'sounds fun' then showed me a photo of candles in jars for centrepieces."

Sucking my teeth, I think back. Back to when I hadn't had the image of my fiancé and another woman seared onto my brain.

Some of Jamie's words sound familiar. I had shown him a photo of centrepieces. He'd been flicking through his tablet. He said the centrepieces were nice, I remember that much, but I don't remember the part about him meeting his friends.

"I don't remember that," I say, softer now.

"Just because you don't remember something doesn't mean it didn't happen. It's not my fault you weren't listening."

Stung, I stick my chin out. "Well, even if you did tell me, you still should have called when you realised I was trying to contact you. I've been worried sick!"

Jamie pulls his phone from his pocket and shows me a black screen. "My phone died at lunchtime. I didn't have my charger in the car. Anything else you want to accuse me of? Any more shouting you want to do?"

Wounded, I shrink away from him.

Once upon a time, I'd have been mortified at this display of irrational anger. Shouting at Jamie the second he walked in the door without giving him chance to breathe never mind explain was not like me. Past Cassie would never have let this happen. Had she forgotten Jamie's plans, she would have apologised with a kiss and asked if he'd had a good time. She would have believed him.

But *past* Cassie didn't know Jamie was cheating and lying about his job, did she?

I pull my shoulders back. "I didn't know where you were."

"I'm not saying sorry for having plans you forgot I told you about," Jamie says, undoing the top button of his shirt. "You've got yourself worked up over nothing."

His cool dismissal whips across my chest. He looks so indifferent to me, so done with my outburst, that a hot wave of shame runs over my body.

I have no recollection of Jamie telling me about meeting his friends.

The fact that I could forget that worries me. What else had I barely listened to over the course of our relationship? What other moments had I been distracted in?

Then the worst thought hits me… am I to blame for his cheating? Did I not listen enough, not care enough, not give Jamie the same attention he gave me?

Tears prickle my eyes as Jamie turns his back on me. "I'm sorry," I whisper, apologising for so much more than forgetting his plans.

"What?"

"I'm sorry," I say, louder this time, and I'm surprised to hear I mean it.

I want to tell him I'm sorry it's come to this. I'm sorry we've both become people I never thought we would be and for whatever part I played in our demise, but I don't. I can't, because saying those words out loud admits the truth that we are over. A truth that somehow, despite everything I know, I still can't believe is real.

"I know it's not an excuse, but I've got a lot on. I forgot you were out. I made a special dinner so we could have some time together, and now I've ruined it."

Jamie softens and walks towards me with his arms outstretched. I want to shy away from his touch, but my body won't listen. It yearns for Jamie, desperate to be beside him where it thinks it belongs.

Jamie's arms wrap around me and, even though I hate myself for it, I sink into him.

"I know wedding planning is stressful, but don't let us forget who we are in all this, okay? You see your friends, I see mine, it's the way we've always been. One of the things I love most about you is that you let me have my space."

I burrow into his neck. I know that Jamie's version of space gave him all the room he needed to have an affair. I know he's used it to hide his employment woes. This arrangement isn't the trusting partnership I thought it was, but in his arms I want to believe everything is perfect, the way it always seemed to me. I hate myself for it, but I want him. I want us. I want it all back the way it used to be.

I lean into Jamie, my body collapsing into his.

"Hey," he whispers into my hair. "Are you okay?"

"I'm so stressed."

"Cass, if you need me to do anything for the wedding, just say. I can't flower arrange or braid hair or whatever it is you're trying to sort, but I can help, okay? I'm going to be your husband soon. It's my job to stop you feeling like this."

I pull away from Jamie and study him. I note the faded freckles across the bridge of his nose. The crinkles around his eyes from the early mornings and long nights that come hand in hand with teaching. I take in every detail of the man I love. The man who has broken my heart.

"I'll sort it." I kiss him hard on the lips and head into the kitchen, picking up the dish of cold enchiladas and throwing them in the bin.

"I could have taken them for lunch tomorrow," Jamie says.

"They were burnt."

"It's a shame they were ruined. It seems sad for all that effort to go to waste."

All that effort to go to waste… his words break me in a way he doesn't know.

"Come on, let's get you to bed. You need an early night." Jamie stretches out his hand. I take it. I follow him to our bedroom and pull my pyjamas from underneath my pillow. He watches me undress, a playfulness dancing in his eyes. "You're beautiful," he says. "I'm so lucky."

I meet his gaze across the low-lit room. "Do you really think so?" I ask, hating myself for caring what his answer is.

"Always. Even when you shout at me for going out with the boys," Jamie grins. I let out a small, strained laugh and climb into bed, and Jamie tucks me in.

"Aren't you coming to bed too?"

"Not yet. Soon," Jamie replies, kissing me goodnight.

I watch him go then close my eyes, willing myself to fall into rest, but the image of Jamie with Tara swims into my consciousness. It screams, reminding me of the truth concealed behind these fraudulent, loving moments.

Holding back a sob, I throw back the duvet and reach for my phone. I search for Ricky's Facebook profile and see he's shared a story. I click on it and an image of a beer fills my screen.

I exhale, my relief so strong I can taste it. Jamie did meet his friends. He wasn't lying to me, not this time.

Shaking my head, I close the photo, but as I do something in it catches my attention. I reload the image and break all over again.

Through the liquid in the pint glass is a woman's hand. There are no other drinks on the table but hers. Ricky was out, alright, but not with Jamie and Pete.

Jamie lied, again. Genuinely, convincingly, without breaking a sweat. He never planned a night out and told me about it. I hadn't forgotten anything. What he described never happened. Jamie made me think I was crazy, but I'm not crazy. I remember that conversation exactly how it went down.

I put my phone on the bedside table and push my face into my pillow, suffocating myself and the urge to scream.

Jamie's lies were so slick, so well thought out, they send a shiver down my spine, but the lie isn't the worst past. The worst part is that he knew he could make me doubt myself before I would ever doubt him.

Tears soak my pillow as I wonder how often over the course of our relationship Jamie has lied without me having even the slightest suspicion everything might not be quite what it seemed. How many other fictitious conversations had he made up to fool me into doubting myself and believing him?

And the worst question of all - how could I have fallen victim to

103

Jamie's lies *again*?

"No more, Cassie. No more!" I scold myself. I say it again and again, hoping that sometime after hearing those words for the hundredth time, they sink in.

16.

Jamie's lies are still bitter on my tongue when I wake up but autopilot takes over. I make breakfast for the both of us. I pour Jamie a coffee. I do everything a good fiancée should, all with happiness on my face and a hollowness in my chest, counting down the minutes until I can flee to work.

"Don't forget dinner at my parents' tonight," Jamie calls after me as I make my way towards the front door.

I blink. "It's the third Thursday already?"

Jamie appears in the hallway, grinning. "You forgot?"

Grimacing, I nod. "Can I blame wedding planning?"

"Blame whatever you want, as long as you show up on time."

Forcing a laugh, I wave goodbye then head to my car.

I can't believe I forgot about dinner. Every third Thursday of the month, Anne and Martin host a dinner for their two children. Alison brings her husband Mike and their sons, Ethan and Joel, and Jamie brings me. The dinners are a militant Patrick tradition. They cannot be missed. Jamie and I have even changed holiday dates to accommodate it in the past, yet my mind has been so focused on Jamie and Tara I completely forgot about it.

As I drive to work, my mind wanders to memories of my first Thursday dinner with the Patricks. A lifetime ago, with so many memories interspersed between then and now.

On the journey to their house, I was so nervous Jamie put his hand over mine to try steady it. "Don't worry, they're going to love you," he soothed but I couldn't respond. By that point, I was so in love with Jamie I couldn't imagine my life without him in it. Being hated by the in-laws made the idea a possibility, so I wore my best 'parent pleasing' dress and even went to a bakery to pick up a cake for dessert. I hated how much making a good impression meant to me, but the truth was I wanted Anne and Martin to love me because I loved their son more than I'd ever loved anyone before.

It turns out, I had nothing to worry about. Anne and Martin were wonderful, warm people and we hit it off straight away. A librarian for over thirty-five years, Anne took a particular shine to me when she discovered I was an avid reader. I left my first Thursday dinner armed with a list of book recommendations and the blissful memory of Jamie's proud beam as Anne hugged me goodbye and said, 'I am so happy my son met you!'.

The memory chokes me all day. Shari even comments on my quietness at lunchtime.

"I'm just thinking about how much work we've to do before the end of term," I lie. The statement is enough to shift all attention from me and get everyone talking about their stresses instead.

Only Debbie doesn't move on. She leans close and whispers, "did something happen last night?"

"I'm not talking about this in the staffroom," I reply.

Debbie focuses back on her lunch, but my peace is short-lived. At the end of the day when it's just the two of us in the classroom, she corners me. "Have you left him? Is that why you're so quiet?"

For a split second, I debate saying yes just to get Debbie off my back, but if I'm to eventually convince Debbie I'm going through with the wedding, I can't have left my fiancé. So, steeling myself for her horror, I shake my head.

"Cass! Why can't you make this step?"

"I've told you Debbie, I need to know everything before I speak to him about it."

"What more is there to know other than he's a liar? I really don't think knowing where he meets his mistress or how much he spends on her is going to make you feel better."

I flinch at the ugly truth in her words. "I'm dealing with this in my own way. For now, it's easier for things to carry on as normal. I mean, I'm going for dinner tonight at his parents' house."

Debbie blinks. "You are joking, aren't you?"

"They're good people, Debbie. They'll be hurt when they find out what's happened."

"Hurt by him, not you! You're the victim in this."

I bristle. Victim. How the word spears me. "Debbie, you're asking me to dismantle my life -"

"I'm asking you to put yourself first."

"And I'm asking you to trust me."

We hold eye contact, a tension simmering between us until Debbie sighs. She leaves me in peace to mark today's work. When the task is complete, I set off for another night of faking it.

Only tonight I won't just be faking it – I'll be trying to find out why Anne and Martin sent Jamie that money. My heart skips a beat at the thought.

Jamie's leaning against his car and typing on his phone when I pull up outside his parents' four-bedroom semi-detached. He slides his phone away and opens my door for me. "You remembered to come! I'm so proud," he grins. When I'm free of my car, he wraps me in his arms. "Guess what I've been thinking about today?"

"What?"

"I've been thinking how the next time we go to Thursday dinner, we'll be married. How exciting is that?"

"So exciting," I reply, burying my head in Jamie's chest so I can hide my upset.

"Get a room, you two," comes a sudden holler from behind. I turn to see Alison, the source of the shout, climbing out of her family car further down the road.

Jamie takes my hand in his and we make our way towards his sister. "I win again, the most punctual Patrick!"

Alison sticks her tongue out at her brother then hugs him. Ignoring their affectionate embrace, I go to help Ethan and Joel out of the car but before I can reach them Alison grabs me. "How are you, my almost sister-in-law?!"

"Steady on, Alison, don't shout at the poor girl," Mike says. "I swear the pitch of her voice is getting so high, I can't hear her anymore."

"So that's why you didn't do the washing up when I asked you to last night…" Alison jokes before thrusting a bottle of champagne into Jamie's hands. "We brought a little treat for tonight."

"You didn't have to do that."

"Please, it's almost time for my baby brother's wedding! There's a lot to celebrate." Alison grabs my wrist. "How excited are you, Cass? I can't sit still whenever I think of the wedding!"

Mike pulls a mock-horrified expression. "Does that mean you'll continue to be in a permanent state of cheer until the big day?" Alison bats his arm, and the pair exchange a smile.

The brutality of watching their genuine love play out before my sham version is cut short by the well-timed distraction of Ethan and Joel tumbling out of the car. They wrap their arms around Jamie's waist, their excitable babble filling the air.

"Uncle Jamie, I got ten out of ten on my spelling test!"

"I played football at lunchtime!"

Their enthusiasm is contagious. "Hi boys!" I chirp, ruffling Ethan's hair. He brushes it back in place and grins impishly at me. Ethan looks so much like Jamie it's hard not to imagine him being our son, but I sniff and straighten up. No imagining my could-have-been future, not tonight.

"Come on. We're late, and you know how much Anne hates that,"

Mike announces, throwing his arm over Alison's shoulder and steering her towards the house.

We chat as we walk towards Anne and Martin's suburban dream home, barely stepping onto the driveaway before Anne throws open the front door. "You're here!" she cries. Her cheeks are pink, her eyes shiny. She hugs her family one by one. When she gets to me, she squeezes extra tight.

The warmth of Anne and Martin's home waves us in, the air thick with the scent of a homecooked meal. Martin emerges from the living room and claps Jamie on the shoulder. It stings to see Martin's pride as he greets his son, the man he believes to be simply wonderful.

I turn away to hang my coat up then follow everyone through the house, walking past Alison and Mike's wedding photo, snapshots of Ethan and Joel as babies and prints of Jamie and me in Thailand.

"Let's get a glass of wine and have a girly chat! Lord knows I need one living with three boys," Alison says, linking my arm.

"A girly chat," Ethan whines.

Martin swoops to his grandsons. "Don't worry, I've set some footy nets up in the garden. Want to play?"

As Ethan and Joel shriek in delight, my heart tugs. Any future children I may have won't experience Martin's adoration and fun-loving nature. In fact, in a few weeks' time, I'll never attend a third Thursday dinner with the Patricks again. There will be no more book swapping with Anne, no more giggles with Alison. No more of this life that I love so much.

My crushing sadness is interrupted by a shout from Ethan. "Mum, watch us play!"

"Ugh, I knew they'd ask that," Alison groans, dropping my arm. "I'll go outside with the boys but don't you two talk wedding without me!"

"We wouldn't dream of it," Anne replies, winking at me when Alison isn't looking.

Jamie's hand grazes my waist. "I'll be in the garden too, showing my nephews how to play." He pecks me on the cheek then scoops Joel into his arms and carries him outside. Anne claps her hands, beaming at this display of affection, and suddenly being here is too much. My bottom lip wobbles, and I don't know how to stop it.

When everyone has gone, Anne reaches out and touches my forehead. "Are you okay, love? You're a bit pale."

"I'm fine, I just could do with that wine."

"A girl after my own heart," Anne jokes, leading me into her farmhouse style kitchen. She grabs a fresh wineglass, sits it beside her half full one, and pours me a drink. "So, how is everything going with the wedding?"

"Are you sure we shouldn't wait for Alison to talk about this?"

"Oh, she'll be fine. She can catch up on the details over dinner."

My intestines plummet, but I don't let it show. "It's going well, thanks. I mean, it's stressful, but one of Jamie's friends is going to help me with the last few bits. She's coming around on Saturday."

"Oh, isn't that kind! Jamie always knows the best people."

"She seems lovely," I reply through gritted teeth.

Anne passes me my wine. I take a large gulp and Anne raises her eyebrow. "Is that how it's going to be tonight? Well, let me join in with the festivities!" she grins, downing the rest of her drink. She grimaces at the acidity when she swallows then laughs. "Oh, Cass, I can't tell you how excited I am for the wedding! I've had two glasses of wine before you came to celebrate. Martin will probably have to put me to bed in half an hour or I'll end up spilling all my secrets!"

My vision lingers on Anne's empty wineglass, then her flushed cheeks. A shameful burn tingles my toes, but I'm too invested in unveiling the truth to care about guilt and remorse.

"An early night sounds perfect," I reply, topping us both up. "Cheers."

We clink glasses and drink. When our toast is finished, Anne studies me. "If you don't mind me saying, Cass, you're looking tired. Wedding planning must be more stressful than I remember."

"Stressful, time consuming, confusing, expensive… shall I go on?"

"Well, you're doing a good job juggling it all."

"It doesn't feel like it. Sometimes I look at our bank accounts and want to cry," I push, taking another drink.

Anne mirrors me, then squeezes my hand. "Jamie said it was getting a bit expensive, and you've still to book your honeymoon, haven't you?"

With the conversation on money, my palms sweat, but I nod as if this exchange is the most normal in the world. "Jamie's trying to find a bargain, but who knows if he will get one. Everyone hears wedding and the price is at least double what it usually is."

"I must admit, Martin and I had a shock ourselves when Jamie told us how much things cost."

"It is a lot. It almost makes you wonder how anyone can afford a wedding."

"Tell me about it. Ten thousand for a venue alone, never mind the food. I couldn't believe it when I heard," Anne grimaces.

Alarm bells ring in my mind. "Ten thousand?"

Anne takes another sip of wine. "For your venue. Jamie said they snuck all those extras in after you had to postpone the wedding. Very cheeky to do that in the middle of a global pandemic if you ask me, but that's business these days, isn't it?"

"Very cheeky," I hear myself say over the blood pounding in my ears. "We couldn't believe it when they gave us the final bill."

"I know. Poor Jamie was distraught thinking you might have to cancel the wedding or go without a honeymoon. He just wants you to have the perfect day." Anne's eyes mist over as she looks out of the window to her family in the garden.

I don't follow her gaze. "We aren't cancelling the wedding."

"Oh, I know, and thank goodness because we're all so excited for it! Martin and I were happy to help out."

And there it is – a thread to pull. I grip my wineglass so Anne can't see my hands are shaking. "Help out?"

Anne's face drains of colour and she rests her hand on her chest to steady her heartrate.

I know what's coming before she says it, but I pray it's not the case. Somehow, despite everything I've found out, I pin all my hopes on Jamie not being the person deep down I know he is.

"Oh, Cassie, I forgot… I forgot you didn't know. It's the wine – I've had too much. I shouldn't have said a word! Forget I said anything, please? Jamie will be so upset if he knows I've told you," Anne babbles, her neck red and blotchy.

"Say anything about what?" I ask, my voice rising an octave.

Anne grabs my hand, her eyes darting outside to see if anyone has heard us through the open kitchen window. "Jamie came to us at the start of the year to say you couldn't afford the wedding," she rushes. "He said he'd overestimated how much he could save and promised you the most wonderful honeymoon, but he couldn't quite make the numbers work to do it all. It was awful – he was crying like I've never seen him cry before!"

Through a dry mouth, I ask, "What did you do?"

"It was nothing, Cass. I mean it, it was nothing. Martin and I have been saving since the children were born. We were going to give you some money to help with the deposit for a house anyway, but we gave Jamie the money a little sooner to tide you over. Jamie asked – Jamie *begged* – us to not tell you. Please don't tell him I've let this slip! He'll never forgive me. Heck, I'll never forgive myself."

I can't watch Anne's desperate pleading any longer. I turn and look out of the window to where Jamie is running around, his t-shirt pulled over his head to celebrate a goal. Alison's laughter ricochets around the garden while poor Martin lies tangled in the net of goalposts. The scene is a snapshot of family bliss, with Jamie front and centre. The perfect son, the perfect brother, the perfect uncle.

But he's not. He's not who any of us think he is.

"How much did you give him?" I ask, my voice barely a whisper, because even though I know the answer, I need to hear her say it.

Anne bites her lip. "Fifteen thousand."

I lean back on the counter to keep myself upright, my entire body begging to collapse.

"Please don't be angry, Cassie. He did it with the best intentions. He did it for you! We were going to give you the money anyway. We've had it in a savings account for years to give to him when the time was right. Jamie was going to tell you when you were married. Some of the money is to help with the wedding and the honeymoon, then the rest is for the house. Jamie promised us that."

"Jamie promises a lot of things," I snap, then I catch myself. "And he always keeps them."

"He does. He's such a good boy," Anne says, her body sagging with relief now she knows I'm not going to storm outside and shout at her son for taking money and not telling me about it. "He adores you, Cassie, I hope you know that. This wedding is going to be perfect!"

"It really is," I whisper.

17.

The truth about the money sits heavy on my chest but thanks to a last-minute need for me to present a data overview for a Governors' meeting, work is so hectic the next day that I barely have time to breathe, never mind think about it. I stay at work late and come home shattered, with nothing but the need for rest on my mind.

However, as soon as Saturday rolls around, I transform into an anxious mother waiting for their child to perform on stage for the first time.

Even though the thought of having Tara in my home makes my skin crawl, I still want to impress her. I want her to look at me and think, 'How can we hurt this wonderful woman?', to see I'm a real person, not someone she pretends doesn't exist while she mounts Jamie whenever she tells Nico she's going to Zumba.

With the snacks I bought for the occasion laid out on the dining table and the apartment tidier than a showroom, I slip into a flattering floral dress. Taking in my reflection in the mirror, I'm ready to face the other half of the toxic duo.

"Wow! You look nice," Jamie says, strolling into the bedroom.

"Thanks, so do you," I reply, then I spot his car keys in his hand. My eyebrows furrow. "Are you going somewhere?"

"Yeah, I'm off to play golf with Jonah."

"But Tara will be here in a second," I protest.

"Here to help you with the wedding, not to see me. I don't need to be here, do I?"

"I'd have thought you'd have wanted to be."

"Do you really want my input today? Flowers are all the same to me, remember?" Jamie says, holding my body against his. His hands rest on my bum, and it takes all my strength to not knee him in the crotch.

I put my hands on his chest to keep a distance between us. "We won't be talking about flowers."

"You know what I mean. It's probably best I stay out of the way."

"Don't you think Tara might think it's rude if you aren't here to say hello?"

"I don't think Tara will think anything about me not being here. She knows what I'm like with creative stuff," Jamie shrugs. "How about I get us a Chinese on the way back to make up for my absence?"

"Fine," I sigh.

I tell myself it's a good thing Jamie isn't going to be around when Tara's here. That way, I can dig for answers. But if I'm honest, I'd wanted to observe their dynamic once more. I wanted to see how Jamie reacted to the woman he is seeing behind my back sitting on *our* sofa, eating *our* food, talking to me about *our* wedding. It's almost insulting that he doesn't think that's worthy of his attention.

Ten minutes after Jamie leaves, the intercom to our apartment buzzes. I bound over to it, a muddled jumble of nervous energy, hatred, and excitement. "Come on up!" I trill through the speaker.

Taking one last look at myself in the mirror, I smooth down my dress. I look normal, nice, unsuspecting. A woman you'd want to befriend, not betray. Too bad Tara's already done the latter.

She knocks on the front door, and I open it with a smile. "Tara! Thanks so much for making the time for this," I say, pulling her into a hug. She's so slender I could snap her in two if I squeezed hard enough. I let her go before my arms take matters into their own hands and do just that.

"Oh, it's no trouble," Tara replies, gripping the sleeve of her jumper like it's a comfort blanket.

As she removes her shoes, I study her plump lips, her small but pert cleavage, her handbag that costs more than any I own. The shopping sprees on Jamie's credit card flash in my brain. I shake them away and focus on the woman before me.

Physically, she's so different to me it's hard not to compare myself to her, but I'm furious at myself for doing so. I am not in competition with this woman – I have been hurt by her. Jamie has forced us to stand side by side, but I'm not going to mark us both out of ten and compare scores, no matter how tempting it is.

"Shall I make us a cup of tea?" I ask.

Tara nods and I gesture for her to go ahead. I follow her, watching as she studies the framed photos documenting my relationship that line the walls. Her face never slips to show how she feels, but I can only imagine how witnessing our happiness must crush her.

When we reach the kitchen, Tara speaks. "You have a beautiful home."

"Thank you. We're saving for a house but saving and paying for a wedding at the same time isn't easy."

"Nico and I found it hard enough to save for a house so I can't imagine being able to afford both."

"Homeowners, congratulations!" I say, glossing over the fact that I already know that scrap of information thanks to social media. "Is a wedding next?"

"Oh, I don't know. We're happy as we are for now."

"Do you not want to get married?" I ask, flicking the kettle on.

"I do one day, but I'm still young, you know?"

I nod because I do know. I know exactly what it's like to be twenty-six and feel like your whole life is stretched out ahead of you, a seemingly endless rainbow of possibility. Decisions like marriage and children seem as frivolous as deciding where to go for drinks on a Saturday night. Life is too *fun* at twenty-six. Being in a relationship is great, but so is getting the handsome stranger at the bar to buy you a drink and, if you're Tara, sleeping with your engaged co-worker.

I drop two teabags into two mugs, trying to shake the mental image of Jamie's lips on hers, of Tara's hands running through his thick hair.

"There's plenty of time for marriage," I manage to say. "Sugar?"

"No thanks, I'm trying to cut down."

I fight the urge to roll my eyes, then pour steaming water into the mugs. "I'll let you pour your own milk. Jamie always says I never put enough in."

Tara blinks at the mention of Jamie's name. Her expression stays serene, her blink the only betrayal of her composure, but I saw the moment what she is doing and who she is hurting registered.

Tara pours a splash of milk into her mug then we take our tea to the dining table. Spread out in front of us is my wedding file and an assortment of decorations I've already made. I've also created an information pack for Tara which includes her invitation, a list of suppliers we're using, a printout of our colour scheme and a copy of the guest list which includes everyone's contact details.

"Tell me you're a teacher without telling me you're a teacher," Tara jokes, flicking through the pack.

"I know, it's almost a sickness, isn't it?"

We laugh, an intimate moment that's not lost on me.

"So, what is it you need help with?" Tara asks.

"What don't I need help with?" I joke. "I have most things under control, but there are a few things left. One of our jobs today is to go through the guest list. We need to check final numbers and dietary requirements so we can match them to the table places, then create thank you packs for the bridesmaids and groomsmen."

"Thank you packs?"

"Apparently these days it's not enough to give favours to your guests, but you must also give gifts to your wedding party."

"As if getting a free meal and new dress isn't enough."

"Exactly!" I giggle, but then I catch myself. I'm not here to make friends with this woman. "Other than those gifts, the biggest job to do is the favours and the ceremony packs. Our favours are a mixture of retro snacks in little jars. I was thinking today we could fill the jars and label them with the guest's name if that's okay?"

"Of course. And the ceremony packs?"

"This is where I need your help the most. I saw an idea online a few weeks ago and thought it was so original. Basically, when the guests arrive, I want an envelope to be waiting for them. Inside I want one card saying thank you for coming and another that has the 'story of our love' written on it."

Tara pouts. "That's so cute!"

"Thank you, I thought so too. The problem is I don't know what design to use. I remember Jamie telling me how creative you were so I thought you might be able to help."

A smug sense of satisfaction washes over me as Tara's cheeks flush at the mention of Jamie complimenting her. "I'm not that good," she says, shifting in her seat.

"You'll be better than me, trust me. Jamie doesn't have a creative bone in his body either so he's no help."

Tara can't help but smile at this. "He's terrible, isn't he? It would almost be worth asking him to design the card just to see the mess he produced."

I force a laugh. "He is Mr Uncreative, isn't he? That's why I'm hoping your artistic skills save us. I'll send you the words and the photos to use, but if you could design the thank you and love story card, I'd really appreciate it. Is it something you think you could do?"

Tara doesn't take a second to think about it. "Sure! I'll email you a final design, then if you like it, I'll get them printed for you."

"You'd even sort the printing?"

"Of course. If it helps, then it's the least I can do."

The temptation to snap, 'The least you can do to make up for fucking my fiancé' bites me, but thankfully the words stay in my head.

"Tara, that's amazing! You're so kind," I gush. "There is one thing, though. I want these cards to be a secret. I've told Jamie I'm going to have a special keepsake commissioned but he doesn't know what it will be. I want him and all the guests to be surprised, so I'm afraid that means not showing them to anyone, not even Nico."

Tara laughs. "Nico's about as creative as Jamie, so I won't be asking for his input with the design! Don't worry, I won't show the cards to anyone but you."

I can't hide my joy. I reach out and squeeze Tara's delicate hand. "I don't know if I'll ever be able to thank you enough for saying yes to this."

"It's no big deal, really. Now, shall we get started?"

For the next two hours, we crosscheck lists, wrap gifts for the bridal party, and package and label eighty-eight jars filled with an array of sugar-laden treats that will never be eaten. While we work, we chat.

It pains me to learn that I have a lot in common with Tara. We both enjoy nineties pop-punk music and think the films we watched as children have a lot to answer for when it comes to outdated gender roles. Tara's favourite clothing stores are the same as mine. We even go to the same hairdresser.

Finding out how similar we are somehow makes things worse. Had Tara been my opposite, I might have been able to somewhat understand why Jamie strayed. Tara might have shown him an alternate life or brought out a side of him I suppressed. His cheating wouldn't be excusable, but at least I'd be able to coddle myself with a reason as to why he would throw our life together away.

But Tara is so similar to me it's almost predictable. Everything down to her favourite restaurant is the same as mine. At one point, we even say the same answer at the same time.

As I screw the lid on a jar, I wonder why Jamie would cheat on me with… well, me.

I try telling myself the reason must be physical but comparing my body to Tara's feels shallow. Sure, we are different. My boobs are bigger, my hips wider, my hair the same length only brown not blonde. There is nothing repulsive about her and nothing overly enticing about me. We are just two women, two bodies, both attractive in their own way.

To reduce Jamie's need to break every promise he ever made to me down to the fact that Tara's legs are three inches shorter than mine downplays the situation. I refuse to sign his actions off as some primal desire to have sex with something pretty.

"All done!" Tara beams after finishing writing the last label for the last jar.

I whoop and survey our handiwork. "It's so strange thinking these are for my wedding," I say. My heart twists at my words.

"Tell me about it. It's strange to think you'll be married to Jamie in two weeks' time. You must really love him," Tara says softly, toying with the pen in her hands.

Our eyes meet and the dynamic between us shifts. Everything is held under a microscope. I don't break eye contact and neither does Tara. The moment flickers between us. Tara's face is a mask, but through her stoic expression I see a torrent of pain flowing beneath the surface.

Suddenly, Tara's phone pings. We jump at the interruption. She picks it up and all colour leaves her face. "I have to go. I told Nico I'd only be gone a few hours."

The bluntness of Tara's exit isn't lost on me, not that I let my expression show it. "Of course! Don't let me keep you longer than I already have, but please know how grateful I am for your time today."

"It's no big deal. Just send the wording for the cards and I'll sort them. I'd better dash, though. I promised Nico we'd go out tonight and we have a few errands to run before we can head out."

I lead Tara to the front door. "Are you going anywhere nice?"

"Nico fancies that new Italian, Bella. I don't know if you've heard of it?"

I freeze. That restaurant was on Jamie's bank statement. A venue of one of their dates.

"I wasn't too impressed the last time I went, but Nico wants to give it a try, so why not?" Tara shrugs.

The bottom of my body gives way as Tara slips on her shoes. I wrap my arms around myself, holding it together when all I want to do is roar. How dare she mention one of the places she's been to with Jamie so casually, so carelessly? How arrogant, how smug, can one person be?

As I thank Tara for her help and wave goodbye, a renewed sense of purpose charges through me. Tara can tell me witty anecdotes and suggest films she thinks I might enjoy all day long, but she can't blind me. I'm not going to lose sight of the end goal here. I'm not going to stop until I have shown them both how wrong they were to do this.

Tara Cartwright is going to rue the day she ever mistook me for a fool.

18.

My shot nerves after an afternoon with Tara tell me I'm in desperate need of some self-care, but there's no time for that. Every free moment I have must be spent understanding how my life imploded and building up to revealing the truth in the best, most impactful way. With that in mind, I resort to doing something I never thought I would do – researching cheating.

Within a few minutes of scouring the internet, I'm overwhelmed.

I find numerous checklists of clues your partner could be unfaithful, each tinged with a pitying tone that asks, 'How could you not have spotted this sooner?'.

I read countless articles on the websites of glossy magazines with titles like '*How to Stop him Cheating*' and '*Is Cheating Always Bad?*'. They're all subtly laced with judgement and linked to articles hinting you're not good enough as you are, ones shouting '*Lose 6lbs in a week*' or '*How to Get the Best Revenge Body*'.

I discover influencers and bloggers sharing infidelity experiences, their online diaries devastating but the comments underneath even more upsetting. Muddled in the mix of messages of support are ones like, '*is it a surprise they cheated when you look like that?*'.

Then I find an article that takes my world and tears it completely in two.

The Curse of Modern Relationships
by Sara Hosseini

These days, love is one swipe, one friend request, one follow away. With a multitude of options at our fingertips, we can be anyone, but we can also be left for anyone. Knowing that, is it a surprise to learn that controversial psychologist Brenna McNeil claims that for most of us, dating is a game of reshaping ourselves to be the perfect partner through fear of being alone?

"We've all had the conversation about a friend where we claim, 'they've changed' since entering a relationship," Brenna says. "Sometimes that's a positive – self-destructive behaviours are tamed, ambitions are supported to then be met – but other times we watch people shrink themselves for the promise of love. We berate them for it, but the reality of all modern love matches is that at any moment your partner could download an app or add a friend and enter a whole new world of dating possibilities. Without necessarily realising it, most people change who they are to minimise the risk of that happening. Watering ourselves down can be argued as a sign of self-protection, much like marrying into wealth was in the past."

Some say Brenna's argument is compromise, a normal part of all relationships, but Brenna's response is: who is compromising? How much are they giving in or giving up, and are those compromises being returned?

I read that section again and again, the questions burning in my core until they set me alight. Through the heat of the flames, the haze of love I've been blinded by for so long evaporates and, finally, I see.

The signs something was amiss with my relationship have been there all along. When I look at Jamie's life, all I see are the gaps in what I know. The vagueness in his social plans, the separateness of our friendship groups. Jamie meets my friends regularly, but the gesture is rarely returned. Where are the invitations to drinks with Jamie's friends? Why don't we go to their homes for dinner? Pete living in Edinburgh is often the excuse, but Pete isn't Jamie's only friend. Ricky is his best man... when did I last see him?

Jamie lives exactly the way he wants to, no questions asked, but the same can't be said for me.

With squirming clarity, I think back to the major arguments in our relationship. There haven't been many and they always ended quickly. I used to think our ability to de-escalate a situation was a strength and I would brag, a little smugly I admit, that we never argued, but looking back I wonder if that's something to brag about at all.

Our first row happened because I was late home after meeting my friends for drinks. Jamie was livid, shouting about how he thought something awful had happened to me.

"Just the other week, Ricky told me about this guy he works with whose girlfriend was raped getting home from a night out. I've sat here watching the clock, terrified something might have happened to you. Do you have any idea how worried I've been? I'd never forgive myself if you got hurt and I wasn't there to protect you."

"I'm sorry, I didn't think staying out was such a big deal," I'd protested.

"Not a big deal? Cass, are you serious?" Jamie cried. Tears spilled down my cheeks as he painted fearful visions of alternate timelines, ones I felt ignorant for not living in catatonic fear of. Once I agreed to him picking me up at a pre-agreed time whenever I went out, our argument stopped. I told my friends it was romantic he wanted to make sure I was safe, a sentiment I told myself every time he rang twenty minutes earlier than agreed to say he was waiting outside.

Then there was the time my childhood friend Aran suggested catching up and Jamie offered to come along too.

"That's sweet of you, Jamie, but you don't know him. Besides, I've not seen Aran in forever! We've so much to catch up on, so much you won't know about. You'll be excluded from the conversation."

"I thought you'd want me to meet your friends," he'd pouted. I couldn't stand the disappointment on his face, so I took Jamie along under the guise I wanted the two to meet.

As predicted, the conversation was awkward and stilted. I walked away feeling like my friendship with Aran had faded. Jamie even commented on it, saying, 'I thought you two were close?'. Those words were enough to put doubt in my mind. I haven't seen Aran since. I didn't even invite him to the wedding.

It's only now I think about it that I realise most of our arguments have been about me doing something Jamie didn't like, and every time it was me who changed my behaviour. For Jamie, for our relationship, I clipped my wings, but manipulation was weaved into each of those choices.

Giving up personal training sessions with my instructor Ryan so Jamie and I could run together wasn't so we could have a joint hobby. Jamie booking a surprise weekend away over Lily's birthday celebrations wasn't so we could have a romantic break, but so I wouldn't go out with my single friends.

As the list of Jamie's controlling behaviour grows, the one constant with them is me. Me and my willingness to bend to whatever Jamie wanted, all because he made it seem like the right answer. The only answer.

By the time Jamie arrives home, I'm trembling from the aftershock of the truth.

"Hey!" he chirps, leaping onto the sofa beside me. "Did you have a good day with Tara?"

My body clenches in his presence, but I force a smile. "It was good, thanks."

"Glad to hear it! What did you get up to?"

"Oh, we got so much done, I don't even know where to start! I feel much better about everything. Tara's help has even given me time to plan a few extra surprises for the big day."

Jamie wiggles his eyebrows suggestively. "Surprises, eh? Like what?"

"Just a few more decorations and a keepsake for our guests."

"Can I know anything about them?"

"If I told you, they wouldn't be a surprise, would they?" I reply. Jamie laughs and swoops in to kiss me, but I squirm in his arms. "Where's the Chinese?"

Jamie throws his head back and groans. "Urgh, I forgot!"

Reaching for my phone gives me the perfect opportunity to break free of his grip. "Never mind, we can order one."

"I don't fancy a Chinese tonight, actually."

Instinctively, my mouth opens to say 'okay', but I stop myself. "Really? Well, I'd like one."

Jamie pulls his phone from his pocket even though mine is in my hand, ready to use. "Let's see if we can find something else."

"But I'd like a Chinese."

"It's easier if we order from the same place."

"I'd like a Chinese," I say, my voice shrill.

Jamie blinks, his face a picture of irritation. "Alright, Cass, you don't have to be so hysterical. Order what you want." With that, he goes into the kitchen in a huff, but I barely even notice him leave the room.

What we have for dinner is such a small decision but in the context of what I now know, it's so much bigger than that. What starts with me not eating what I want because he doesn't feel like it quickly moves to me cancelling plans with friends because Jamie can't be bothered or turning down a job opportunity because it means less time together. And I did it, every time, for him. I gave up so much until I'm not even sure of my own voice anymore. The music I listen to, the clothes I like, the dreams I have... who do they belong to, really?

I order the Chinese on principle, but when it arrives, I barely touch it. There's no room in my stomach for food when it's already so full from digesting the warnings and truths I have ignored for so long.

19.

With the realisation of how much I've melted myself down to fit the mould of 'Jamie's Ideal Woman' fresh in my mind, I can't rest. I itch to peel my skin from my body, to wrench myself from this lie of a life. I need space, need to breathe, need to be anywhere but in our apartment.

My knees weaken with relief when I check my diary and discover I have plans, even if they are wedding orientated plans with Anne.

Months ago, back when I thought I'd be marrying the love of my life on our wedding day and not outing him as a cheat, I asked both my mum and Anne to collect photographs from our childhoods. I wanted to create a timeline that showed us growing up as two separate people then coming together as one. The idea seemed cute at the time. Now? Not so much.

Barricading my sadness inside, I get dressed then go to Jamie. I find him in the kitchen, humming along to the radio and making a coffee. "I'm heading out now."

"Where are you going?"

"To your parents' house. I'm picking up the photos."

Jamie stops stirring sugar into his coffee. "What photos?"

"The photos for the timeline at the wedding."

"The baby photos?" Jamie asks. When I nod, he groans. "Cass, do we have to do that?"

"Why not? It's cute!"

"Surely at our wedding people want to see photos of us as a couple, not me with my first bike or building a sandcastle when I was four."

I draw Jamie close to me. "It's meant to represent the idea of two people and two lives coming together."

"And we have to do it by using cringey childhood photos?"

"How else would we do it?"

Jamie sways me in his arms and sighs. "Fine, but you've only got yourself to blame if people are too busy laughing at me to compliment you on your dress."

"I'll take the blame, don't worry. Besides, baby photos are supposed to be laughed at."

Jamie lets out a strangled noise and kisses me. I follow his lead then say goodbye.

As soon as I leave the apartment I find air, but the sensation of finally being able to breathe is short-lived. Seeing Anne again after her money bombshell is going to be awkward. She radiated with tension throughout the Thursday dinner, even with the distraction of her grandchildren. Who knows how sitting together one on one will be?

My stomach brews on the drive to her house, my nerves fizzing to delirious new heights when Anne opens the front door to greet me. "Cassie," she enthuses, ushering me inside. "Would you like a cup of tea?"

I nod and we head into the kitchen. While the kettle boils, Anne prattles away, sharing stories about people she works with, people I've never met and never will. She barely takes a breath between her words, and I realise how nervous she is around me now. I find myself hating Jamie more for putting his mum through this.

When the tea is made, we move to the living room where a small stack of photographs waits for me on the coffee table.

"Did you go through them already?" I ask, thumbing the pile.

"Oh no, dear. These are all the photos we have of Jamie when he was young."

I eye the stack again. There are no more than twenty photos here, tops, but that isn't the Anne and Martin I know. They're people who ask for family photos on every special occasion, the kind of parents who when talking about their children growing up remember specific details as though the memories happened the day before. I expected numerous volumes of photographs documenting every pivotal moment of Jamie's life.

Anne must sense my shock. "I promise we took more but Jamie threw them out."

"He did? Why?"

Anne takes a delicate sip of tea and shrugs. "It was quite strange, really. He came back from university his final year in a funny mood. He was sullen and closed off, wouldn't tell me what was wrong, kept insisting it was nothing. Then one day I found him looking through his childhood photos. I thought it was sweet until I saw he was crying."

The tea curdles in my stomach. "Why was he crying?"

"I never got to the bottom of it, but I think it was to do with feeling embarrassed. Jamie didn't have the university experience most people talk about. You know, the falling in love and making a whole host of new friends. Jamie was a lovely boy, but he was somewhat of a loner. He was awkward and… well, he was miles away from the man you know him as today. University was a strange time for him, like it is for most young people, I suppose. Lots of figuring himself out and learning about what he wanted in life. I think seeing those photos of who he used to be upset him."

Questions fill my mouth but I hold them in so I can take a moment to see what was so bad Jamie wanted to erase it from history. I take the first photo from the pile, a snapshot of Jamie around the age of seven. He's all knobbly knees and missing teeth, like any other seven-year-old. His clothes are cringey in a 'why-did-my-parents-dress-me-like-that' way, but they're nothing to be ashamed of.

But there is something strange about him, a seriousness that comes across even in photos. I flick through the next few photographs and find the same thing. There's an intensity to his features like he's trying to play the part of a happy child but not quite meeting the mark.

"I don't know what he's embarrassed for. He was cute," I say for Anne's benefit.

Smiling, Anne reaches for one of the photos, a shot of a sleeping baby Jamie nestled in her arms. She strokes her thumb over his cherubic cheeks. "Wasn't he? I used to watch him sleep for hours. We tried so hard for another baby after Alison. Three years of trying, three years of tears, then he came along. My miracle."

Anne's eyes mist with tears and my throat closes. I always knew she shone with pride whenever she spoke of Jamie, but I thought that was like any parent. I didn't know about her struggles.

Even though I'm not responsible for any of Jamie's actions, I still burn with the shame of his betrayals. How is Anne going to feel when she finds out the truth? The way she looks at him, the adoration in her voice... the truth will break her.

"I saw how much the photos upset him, but I couldn't let him throw them all away. They're memories, aren't they? They're precious. I've never told him this, but I snuck in the bin after he'd finished and fished a few out. There are probably photos in here he doesn't know exist anymore, but I had to keep them."

"You did the right thing."

Anne smiles. "I know I did. I think Jamie will secretly be thrilled when he sees these at the wedding."

"Me too," I reply, but as I glance at Jamie's surly expression in a photo from his ninth birthday, I'm not so sure.

I chat to Anne about the wedding for a few hours before making an excuse to get going. She hands me a stack of books, including two she wants to lend my mum, then I leave.

I walk to my car on unsteady legs. There's a pounding in my head that wasn't there this morning, an adrenaline in my veins that's making me uneasy. All I can think of is the photos of Jamie and his desire to eradicate them from history. Who hates themselves so much that they would throw out every token of their past? What does that say about a person?

Gritting my teeth to stop myself from shivering, I start my car then feel my phone vibrating in my pocket. Seeing Mum's name on the screen, I answer the call. "Is everything okay?"

"Yes, don't worry, I've just got exciting news - I've finally found the shoes to match my dress!"

I can't help but smile. A month after we got engaged, Mum found her perfect wedding outfit, a pale blue dress with a matching fitted jacket. She bought it on the spot, but finding the perfect shoes? That's been a different story.

"If you're free, why don't you come over for lunch? I'll show you the shoes."

I weigh up my options but with my alternative plan being an afternoon with Jamie, there's no real choice to make. "Sounds great! I'll be there soon," I reply.

Only on the drive to Mum's, my desperation to be anywhere but home wavers.

How can I stand face to face with my mum and lie? Faking it to Anne and Martin is hard enough but lying to my mum is something else entirely. She knows me better than anyone. For a long time after my dad died, we only had each other. Because of that, we built an impenetrable bond, the kind no words can do justice to describing. Even when Mum met my stepdad Colin, we stayed as close as ever. My worry is that closeness means with one look she will see through me, and then it will all be over.

I turn the volume of the radio higher to drown out my anxiety before it gets the better of me, but the churning in my stomach warns me that's easier said than done.

The familiar streets of my childhood close in on me as I drive along them. I grip the steering wheel, a slick of sweat on my brow. I'm about to turn onto Mount Terrace when my stomach lurches, vomit pushing up my throat. I clamp my lips together and swallow. It burns on the way down, then shoots back up my throat again a second later.

Nerves fried, I pull over. I pray for this feeling to pass, but as my stomach flips once more, I know that's wishful thinking.

With a quaking hand, I call my mum.

She answers on the second ring. "Hello, love. Will you be long? Colin's about to nip out and grab lunch for us."

The mention of food sends a ripple through my abdomen. "I'm sorry but I'm not going to make it to yours. I was just nearly sick in my car."

"Oh, Cass! Are you okay?"

"Yes, no, I don't know… I need to go home." Another wave of nausea crashes through me and I groan. "I'm definitely not well."

"Oh, sweetheart! Don't worry about coming over. Get yourself home. I'll call Jamie and let him know you're sick. Rest up, okay? I love you."

"I love you too," I say before I hang up.

Tipping my head back, I focus on my breathing. My shirt is now stuck to me, large, damp patches staining my underarms, my skin aflame.

What is happening to me? I thought the mental torture of Jamie's actions was bad enough, but now there's this physical agony. That cheat, that thief, that sour-faced child… he's killing me, bit by bit, he's killing me.

20.

I crawl into bed as soon as I get in, feeling too horrendous to even show Jamie the photos I'd collected from Anne. Even though I sleep all day, I wake the next morning feeling nothing short of horrific. My body trembles with fever, but there is no room for illness. Today is the day I am meeting Patricia Campbell. The day I will finally get answers. A day I cannot miss. I need to go into work as if everything is normal, then apologetically claim I have a doctor's appointment and duck out at lunchtime. Doing anything other than following that plan isn't an option.

So, even though swinging my legs out of bed sends spurts of agony throughout my body, I get up.

Jamie winces when I stumble into the kitchen. "Babe, no offence but you look like shit."

"I feel it."

"Then get back in bed."

"It's the last day of term on Friday, I can't be sick," I protest, wrapping my dressing gown around my shivering body.

"If you go in, you'll only make yourself sicker. You need a day in bed."

"I can't -"

"There's no can't about it, that's an order," Jamie states, leading me back to the bedroom. "Seriously, Cass, you can't go to work today, not like this. I'll call and tell them you're sick."

I want to protest, but the walk to the kitchen sapped all my energy. Joints aching, I climb under the duvet and listen as Jamie calls work. He then potters about the apartment getting ready for his day before coming into the bedroom to check on me.

"Rest, okay? I'm serious, don't move a muscle. I'll be home as soon as I can to look after you."

"My hero," I whisper. Clutching the duvet to my chest, I wave goodbye from bed as Jamie sets off for 'work'.

When the front door closes, I intend to drag myself into the shower. I want to meet Patricia as a woman in control, not a woman on the edge of insanity, but my body is too heavy to move. Before I know it my eyelids droop and I fall asleep.

Feverish dreams suffocate me. I'm taunted by visions of a naked Jamie and Tara rolling around in the very sheets I'm laid in. Jamie's eyes lock on mine as he kisses her, an undeniable mocking shining in them.

I wake with a sudden start, horrified to see it's half past twelve.

Tearing back the duvet and ignoring the pounding in my head, I throw on yesterday's clothes and clean my teeth so hard my gums bleed. Pale and sweaty, I run to my car.

I hit every red light on the way into the city. "Come on!" I rage, drumming my throbbing fingers on the steering wheel. Sweat drips from my brow, but I can't tell if it's my fever or the panic of being so late that's causing me such distress.

Finally, I park in an overpriced carpark then I run to Caffeine, the coffee shop Patricia suggested we meet at. Rough would be a kind way to describe the greasy establishment. With sticky tables, dirty windows, and peeling paint, it's the kind of place I'd usually steer clear of, which makes it perfect for what I'm about to do.

I push open the front door, and the smell of cooking oil waves me in.

Patricia is sat by the window, as promised. She's wearing a shocking pink vest and greying white jeans with multiple rips in them. She's already ordered a coffee and is tapping away on her phone, her fake nails hitting the screen like tiny hammers.

I approach her. "Patricia?"

Her heavily drawn eyebrows raise when she sees me. "Wow, Abby, you must like a lie in more than I do," she jokes, but there's a hard edge to her voice.

"I'm so sorry I'm late. The ex, you know?" I sigh, hoping she won't ask for more detail.

Patricia's nastiness crumbles instantly. "Oh, I know *that* story. Let me guess, late for picking up the children because he's with his new woman?"

I roll my eyes. "How did you know?"

"Men, they're all the same! If he bothers you again, let me know. I'll come around and tell him what's what."

Eying the multitude of rings on Patricia's fingers and her once-broken nose, there's no doubt in my mind Patricia could tell an ex what's what.

"I tell you, there's nothing I hate more than men. Except maybe liars. And lying men? The absolute worst." Patricia signals over a waitress who doesn't look old enough to be in school, never mind working. "What d'you want?"

"A cappuccino, please," I reply, wriggling out of my coat. Instantly, I regret the decision. I shiver even though my clammy hands and damp forehead tell me I'm anything but cold.

"So, your children – two boys?" Patricia asks, adding another sugar to her coffee.

"Alfie and Matthew," I reply, startling as I realise I've used two names Jamie mentioned liking when we talked about names for our future children.

"Nice. I've got an Alfie myself, an Alfie-Ross. They love Meadow Park. My other boy, Riley, he gets in a bit of trouble every now and then, but he's a little shit, so what can you do?"

"My Alfie's too quiet for trouble," I respond, glossing over the fact Patricia called her son, who I know to be no older than six, a shit.

"We'll have to pair him up with Riley. They can help each other out.

Yours can calm Riley down, mine can make yours man up."

My left eye twitches but I push myself to nod. "That sounds great."

"So, what do you want to know about Meadow Park?" Patricia asks, nodding briskly at the waitress as she sets down my drink. Wrapping my hands around the warm mug, I launch into the speech I've been rehearsing for the last few days.

"It matters to me that the boys have stability at school. Our home life is so chaotic at the minute, you know? Alfie had three different teachers last year because of staffing changes, and it really impacted him. Meadow Park seems nice, but I heard there was a bit of trouble with one of the teachers there not too long ago. Apparently, it was so bad he even left the school at Christmas."

Patricia's eyes sparkle. "Are you on about the lovely Mr Patrick?"

My brain pounces at the mention of Jamie's name. I stir sugar into my cappuccino to keep my hands busy so Patricia won't notice they're shaking. "Was that his name?"

"Oh yes! The arse of an Olympian and arms that could toss you around the bedroom, if you know what I mean!" Patricia fans herself with her hand. I grip the handle of my mug and swallow the urge to smack her around the head with it. "There was a scandal about him alright."

"What happened?"

"Shagging another teacher, wasn't he?" Patricia shrugs. "No one knows who, but I reckon it was Mrs Mead. She's got huge boobs, and I mean *huge*. How could any man resist?"

I try to smile in response, but my face won't obey orders.

"Rumour has it, Mr Patrick had been trying it on with an apprentice too, even though she's only eighteen. I reckon that's lies, though. The school were just trying to make him out to be a bastard rather than a sex god! But he was definitely shagging another teacher, everyone knows that. I nearly got a piece of him myself too, but he got the boot before I could get in there," Patricia sighs, sucking her teeth. "I tell you, whoever he ends up with is one lucky lady!"

I don't bother replying. Instead, I put my drink to my lips and stifle a scream.

So, Jamie's affair with Tara cost him his job. It all makes perfect sense. Of course he can't tell me why he isn't working anymore – that would mean admitting he wasn't only staying back to mark books. That would mean admitting the truth, the truth everyone has already found out, even the parents at the school gates... everyone but me.

"I can't believe he cheated," I whisper.

Patricia frowns. "He didn't cheat. He's single."

"Right, yeah," I fumble.

"If only I had a photo of him to show you, you'd see what all the fuss was about. I can't imagine how hot their hook-up was. I bet they did it in a classroom."

Suddenly, the ugly truth, Patricia's fawning and the heat in the café is too much. My mug slips from my hands. Its steaming contents pool across the table, spreading out and taking over everything, just like Jamie's lies.

Patricia grabs her phone and leaps to her feet before cappuccino soaks her white denim. "Watch it, you idiot!"

"I'm sorry, I'm so sorry," I babble, grabbing paper napkins to mop up the cappuccino that's now dripping onto the floor. I bend to wipe it but as soon as my head moves, the room spins.

"Are you okay?" the waitress asks, rushing over with a cloth to help me clean the mess.

"Yes... no... I don't feel very well."

"You look horrible," Patricia sneers. "You're all sweaty and disgusting."

"I think I need to go home."

"Here," the waitress says, helping me to my feet. My hand in hers is soaked with sweat. I want to apologise, but I can't find the words. My throat is too clogged with emotion, my body too on fire to focus on anything but finding air.

My eyes land on the front door.

"I'm sorry about today. I'll make it up to you," I call in Patricia's direction before stumbling outside. Blinding sunlight screeches at me. I hold onto the wall to keep myself upright as I struggle down the street, sweat pouring from every pore.

"Abby! Where are you going? You haven't paid!!" Patricia hollers after me, but I don't stop. I'm scared that if I don't keep moving, I'll vomit down myself.

I push my way through elderly shoppers, university students and mothers with young children, the crowds seeming bigger and bigger, the surroundings louder and louder until eventually, somehow, I make it back to the safety of my car. Spilling inside, I slam the door on the rest of the world.

Resting my chin on the steering wheel, I stare at the concrete wall ahead, breathing until I'm no longer seeing double. Only when my vision clears, all there is for me to see is the raging, ugly truth.

To know Jamie is cheating with Tara is one thing, but to know their affair cost him his job is another. Every morning when Jamie kisses me goodbye, he's covering up his betrayal. Every night when he tells me fictitious work stories, he's fuelling his lie. What he has done doesn't play on his conscience at all. His affair and the damage it's caused is as much a part of his life as brushing his teeth is.

"Bastard!" I screech into the silent abyss of my car.

I don't know how long I sit there waiting for the truth to stop feeling like a cruel, merciless taunt, but it never does. Everything about what Patricia told me hurts in the worst possible way, but the main thing is that it's the truth. It's what I wanted to find out, right?

Right?

<u>21.</u>

When I get home, I check my phone to find a message from Patricia raging that I owe her money for the drink I '*poured all over her like an idiot*'. I don't respond and I don't send her the money. The last thing I need is a link from my bank account to hers. Instead, I deactivate the Abby Dunne Facebook account and pray I never have to use it again.

I spend the rest of the day wrapped in a huddle of blankets, fighting off the shivers that ransack my body, but no matter what I do I can't stop the trauma of the day from reverberating through me.

Debbie tries calling me when she finishes work, but I let my phone ring out. She calls three more times until I pacify her with a text saying all is well. Her pressing concern must exhaust me because before I know it, I'm asleep on the sofa.

I wake to find Jamie stood over me with a bouquet of flowers in his arms. My throat closes with terror and I struggle to a seated position. "Were you watching me sleep?"

"What? No," he laughs. "I've just got in. I wanted to surprise you with some flowers."

He offers me the bouquet and I take it, burying my face in the blooms so I have an excuse not to look at him. "They're beautiful, thank you."

"I'm glad you like them. How are you feeling?"

"I've been better."

"Oh babe," Jamie pouts. He reaches out to cuddle me, but I hold my hand up to stop him.

"I don't want you to catch whatever bug this is."

"I guess we can't have both of us down and out, can we? Although a day in bed with you does sound great," Jamie jokes, flopping onto the other end of the sofa. He kicks his shoes off as he turns on the television. They land with a soft thud in the middle of the room. Jamie selects an American sitcom to watch and nestles into the sofa, making himself comfortable.

I try to follow what's happening on the screen but the canned laughter and cutesy outfits grate against my tension, leaving me exhausted once more. "I think I need to sleep," I say, pushing myself to stand.

"You're probably right. Do you want me to bring you a drink or anything?" Jamie asks. I shake my head and move to leave the room but before I go Jamie grabs my hand and kisses it. "There. You can't get mad at me for that kiss."

"I could never be mad at you," I lie, then I free myself from his choking presence.

At the end of the hallway, I spy Jamie's coat and laptop bag. My legs carry me towards them without being instructed to. I check them for clues as to where he's been today, but neither contain any secrets. Inwardly I curse, but then it strikes me that Jamie is alone in the living room. Jamie who lies everywhere, even at home.

Biting my lip, I make my way back down the hallway. Through the gap in the doorway, I spy Jamie typing a message, no doubt to Tara. When the message sends, he puts his phone away and reaches down the side of the sofa for his tablet.

His tablet.

How had I not thought of that before?

My chest flutters with possibility. Pushing myself to be braver, I take a tentative step forward. I hold my breath, terrified Jamie will catch me spying on him, but he's too engrossed by his screen to notice he's being watched.

Jamie enters his tablet's passcode and I make a mental note of it – 363036. I repeat the numbers on loop, all the while my throat pulses with the thunder of my heart.

With a yawn, Jamie adjusts his position on the sofa. He might be comfier, but his bulky frame now blocks a chunk of the screen, so I step to the right. Closer to Jamie, closer to the truth, and closer to being caught.

Jamie opens his saved photos and selects a folder. I crane my neck, trying to place the images, but I never get chance to see them properly with his body covering most of the screen. I can only make out the odd flash of interiors or curve flesh, but little else. Frustration bites me. I take another step forward but as soon as I do, my blood turns to ice.

Women.

Jamie's looking at photos of women, crude ones taken by someone desperate to see them at their most erotic, most vulnerable angles.

My already unsteady legs give way and I stumble, grabbing the wall for support.

"Cass?"

Jamie's head snaps around and I meet his gaze. There's a flash of something I've never seen before in his eyes and my knees lock in fear.

"I… I needed a drink of water."

"Why didn't you ask me to get you one?"

"My throat hurts, I didn't want to shout."

Jamie stands and drops his tablet on the sofa, the screen now black. "Have you been up long?"

I shake my head.

"Good, you're too sick to be walking about. Let's get you back to bed."

With his hand on the small of my back, Jamie leads me into the bedroom. My body stiffens at his touch, but I let him lead me. He pulls back the covers and I climb into bed obligingly, gripping the duvet so tight I can see the whites of my knuckles.

Jamie places my phone on the bedside table then leans over me, his arms on each side of my body, pinning me inside the duvet. "If you need anything, text me. Don't get up. You're meant to be resting."

"I'm sorry."

Appeased, Jamie nods. "I love you," he says. Only when I say it back does he leave the room and only with him gone do I dare exhale.

I lay back against my pillow, my thoughts racing. The way Jamie looked at me… it was like staring into the eyes of a stranger, and a terrifying one at that. The hairs on my arms stand to attention at the memory, my fear bringing into clarity the glaring truth. Jamie didn't want me to see what was on that screen. That can only mean one thing - Jamie's tablet contains the rest of his secrets. To uncover them, that's where I need to look.

22.

Morning sun streams through the gap in the bedroom curtains. I wince at its intrusion. "I can't go back to work today, there's no way."

"I think you're right, Cass. You still look pale," Jamie says sadly. "I'll call work and let them know you won't be in today, okay?"

"Thank you," I reply.

I listen out to Jamie's morning routine from the confinements of our bed. He makes himself breakfast, showers, and dresses, then he brings me a cup of tea and a book. With a kiss on the forehead, he leaves.

As soon as the front door closes, I sit up. My head is cloudy with the remnants of illness, but nothing could stop me from hacking into that tablet today.

I plant my feet on the floor and force one foot in front of the other until I reach the living room. Pulling the cushions from the sofa, I locate Jamie's tablet. I type in his passcode and the tablet unlocks, the screen filling with a multitude of apps.

I'm in.

I head straight to the camera roll, but my excitement is short-lived because as soon as it loads, hundreds of photos of our relationship confront me. Snapshots of nights out, weekends away, walks on beaches, and lazy Sunday mornings. Our relationship in all its glory, the way it looks to the outside world.

The way it looked to me.

My vision blurs as I click on a photograph taken on New Year's Eve.

We're both a little tipsy. My red lipstick is smeared across Jamie's beaming mouth. Arm in arm, we're two people in love.

But that can't be true, can it? Jamie had lost his job because of his affair with Tara by that point. He might have his arm around me in the image, but behind my back it's around someone else.

I jab at the back button, not wanting to see memories of my idiotic self any longer. The tablet skips backwards until I'm presented with a list of photo albums. I scan their names. New York, Edits, Summer 2021, X.

X?

I click on the album and the screen fills with photos and videos of women, all of them either semi-nude or completely naked. It's such a confronting find that I almost drop the tablet.

Trembling, I click on the first photograph. It's of a woman with large, fake breasts and glossy, parted lips. Her eyes bore into mine from the screen. I shudder and swipe to the next photo, this time of a self-conscious redhead, her hands struggling to cover herself. The one after is a photo of a brunette in see-through lingerie.

Photo after photo flicks past my line of sight, each one splintering another piece of my soul, but even through my heartache something about them seems odd to me.

None of the images are professional. Some are so poorly shot they're bordering on unflattering. They look like photos of real, everyday women, only real, everyday women at their most intimate. Some are photos they've taken of themselves, some are photos taken by someone else in the room, but all are most definitely amateur.

Frowning, I skip to the next image, only my blood runs cold as soon as I see it.

It's a photo of a naked woman laid on a floral duvet, her legs spread wide and her smile inviting. She's taken the image herself using a mirror at the end of the bed to capture her reflection. Badly dyed hair tumbles over her bony shoulders, her raised eyebrows so thick they look drawn on with a marker pen.

It's a photo of a woman I recognise.

It's a photo of Patricia Campbell.

23.

I stare at the photo for what feels like an eternity. I half expect Patricia's features to rearrange so I can shake my head at how paranoid I must be to think Jamie would have a nude of Patricia Campbell, but it's still her face I see before me. There's no mistaking it's her and there's no mistaking what this means - my fiancé *was* flirting with Patricia, just like she said he was. He was flirting with all the women in these photos.

I can't hold the vomit back. I rush to the kitchen and throw up in the sink, shedding my stomach of its meagre contents.

"Fuck," I exhale, gripping the counter for support.

For a moment, I debate stumbling to my car and showing up at my mum's front door with my arms outstretched and the tablet in my hand, but I can't. Now I've scratched the surface of Jamie's treachery, I need to uncover it all.

Chills race through my body as I make my way back to the sofa and pick up the tablet once more. Patricia's 'come to bed' smile flashes on the screen. I skip past the photo quickly and flick through more of Jamie's pornographic stash until I see another familiar face. Another parent from Jamie's school.

A few months ago, we were doing the weekly food shop when Jamie saw her on the next aisle. He grabbed my hand and pulled me in the opposite direction.

"What are you doing?"

"Cass, we've got to hide! That woman is crazy! She threatened to slash

Arron's tyres the other week because she said he gives out too much homework. I kept her son in at break time the other day. Who knows what she'll do to me!"

I laughed at Jamie's dramatics but complied, knowing there were some parents I'd hide from if I saw them in public too, but this photo explains the real reason for his frantic actions and the memory burns. Another twisted experience, another wicked lie. Another time the truth was in front of me, but I was too blind to see it.

My eyes rest on the photograph on the screen and I sigh. I don't want to see another naked stranger my fiancé has seduced. I've seen enough.

I close Jamie's photos and scan the rest of his home screen for places to investigate. I spot the thousands of email notifications he has and open the app. Skimming down the list, I ignore generic marketing messages until one subject line catches my attention.

'LaydeeeeKilla07 commented on your post'.

Curiosity piqued; I open the email.

You're the man!!! These posts make my day. I wish I could get as many women as you. Teach us your ways!

My throat closes as I reread the message and try to understand what it means, but nothing about it makes sense. Why would someone say that to Jamie? What posts make their day?

In the email there's a link to reply to the comment. I click it and a webpage for a blog called 'The Good Bad Guy's Guide' loads. It's a website with the most basic setup but the unimaginative design hasn't impacted its appeal or popularity. Despite only being published two days ago, the post *'LaydeeeeKilla07'* commented on has almost fifty comments already.

Gripping the tablet tight, I read.

What a night I've had!

While good old wifey-to-be waits for me at home, T and I hit the town. After five cocktails for her (they make her loose), we split the bill and head back to hers. I'd describe the house, but as always, I barely noticed it. As soon as the front door closed, we were on each other, clothes gone.

I clamp my hand over my mouth.

This isn't any website I've found… this is Jamie's website. These words, this night, they belong to him.

Horror rolls down my body as I skim over the next few sentences detailing everything Jamie and Tara got up to. What he did with her while I was at home, planning our wedding and waiting for him to return. Their erotic affair, narrated for me by Jamie himself.

Bile burns my throat as I click through months of backdated posts, each one describing illicit hook-ups not just with Tara, but with a multitude of women. Jamie never says their names, instead referring to them by their first initial, but one constant is T. T who he's been meeting since the middle of last year.

I press my knuckles to my mouth to hold in a scream as the foundations of my life shift beneath my feet. I feel myself slipping, falling through the cracks, my spirit depleted by a man who has repeatedly betrayed me then shared the news in a public arena. To him, to the world, I'm nothing more than wifey-to-be, a placeholder, a pair of arms to return home to when he's done.

I force myself to find what else Jamie's written about me. I find the posts quickly. Peppered between narratives about his cheating escapades are ones about his homelife and the joy he takes in living a double life. They all have sarcastic titles like *'Wifey-to-be did good today'* or *'How to have a fiancée AND get laid too'*.

Every fibre of my being tells me not to read further but I ignore the warnings and plough through the posts, each word wounding like a bullet.

Wifey-to-be is honestly the most naïve person on the planet. It's probably why I proposed to her, knowing I'll never find someone as clueless again. She thinks she's too worldly-wise, too strong, to be cheated on. It's enough to make me laugh.

I've told her I had two staff meetings this week and she didn't question me once. It's almost too easy but I'm not complaining. I get to do what I want and come home to a clean home and grateful lover – what more could a man want?

Wifey-to-be is so eager to please. I love seeing how far I can push it with her. Whatever I say, whatever I do, she's still there. She's still saying yes. Men, do yourself a favour and find a partner like her. You won't regret it.

I can't breathe through the vulgarity of his words, can't focus on anything other than the fact that my identity has been stripped back and warped into something so worthless. I'm not Cassie, not a friend, a daughter, a person. I'm wifey-to-be, the butt of the joke in this sick section of the internet.

When Jamie's bragging gets too much to stomach, I read the comments beneath his posts. They're almost as bad as Jamie's anecdotes. Not only are people engrossed by his writing but they're cheering him on, asking for more and wanting Jamie to push his treachery even further.

Would love to send a feminist this site. It would shut them up LOL

We need 2 meet 4 a pint. I need more of these stories!! Have you ever been with one of wifey's friends? An idea for nxt time...

U r a KING

The words scratch into my soul, embedding in a place where they will scar and stay forever. My most personal betrayal, the worst way someone can hurt someone, encouraged, celebrated, and devoured on the internet for entertainment. I don't know who makes me angrier, Jamie or his fans.

Unable to face reading anything else, I go to lock the tablet, but the title of a linked post catches my eye - '*The Evidence in Front of Her*'.

You know how I told you it was getting too easy to hide it all from wifey-to-be? I've started leaving shit out for kicks to see if she picks up on it. She never does.

There's a box in our home. She thinks it's full of cute memories. She couldn't be more wrong. Every time she goes into the room I keep it in, I laugh. Sometimes I even send her in there for the thrill of it.

I don't need to read more. I fly into the second bedroom and drag Jamie's memory box from the wardrobe. It's heavier than I remember. Heavier than a box filled with stuffed animals and childhood mementos should be.

I flick the lid off and fall to my knees.

Inside, I don't find Jamie's handmade Mother's Day cards or the ratty blanket he slept with until he was almost in secondary school. Instead, I find a lacy bra that smells of perfume that isn't mine. Photographs taken in an array of hotel rooms I've never been to, all starring different women in various stages of undress. I find sex toys I've never seen before, never mind used. Tissues with lipstick kisses pressed onto them. Tickets dated during times we were together for events I never attended. Numerous business cards and scraps of paper with phone numbers scrawled across them.

The box, the photos, the blog… it all makes sense. Jamie is a collector, a collector of women. Tara's just the tip of the iceberg, and I'm the coverup he's using to get away with it all.

Finally, I've found the truth.

24.

I don't know how long I sit on the floor staring at that box of deception. It's like I'm entranced by the lingering smell of stale perfume permeating the room.

I can't believe it. Even with the proof right in front of me, it still won't sink in.

Day after day, I've walked past evidence that would tell me cosy nights in were not on Jamie's list of priorities. While I sleep, a few feet away from my head lies a trunk of information with the power to transform my life into something more twisted than any nightmare.

My hand trembles as I pick up the bra. Whoever owns it has small boobs and expensive taste. I imagine her as a blonde with a few thousand followers on Instagram. Neat abs she swears she doesn't exercise to maintain. Jamie will have taken her somewhere nice. I imagine her laughing at his jokes, flashing her perfect teeth, her full lips coming towards his at the end of dinner to assure him he'd impressed her enough to take off her minuscule underwear.

I drop the bra, the skin on my hands burning, and focus on what else Jamie deemed necessary to keep instead of his childhood possessions.

The first thing I notice is a designer wallet. Inside I find a photo of Alison's dog alongside two credit cards in Jamie's name. One is for the account I saw listed on his phone, the other for a different bank. I grab my phone and copy the details of both cards into my notes, then put the wallet back.

Rooting through the rest of the box, I find more examples that show how little I know the man I live with. Sleek black business cards with 'The Good Bad Guy's Guide' web address printed on them. A passionate love letter from someone called Cynthia. A beermat from The Silver Fox pub with a phone number scrawled across it. Before I can talk myself out of it, I dial the number.

"Hello?" a female voice answers.

I stumble over my words. "I found your number in a box... in Jamie's box."

"Jamie's box?" The voice is sharp, defensive.

"I know you didn't do anything wrong, but I need to ask – Jamie Patrick, do you know him?"

The woman replies straight away. "No, I've never heard of him."

"Really? Because your number is on a beermat in this box. It's from The Silver Fox –"

I swear I hear the woman gasp. "Did you say The Silver Fox?"

I curl my nails into my palms before replying. "Yes."

"Look, I don't know why or how you've found my number, but I haven't been to The Silver Fox for a while. Not since I met Todd."

"Todd?"

"Todd. I didn't get his last name, and I don't want to. I know you don't know me but if your partner knows Todd then you need to run."

An icy fingernail traces its way down my spine. "Why?"

"Because Todd is a psycho! I met him a few weeks ago. We got chatting, we kissed. He wanted to come back to mine, but I said no and gave him my number instead. We messaged for a bit but every time we spoke, he tried to turn it sexual. When I made it clear I wasn't interested in a casual thing, he threatened me. He said he knew where I worked, where my family lived. I blocked his number. I haven't heard from him since, but I don't trust him not to show up again. Men like Todd don't take kindly to being rejected. I haven't dared to go back to The Silver Fox."

The woman's story sits heavy on my chest. Sure, she says she met a man called Todd, but with everything I've found out would it be such a stretch to think that Jamie would change his name so the women he meets can't find him online?

"I'm sorry I can't be more help –"

"No, you've been great. Thanks," I say, then I hang up and block the number as if pretending the call never happened could wipe it from my mind.

Grabbing another two beermats with phone numbers written on them, I debate making more phone calls but what's the point? Everything I need to know is in front of me. Everything is published on the internet for public consumption.

What I've found changes everything. Jamie isn't a man who deserves to be humiliated on his wedding day - he is a man who deserves to be ruined in a way that means he can never break another heart or lie to another soul again. Telling everyone about him and Tara won't be enough. He deserves more.

My mind runs wild with thoughts of what to do next. I start by stuffing every token of Jamie's other life back inside the box and cramming it into the wardrobe. Slamming the doors shut behind me, I then text my mum to say my car is playing up and ask if I can borrow hers to pick up some wedding bits.

Next, I email work to say that while I'll be back tomorrow, I'll be in late so I can go to the doctor.

Creating another new email, I type a message to Tara.

Hey Tara,

Sorry for the delay in sending this to you – I'm sure Jamie has told you I've not been well. I'm (finally!) better so I thought I'd send you the text for the love story card:

Those who know us say we are 'meant to be' but what does that mean?

It means surprise minibreaks, waiting in A&E for 5 hours when one of you falls and breaks their arm, not watching an addictive TV show until the other is there, cooking when you know the other has had a bad day. It means sharing your deepest, darkest secrets and knowing they will be safe. It means you have someone to hold your hand through every storm. It means you've got all of each other, the good and the bad.

Today is a day to celebrate a tale as old as time. Boy meets girl, they fall in love, they live happily ever after.

Happily ever after might sound naïve, but when you have your true love in your arms it doesn't seem farfetched at all. Not even 'ever after' sounds long enough to spend by each other's side.

Hope it's not too many words for your design – and not too cheesy! Thanks again. You're the best!
Cassie xx

I reread the message, my lips curling at the irony of every word. With Tara's design skills, I'm sure the card will end up a beautiful keepsake, only it will be one our guests will never see. Not with those words, anyway.

Glancing at the time, I snap my laptop shut and get dressed so I can pick up Mum's car. When a taxi drops me off at her house, her only question is why I'm not in work today.

"I'm not fully better yet. I thought one more day of rest would help."

"I hope it does, sweetheart. Take care of yourself, okay?" she says, handing over the keys.

Before I return home, I make a detour to a phone shop and locate an eager sales assistant.

"I broke my phone the other day. I'm looking for something basic until I pick a new one," I lie.

He shows me a burner phone, the oldest model they sell, one that's so chunky it could smash a window. It can access the internet and email, but there's no Cloud, no connecting to external devices. It's perfect.

"I'll take it, and a pre-paid SIM card," I say. I pay for the phone in cash and leave the shop on cloud nine, the phone and all the possibilities it brings burning in the carrier bag.

After setting up the phone and adding the Abby Dunne email to it, I stash it in the glove compartment of Mum's car and drive home. Parking further down the street so Jamie won't spot the car, I head inside and hide the keys in my laptop bag.

After all that action, I'm worn out. I stretch out on the sofa, a heaviness pressing on my limbs, and I drift off into perfect blackness.

When he returns home that evening, Jamie finds me curled under a blanket, dressed in the same pyjamas he saw me wearing that morning. "Feeling better?"

"Much," I reply.

Jamie cheers and pulls me to my feet. He dances me around the living room, his hands clamped on my waist, his happiness bouncing off the walls. I laugh along like I'm supposed to, all the while trying to suppress the screaming inside me that shouts I don't know this man at all, or what he is capable of.

25.

The shrill sound of my alarm wrenches me from the peaceful grip of sleep. Jamie's arms make themselves at home around my waist. "How are you feeling today?"

Despite the pounding in my head, I reply, "All better."

"Finally," he cheers, rolling on top of me. I giggle even though being caught under his bodyweight doesn't feel like anything to laugh about, then press a kiss onto his shoulder.

"I need to get ready. Shari's giving me a lift to work so she can fill me in on all the drama from while I was away. Apparently, there's a lot," I explain, hoping the excuse is good enough to stop Jamie wondering why my car will still be in the garage when he leaves.

If he's suspicious, he doesn't show it. "Sounds fun. I can't wait to hear all about it tonight!"

After showering and dressing in record time, I root through the second bedroom and locate a blonde wig from an old Halloween costume. The hair is matted and made from plastic, but anything that will help conceal my identity is fine by me. I hide the wig in my laptop bag then say goodbye to Jamie.

Scurrying out of the apartment, I dash to the safety of Mum's car. Rain lashes the windscreen, the torrential weather a blessing. I pull the wig over my hair and throw the hoodie I left in the car the day before over my work clothes.

Then I wait.

Crouching low, I watch the door of our communal garage. Two neighbours leave before Jamie's red car comes into view.

Gripping the steering wheel, I pull out after him. I keep a safe distance between us, but the mix of the rain and Mum's generic car seems to be more than enough camouflage. Jamie drives along, blissfully unaware I'm three cars behind him.

Instead of turning down Hall Road to drive towards Meadow Park Primary, Jamie continues towards the city. Even though I knew it would happen, I still smirk with the triumph of catching him out.

But Jamie doesn't stop in the city. Instead, he joins the motorway, travelling even further away from the school he supposedly teaches at. I keep on his tail, dry mouthed and wondering where the hell we are going.

Twenty minutes into the journey, Jamie signals to exit the motorway. I follow him, eyebrows raised. How far from home we are, how few people know either of us out here.

Jamie drives for another ten minutes before pulling into a multi-storey carpark attached to a shopping centre. I don't have a choice other than to follow him.

Inside the carpark with no rain to distort Jamie's view and me in the car behind, I'm as visible as can be. The wig might momentarily throw Jamie off, but one lingering look in his rear-view mirror is all it would take for him to recognise me and for everything to be over.

Blood thumps in my ears as Mum's car rolls behind Jamie's. I keep my speed slow, my reflexes ready, but none of my precautions seem enough to keep me out of sight.

On level three, Jamie swings into an open parking space and turns off the ignition. I scan my surroundings for another free spot, but I can't see one. My palms slip on the steering wheel as I drive down the next lane, hunting for a gap that doesn't exist.

"Come on!" I hiss, watching in horror as Jamie saunters out of his car and makes his way towards the lifts. I scour the sea of vehicles before me, desperate for vacant space but finding none.

This can't be it. This can't be where I lose him.

I glance at Jamie in time to see him push the call button for the lifts. A desperate squeal bursts from me and, for one wild moment, I contemplate abandoning Mum's car in the middle of the carpark. Anything but lose Jamie.

Suddenly, a battered blue car reverses out of a space ahead of me. Accelerating too fast, I pull into it before anyone can steal it from me.

As I run across the carpark, I watch Jamie disappear into a lift alongside four other people. The doors close. The numbers on the panel above descend to reach the ground floor while I frantically jab the button to call another. One arrives, but not quickly enough. I press the button for the ground floor and cross my fingers so tight my bones scream, praying this isn't where everything falls apart.

No one else gets into the lift so I travel to the ground floor in one smooth ride. Stepping out into the bustling shopping centre, I search the crowd. Faces blur, none of them the one I want to see, but then I spot Jamie's broad shoulders in the distance.

I'm after him in seconds, weaving my way in and out of the crowd. He walks out of the shopping centre and down the high street, taking a right at the end of the road.

Blind to the rest of the world, I pursue Jamie, accidentally knocking into a man in a smart suit as I do so.

"Watch it!" he snaps, but I don't have the breath in me to apologise.

Ahead of me, Jamie pushes open the door of a coffee shop so hipster it hurts. It must be part of the job description that you have a beard and a topknot to work there. It's not a place I'd have said Jamie would go to, but there he is, sitting on the third table from the window and setting up his laptop as if it's where he belongs.

Keeping my hood up, I sit on a damp bench nearby. The cheap wig itches my scalp, but I push past the irritation and glue my eyes to Jamie.

He taps away on his laptop as if he is working, but with no job I can't imagine what he's doing. Probably writing his next vile blogpost or composing a dirty message to send to one of his many lovers. Every so often he scans his surroundings but what he's looking for I've no idea.

Only when a petite blonde in a tight pencil skirt enters the coffee shop, I realise.

The pair exchange coy smiles, then Jamie focuses his attention back on his laptop. The woman smooths down her hair as she orders a drink, stealing glances at Jamie whenever she thinks he's not looking. Jamie senses he's being checked out. His chest puffs forward and he frowns at the screen in front of him like he's in the middle of something important. I almost laugh at this display of bullshit, but I'm too in awe of his dedication to the role of 'businessman at work' to find it amusing.

Suddenly, Jamie is on his feet, leaving his laptop unattended and approaching the counter. The woman watches as he places an order, then he turns to her, initiating conversation.

Despite telling myself I don't care, witnessing Jamie charm his next victim still punches me between the ribs.

The pair talk, playful and giggly. The barista hands the woman her coffee in a takeout cup, but she doesn't leave. She stands beside Jamie, laughing at something he's said. They walk away from the counter together. I shrink into my hood, all the while wondering how Jamie would spot me when he only has eyes for the woman in the pencil skirt.

She might have ordered her drink to go, but whatever line Jamie spun her is enough to change her mind because they both take a seat at his table.

After a few minutes of conversation, a waitress sets a coffee and a croissant on the table. Jamie offers the woman half his food, a true pseudo gentleman. She declines, but his generosity has her beaming. More than that, whatever he's saying is soothing her nerves because she's no longer patting her hair self-consciously and toying with her takeout cup.

But what *is* he saying? I can't exactly sit next to him to find out. All I can do is watch through a window, but what does that tell me other than what I already know? I need someone on the inside, someone who can listen for me.

I look around and spot a student reading a book two benches away from me. She's wearing an oversized hoodie with the logo of a band I've never heard of printed across the chest. A 'piss off, world' vibe radiates from her, but with all the other benches empty, she's my only option.

Tentatively, I approach her. "Excuse me," I interject, trying my best to ignore the wary grimace she shoots me. "I was wondering if you could help me?"

She pauses, looking me up and down. "With what?"

"There's a man in there," I say, pointing to the coffee shop. "He's sat with a woman. I need you to find out what they're saying."

The girl lets out a sharp laugh. "Are you crazy?"

My cheeks burn. "I'll pay you. However much you want, I'll pay."

"I don't care, I'm not spying on someone."

"It's not spying –"

"Trust me, it is."

The judgement in her voice crucifies me. For the first time, I become aware of how strange I must look, sculking outside a coffee shop in my terrible disguise and begging someone I've never met before to spy on Jamie. It's almost embarrassing, really.

But what choice do I have? I've been pushed to this point, and I need this girl's help.

I take a deep breath. "The man in there is my… he's my friend's fiancé. He's cheating on her. He's supposed to be at work right now, but I found out he lost his job at Christmas. She doesn't know." My voice wavers. I don't want to cry, not here, not now, not in front of this alarmed teenager. "I need to save her from him. I need to know what he's saying. Please."

The girl studies me for a moment that seems to last a lifetime before slotting a bookmark into her book. "Okay, I'll do it."

My knees weaken. "Thank you, thank you so much." I point at Jamie. "That's him."

The girl nods. As she puts her belongings into her bag, I hold out some cash for her to buy herself a drink with. She shakes her head, her pity evident, then she marches into the coffee shop.

I chew my thumbnail as I watch from the bench. The student slinks over to the table next to Jamie's, sitting in the seat closest to the window and blocking my view, but it doesn't matter. What matters is that I have ears where I need them.

By the time Jamie's pencil skirted companion leaves the coffee shop, speed walking because her flirty escapades have probably made her extremely late for work, my bum is numb from sitting for so long. A few minutes later, the student walks out.

I jump to my feet. "What happened?"

She lets out a long exhale. "Well, he's one smooth guy."

My heart sinks. "He's that good?"

"Oh, very." She sets off walking and I follow. "He was telling her all about owning a rescue dog and caring for his disabled sister. I could almost hear her ovaries calling out, begging him to be the father of her children."

I can't hide my shock. "But that's all lies!"

"That's not what he told Jenny, or Jen – he was calling her Jen by the end of their chat. He made himself sound like a real catch. Todd's a great guy, alright."

I balk at the name, the memory of my phone call with the woman from The Silver Fox flashing in my mind. "Todd?"

"That's his name, right?" the student asks, then she bites her lip. "Wow. Well, that's what he told her his name is. Todd Goldman."

If it wasn't so tragic that this was my life, I'd laugh out loud at Jamie's ludicrous choice of fake name.

"Did he say why he was working in a coffee shop?" I ask.

The student shakes her head. "He said he had a meeting in the city later but that's it. He kept work chat pretty vague, to be honest."

"Probably because he doesn't really have a job."

"Probably," she shrugs, then she stops. "I need to go to class now. I'm sorry I didn't find much out for you, but I hope it helps your friend."

"No, you've been great. I can't thank you enough." I fumble for my purse, but the girl puts her hand on my arm to stop me.

"Keep your money, I don't want it. I'm sorry this has happened. Your friend's better off without him, though. He has Jen's number and they're meeting at the weekend."

"This weekend? The weekend before the wedding?"

The girl's eyes widen. "She's not actually going to marry him, is she?"

I shake my head. "No, I'm going to make sure of that," I reply, then I walk away before I start crying in public.

26.

Back in the safety of Mum's car, I replay my conversation with the student, letting the name Todd Goldman roll around my brain until I have a brainwave. I pull out my phone and search for 'Todd Goldman' on social media.

To my amazement, there he is – Todd, or should I say Jamie.

The profile says he lives two cities away but there's no doubt that this is Jamie. Every photo features him. From selfies of him wearing well-cut suits in expensive clothing stores to snapshots of nights out with friends to images of Jamie with Alison's dog, his face is everywhere. The only image Jamie's not in is a scenic photograph of Rome I took last summer he's used as his cover photo, something that irritates me more than it should.

Scanning through Todd Goldman's friends list, I discover most people on there are women. No doubt they're all ex-conquests or people he's currently charming.

I tip my head back and fill my lungs with air.

This profile proves it once and for all – Jamie is living a double life. Sometimes he's Jamie Patrick, sometimes he's Todd Goldman, but every time he is a liar, a cheat and someone who deserves to be played at his own sick game.

I sit for about three seconds before wrenching open the glovebox and grabbing the burner phone I bought yesterday. I save one number to it - the only number I need.

Before I can talk myself out of it, I send a text.

Hey Todd/Jamie/whoever you are today... does Cassie know she's not your only one?

My body hums with tension, but somewhere inside me, a small spark of joy ignites as I picture Jamie's face when he reads that message.

Slipping the phone into my pocket, I set off driving. I drop Mum's car at her house then take a taxi to work. My students give me a hero's welcome, cheering as soon as I enter the classroom. I paint on a smile and throw myself into the day. Apart from Theo flooding the boys' toilet, everything goes smoothly and home time rolls around in no time.

Waving the last child out of the door, I wander back into the classroom.

"Hey," Debbie says when I return, her tone not dissimilar to a therapist's. "Are you feeling better now? You're still a little pale."

"I guess that's how you look when you haven't been able to keep anything down for a few days," I joke.

Debbie face twists. "Oh, Cass. I've been worried about you."

"It was just a stomach bug."

"I think we both know it's more than that."

I perch on the end of my desk and Debbie joins me. We sit together in companionable silence. I debate resting my head on her shoulder, but I hold back. As wonderful as it is having Debbie by my side, it's drawing closer to the time I must pretend to her that I'm still marrying Jamie. It's a lie that might just kill me, especially after what I've found out these last few days.

But until that moment, I have her as my confidant. "I have something to show you," I say, reaching for my phone. "I hacked Jamie's tablet while I was off sick. I found this website on his internet history."

I load 'The Good Bad Guy's Guide' and hand Debbie my phone. She selects a post and I watch her eyes dart across the screen as she reads. She's barely finished the first sentence before they widen, then she lowers the phone. "Did he… did he write this?"

"No," I lie because I still can't bring myself to admit that the man I let into my bed and my life wrote those things.

Debbie glances back at the phone, her nose scrunched up. "That's the most disgusting thing I've ever seen."

"I know."

Debbie blows a puff of air out of her mouth, one so strong it ruffles her fringe. "If this is the type of thing he's reading, Cass, you need to run. For your own safety. Anyone who can read that and be okay is someone to fear."

Even though my brain niggles that Debbie is right, I do my best to shake off her words because I can't run. I refuse to. Jamie's told too many lies and hurt too many people. Someone needs to show him he can't do that. Someone needs to take him down.

"Do you really think it's that bad?" I ask as I take back my phone.

"Cass, how could you ask that? There's violence dripping from every word!"

Hearing someone else describe how horrendous Jamie's website is brings a new sense of shame to my situation and I hang my head. "What do you think makes someone write something like that?"

"Who knows, Cass. Childhood trauma? A warped sense of entitlement? A bad breakup they could never get over? Being a total pig? I've no idea but trying to rationalise it doesn't change the fact that what's written is nothing short of vile." Debbie shifts towards me. "I need to go in a second, Cass. Phil's picking me up to do the weekly shop, but I feel weird leaving you like this."

"I'll be okay, I promise. I'll finish up here and go home," I reply but mentioning home only makes Debbie's concern deepen.

"I need to ask you something and I need you to answer me honestly. Are you in danger?"

I chew my lip. "I… I don't think so."

"But you don't know for sure?"

"Does anyone know for sure?"

"Cassie, now isn't the time to be cryptic," Debbie says gently.

"I know, I know, it's just…" I look at Debbie's kind face and the resolve I was clinging onto breaks. "The Jamie I see at home is so hard to marry up with the version I know exists. I know he's cheated, I know he's lied, but everything about him tells me he hasn't. Sometimes it feels like I've dreamed it all."

"But you haven't, Cass. You've got the photo. You've found out he doesn't have a job anymore. What more do you need to see? The man is not who he says he is."

"I know but you're asking me if I'm in danger when a part of me still can't believe this is my life. I mean, up until a few weeks ago I'd have laughed if you told me Jamie was having an affair. I've never seen him be violent or even particularly angry, but then…"

"But then what?"

"But then the Jamie I know isn't the man who is jobless and having an affair," I admit.

"I think you should leave tonight. Screw the wedding, screw sorting money and the apartment. You don't know this man. He could hurt you."

"He wouldn't."

"Are you sure about that?"

An ominous shiver runs through my body at Debbie's words. I try shaking it away but it holds tight, wrapping my spine in its ice-cold grip. "I think… I think I need to process what I've seen and take some time to work out what to do." I straighten up and squeeze Debbie's hand. "Honestly, I'll be fine. You head off."

Debbie wavers, her desire to fix things at loggerheads with her plans to meet Phil. "Call me tonight if you need a chat, okay? You shouldn't be dealing with this on your own."

"Thanks, Debbie," I reply. I wave goodbye but even when she's gone, her worry lingers. It invades my lungs until it's all I can breathe, and I can't help but wonder what Debbie read to make her react so strongly. I reopen 'The Good Bad Guy's Guide' and read the post that's loaded on the screen.

Stay with me, men, because this is an important message.

I went out this weekend. Told wifey-to-be I was with work friends, but really I met some finance wanker I got chatting to in a coffee shop a few weeks ago. One who loves to show off and claim he's top dog. He thought I was lying when I said how many women I'd slept with in the last month. We went for drinks and I proved my point when he saw the amount of numbers I got in one night. After that, he was hooked.

It was a sweet arrangement. He paid the bills and I showed him how to pick up women. Easy trade (am I talking about our deal, or the women he ended up with...?)

But this weekend, finance wanker decided to get us kicked out of a bar. He grabbed someone as they walked past. The bouncer was on him straight away. It didn't matter about the size of his wallet or the amount he'd spent, not when little-miss-short-dress complained about unwanted advances.

Unwanted advances? Try telling your outfit that...

Anyway, I digress. My point is that what finance wanker doesn't realise is you don't need to grab them. You don't need to chase or intimidate or demand, not at first. You let them come to you. You let them think it's their idea.

Then you exercise your power. Then you become all consuming. That way, when you walk away, they think they've only got themselves to blame.

Look at wifey-to-be – I can do anything and it's okay. I could hit her across the face and she'd still look at me like she was thankful for it. Sometimes I even debate doing it just to prove I can.

Take note, men. You can do whatever you want, you've just got to play the game the right way.

I bring my trembling hands to my mouth to suppress a scream. My mind races with visions of all the times I've slept beside Jamie, unconscious in his presence and completely unaware of this side to him. He could have hurt me. He *wants* to hurt me. What will happen when he finds out what I've done, this man who fantasises about hitting me and exercising his power over others?

I press my face into my hands and run through my revenge plans, checking them for gaps. If Jamie finds out what I plan to do to his life before the wedding day, he could... well, it doesn't bear thinking about.

"You look lost in thought."

I jump at the unexpected sound of Shari's voice and look up to find her in the doorway. "You scared me."

"Sorry, I didn't mean to. I was going to come in here and complain about my day, but you look even more stressed than I do. Everything okay?"

I let out what I hope comes across as a carefree laugh. "Yeah, there's just a lot on with the wedding, that's all."

"Oh, it will be fine. I've been a bridesmaid three times now. It all works out in the end, I promise," Shari replies. We share a smile then she steps backwards. "Anyway, I'd best go find someone else to offload to."

"We can chat if you want to?"

Shari waves her hand to dismiss me. "The golden rule of offloading is that you can't dump your problems onto someone more stressed than you, but I appreciate the offer. Make sure you head home soon, and try not to worry about the wedding, okay? It's only one day."

"One day that's the start of the rest of my life."

"Just the start of a new chapter, one that's hopefully even better than the one before," Shari calls as she walks away.

I stare at the empty doorway long after she's gone. Shari's right, this is a new chapter. Not the chapter I thought I was going to write but one I need to write.

If I do everything exactly as planned, no one will be in danger. If anything, they will be safer than they are now. With Jamie outed, everyone will know him as the monster he is. Once they know that, he will never be able to hurt anyone again.

A phrase from Jamie's website echoes in my mind – *'you've just got to play the game the right way'*. I smirk. I plan to do exactly that, plan on playing the game even better than Jamie himself. Not just for me but for every woman he's ever written about. Every woman he hopes to feature on his website in the future. Every person who has swallowed one of his barbed lies or fallen victim to his false promises.

With a renewed sense of purpose, I dig the burner phone out of my handbag and find a text waiting for me.

I think you have the wrong number

My nostrils flare as I type my response.

You WISH I had the wrong number. But how could I when you gave it to me? Or do you give your number to that many women we all blur into one. Maybe I should tell Cassie that part too?

I hit send then slip the phone into the drawer of my desk. Waiting until tomorrow to read Jamie's response is going to be torture but it's worth it to make him sweat.

As I pack away my pencil case and get ready to go home, my fingertips tingle. This is it. Wheels are turning, plans are in motion. I couldn't be more ready for it, fallout, fights and all.

27.

I arrive home from work to an empty apartment. I check my phone for a message from Jamie explaining his absence but find none. Almost a week to go to the wedding, and I've no idea where my fiancé is or who he's with. I snort, even though there's nothing funny about it.

Padding into the living room, I flop onto the sofa and pull out my laptop. Checking my emails, I see that Tara has replied.

Hey Cassie,
So sorry to hear you've been unwell! I'm glad you're feeling better now.
What you wrote was beautiful! I've created both cards. If you click
here *it should take you to the website to view the proofs. My username is this email and password is tara0274!*
If you want anything changing, let me know. Otherwise all you have to do is approve the card for printing, then they will be delivered by the start of next week. I've set the address as my house so that I can write the envelopes for you too. Exciting times!
Tara x

I roll my eyes at Tara's perky friendliness then follow the link to see her design for the cards. When the page loads, my heart sinks.

They're stunning. Really, truly stunning. Simple, elegant, and classy, Tara has made two beautiful keepsakes, but the love story card is the real showstopper. Framed inside a heart is a beaming photo of me and Jamie.

The background is an intricate lace pattern that looks so realistic I almost touch the screen to feel it. They're exactly what I asked for and more.

I don't allow myself even a second to dwell in self-pity. I approve the design then minimise the page.

With Tara's cards sent to print, I use the Abby Dunne email to make a new profile on the printing website. I copy Tara's love story card and set about editing it, deleting every blissful sentiment and replacing it with an equally emotional verse.

You think you are here today to see a wedding, but you are wrong. Jamie Patrick is not the man you think he is.

Jamie is a liar and a cheat. His lies have even cost him his career, but they haven't stopped him. He has a fake name and fake social media accounts that he uses to entrap women. I tried to get Jamie to come clean about his actions and tell Cassie the truth, but as always Jamie thought he could lie his way out of it.

With that in mind, I could stay silent no more.

Jamie Patrick is a manipulative shell of a man. There is no limit to his deception. I am through with him, but I thought you all deserved to know the truth about the man stood before you today.

I've just processed the order when Jamie arrives home. I stiffen at the sound of his footsteps, snap my laptop shut, and go to him with open arms.

"Well, someone's pleased to see me," he grins.

"What can I say, I've missed you."

"I might stay late every night if this is what I'll come home to," Jamie jokes, shrugging his coat from his shoulders.

"How come you stayed late?"

"Oh, you know how it is. Stuff piles up, doesn't it?"

I can't be bothered to respond when I know the only thing piling up in Jamie's life is the number of women he's sleeping with. I walk away, speaking to him over my shoulder. "Did you have a good day?"

"Not bad, but something did come up."

"Oh?"

Jamie follows me into the kitchen and pulls a beer from the fridge. "I was talking with some of the other teachers, and they were saying how nice it would be to go for a few drinks to celebrate the wedding. We were thinking of heading into town this Saturday."

The student's words about Jamie meeting Jen from the coffee shop on Saturday spring to my mind. "This Saturday? You said yes to going out on the last weekend before the wedding?"

Jamie groans and runs his hands through his hair. "I know, what a nightmare! But you have your dress fitting so you'll be out with your bridesmaids. I thought – I hoped - you wouldn't mind if I went." Jamie looks at me through large, apologetic eyes, a performance so convincing I blink a few times to break free of its spell.

"It's the end of term tomorrow. Why can't you go for drinks after work like I am?"

"Our end of term drinks are cancelled because no one can make them. Saturday is the only day that worked for everyone."

I sigh and lean against the kitchen counter. "The last weekend before the wedding..."

"I know, but what could I say? They're not coming to the wedding, they won't get to celebrate with me then."

"We could have invited them."

"Cass, I struggle with the idea of paying that much for a meal for my cousins and I grew up with them, never mind my colleagues."

"It's not about the money. They'd have loved to come."

Jamie points the neck of his beer bottle at me. "They'd have loved a free night out, you know that as well as I do. I want our wedding to be about me, you and our future, not about who can score the most free drinks. I'll go out with them on Saturday so they feel a part of it and then next week is just for us, I promise. Deal?"

I swallow hard. Despite his act, I know the only person Jamie will be with on Saturday is Jen. If I say yes, I'm allowing my fiancé to cheat on me.

But what's the point in saying no? If he doesn't meet Jen this Saturday, he'll still meet her another time. And if it isn't her, it will be someone else.

"Go on then," I shrug, ignoring the chunk of my dignity that shatters at those words.

Jamie rushes to me and instinctively I take a step backwards, but he doesn't notice. Instead, he lifts me up and kisses me all over. "You, Cassandra Edwards, are the best! It's no wonder I asked you to marry me."

"Put me down, you idiot," I laugh.

Jamie squeezes me then obliges, lowering me to the ground. "I have some other news," he says, and I prepare myself for another lie. "Do you remember my friend Jaz from university?"

I shake my head.

"I've never mentioned Jaz before? Weird, she was one of my closest friends. Anyway, she's head of a school called Craven Primary, have you heard of it?"

Again, I shake my head.

"Well, Jaz messaged me this morning about a teaching position going there. It's about forty minutes' drive away, but the job sounds brilliant. Head of English and Computing, pay rise, great prospects for promotion."

My eyebrows arch. "A new job?"

"A new job. What do you think?"

"But I thought you liked Meadow Park?"

"I do, I did, but I can't see myself progressing more there than I already have. If we want a house and a family then I need to make more money. Plus, a new challenge sounds great. Craven's a really good school."

I look into Jamie's bright, eager eyes, eyes that don't betray any hint of the real reason for this sudden desire for change, and boil with anger. This has nothing to do with money or a need to excel in his career. If he gets the job, he can use his parents' money to tide him over until he starts at Craven Primary. If he gets the job, he gets away with his lies.

"Say something," Jamie says, breaking into my thoughts.

I force my lips to stretch into a smile. "If you want to go for it, then I support you all the way."

Jamie sweeps me into his arms. "Thank you, thank you so much! You've no idea how much this means to me." He backs out of the hug so he can see my face. "I have my interview the week after the school holidays, but Jaz pretty much told me I've already got the job."

"That's amazing," I enthuse.

"I know, right? Marriage, a new job, an exciting future. It's all going to happen for us, Cass. I can feel it."

As Jamie pulls me into him once more, I hold tight, all the while wondering how easy it would be to reach for a knife on the counter and drive it into his deceitful, black heart.

28.

Even though the last day of term is usually something all teachers fantasise about, I drag my heels getting ready for it. Queasiness flows through me the entire drive to work. As soon as three o'clock hits, there will be no Miss Edwards persona for me to hide behind, no daily distraction to remind me that I am so much more than Jamie's actions.

More than that, today is the day I must tell Debbie I'm going through with the wedding and that I've forgiven him. My insides shrivel as I imagine her reaction to the news, and the shame I'll feel delivering every false word.

The only thing that makes me feel better is opening my desk and finding a message waiting for me on the burner phone.

Gave it to you when? Who is this?

It's not the most exciting reply I've ever received, but what did I expect Jamie to do - offer a full confession? Beg for the anonymous texter to save me from the heartache of the truth?

I push my disappointment aside and respond.

You don't remember me? That makes me so sad! Perhaps I should message Cassie and tell her EXACTLY who I am

I leave the phone on my desk and go to fill my water bottle. I've barely reached the classroom sink when the phone buzzes. Seconds later, it buzzes again.

I smirk. Double texting means one thing – Jamie's rattled.

Even though I'm dying to know what he's said, I refrain from reading his responses because I know there's little more Jamie hates than waiting for a reply. I leave him to stew and set up for the day, tossing English books onto tables as if I don't have a care in the world.

"Someone's in a good mood," Debbie says when she enters the classroom.

Unease takes hold of me when I see her, but I try to not let it show. "What can I say, it's the last day of term."

"And you're looking forward to the holidays?"

"Why wouldn't I be?"

Debbie tilts her head. "Is that a trick question?"

I laugh and turn my back to Debbie, but I feel her eyes fix on me.

"Cass, what's going on?"

The confidence I built up before her arrival wavers. I clutch the books to my chest but one look in her concerned eyes and I crumble. "Shari needs to speak to me about a trip she's hoping to plan next term. Are you okay to finish setting up?"

I rush out of the classroom before Debbie can reply, hiding out with Shari under the guise of finding out more details about our end of term drinks. One minute before the children are due to arrive, I slink back to my classroom.

"Everything sorted?" Debbie asks.

"Yes," I reply, then I head straight to the door to invite the children inside.

The whirlwind nature of working in a school means I successfully avoid deep chats with Debbie all day.

At ten past three, I wave goodbye to the last student and close the door. A sense of peace washes over me. Reaching the end of term means one thing – the wedding is closer than ever. I might be down the distraction of work, but for the next week all I have to do is keep my head above water.

Only as soon as I enter the classroom and see Debbie waiting for me, I feel myself being pulled under.

"The last day of term, can you believe it? It's been a blur! I can't wait for the break, although it is going to be strange not knowing how you're getting on," Debbie says. She watches me with that all too familiar pity lining her features. "Are you going to be okay over the holidays?"

"Why wouldn't I be?"

"Well, you were meant to be getting married…"

And just like that, it's here. The moment I've feared since I first decided on using my wedding day for revenge.

I look at Debbie, taking a mental picture of the last time she will see me as anything but a fool, then I speak. "But Debbie, I am getting married," I say.

There's a beat of silence before Debbie speaks, one that's filled with such hope I'll take back what I've said it almost kills me.

"You're… you're what?"

"I am getting married." The words line my throat like honey, thick and cloying. I make a move towards my desk but Debbie grabs my arm to stop me.

"Cass, he's *cheating* on you."

"He's not cheating on me. He just kissed someone," I correct.

"You asked him that, did you?"

"I did. We got everything out in the open like I said we would. Jamie told me it was just a kiss, a one-time thing."

"Well, it didn't look a one-time thing to me!"

Debbie's analysis of the kiss pierces my soul. "It meant nothing, Debbie."

"Even if that is true, he was willing to throw your relationship away for a meaningless kiss. That's appalling! And he lied about his job, remember? What was his excuse for that?"

My cheeks burn as Debbie lists off the lies my fiancé told me. "He was struggling mentally. He needed a break from teaching –"

"And he couldn't tell you that? His answer to his problems was to secretly quit his job and kiss someone else... you can't marry him after that! Surely you can't marry him after that?" Debbie crumples. "You told me you were sorting it."

"But Debbie, I did sort it."

"By forgiving him?!"

My jaw clenches, the pain of pretending to be someone I'm not scalding. In this moment, I hate myself more than I've ever hated anyone, even Jamie. "He made a mistake. One mistake, one kiss. It's nothing. Definitely not enough to throw a relationship away for."

"You can't be serious, Cass! You know as well as I do it was more than that. Besides, if he's done it once, he'll do it again."

"You don't know that."

"I do and so do you! You're too clever to fall for those lies, too young to attach yourself to him and have him ruin your life."

My head snaps up, my lips curling into a snarl. "He is *not* going to ruin my life."

Debbie flinches at the fury in my voice. She takes a step back, her eyes trailing over me. They take in every inch of my face, the way my chest rises and falls with the anger of my breathing, then she raises her hand to her mouth. "Cass, what have you done?"

I blink. "What do you mean?"

"I know you, Cass. You're not marrying him. You wouldn't do that, you're too smart. So why are you going through with this wedding?"

"I told you, we've worked it out," I reply through gritted teeth.

"And I'm telling you I don't believe you."

Debbie's words hang in the air. She holds my gaze, and all the while my heart pounds with an intensity like nothing I've ever felt before.

This wasn't supposed to happen. Debbie was supposed to be angry at me for staying, shout maybe, but not believe me? I never planned for that.

"What have you done, Cass?" Debbie whispers.

My mouth fills with lies but as Debbie shakes her head, the words die on my tongue. I stare at her, this woman who has been by my side since this ordeal started, and I crack. "I did what he deserves, what they both deserve."

"Cass, no! This isn't how your story is supposed to go! You need to tell me what you've done so we can fix this."

"There's no fixing this, Debbie. Besides, I don't want to."

"Tell me what you've done, Cass."

"You're better off not knowing."

Debbie runs her hands through her hair, her breath ragged. Her eyes scan the room as if searching for answers on how to take this back, but she finds none. "Did I make you do this? Did I put you up to it by saying what I wanted to do to Tony?"

I shake my head. "I'd have done it regardless."

"Why, Cass? Why would you do this? Whatever you're planning, it's not going to make you happy! I can't let you make this mistake. If you were my daughter -"

"But I'm not your daughter, am I? I'm the loser you saw get cheated on."

"Cass, you're not a loser!"

"Don't try make me feel better about this!" I shout, my voice so shrill I feel my throat tear. "I know what will make me feel better, and it's watching Jamie's world fall apart. Did you honestly expect me to just walk away? Jamie cheated, he lied, he fucked me over, but he's going to regret it. He deserves it, Debbie. You know as well as I do how much he deserves it, and you only know five percent of what he's done."

Debbie's face twists. "His punishment isn't for you to decide, Cass. Not like this. You're making a mistake."

"Debbie, I am going through with this wedding. I'm going to come back after the school holidays as someone whose relationship fell apart, but whose life didn't. You are going to come back next term as a woman who has had a great break with her family. I will smile at you and be

179

happy for you. I want you to do the same for me."

"Cass –"

"Debbie, please," I say, my voice cracking. "You will not change my mind. I have to do this. I have to make him hurt."

"You don't!"

"I do!" I shout back, my cheeks dampening as my tears fall. "That man has cut me open. He has changed the way I look at the world forever. How can you ask me to walk away? To carry on as if nothing happened? Well, I refuse. I refuse to be his victim. I refuse to let him walk away the winner."

"Cass, no one will be a winner if you go through with this."

"With what I've got planned, I will be."

Debbie shrinks before me, her chin wobbling. "I can't change your mind, can I?" she asks in a small voice.

Wiping my eyes with the back of my hand, I shake my head. "What you can do is give me your silence. You can never say I knew, ever. This conversation stays in this room. Please, Debbie, I need your silence."

"Cass…"

"Please, Debbie."

Debbie gulps. "What you've done… is it legal?"

Flashbacks of drugging Jamie, hacking into his personal accounts, and using photos of Alison's sons to create a fake account flick through my mind. Then there's the burner phone I'm using to harass him.

Afraid of Debbie's reaction if I tell the truth, I nod.

"Can it be reversed?"

Again, I lie, this time with a shake of my head.

Debbie closes her eyes, drained. "I can't believe you want me to lie about this, Cass."

"Not lie, just say nothing like you have been doing for the last few weeks."

"The last few weeks when I thought I was helping you!"

"You were helping me, you are helping me," I say, reaching for Debbie, but she moves away so I can't touch her. In her eyes I no longer see sadness or pity but something else, something even more crucifying – disappointment.

"I wish you all the best, Cassie. Lord knows you're going to need it if you're going to destroy that man."

"Debbie," I begin, but she pushes past me and grabs her handbag from the classroom cupboard.

At the door, she pauses. "You have my silence, Cass, but you've lost all my respect. If you go through with this, you're never going to get that back."

Debbie leaves the room, but her words stay behind, punching me in the stomach until I'm doubled over.

29.

As tradition at the end of every term, my colleagues and I gather at the nearest pub to celebrate surviving the pressures and stresses of teaching. After my showdown with Debbie, a night of losing myself in alcohol has more appeal than ever. I even invite my friends to prolong the evening. Alisha is inevitably working late, Laney already has plans but Lily texts that she will be there when she finishes work.

Our pub of choice is The White Bear, a venue with sticky carpets and bleary-eyed regulars, but cheap drinks and decent music. Debbie is notably absent, a gut-twisting realisation I do my best to shake off as we take a seat around four tables we've pushed together. I reach for my wine, but Shari stops me and silences the group.

"Before we start gossiping about bad management and annoying parents, there's something special happening this term. Something we must toast. Or should I say, someone."

Every eye lands on me. I squirm under the intensity of the attention but Shari nudges me in the ribs.

"Don't be coy, Miss Edwards! We all know how excited you are for this wedding. It's sickening really, but we love you so it's okay."

Laughter rings out around the table. I try joining in, but the lump in my throat won't let me.

"We can't wait to hear all about your special day when we're back after the holidays, but until then please forget work exists and enjoy every moment of your wedding." Shari raises her gin and tonic in the air. "If you'd all like to join me in toasting Cassie and Jamie – may they live a long, happy life together!"

"To Cassie and Jamie!" everyone choruses, then we clink glasses. I take a gulp of wine, wincing as it burns my throat the way only cheap alcohol can, then drink until I've drained my glass.

As everyone breaks into conversations in smaller groups, Shari puts her arm over my shoulder. "Jamie is one lucky man," she whispers in my ear. "I hope he knows it!"

"Not as much as he should do."

Shari laughs, not for one second realising I'm telling the truth. "By the way, do you know what happened with Debbie?" she says. "Fiona saw her leaving work and said Debbie looked like she was about to cry."

Snakes of guilt twist in my gut, but I shake my head. "I hope she's okay."

"Me too. Debbie's the best. If something at work has made her cry, then there's no hope for the rest of us."

I reach for my bottle of wine to top up my glass. When Shari turns to speak to Caroline beside her, I down my drink, grimacing with every desperate swallow. I go to pour another but the last mouthful I had still stings my oesophagus. I look around the table, the echo of Shari's speech bellowing in my mind, and suddenly everyone's animated faces swim before me.

"Excuse me," I say, sliding out of my seat and pushing past my colleagues.

I fight my way towards a dilapidated bathroom that reeks of budget bleach. Once locked inside a cubicle, I sit on the lid of the toilet with my head in my hands. The way Debbie looked at me flashes in my mind. Her horror, her upset… it's enough to make me shudder.

Sighing, I check both my phone and the burner phone. One has a message from Jamie wishing me a good night with my friends, the other something much less polite from him.

Clearly you get your kicks from messaging strangers. I feel bad for you. What a sad, lonely life you must lead. Why don't you do the world a favour and top yourself? I can recommend a bridge to jump from if you want

Every letter of Jamie's cruel message ricochets through my body, leaving a trail of devastation in its wake.

He's right - a sad lonely life is exactly what I lead, and after today it's even lonelier. Debbie could barely look at me when she left the classroom. Her disappointment was so potent I'm still choking on it, but what did I expect? After asking Debbie to lie for me, I deserve to hurt like this. If anything, I deserve to hurt more.

I don't think twice about how to inflict that pain. I load 'The Good Bad Guy's Guide' and discover a new post was published earlier today.

Isn't it funny how you can meet a woman and think 'wow, she's a 10/10' but then quickly realise she's actually a 2/10? I've collated a list of my top ten reasons of how those tens become twos – let me know your ten reasons in the comments!

1. *She nags. Enough said*

2. *She reads horoscopes. Again, enough said*

3. *She calls herself a 'girl boss'. I shudder at the phrase*

4. *She's got a lot of exes. I don't want second-hand goods, thank you*

5. *She mentions the word 'feminism'. Seriously, if she says it once, RUN*

6. *She says the words 'red flag'. Trust me, that's a red flag*

7. *She has body hair. Waxing has been around for years now, right?*

8. *She has any or all of these: an annoying laugh, a fake laugh, or a posh laugh*

9. *She references romantic comedies at any point in the date*

10.   *Unpainted toenails. I don't know why, but they just get me*

It was hard to narrow it down to ten, if I'm honest, but this is my list and I'm sticking with it. This list could save you from a potential dating disaster. You're welcome!

Still, I guess even a 2/10 is worth taking home for the night...

Bile rises in my throat, but anger rises quicker. I reread the list, taking in every judgement and derision, then boil over. I type 'you're disgusting' in the comment box then hit send. Before the message posts, it asks me for a name and email address. I've never been more grateful to have the Abby Dunne alias.

With my comment posted, a beacon of truth underneath Jamie's hideousness, I re-join my colleagues and my wine, drinking until the edges of my pain are ever so slightly numbed.

Lily shows up around seven. She waves, standing back and judging how drunk we all are. It's a short assessment – we're well on our way to a raging hangover.

"I'm guessing I need shots, and I need them now?" she asks.

I leap out of my seat. "Yes, let's do it!"

Lily takes my hand and weaves me through the crowd towards the bar. I cling to her, wishing she could lead me through everything in my life this decisively.

"Two shots of tequila and a bottle of Pinot, please," she says, then she glances at me and waves the barman back. "And a glass of water for my friend."

"Lily, I'm fine."

"How many fingers am I holding up?" she asks, holding three fingers in the air.

I stick my middle finger up at her. "How many am I?"

Lily throws her head back, laughing so freely that an unexpected wave of emotion washes over me. I rest my head on her shoulder.

"What's wrong with you?" she asks.

"Oh, nothing. Wedding stress."

"I've got a fix for that," Lily says, wriggling me from her shoulder and pulling out her phone. She types something then rests the phone on the bar with a timer displayed on the screen. "You have five minutes to talk about the wedding, then we put a line under the conversation, you forget about it, and you enjoy your night. I love you, Cass, and I'm so excited for your wedding, but it's one day. It's not worth crushing yourself over. Plus, I refuse to let us be the kind of women who only talk about men and marriage and babies. I want to hear about your wedding, but I also want to hear about you, okay?"

I lift my vision to meet Lily's. When she spots the tears brewing in my eyes, her face fills with alarm.

"Shit, I thought this was a good idea! You're not offended, are you?"

"Not at all. I promise you've said the best thing you could have."

"That's settled then," Lily says. She reaches to start the timer but I push her phone towards her.

"Don't bother. Trust me, I'm done with wedding chat. Let's talk about our jobs and travel and TV and -"

"And anything that's not what some b-grade rom-com would have you believe women talk about," Lily grins.

The barman returns with her drinks then we join my colleagues. Lily stays with me long after they leave. We talk about our careers and our goals for the next few years. We talk about the books we want to read, the latest political scandal, the celebrities we used to admire when we were younger and what they're up to now. We talk about everything but relationships, and for the first time in a long time, pieces of my soul come back to life.

But five wines in, I steer the conversation onto dangerous territory. "Lily, can I ask you something? Something about Andy?"

Lily blinks at the mention of the taboo subject then nods.

"How did you get over him? How did you forget what he did?"

Lily studies her drink, wiping condensation from the glass with her finger. "I didn't forget what he did, and I don't think I ever will, but I learned to be okay with it. I don't hate Andy like I once did. In fact, I don't hate him at all. You can't be angry at someone for feeling like they wanted more in life or wanting to make a change. If leaving and travelling was what he felt he had to do, who am I to say otherwise? I'm happy he got the life he wanted. In a way, I'm even proud of him for making that step. I just wish he'd told me how unhappy he was first. I wish he'd given us the chance to end in a better way than we did. I deserved that."

I study Lily, my amazing best friend who rebuilt her life after it was demolished. Will I have her strength when it's my turn to do the same? Years down the line, will I be able to speak about what Jamie's done with such measured consideration?

Suddenly, Lily's eyes meet mine. "Why are you asking me about this, anyway?"

"I don't know, I guess with the wedding coming up, it's got me thinking of old times and how things might have been."

Lily smiles a wry smile. "Now that's a rocky path to walk down. Look, all you need to know is that I'm happy. It might have taken me a little while to get there but I finally look back on that time of my life with fondness. I see the memories for what they were and the lessons I've learned. I'm happy now. Happier than before, even. I promise."

"I don't think I've ever told you how proud I am of you for getting through it all, have I?"

Lily laughs, a blush creeping up her neck. "Oh no, we can't be at that point in the night already. I'm too sober for mushy comments and sickly kindness."

"I'm not. I mean it, I can't tell you how much I love you."

Lily grins and shakes her head. "I think that means it's time for home, don't you?"

My heart sinks at her words but I know she's right. Even though Jamie's not meant to pick me up for another hour, I need to go home. I've had too much to drink. The edges of my world are blurry. Drunk, vulnerable and in the arms of one of my best friends, I'm as close as I'll ever be to telling the truth.

Ten minutes after texting Jamie to say I'm ready to leave, he replies that he's on his way. When he arrives, Lily bundles me into the passenger seat of his car. "Sorry, Jamie. She's a little worse for wear."

"It's no bother, as long as you both had a good time."

There's something about Jamie's false kindness that breaks me. I reach for Lily, but she folds me back inside the car. "You, my friend, need to go home and get some sleep," she says, closing the door and tapping her fingers on the window to wave goodbye.

As Jamie drives back to the apartment, a weighted blanket of sadness wraps around my shoulders. I flop my head against the window, staring out at the world until my vision blackens and I drift off to sleep, drunk, sad, and lonelier than ever.

30.

My head pounds as the shrill ringing of my alarm tears me from the grip of sleep. I jolt upright, the familiar surroundings of my bedroom taking a second to register through my haziness. I don't remember getting into the apartment last night. Jamie must have helped me. I cringe at the humiliation of needing him then grab my phone to turn off my alarm. The words 'final dress fitting' flash on the screen and I groan, flopping backwards. I bury my face in my pillow, willing time to fast-forward to the part where everything wedding related is done with and Jamie is no longer in my life.

It's like thinking of Jamie conjures him as he chooses that moment to enter the room carrying a cup of coffee. His perky alertness contrasts sharply with my sullen exhaustion. "You need to get up, Lily will be here soon. Besides, it's dress day! Isn't this the day all girls dream of?"

"That's the day you pick your dress. I'm only trying it on again today. Besides, I'm tired," I huff.

"I know, that's why I brought you a coffee."

I haul myself to a sitting position and take the mug from him, but I know it's going to take more than a cup of coffee for me to get through today.

In record time, I shower and get dressed. My eye bags are so dark no cosmetics could conceal them, but I do my best, layering my face with makeup until I look somewhat human. When Lily messages to say she's outside, I take one last determined look in the mirror then head downstairs to meet her.

Lily laughs as soon as she sees me. "Hey party animal! How are you feeling after last night?"

"Horrific."

"I knew you would be. I made sure I was on time so I didn't miss a single moment of your suffering."

"You're evil," I groan.

"It's called being a best friend," Lily winks, then she peels the car away from the curb and sets off towards Happily Ever After, my bridal boutique of choice. I hate previous Cassie for shopping at a store with a name that's now spiked with so much irony. I sit in a tense silence as the air around me thickens with anticipation, the intensity of my hangover quadrupling in its presence.

When we pull up outside the boutique, Mum, Laney, and Alisha are already outside waiting for us.

"We're later than Laney?!" Lily exclaims as she climbs out of her car.

"I told her I was picking her up thirty minutes earlier than I did," Mum confesses. "Even then she wasn't ready on time."

The group descends into laughter, and even I find myself joining in. For one blissful second, I forget what I'm about to do and enjoy a moment with the people I love the most, but then Alisha's arm links mine. "Come on then, Cass. Let's see you in your gorgeous dress one final time before the big day!"

I let her lead me inside, but as soon as we enter the store I want to leave. Glitzy gowns in bright shades of white assault my eyeballs. The scent of a sickly-sweet candle wafts through the air, the fumes making my head spin.

From behind the counter, a young shop assistant bounds towards us. "You must be the Edwards party," she enthuses. "I'm Maddie. Come with me. We'll do the dress reveal through here."

We follow Maddie through the shop, passing dreamy dresses that my hands itch to tear apart until we reach the back of the store. Pale pink chairs arranged in an expectant formation greet us. We take a seat, the atmosphere fizzing.

"This is it. The last time you'll try on your dress before the big day!" Lily cheers.

"I've got tissues at the ready," Mum adds.

"Steady on, she won't look that bad," Laney jokes. "Although I won't lie, Cass, the hungover sheen you've got going on right now really does contrast with the white of these dresses."

I groan. "Don't, Laney, I feel terrible."

"I bet you don't feel as bad as Laney did that time she threw up in a plant pot in a shopping centre," Lily says, and instantly my focus is drawn from the pain of this moment onto tales of the worst hangovers we've experienced.

I'm giggling along with another of Laney's wild stories when Maddie reappears. "Cassie, if you'd like to follow me."

My body stiffens, shouting that there's nothing I'd like to do less than follow her, but I stand. Mum and my bridesmaids squeal as Maddie leads me to the changing room around the corner. She holds the silky curtain and turns to me, beaming. "Are you ready?" she asks. I nod and Maddie peels open the changing room curtain.

There, hung before me, is my dress.

It's as beautiful as I remember. More so, if anything, which only adds insult to injury.

I try to think of the woman who chose this dress, but she's so far removed from who I am it's impossible to imagine her. Another life, another Cassie.

I'd gone wedding dress shopping with my mum and my bridesmaids. I tried on five dresses I thought would suit me based on hours of diligent research, but none were right. I felt like a child playing dress up, someone pretending to be what they thought a bride should be.

Then the assistant brought me another dress. "Your mum said to try this one."

It wasn't anything I'd have picked for myself but from the moment it slipped over my skin, I knew it was the one. I didn't even need to see myself in a mirror.

Mum cried the instant she saw me. "You're lit up," she sobbed.

Taking in my reflection, I knew exactly what she meant. A woman illuminated by love, secure in her future, and smothered with happiness.

As I climb into my dress again, the same wave of adoration washes over me, only this time a tsunami of sadness wipes it out. My hands tremble as I touch the intricate appliqued flowers while Maddie fastens the back.

"Hurry up, we're dying of excitement out here!" Alisha shouts. Everyone cheers in agreement. Their happiness jars with the tension in the changing room.

"Are you ready to show them?" Maddie asks.

I want to yell no, to rip the most beautiful dress I will ever own from my body and run out onto the street in my underwear, but instead I nod. Then, as abruptly as a bikini wax, Maddie pulls open the curtain and leads me to my audience.

Gasps ring out as I round the corner.

"Cass, I don't even know what to say," Alisha whispers. "You're a vision."

"Look at yourself," Mum orders. "Look in the mirror and see how beautiful you are."

A choking hand wraps itself around my throat at her words. I don't want to see myself but what can I do? I must perform. I must become the bride.

So, I face the mirror.

My gaze fixes on the hem of the dress first, studying the delicate flowers skimming the floor. I draw my eyes up my body, noticing how the dress flares out at exactly the right point by my knee, how the hips I'm usually insecure about seem beautifully curved. My waist appears small, my breasts full, my silhouette perfected.

Then I catch sight of my melancholy expression, the one thing betraying my secret wish that this moment was part of a different story, and a single tear escapes me.

"She's crying!" Alisha coos.

Everyone crowds around me, gushing about how beautiful I am and how lucky Jamie is. I soak up the compliments, not once looking back at my reflection to see what could have been. I play the role of overjoyed bride and keep my tears on the inside where they rain down on me, a monsoon of broken hopes and dreams.

31.

My head is splitting by the time I'm dropped off at home after lunch with my bridal party. I drag myself into the lift and jab the button for the fourth floor, thankful that the only thing standing between me and my bed is this short ride.

"Jamie?" I call out into the apartment when I get in, but there's no reply.

I wonder if he's out with her already. Jen from the coffee shop. Jen who thinks she's meeting Todd, businessman, dog owner and all-around great guy. I imagine Jamie with her, how he'll pull out her chair and hold the door open for her. He'll listen to what she has to say, mention details from their first meeting so she thinks she's special enough to be remembered. He'll make her feel like she's the only woman in the world, exactly how he made me feel.

I bite the inside of my lip to stop myself from crying. Thankfully, the well-timed sound of a key in the lock of the front door tells me tears aren't an option right now anyway.

"Hey babe," Jamie calls when he enters the apartment. I hear the soft thud of his shoes landing on the floor as he kicks them off, then a few seconds later he joins me in the living room.

"You're very sweaty," I comment, nodding at his damp forehead.

"I thought I'd squeeze a run in before I went out. Did you have a good day?"

I feign enthusiasm. "It was great!"

"And the dress?"

"Perfect."

Happiness takes over Jamie's features. "Oh, Cass, I can't wait to see you in it! You're going to make the most beautiful bride."

"Thank you. I really hope you like it," I reply, then I glance at the time. "When are you going out?"

"We're meeting at eight."

Even though I tell myself to act nonchalant, a burning sensation sweeps over my body. I look to my feet, furious with myself for showing Jamie I care.

Jamie reaches for me. "Hey, don't be upset. You know I'd spend every Saturday night with you for the rest of my life if I could. In fact, I intend to, but I can't get out of this, not now. It's too late. Just know that I love you more than anything in the world."

Maybe it's from spending a day with people who are still under the impression we are happy or maybe it's because I can't bear it anymore, but hearing Jamie say how much I matter to him is too much and I dissolve into tears.

In an instant, I'm wrapped in Jamie's arms. "Cass, don't cry! I hate to see you upset."

"I'm fine," I reply, a response that might be convincing if I wasn't sobbing as I said it.

"It's a big time, isn't it? There's so much going on. Why don't you take tonight to unwind? Watch some television and have a little me time."

"I think I will," I sniff, knowing all too well that no amount of 'me time' will make me feel better. "Will you be home late?"

"Maybe," Jamie admits, his face twisting. "You know how these things are. They start off innocently then the next thing you know you're six shots in with the dinner ladies bitching about the new student teacher."

I laugh at his joke like I'm supposed to. "I guess so. Do you want me to pick you up?"

"No, don't put yourself out. Not when you need some time to rest."

Jamie's answer doesn't surprise me, but it still hurts. "Thank you for thinking of me," I manage to say. "Now get in the shower. You stink."

Jamie laughs then goes to get ready. In the aching silence of his absence, I lie down on the sofa, resting my arm over my head to shut out the world.

"Looks like the restful night has already started," Jamie grins when he enters the room a short while later, impeccably dressed and smelling of his favourite aftershave. He makes a move to join me but then his phone buzzes. With an apologetic grimace, he takes my hand. "I'd better set off."

"Have fun," I say.

After kissing me goodbye, Jamie leaves. The scent of his aftershave lingers in the air long after the front door has closed. I turn on the television, grab a book, anything to occupy my time, but nothing can distract me from thoughts of Jamie and Jen. So, I grab a bottle of wine and the burner phone, then cuddle up on the sofa and get typing.

Does your fiancée know you're out with another woman tonight?

Thirty-four minutes later and after gnawing my thumb so aggressively it bleeds, the phone bursts into life with a response.

The real question is - do the police know you're harassing a man?

I smirk as I reply.

Let's imagine that, shall we – 'Jamie, why are you going to the police station?' 'For questioning, darling. I'm being harassed by someone who wants to tell you what I get up to behind your back. By the way, did I mention I was cheating on you?'

My response is clumsy, but I want to reply fast. The longer Jamie is on his phone, the ruder he will appear, and the more likely Jen is to walk away. She doesn't need dragging into this mess. There are already

Jess Kitching

enough bodies in the graveyard of Jamie's ex-lovers without adding her to the pile.

Are you sure you know me at all? I don't think I've ever called anyone darling...

Wine fuels my response.

I've heard pet names are great for cheats to use. That way, they never confuse their lovers with each other. Maybe a tip for the future?

After a few minutes of staring at the television and absorbing nothing of what's playing out in front of me, the burner phone vibrates.

I don't need tips on how to pick up women, but thank you for the offer ;)

I dig my nails into the sofa to stop myself from clawing at my skin. He's enjoying this. Even with someone threatening to tell me the truth, Jamie still thinks he's untouchable.

Hissing air through my teeth, I respond.

Maybe you don't need tips on how to get women, but you do need tips on how not to get caught. Cassie will find out what you've been up to. I will tell her, that I promise you.

Powered by rage, I hurtle into the second bedroom and re-open Jamie's memory box. The artefacts of deceit greet me but seeing them doesn't hurt like it did the first time. Strangely enough, compared to the repulsive things he writes on his website, Jamie collecting mementos from his conquests doesn't seem that bad.

I rake through the contents of the box and source every phone number in there, then send each person the same message from the burner phone.

197

Todd Goldman is not a real person. He is using a fake name, having sex with multiple women, and cheating on his fiancé. If you are in contact with him, do yourself a favour and end it

Over the course of the evening, a few replies trickle in, some asking who is sending this message, some telling me more about 'Todd'.

Omg I knw it! He was a DICK!!!! Threatened 2 snd my nudes to my family and my boss (I knowwwww, y did I send them?!) Deleted & blockd

Wow, thanks for this message. Met Todd at a coffee shop, thought he seemed sweet! You saved me

Y am I not surprised by this? Got wot he wanted n ran...

Every response fuels me to create a subtle vengeful moment, one for each of Jamie's victims. I swill the rest of his protein powder down the sink and bury his favourite shirt in the bottom of the bin. My final stroke of childish revenge is to add the rest of my hair removal cream into his shampoo. It's petty, but right now I'm at that level.

Eventually, brain fried, I crawl into bed and drift into a fitful sleep.

Jamie stumbles home in the early hours of the morning. He uses the bathroom, pissing loudly, then sprays deodorant and slides into bed beside me. My jaw clenches as I breathe in the faint smell of perfume despite his attempt to cover it up.

"I hope I didn't wake you," he whispers. "I've had a little too much to drink."

I roll over. Face to face, the stench of Jen's perfume is stronger than ever. "That's okay. You're allowed to have fun."

Jamie plants a kiss on my lips, the same lips that I know have been on another woman's tonight. Vomit pushes its way up my throat and it takes all my might to stop it travelling further.

When we pull apart, I can't resist commenting on the lack of alcohol on Jamie's breath. "You don't seem drunk."

"Cass, the room is spinning. Seriously, if you could be inside my head…"

"What a place that would be."

Jamie fumbles for my hand and squeezes it, smacking his lips together as if his mouth is dry. I roll my eyes at his theatrics and turn onto my side.

Within seconds Jamie is curled around me, his semi erect penis pressing into my lower back. "You know, we could do a little drunken role play…"

"I'm not drunk."

"But I am."

Another lie. They slip from his lips like infants on ice.

"I'm on my period," I lie.

Jamie groans and pecks the back of my neck. "Worst luck. We've not done it in forever."

"I know, but we best get used to never having sex – we'll be married soon."

Jamie pokes me in the ribs. I jolt from the sharpness of his touch. "We are *not* going to be one of those married couples, Cassandra Edwards. We will be at it constantly."

"You're already at it constantly!" I fight to shout, but I choose to laugh instead.

I remain rigid until I know from his gentle snores that Jamie is asleep. Only then do I allow myself to breathe. Only then do I stop imagining tearing his insatiable dick off and feeding it to the dog across the road.

32.

I leave Jamie to sleep in, partly because I know he must be exhausted from spending all night flirting with another woman but mostly because his body anywhere near mine makes me want to dive headfirst off a cliff.

With no work and no social plans, there's no need for me to pretend life is perfect. I wade through my morning, showering for so long climate justice activists would use me as a poster girl for ignorance. By the time I get out of the water, my skin is red raw and wrinkled. I smother myself in moisturiser, an act of self-care I rarely remember to do.

"You'll be single again soon. You can make time to moisturise every night then," I say to my reflection. The thought sends a shiver down my spine.

In all honesty, I've not paid much attention to life after the wedding. Life after Jamie. Plotting Jamie and Tara's destruction has consumed too much of my time to give thoughts of singlehood headspace. I like it that way. While some aspects of being single were great, I hated dating, and that was when I wasn't entering the field with the emotional baggage of a serial cheat for an ex-fiancé.

But single life worries can wait. Today there are more pressing matters to attend to. Pushing myself out of the bathroom, I get dressed then head into the kitchen where I find Jamie crunching on an overdone piece of toast and glaring at his phone.

"Well, that looks delicious," I comment.

Jamie's grimace vanishes when he sees me. "I know, and I'm usually the chef out of the two of us."

"Don't expect that to change when we get married."

"Noted," Jamie grins. "Have you got many plans today?"

"Another exciting day of wedding prep and admin. How about you?"

Jamie takes a bite of his toast with an audible crunch. "I'm meeting Ricky, remember? We're running over best man duties."

I don't know when this conversation was supposed to have happened – it's probably another situation Jamie wants to delude me into believing existed – but I need him out of the apartment, so I don't fight back. "Vaguely," I reply. "It's good to hear Ricky's taking best man duties seriously."

"Well, he knows this day, and you, mean the world to me."

I react as Jamie would want me to and simper, but the sadist in me spots an opportunity for more self-torture. "Why don't you ask Ricky to come here? It would be great to see him before the wedding. It feels like I've not caught up with him in forever!"

Jamie doesn't miss a beat with his lies. "I would but he's got plans this afternoon. Coming here would be out of his way."

"Well, we'll have to invite him over soon. It's been far too long since I last saw him."

"Definitely," Jamie agrees, even though I know he has no intention of creating those plans. He finishes his breakfast and heads out soon after, who he's really meeting a question I don't know the answer to.

The first thing I do after he leaves is check the burner phone. There are three messages waiting, a number high enough to make me sure I'm getting to him.

And what would the truth be, exactly? That a random number is texting me, insinuating I've done something wrong with absolutely no proof at all

The second, sent an hour later:

No response after all that big talk? What a shame I outwitted you so quickly. I enjoyed having you to play with. You know, like a cat plays with a mouse before it kills it

The third message is my favourite, sent this morning and probably the reason for his burnt toast.

Your number will be blocked today, your pathetic messages erased. I hope you enjoyed your fun while it lasted – I know I did!

With a satisfied smile, I respond.

Oh Jamie, a person must be well rested for acts of revenge. I'm not done with you yet. In fact, I've barely started. Block away, but I'll still find you. I'll still message you. And if I can't get to you, I can always go to Cassie

I press send then reread my exchange with Jamie, every taunting, spiteful word and hatefilled sentiment, and the darkness surrounding me creeps in even further until I can't see past it. I sigh and go to lock the phone, but something stops me in my tracks.

There's an email notification on the burner phone, but that can't be right. This phone is linked to the Abby Dunne email, and I've not used it for days.

Chest fluttering, I open the app and choke when I read the subject line of the email.

The Good Bad Guy's Guide replied to your comment

Panic swells in my lungs, then I remember – the other night at the pub. Me, tipsy and angry, reading Jamie's latest post. My stupid need to retaliate in whatever small, petty way I could.

How could I be so stupid?

My heart drums in my ears as I race through the potential consequences of Jamie knowing the name Abby Dunne.

I open Facebook to confirm that, yes, the fake account is closed. Jamie will never be able to find the profile and see the photos of Ethan and Joel I stole and used as if they were mine to do so. He will never know I met Patricia Campbell. He will have this email address, but so what? There's nothing tying me to it. It's just an email belonging to someone who finds his website offensive which, judging by the content he shares, won't be the first time he's received a message like that.

Abby Dunne will mean nothing to him, I decide. I repeat the sentence again and again until my heartrate slows.

I follow the link to 'The Good Bad Guy's Guide' to delete the comment, but before I do, I read Jamie's response.

Ah, another hysterical woman has found my site… welcome! Did you get lost on the way to reading one of those 'why am I still single' articles? Let me save you some time – it's not him, it's you

Words don't do justice to describing the feeling that comes over me. It begins at my toes, a scalding flickering of rage that climbs up my body, coiling around my legs, then my torso, then my chest, until it's wrapped around my throat.

What I've planned isn't enough, I realise. It won't damage Jamie in the way I want to, the way I need to. He needs to be plundered of whatever worth he thinks he has, ruined in a way he can't come back from. He needs to hit rock bottom, with a mountain to climb before him that's so big he will doubt he can make it.

Luckily for me, I know just what to do to make that happen. And the best part is, I'll be using Jamie's own flaws against him for it to work.

After deleting the comment and removing every trace of Abby Dunne from that hideous website, I grab my other phone and open the notes saved on there. Jamie's credit card numbers shine on the screen, a beacon of opportunity.

Jamie's debt is bad and so are the lies he's told to cover up his financial woes, but they could be worse. Much worse. I could make them that way.

Financially ruined, he won't be able to fund his dates. You can't lie about what you can provide someone with no money to back it up. If I do this, who knows how many women I'll save from his lecherous advances. Besides, I'll carry the pain of what Jamie's done forever, so why shouldn't he carry crushing debt forever? Why can't he remember me every time he checks his account and sees the colossal mound of money he must earn to break even? It's a win-win situation for everyone. Everyone but Jamie.

And it will be so easy for people to believe he did it himself. He's already in debt. He has a history of it too. All I'll be doing is pushing it that little bit higher.

It's so perfect I could yell at myself for not considering it sooner. I grab my laptop, ready to get to work, but as my school username appears on the screen I freeze.

Revenge needs to be slick. Untraceable even. I've already made the Abby Dunne email and social media accounts on this laptop, which wasn't smart, but using Jamie's credit cards is something else entirely. It's fraud. When he finds out what I've done, he will go to the police. They will investigate his claims. If I make even one transaction on my laptop, I'll be arrested. A criminal record could mean I'd lose my teaching licence and with it the job that is such an integral part of who I am.

The only way for this debt to stick is for it to seem like Jamie did it himself. For that, there's only one thing I can use.

Closing my laptop, I reach down the side of the sofa and locate Jamie's tablet. I press in his passcode and within seconds I'm searching for the most elaborate honeymoon in Mexico I can find. I figure seeing as Jamie is outwardly such a loving partner, it will be easy for everyone to imagine he would book the honeymoon of a lifetime as a surprise.

Booking the holiday for the day after the wedding is a little pricier with it being such short notice, but Jamie can afford it, I surmise.

After including all the upgrades and excursions I can, I'm happy this holiday would earn Jamie some real husband points. My eyes bulge at the final total but then I remember how much money Jamie spends on other women and it doesn't seem so bad. In fact, it doesn't seem expensive enough.

I decline adding insurance to the booking, press confirm and that's it – I commit fraud.

I wait to feel a change within me, a niggling guilt telling me I've crossed a line, but it never comes. All I feel is the sweet sensation of jubilation, one that increases when a few seconds later a confirmation email pings into Jamie's inbox, joining the thousands of unread messages already in there.

But there's no time to celebrate, not when there's more to be done.

Flexing my fingers, I go back to the internet so I can upgrade Jamie's holiday wardrobe. It's clear from his credit card statement and Todd Goldman profile he enjoys the finer things in life, so I run with that.

Shopping for Jamie turns out to be fun. To make it look like he's done this himself, I pick out clothes he would wear but I can't resist adding a pair of sandals that look like they were created to be paired with beige socks. I choose the delivery date for Friday when Jamie won't be home, typing in the digits of his second credit card and confirming my order.

While these purchases are perfect because they're so expensive, there needs to be more seediness to Jamie's financial woes for people to really judge him when everything comes out. With that in mind, I sign him up for two dating websites and three pay-for-porn accounts. The financial hit isn't huge, but when Jamie must explain to his parents where their money went, having to show them 'XXX BABEZ' on his statement is going to be worth it.

I try signing him up for a third dating website but when an alert comes up saying he already has an account registered, I take it as my cue to stop.

After searching for various sports results to push my website visits down Jamie's internet history, I lock the tablet and sink into the sofa. Jamie's debt has gone from bad to crushing. By the time he does his monthly budget and realises, the wedding will have already happened. I'll be free of him, and he will be drowning in more debt than ever. My work here is done.

33.

I've barely put Jamie's tablet back down the side of the sofa when I hear the front door open. My heart leaps into my throat.

"Jamie?"

"Who else?" he replies.

I let out a strangled laugh and scan the room, my skin igniting as I spot the burner phone on the coffee table. I dash for it, dropping it into my laptop bag just as Jamie enters the room.

"Hey," I chirp but it's clear my frantic panic was for nothing. Jamie's stony-faced and staring as his phone, oblivious to the rest of the world. "You okay?"

"Sorry, Alison's text me something stupid about the wedding."

I know full well the text that's ruined Jamie's mood isn't from Alison, but I go along with his lie. "What did she say?"

"Oh, it's nothing. You know how she is, fussing for the sake of it."

"Send her to me if you want. I know more about the wedding than you do."

Jamie hugs me, resting his chin on the top of my head. "You are good to me, aren't you? I don't know how you're holding it together. One message from her and I'm broken."

"I've had a few wobbly days but I'm feeling good now."

Jamie leans back and studies me. "You seem like your old self again. Better, even."

"I feel better."

At this, Jamie grins. His eyes linger on my lips, and I pull out of the hug before he can kiss me.

"Did you have a good time with Ricky?" I ask as I head into the kitchen.

Jamie follows me. He picks up an apple from the fruit bowl, tosses it into the air and catches it. "I did. He's all set for the wedding. Mum called me on the way home though. She wants us to go over to hers for a meal on Wednesday. I said we'd go. I hope you don't mind."

I frown. "I'm at a spa day on Wednesday."

"Yeah, a spa *day*. You don't need to be at my parents' house until the evening."

"But we're going for drinks after. It's been booked for months."

Jamie catches the apple, the sound of the fruit hitting his skin a sharp slap. "Cass, they want a moment with us before the wedding. You can still go to your spa day, you just need to cut it a little shorter, that's all."

"But I don't want to cut my day shorter. Can't we go to theirs on Thursday instead?"

"I'm out on Thursday. Ricky told me about it today. It's a surprise he's been sorting all weekend."

I fold my arms across my chest. "You're going out again? What happened to this week being about us?"

Jamie's face sets. "That's not fair, Cass. You're the one who's always busy."

"Busy planning our wedding!"

"A spa day is planning our wedding?"

My jaw clenches. "So now you're saying I can't have a break?"

"No, what I'm saying is I understood your need for a day with your friends. I thought you'd understand my need for a night with mine."

I could scream at his manipulation. "Can't you go out with Ricky after dinner with your parents?"

Jamie pulls a face. "I can't do that. I don't want to put a time limit on how long we'll be with Mum and Dad. That would be rude."

"And leaving my spa day early wouldn't be?"

"Not really. You'll have had an entire day with your friends by the time we need to leave. Thursday is a night Ricky's arranged just for me. I can't exactly cut it in half."

"You've already had a stag do. That was the night for you," I hit back.

"And you've already had a hen do. A meal cuts right in the middle of my event, but it only shaves a bit of time off the end of yours. Why are you being so unreasonable about this?"

Irritation prickles my skin. "I just don't see why I have to be the one to give up my thing and you don't."

"I'm sorry, Cassie, I didn't realise seeing my parents was such a chore for you." With that, Jamie drops the apple back in the fruit bowl and walks past me like I'm invisible.

Alone in the ringing silence of the kitchen, I radiate with rage.

In the past, I'd have conceded without a fight. More than giving in, I'd have talked myself into believing Jamie's version of events. With his plan, we both get to see our friends. When he tells the story, it almost makes sense for me to give up what I want.

Only I'm not writing the story of my life with his pen anymore.

Stubbornness waves me in, begging me to take a seat and leave Jamie to wonder why I'm no longer accommodating his every wish, but there's no room for stubbornness when it comes to revenge.

I order my legs to walk to the bedroom where I find a sour-faced Jamie stretched out across the bed, phone in hand.

"We can go on Wednesday," I say.

"Oh, don't worry about it. If seeing my parents is such an inconvenience for your social life, I'll tell them you don't want to go."

"Jamie, that's not fair."

"No, you're right, it's not fair. They're good people, Cassie. People who have invited you into their lives. You should want to see them. They're going to become your family soon."

"I *do* want to see them. I just said we can go!"

Jamie raises his eyebrows at my shrill tone.

Swallowing my rage feels impossible but somehow, I manage to do it. "I didn't mean to shout," I say through gritted teeth. "Of course I want to see your parents. You're right, your plan makes sense. I'll text everyone now to let them know I'll be leaving the spa early."

Jamie nods, but his hostile demeanour doesn't change. He watches me text my friends, and only when the message is sent does he leave his sulking position and come to me. "Thanks, Cassie. Wednesday night means a lot to my parents and to me. You're going to make the best daughter-in-law, and the best wife."

I nestle into Jamie, focusing on my breathing and not the feel of his flesh on mine, only these days it's getting harder to breathe around him. These days, being wrapped in his arms is like being held underwater, no air and no way out.

34.

I'm either exhausted from the end of term or from living in a constant state of anxiety because when I wake the next morning, it's after half past ten. I roll over and startle at the sight of Jamie in bed beside me reading a book.

"Morning, gorgeous. How good is a no alarm Monday?" he smiles, resting his book on the bedside table and moving towards me.

"So good," I reply. "But how come you're still in bed? You hate wasting the day."

"I didn't want you to wake up alone on the first official day of the holidays."

"That's kind of you," I say, stroking the stubble lining his jaw.

"You know me - I'm Mr Kind," Jamie winks. We curl together in what appears to be a content silence, but inside I'm counting down the seconds until it's appropriate for me to break free. Luckily, my phone provides the perfect excuse by bursting into life.

I blink when I see who's calling. "It's Tara," I say aloud for my own benefit as much as Jamie's, then I accept the call. "Hello?"

"Hey Cassie! Random call, I know, but remember when you said you were looking for necklaces for your bridesmaids? I've seen one I think you'll love. Do you want me to send a photo?"

The shock of hearing Tara's voice still hasn't registered with me, never mind the process of digesting the niceties she's saying.

"Cassie, are you there?"

"Sorry, I'm not awake yet. First day of the holidays, you know?" I fluster.

"Oh, completely! I'm sorry if I've interrupted your morning but I just had to see if you were interested in these necklaces. They're half price and so beautiful! If you want, I'll buy them and drop them off later this week with the cards for the wedding."

"You'd do that?"

"Of course, anything to help. Anyway, I'll stop talking now so you can enjoy your morning, but I'll send a photo of the necklaces. Text me if you want them."

I thank Tara and say goodbye then rest my phone on the bedside table.

"What did Tara want?" Jamie asks.

"She's seen a necklace she thinks I might like to give my bridesmaids."

"That's kind of her."

"It is," I reply.

As promised, a few seconds later a photo pings into my inbox. The necklace is perfect, a fine, silver chain with a delicate star dangling from it. Printed on the box the necklace comes in are the words, '*My wish for you is a lifetime of happiness*'.

"Look," I say, showing Jamie.

"Pretty."

I message Tara asking her to get three necklaces and thanking her for thinking of me, then I lay back on my pillow.

Hating Tara was so much easier before I met her. Wanting to destroy her seemed so simple once upon a time. Even after reading the hatred on Jamie's website, I could still talk myself into thinking picking Tara to be the scapegoat made sense. She wasn't like Jamie's other victims who didn't know about my existence. She's met me. Plus, being with Nico means she's a cheat too. In so many ways she's as bad as Jamie but try telling that to the creeping doubt eating away at the pit of my stomach.

Before I can talk myself out of it, I text Tara again.

Fancy meeting for dinner on Thursday? My treat. You can give me the cards and the necklaces then and I can thank you in person x

A few seconds later, Tara replies.

Bought the necklaces! And, if you have time to meet so close to the wedding, I'd love to. Time and place? X

I arrange to meet her at a bar in the city and thank her once again. Putting my phone back on the bedside table, I turn to Jamie. "I'm meeting Tara on Thursday to say thank you for her help. She's been great, you know."

"Good. I'm glad you've made a new friend. Tara's great."

I study Jamie as he picks his book up once more and continues to read. His face betrays no sign of emotion. Surely any normal man would be on edge at the thought of his fiancée and his lover meeting, especially so close to the wedding when emotions on both sides will be running high.

But he doesn't look bothered. In fact, he doesn't look like he cares about anything other than getting to the end of his chapter.

"Do you care about me at all?" I fight to ask. The words sit there, trapped between my clamped lips. It's a question I have asked myself every day since Debbie showed me that photograph, one I still don't know the answer to. I'm not sure if finding out the answer would make me feel better or worse.

35.

With only a few days to go to the wedding, time passes in a blur of organisational chaos. Everyone warned me it would be this way, but even with their words of caution ringing in my ears I'm still overwhelmed by the onslaught of calls, questions, and demands. Jamie tries to participate, but whenever he answers the phone, everyone only wants to speak to me. It's as if all he must do is show up on the day, whereas at the drop of a hat I'm expected to list the various dietary requirements of our guests or calculate the number of cupcakes needed.

On top of other people's expectations are the expectations I placed upon myself when I thought this wedding would be the happiest day of my life. Personalised name cards and cute favours weren't the only DIY items I planned, so every spare minute I have is spent making signage, gifts, and decorations.

Only when I come to create the timeline for the wedding reception, I can't find Jamie's childhood photos anywhere. I ransack the second bedroom, tearing apart every box of wedding décor, but still I'm empty-handed.

"Jamie, can you help me?" I call out.

A few seconds later, Jamie appears in the doorway. "What's up?"

"I can't find the photos your mum gave me. I know I put them in here somewhere."

Jamie's eyebrows raise at the mountain of stuff piled around me. "Looking for them through all this will be like looking for a needle in a haystack."

"I know but we need them for the timeline at the wedding."

"If you can't find them, you can't find them. Besides, is it such a big deal if we don't make a timeline?"

I stop rooting through a box of candles so I can look at Jamie. "What do you mean? It's what we planned to do."

"I know but will it matter if it's not there? No one wants to see photos of us as children anyway."

Jamie's response comes out so quickly it's almost as if it's been rehearsed. I tilt my head. "Did you move them?"

"What?"

"Did you move the photos?"

Jamie scoffs at my question. "I didn't touch anything, Cass. I'm only trying to stop you from stressing about not being able to find them. All I'm saying is, would it be such a big deal if the timeline was made up of photos of our actual relationship, not our entire lives?"

A fight tingles on the tip of my tongue, my determination to catch him lying so strong it's overwhelming, but with everything going on I don't have the energy.

"We'll still have to find the photos. They're your mum's memories."

"We can find them after the wedding. It's not important to look for them now, not when you're already so busy."

Conceding, I pack everything away, all the while wondering why my fiancé refuses to have anything to do with his childhood. I've never known anyone feel so strongly about the person they used to be, and in my quiet moments I wonder what his revulsion to the past means.

Outside of hiding the photos, Jamie is great. If I didn't know he was a lying, cheating scumbag, his offers of neck massages, endless cups of tea and limitless patience when listening to my rants would have been enough for me to fall in love all over again. I'd skip down the aisle, ready to begin the rest of my life with a man who knew by looking at me when to say, 'She's not here right now, can I take a message instead?'.

But whenever sweet thoughts filter into my brain, the image of Jamie and Tara kissing shoots them down. That image is certain to kill any sentimentality lingering inside me.

Then there's 'The Good Bad Guy's Guide'. Each post locks my knees in fear and embeds the horrifying truth that Jamie is not a man I know, or a man I should feel safe around. I screenshot the worst extracts, although defining which ones are the worst isn't easy when they're all vile.

Is there such a thing as a violent man, or is there just a woman needing a reminder of her place?

Feminism has so much to answer for. It's taken so much and left so many men not getting what they deserve. It's time we reset the balance. Use whatever power you have. Remember, men are the dominant force on this planet.

I use Jamie's words as motivation to plough ahead until vengeance is so close my fingertips can almost touch it.

My edited love story cards arrive on Tuesday morning. They're perfect - beautifully presented in Tara's design, but the words on them shocking enough to break even the most hardened of hearts. I hide them in the second bedroom, buried in a box of wedding supplies so Jamie won't find them.

On top of that, I message Jamie from the burner phone at every opportunity. Once, I even sit with him and hide the phone behind my laptop to send a message.

"Who's that?" I ask as his phone buzzes.

Jamie's set jaw relaxes to answer me. "Ricky. Girl trouble."

"Poor guy. Tell him not to worry. Who knows, he might meet someone at the wedding."

There's something about toying with Jamie like this that's addictive.

Bizarrely, being able to talk openly about his infidelity actually makes him the closest person to me right now.

But no matter how much part of me enjoys the game we're playing, knowing about the darker side to Jamie is terrifying. Whenever he comes near me, my eyes trace the muscles in his arms until fear clogs my throat. Each embrace he wraps me in feels like I'm drowning.

Now I've unearthed his hatred, it's all I notice. I can even see it glinting in his eyes when we're tucked in bed in the darkness. Fear hums inside me, getting louder and louder until it's my first thought every morning and last thought at night.

To make matters worse, quotes from 'The Good Bad Guy's Guide' come to me at the worst times.

She doesn't like you kissing her like that? Make her like it.

When women say no, what they really mean is 'convince me'. I've never heard a no that I can't turn into a yes.

Jamie's words echo in my mind, ruining any moment of peace. When we're sat together on the sofa, his arm around my shoulder, his bicep so close to my throat I feel the heat coming from it. When we're cooking together, a set of knives inches away from his fingers. When we climb into bed, my nightwear flimsy, his presence looming. I live with a constant knot in my stomach and Debbie's question 'are you in danger?' on loop in my mind.

With wedding planning at peak insanity and an undercurrent of terror flowing through everything I do, I'm burnt out. By the time Wednesday rolls around, I'm ready to dive into a hot tub at the spa and refuse to leave. I leap to my feet as soon as Laney texts to say she's outside, but I can't escape the apartment without Jamie pouncing on me.

"Have a great time, and no calls about the wedding. I mean it, put that phone away."

"Don't worry, I'm dropping it in the swimming pool as soon as I get there."

Jamie laughs and leans in for a kiss. His tongue invades my mouth, making my stomach roll. We break apart before my teeth clamp down on it.

"I'll pick you up at half past four, okay?"

Doing my best to ignore my lingering resentment over the meal with his parents, I nod and leave the apartment. I take the stairs, racing down them two at a time to get to my friends as fast as I can.

"Spa day!" Laney cheers when I slide into the backseat of her car.

"Get me in that hot tub!" I wail.

"I told you wedding planning is horrific," Lily says. "That's why I was so relieved when Andy left and I didn't have to do it."

"Yeah, you carried that one like it was a real blessing," Laney grins, then we set off.

The conversation in the car carries on in the same way all conversations with friends you've known forever does – free flowing chat, borderline cruel jokes, and unconditional love dripping from every word. My soul replenishes before we even make it to Serenity Spa.

"This is swanky," Laney comments, pulling into a parking space outside the imposing venue a little too swiftly.

"It is, and these cars cost more than your insurance can pay out, so be careful," Alisha warns, letting go of the dashboard she's been white knuckling the entire journey. "Honestly, Laney, you're the only person I know who's a worse driver after passing their test."

"Why did we make Laney the designated driver again?" I ask.

"Because she's even more of a liability when she's drunk," Lily jokes.

Giggling like schoolgirls, the four of us walk arm in arm towards the spa. As soon as we're inside, my jaw drops.

Serenity Spa is Alisha's pre-wedding treat, and you can tell. I've never seen so much marble in one room. Everything is expensive, polished, and refined. Even the air smells different, cleaner somehow, with a tinge of fresh fruits and eucalyptus.

"Alisha, a day at this place probably costs more than my entire wedding!" I hiss as we make our way towards the changing rooms.

"So what? You deserve the treat!"

We enter the changing rooms – another miracle of marble and fine craftsmanship – and change into our swimwear. Lily's swimming costume is faded, and I haven't tried on my bikini since I last went on holiday.

"I hope you're buying new swimwear for your honeymoon," Laney jokes, plucking the baggy strap of my bikini top.

I stick my tongue out at her and pull on the divine complimentary robe, then together we pad out of the changing room. Gentle instrumental music floats through the air as we follow the scent of essential oils and head towards relaxation.

"Isn't she on the television? You know, that morning news show," Laney whispers, indicating to a toned blonde woman doing laps in the swimming pool in a not-so-subtle way.

"Yes, but the piece of paper you signed when you arrived said you can't talk about who you see in here."

Lily's eyes widen. "Alisha, how rich are you?"

As we turn the corner, the most incredible hot tub surrounded by lush gardens and a manmade waterfall comes into view.

"Who cares how rich she is – look at where she's taken us," I shrug, and together we dash to the hot tub.

I have the best day. The facial makes my skin softer than a newborn's, the massage untangles even my most twisted knots, and my nails are painted a fresh, muted pink. For the first time in a long time, the weight of the truth doesn't crush me. It can't when I'm so light thanks to the love of my friends.

"Alisha, I can't thank you enough for today," I say when we are all back in the hot tub.

"Please, it was the least I could do. As the first bride in our group, you deserve the pampering. After all, you're showing us what we need to avoid."

I choke on a half laugh, half sob, then rest my head on the back of the hot tub, slipping into daydreams of living at Serenity Spa forever.

"I hate to interrupt the fun, but your groom will be here soon," Lily says, pointing to the clock on the wall behind me.

With a sigh so deep it rattles my bones, I turn to my friends. "Time for me to go."

"It's okay. Now we know how rich Alisha is, she can bring us here all the time," Laney grins.

Alone in the changing room, I do my best to muster enthusiasm for the night ahead, but my mood falls flat. All I can think of is how the fallout from this wedding is going to change everything. What's Alisha going to think when she finds out the truth? How will the memories of this day make her feel? Will she be able to set foot in this place again?

And what about the rest of my friends? Will another broken heart make Lily think of Andy? Will watching my life fall apart make Laney even more scared of commitment?

A muffled cry escapes me. Everything about this wedding is a sham, but the people involved aren't. Their feelings, their friendship, their love – that's real. Real and about to change forever, and there's nothing I can do to stop it.

36

"Have you been crying?" Jamie asks when I climb into the car. "Your eyes are red."

"I'm fine, I think it's from the chlorine in the hot tub."

"You'd think a fancy place like this wouldn't pump their water full of chemicals," Jamie says as he pulls out of the carpark. "Actually, I suppose half their clients have their faces full of the stuff, so what does it matter?"

I laugh at his joke and fill him in on my day as we drive to Anne and Martin's. I don't ask him what he's been up to in my absence. I don't have the energy to pretend to care.

When we pull up outside his parents' house, Jamie reaches to the backseat and pulls out a bouquet of flowers. "I thought you might want to give these to my mum. Tell her they're from you. She'll like the thought."

I take the flowers, the weight of them a shock to my relaxed arms. "They're beautiful, Jamie. You can be really sweet, can't you?"

"I'm always sweet, unless you ask me not to be." Jamie winks, then he jumps out of the car so he can reach my door in time to open it for me.

As expected, Anne is ecstatic about the flowers. "Oh, Cassie, you shouldn't have!"

"Where are mine?" Martin jokes, kissing me on the cheek.

"Sorry, Martin, I didn't know if you were a lilies or a roses man," I tease back.

The tantalising scent of Italian food wafts through the air as Martin leads us into the living room. We take a seat and Anne hands everyone a glass of wine.

"So, are we all set for the big day?" Martin asks.

"If we are, it's all down to Cass. I swear, her phone hasn't stopped ringing all week," Jamie says.

"They're probably trying to squeeze a few more last-minute pennies out of you."

Anne catches my eye at Martin's mention of money then looks away. She grabs the bowl of nuts laid out for a pre-meal snack and holds them out. "Never mind the money. It will all be worth it in the end. Nut, anyone?"

The oven timer chooses that moment to announce dinner is ready. Anne practically faints with relief at the interruption.

We move to the dining room for dinner. Martin plays barman, refilling our drinks with theatrical panache, while Anne shuttles in and out of the room until the table is filled with more food than we'll be able to eat.

"You do realise there are only four of us, right?" Jamie jokes.

"Your mum always cooks like she's feeding the entire street, you know that," Martin grins.

"I never know how hungry you'll all be!" Anne says as she takes her seat. Martin reaches to start serving dinner, but Anne bats his hand away from the food. "Not yet, Martin. We need to toast the happy couple first."

Dutifully, we reach for our glasses, holding them mid-air in anticipation of Anne's speech.

"Now, we've always loved our brilliant Jamie, and from the moment he brought the lovely Cassie into our lives, we've loved her too!"

"Here, here!" Martin echoes. "D'you know, Cassie, we were losing hope he'd bring home anyone decent."

"Martin!" Anne bats Martin again, but she's unable to stop herself laughing. "It is true, though. Jamie was such a funny thing when he was younger."

"Alright, cut it out," Jamie says with a roll of his eyes.

"Calling him a funny thing is being polite, my love. What's the saying – 'always the bridesmaid, never the bride'? With Jamie, it was 'always the friend, never the boyfriend'."

"What can I say, I've always respected women," Jamie says to me as if to explain.

"Respected them so much it was like he was scared of them," Martin adds.

"Maybe they were scared of him," Anne jokes. "I wouldn't be surprised with that hair!"

Anne and Martin laugh the way only parents can at their children. They're not being unkind – I've experienced far harsher teasing from my own mum – but I've never heard Anne and Martin joke about Jamie like this. From the look on his face, I can tell it's not a common occurrence for him either.

I watch Jamie from the corner of my eye. A glimmer of something I've never seen in him before glints like sunlight catching the blade of a knife, and a shiver runs down my spine.

"I know you've only seen a few photos of Jamie when he was younger, Cassie, but maybe that's for the best," Anne giggles.

"I couldn't believe you showed her any photos at all! I thought for certain she'd leave him then." Martin points his wineglass in my direction. "Don't you worry, Cassie, you've seen Ethan and Joel, you know how cute your children will be." I feign a polite smile and Martin turns to Anne. "Maybe we should wait to tell her this until after the wedding. There's still time for her to run away, right?"

As Anne and Martin roar with laughter, the tension in the room rises. My skin prickles in the taut atmosphere.

"I tell you, it was like he was obsessed with hair gel. His hair was as solid as a rock with the stuff," Martin says.

Anne giggles but she stops when she notices the surly expression coating Jamie's features. "Oh, don't be like that, love. We're only joking.

I'm just trying to say that we've always loved you and always hoped you'd meet someone worthy of the Jamie we knew, the Jamie we love."

"The Jamie before you started going to the hairdresser and the gym," Martin adds, winking at me. Anne flinches at this additional comment, her eyes pleading with her son to let it go.

The moment suspends, teetering this way and that. I glance at Jamie, my breath caught in the back of my throat, waiting to see what will happen next.

Suddenly, he lets out a strange, booming laugh. "You're right, my hair was tragic, wasn't it? But I must have done something right because I managed to land this one." He reaches out and clutches my hand. Instinct tells me to withdraw it, but I don't think I could pull free even if I tried.

Jamie's eyes crinkle as he smiles, but behind his smile a raging darkness simmers beneath the surface. He looks so manic, so unlike the Jamie I know that for a second I can't breathe.

"To Jamie and Cassie!" Anne cheers, ending the conversation before Martin can say anything else.

"Jamie and Cassie!" we chorus, clinking our glasses together.

The rest of dinner goes without a hitch. We've had such a nice night that by the time we leave, I almost think I imagined Jamie's mask slipping.

The radio hums in the background as we drive home, the soft ballad playing the perfect soundtrack to drift off to. Using the window as a pillow, I give into the delicious daydream of being back at Serenity Spa.

"They were joking, you know," Jamie says, interrupting my thoughts.

"What?"

Jamie shuffles in his seat to correct his posture, his frame filling the car. "My parents. They were joking. I wasn't that weird."

"Oh, I just thought they were teasing you."

Jamie's expression sours. "I guess, but they didn't have to be such dicks about it."

The cloak of anger that covered his features at dinner is back, bringing with it my unease. "I didn't take it seriously, Jamie. Don't worry."

"Good, that's good. I don't want you thinking differently of me, that's all."

"Why would I think differently of you if you were geeky when you were younger?"

Jamie's lips flick into a snarl. "Because no one wants to be with a geek."

My eyes trace him, noting how he grips the steering wheel like it's the throat of an enemy, his veins bulging underneath his skin. For the second time in one night, I'm looking at a stranger.

My throat is tight as I reply. "I wouldn't mind. I've always been impartial to a geek. Science talk is the new sex talk, you know."

Jamie nods, my answer good enough for him. I squeeze his knee, knowing that's what a 'good fiancée' would do. A brief smile flickers across his face, signalling he's okay now. The silence continues, everything forgotten, normality re-established.

Only now I've seen the crack in Jamie's mask, there's no safety in our normality. Every threat I've ever read on 'The Good Bad Guy's Guide' flashes in my mind, screaming with warning. For not the first time, I wonder if the man whose life I am toying with in the name of revenge isn't only someone who has betrayed me, but someone I should fear too.

37.

One of my favourite things about the school holidays is having the 'no work' excuse to stay in bed. Usually, I spend one day curled up under the duvet with a stack of books beside me, reading intermittently and drifting in and out of sleep. Only now the thought of a day with nothing but my thoughts for company doesn't have the same appeal it once did.

I make a move to get up but Jamie rolls on top of me, pinning me to the bed. "Where do you think you're going?"

I struggle beneath him, faking a laugh to conceal my fear. "Jamie, I have a to-do list as long as my arm. It needs completing."

"Nope, today you're going to relax. You need a break."

"But -"

Jamie shushes me then strokes my hair from my face. I lie immobilised underneath him, my body on high alert as his hand moves from my hair to my neck, his thumb lingering over my pulse. "Are you okay? Your heart's racing."

My mouth dries but I pull Jamie's hand from my neck to my lips and press a kiss into his skin. "I'm fine, I promise. There's just so much to do before the wedding."

"Which is exactly why you need a break." Commanding me to stay put, Jamie leaves the room.

My heart rate has only returned to a normal pace when he comes back a few minutes later carrying a cup of tea and a piece of toast. "You didn't have to make me breakfast."

"I wanted to. You've got to start a day in bed the right way, haven't you?"

As I take the food and succumb to his wishes, Jamie plants a buttery kiss on my cheek.

"Have a good day, gorgeous," he calls over his shoulder as he heads for the door. A few seconds later, the television in the living room bursts into life.

With my skin still burning from the reminder of Jamie's hand on my throat, rest is impossible. I reach for my phone. Even though I know it's only going to hurt, I load 'The Good Bad Guy's Guide' and open Jamie's latest piece, a post called '*Is There Nothing I Can't Do?*'.

Apparently, it's not attractive to brag (I can't say I've ever had that issue, women love it when I do) but after the week I've had, how could I not?

I met a woman during the week. I took her out once. I slept with her.

While on that date, I got another woman's number when I was walking back from the bathroom. We've already arranged to meet. I guarantee by the end of the week she'll send me a nude.

I came home to wifey-to-be, still planning the wedding, still doing everything (and I mean everything) I want.

I have it all, lads. And do you know what? It's not enough. I want more and, like always, I'm going to get it.

Nausea radiates through me, every word piercing my soul. I can't tie the two together, the man in the room next door and the man behind this post. The one who brought me tea and toast and the one who brags about his womanising escapades.

But they are the same person. As much as it pains me to admit it, they are.

Simmering, I throw back the duvet and launch myself out of bed.

"Where are you going?" Jamie calls when he senses my movement.

"I'm getting my laptop to do some work," I shout back.

Marching into the second bedroom, I dodge boxes of wedding supplies and locate my laptop bag. I rummage around the bottom of it, my face splitting into a grin when my hand curls around the bulky shape of the burner phone.

"Back to bed – that's an order!"

My body jerks at the sound of Jamie's voice and I turn to find him striding towards me. My brain screams. Rising to stand, I slip the phone into the pocket of my pyjamas. "I have some planning -"

"Work and weddings are banned. You need to relax."

Jamie rests his hands on my waist and steers me back to bed. My trembling body obeys him, too terrified to protest. The phone hangs heavy in my pocket, clanging against my leg with every step I take.

As soon as I reach the bed, I dive under the duvet. "I'll relax, I promise. I promise!"

"Good. Don't make me have to tell you off again," Jamie warns, grinning like this is all a game, then he leaves the room.

After reminding myself to breathe, I lie back against my pillow and pull the burner phone from my pocket. There's no way I can text Jamie now, not when I don't know how much he saw.

With nothing else to do, I slip the phone under my pillow and close my eyes. To my surprise, I fall asleep. By the time I wake up, it's well after lunchtime.

I pad into the living room, disorientated and groggy. "I can't believe I slept for so long."

Jamie puts his phone facedown on the sofa. "You needed it. You've looked exhausted for days."

"Don't you know how to make a woman feel special," I joke.

"You know what I mean. I've been worried about you. It's nice to see you finally relax. Why don't I run you a bath? I know it's not quite a spa day but at least you can relax some more before you meet Tara."

"A bath sounds perfect, thank you."

"Consider it done," Jamie says, taking my hand and kissing it before leaving the room.

I wait until I hear water running in the bathroom before picking up his phone. Two messages wait for him, one from an unsaved number, the other from 'T'. Anger flutters in my stomach and for a moment I debate seeing if Jamie's tablet passcode would grant me access to his phone, but the thought of reading more of his second life drains me. I put his phone back where it was and go to the bathroom where a rose scented scene greets me.

"You used a bath bomb," I smile.

"It's got to be the perfect bath for the perfect woman, right?"

I groan. "That compliment is almost too sickly for me to acknowledge. Thank you, though. This is just what I need."

When Jamie leaves the room, I strip naked and stand in front of the mirror. My hand traces my stomach, a little rounder now than it was when I was last single but I'm okay with that. I've softened into my body as I've aged, learning to appreciate it in a way I never did when I was younger.

But then it hits me - one day I'll be naked in front of someone else. Someone new. All those fears of someone seeing me without clothes for the first time, those anxieties of 'will I be good enough?', they will soon be back in my life.

Suddenly I feel more exposed than ever.

Turning away from my reflection, I'm about to step into the tub when I see that the only towel in the bathroom is still damp from Jamie's morning shower. Holding it around my body, I go to get a clean one from the second bedroom.

When I push open the door, I find Jamie already in there. He springs to his feet, a guilty flush covering his cheeks. I look from his rigid frame to the floor... the floor that's now littered with the contents of my laptop bag.

"What are you doing?" I ask, my heart in my throat.

"Me? I was looking for a pen."

"In my laptop bag?"

Our eyes connect and a current of fizzing electricity passes between us. My heart pounds, the realisation that Jamie suspects I'm sending him the texts punching through my body with every terrified beat.

"I didn't know where they'd be. I thought you might have one."

I march past him towards the desk and pluck a pen from the top drawer. "Pens are in there, where they've always been."

Jamie hits his forehead with his palm. "Of course, how could I forget! Thanks, Cass."

My legs tremble as I walk away and grab a fresh towel. I want to press my face into it and breathe in the calming scent of washing powder, but I must act normal.

Before I leave the room, I stop in the doorway. Jamie's on his knees, cleaning away the scene as if putting my notebook back can make us forget this invasion of privacy ever happened.

"Jamie?"

He looks up at the sound of his name and his features rearrange into a strange, alien smile.

"Next time you need something, please ask. Going through someone's stuff without asking them first is a bit weird."

Jamie lets out a small laugh. I don't join in. I walk away and close the bathroom door, the click of the lock doing nothing to convince me that I am safe from that man or his suspicions.

38.

I'm on edge for the rest of the day. Whenever I catch Jamie smiling at me, my brain panics he's smiling because he's caught me out. When he doesn't ask if I want a cup of tea as he makes himself one, I think it's a petty act of revenge. We coexist in a strange, uneven atmosphere until it's time for us to go on our separate nights out.

"Say hi to the boys for me!" I call after him as we climb into our individual taxis. He blows me a kiss and with that, we are on our way. Two different cars, two different directions, two different nights.

In the safety of the car, I check my bag for the burner phone. I know it's there because I put it there, but I still exhale as my hand curls around its bricklike form.

Only my relief is short-lived. I know I'm going to have to do more than stop Jamie finding the phone to clear my name from his suspect list.

Formulating a plan in the short journey to the city, I ask the driver to drop me off a few streets away from where I'm meeting Tara. I purchase the items I'll need in cash then speed walk to the bar.

I spot her as soon as I enter the vintage-inspired setting. Perched at a table for two and flicking through her phone, nothing about Tara betrays any nerves at meeting me. I rush to her side. "I'm so sorry I'm late! I had to do a bit of shopping and misjudged the timing."

"Oh, it's no bother. Did you get anything nice?"

"Just a few last-minute wedding bits," I reply, taking a seat.

"Speaking of the wedding, thanks for fitting me in so close to the big day. I'm impressed you're free."

"Honestly, you're doing me a favour by being here. Jamie's out tonight. I'd have gone crazy worrying about all the last-minute jobs that need doing if I'd stayed in on my own."

"Well, I'm happy to be your distraction. Plus, there shall be no worrying about last-minute jobs because everything is here, ready to go." Tara points to two large bags stashed under the table. "The necklaces and cards are all in there. The cards need sealing in the envelopes, but I didn't want to do that without you checking them first."

Tara pulls out a thick, white envelope and hands it to me. Written on the front in her beautiful cursive script are the words '*Dear guest*' and the date of the wedding. As I pull the cards out to inspect them, a sprinkle of confetti showers my lap.

"Oops!"

"I did worry the confetti would get everywhere. If you don't like it, you can take it out."

"No, I love it! They're going to be such a wonderful surprise," I reply, studying each card one at a time. My lie of a relationship, my false happiness printed onto the page. A beat of pain ripples through me. I dab my eyes, furious at myself for crying in front of Tara. "Sorry, my emotions are everywhere at the minute! They're perfect. I can't thank you enough."

"I'm so glad you like them! We can seal the envelopes now if you want and save you a job?"

"Oh no, I didn't invite you out so you could work on more wedding prep! I'll do them tomorrow. Now, let me get us both a drink! Is wine okay?"

Tara nods. "Wine's perfect."

I slide from my seat and walk towards the speakeasy style bar where it takes me no longer than ten seconds to realise I'm invisible in this crowd. The barman serves every young woman with her cleavage spilling out of her dress before the teacher in her jeans, nice top, and sensible heels, and it hurts.

Just as I think my sadness couldn't sink any lower, a group of three men jostle their way to the front of the queue. One of them barges through so aggressively that he elbows me in the ribs. "Sorry, love," he says, not once looking in my direction.

My eyes burn with indignant tears as I realise that this is what my life is going to be like in a few days' time. Gone are the cosy nights of cuddles, the comfort of knowing someone has you and you have them. In its place will be loud bars, overpriced drinks and fighting for attention from men who don't even have the patience to join a queue.

While I wait to be served, I list all the things I loved about being single – independence, more time for my own hobbies, making choices simply for myself. The list is long but still before my newly single life has even started, I'm already tired of it.

"A bottle of Pinot, please," I say when the barman eventually acknowledges my existence. Once I've paid, I push through the crowd and make my way back to the table.

Tara perks up when she sees me approaching. "A bottle to share, not a glass each - I like your style!"

"Isn't every night a bottle of wine night in the school holidays?"

Tara laughs, I take my seat and we fall into easy, flowing conversation, just as we did that day in the apartment. The only time irritation bites me is when Tara complains about Nico. "He's so harsh sometimes, you know? Everything is so black and white with him. If he makes his mind up about something, that's it. There's no convincing him otherwise," she says.

"Is that such a bad thing?"

"It is when you're someone who doesn't see the world like that. Not everything is good versus bad, right versus wrong," Tara explains, and I have to bite my lip to stop myself from snapping, 'Is that why you think it's okay to cheat?'.

We skirt around mentioning Jamie until three glasses of wine in, with the edges of her words slurring, Tara leans forward. "So, tell me, how did you know you wanted to be with Jamie forever?"

I blink at her question. "I just did."

Tara doesn't take her eyes off me, wanting more, and I know I'm going to have to dig deep to make it through this conversation.

"Life makes sense when I'm with him, *I* make sense. He brings out the best in me. It's not that I wasn't happy before I met him because I was, but I was always looking for something. With Jamie, I don't need to look for anything else. My life already is exactly the way I want it to be," I confess. I study my wineglass, splintering at the searing honesty in my words. "I… I love him, that's why."

Tara takes me in. "You do, don't you?"

I look at her, unable to stop the tears pooling in my eyes but also not wanting to hide them from her. She needs to understand what they have done to me. She needs to see my pain so that on the day of my wedding, she understands why I did what I've done, why I chose her to take the blame.

"I do. With all my heart, I do."

Tara holds her composure for a second, then her face twists. I freeze. The truth is right there on the tip of her tongue, I can sense it.

If she tells me about their affair, everything is over. The cards I've designed will be wasted. There will be no wedding day humiliation for Jamie. Instead, I'll have to confront him without ever knowing the sweet triumph of evening the score.

The world pauses, the two paths of my future laid out before me, pointing in completely opposite directions.

"I… I need to use the bathroom," Tara rushes. She scrambles to her feet and leaves the table. I watch her walk away, staring after her even when she is no longer in sight.

I've never been someone who can sit alone in public without a distraction, so I pull out my phone. Waiting for me are two texts, one from Laney telling me one of her wedding nails has broken, the other from Shari.

Hope this isn't weird to message but I've just seen Jamie go into The Shed with a blonde, tall, big boobs?!

Even though it's not a shock to discover Jamie's out with another woman and not his friends, my lungs still constrict. I type a breezy response, one betraying no hint of the frustration flowing through me.

He's out tonight with his sister – she's stunning right?

A few seconds later, Shari's reply pings through.

So relieved it's his sister! Hope you don't mind me texting. You can never be too sure these days, can you?

I respond reassuringly and drop my phone into my bag, then reach for my wine.

Part of me wants to laugh for thinking Jamie would act differently with it being so close to the wedding, but going to The Shed? That's a new low, even for him. With our mutual love of indie-rock, it was 'our place' when we first started dating. We'd go every few weeks, singing along to our favourite songs and dancing together without a care in the world. The bar staff probably still recognise him.

I shudder at the humiliation of it all, but through my disgust, an idea pops into my mind. I grab the burner phone from my bag.

The Shed? That's your romantic venue of choice these days? I'm so happy I got the fancier treatment

Grinning, I hit send. Jamie knows I'm out with Tara – I even put a customary shot of our drinks on social media. The Shed is almost ten minutes away from here, and Jamie hadn't told me where he was going. How could he suspect the messages are from me when I'm somewhere else and have no idea where he is?

To strengthen my alibi, I send Jamie a photo of the empty seat opposite and a message reading:

Tara's been gone for ages. She said she was nipping out to make a call... have I been stood up?! Hope you're having a good night

I sit back in my chair, pumped at the perfect alignment of this moment until a voice behind me makes me jump.

"I didn't realise they still sold phones that old!" Tara exclaims, plonking onto her seat.

Blushing, I slip the burner phone into my bag. She wasn't supposed to see the phone. Not yet. "My phone's been playing up. I got a cheap one to tide me over until my upgrade."

As Tara tells me about her new phone, I pour the last of the wine and tell myself it's time to go soon. The more we drink, the closer we get to spilling the truth. We've already walked on dangerous territory, and I don't need to explore it further.

My mouth sours from the taste of alcohol, but I finish my wine. "I'd best be off. There's so much to do tomorrow and I can't face tackling it all with a hangover," I say.

Tara doesn't protest. She hands me the bags of cards and thanks me again for my time. After saying goodbye and paying the bill, I head outside to find a taxi.

Once tucked in the back seat, I make it clear to the driver that I'm not up for conversation. He turns the radio up to fill the awkward silence and I check both phones. There's a message from Jamie asking how long Tara had been away from the table.

About 15 minutes. I started to think something had happened to her

On the burner phone, I find a message from him stating stalking is a criminal offence. The word 'criminal' leaps at me from the screen, throbbing in my field of vision until it's all I can see.

Criminal – that word describes me now. As soon as I used Jamie's credit cards, it applied to me, an admission that doesn't stop tormenting me until I make it home.

In the safety of the apartment, I put Tara's cards in the second bedroom then carry the supplies I bought before meeting her to the master bedroom. I tip them out, eying the components of the next lie I will tell. I don't know what number lie this is. They're all blurring into one.

I was never much of a liar before, but I can't say that about myself anymore. A liar, a criminal... what else can I add to the list? What other parts of myself will I lose to vengeance?

Fighting off tears, I find myself reaching for my phone and searching for the number of the last person I thought I'd call.

"Is everything okay?" Debbie says when she picks up.

I close my eyes at the familiar sound of her voice. "Thank you for answering my call. I wasn't sure if you would."

"I'm here for you whenever, Cass, you know that. You've not answered my question though. Is everything okay?"

I bite my wobbling lower lip. "Honestly, Debbie, I don't know."

"Do you need me to come over? Are you okay? Are you hurt?"

"I'm fine, I... I just need to ask you something."

"Anything."

"Debbie, am I a good person?"

I hear the heartbreak in Debbie's voice as she speaks. "Oh, Cass, of course you are. You're the best, you really are. Look, whatever you've done, it's not too late to back out or undo it."

My chin quivers. Debbie has no idea - it is too late. I can't undo a transaction or eradicate debt, but more than that, I can't let Jamie get away with what he has done. I can't put any more unwitting women in his firing line or let Nico live his life thinking he is with the woman of his dreams. I don't want anyone else to be hurt in this, only the people who have hurt me. I want them gone, ruined, broken.

I blink away my tears. "I should let you get some sleep. It's late."

"Cass –"

"Goodnight, Debbie," I say, then I hang up, silencing Debbie and any thought of this story ending differently than it will.

39.

The first thing I see when I open my eyes the next morning is Jamie. He grins, planting his hands on my hips and pulling me close. "Good morning, my lovely fiancée."

I try not to react to the staleness of his breath and instead force a smile. "Good morning, my too-awake-at-this-time fiancé. What time did you get home last night?"

"Oh, who cares about that when there are more exciting things to discuss! I mean, do you realise tomorrow we become husband and wife?"

"Now isn't that an exciting thought?"

"It's the best!" Jamie cheers, his grip on my hips tightening. "What shall we do for our last day together?"

"I think you mean last morning. You're going to your parents' house at ten."

Jamie groans, burying his head in my neck. "Please don't make me go! I'd rather stay here with you."

"Jamie," I giggle. "You know your parents can't wait for you to stay over for your last night as a single man. Besides, I'll be at my mum's today too."

"Well, I'm still grumbling," Jamie mumbles, pressing his body against mine.

"Breakfast," I say, pulling away. "Let's make breakfast together." Jamie bites my lip playfully then jumps out of bed. I make a move to follow him before stopping. "Wait, I have an idea! Did you check the mail yesterday?"

Jamie shakes his head. "I haven't for a few days, why?"

I squeal. "We might have been sent some cards and gifts before the wedding!"

"Isn't that exciting! I tell you what, why don't you get the mail while I make breakfast?"

"Deal!"

When Jamie leaves the room, I quickly get dressed then pull the supplies I bought last night from under the bed. With only a few minutes to sort everything out, adrenaline makes me clumsy. My hands fumble as I tamper with the product, but I manage to do it. Slotting it into a parcel box and writing our address on the package in chunky capital letters, the final part of my remove-me-from-Jamie's-suspect-list plan is complete.

"Be back soon!" I shout, slipping the parcel underneath my shirt. I rush downstairs to the entrance of our apartment building where I discover that a handful of cards addressed to 'the Patricks' have been delivered. Ignoring how much seeing my almost surname hurts, I turn to the parcels lined up against the wall. Some are for other residents, but most are for us.

Taking the package from underneath my shirt, I carry the mountain of mail back to the apartment.

"We've got gifts!" I cheer when I enter the kitchen.

Jamie looks up from buttering a piece of toast. "Presents? This must be our lucky day."

"I think you'll find tomorrow is our lucky day," I joke, spilling the mail in my arms onto the counter. I grab two parcels and wave them in the air. "Can we open them today? Please, please, please?!"

"Go for it."

"Which one first?"

Jamie points to the parcel in my right hand. I don't have to fake my excitement at him picking that one. I tear open the parcel until a box for a pregnancy test is revealed.

240

I hold it up, my expression a picture of confusion. "What the…"

The colour drains from Jamie's face. "What is it?"

"A million pounds, what does it look like? It's a pregnancy test!" I peer into the box and grimace. "It's open too. Jamie, I think it's been used."

Jamie goes to pluck the test out of my hands, but I stop him.

"Be careful. If it's been used, it means someone's peed on it."

Jamie wrinkles his nose and grabs a towel. There's a tremble to his hands as he pulls the test out of the packaging. His expression doesn't change, then he slips the test back in the box. "How weird."

"Weird? Jamie, someone sent us a used pregnancy test!"

"Exactly, that's weird."

"Was it positive?" I ask, knowing all too well the answer to that is yes because I drew the line on the test myself.

Jamie doesn't even flinch when he lies. "No."

I flip the parcel over in my hands. "There's no note with it."

"Maybe it wasn't for us."

"But it was in with our mail. It's addressed to us, see?" I point to the writing on the parcel. "Jamie, what does it mean?"

"I've no idea. Maybe someone's messing with us. You know, a pre-wedding joke."

"Pregnancy isn't something to joke about."

"Some people have a weird sense of humour," Jamie shrugs, dropping the test in the bin and wrapping his arms around me.

"Well, I don't find it very funny."

"Neither do I."

I look to the bin, but Jamie turns my face to his. "It's probably Ricky playing a practical joke, you know what he's like. It'll be about us wanting a baby after we're married." Jamie widens his eyes as if he's remembering something. "You know, I was talking to the lads last night about how much I want a family with you. I bet they sent this as a wind up. Come to think of it, that even looks like Ricky's handwriting."

"Your friends don't seem like the sort of people who'd do that," I press.

"Weddings transform even the most normal people into arseholes. Josh wanted to get me so drunk on my stag do I tattooed his name to my chest, remember?"

I stare at the bin. "I don't know. There's a bit of a difference between a tattoo and a pregnancy test..."

"Hey, you trust me, don't you?" Jamie says, tilting me to face him.

My body tingles with terror but I force myself to nod.

"Then listen to me when I say this is nothing, okay? Trust me, I'll get Ricky back for this."

Nodding, I fall into his arms. "I hope you do because it really wasn't funny."

"I will. Nobody messes with my fiancée and gets away with it." Jamie keeps me in his embrace for a moment before ushering me out of the kitchen. "Now go lie down and let me bring you breakfast in bed."

As I leave the room without questioning things further, the tension in the apartment evaporates, but Jamie's not the only one to relax. After that, surely there's no way Jamie will suspect me as the person texting him now.

40.

While Jamie is in the bedroom packing everything he needs to stay with his parents before the wedding, I go to the bathroom and text him from the burner phone.

Did you enjoy your present?

"Babe, don't forget your toothbrush!" I call out as I press send.

"Lifesaver! Can you bring it here?"

After hiding the phone in a box of tampons, I leave the room and take Jamie his toothbrush.

"Thanks. I guess you don't want to say 'I do' to a man with stinking breath?"

"Not even a little bit," I reply. I watch him add the shoes he will wear to the wedding to his bag, and a strange sadness washes over me. "Can you believe we're getting married tomorrow?" I flinch at my question, not sure why I started this conversation.

Jamie's eyes lock on mine. He looks so happy that for a moment I really believe he wants to spend the rest of his life with me, and somewhere inside me, another crack appears.

"I'm on countdown to it, Cass. I have been from the moment we met. I always knew you'd be the person I married."

"Don't be silly," I laugh but Jamie shaking his head silences me.

"It's true. As soon as I saw you across the bar, I knew you were The

One. Everything clicked into place. You make me so happy, Cass. I have been from the moment I met you."

Inside my chest, my heart breaks all over again. "Jamie…"

"You don't have to say anything. I just want you to know it's true. I can't wait to marry you tomorrow. I can't wait to spend the rest of my life with you."

With those words, Jamie kisses me, raking his fingers through my hair and knotting them in my curls like he never wants to let go.

Somehow, I find myself kissing him back. Really, truly kissing him back.

His lips press harder onto mine and I push my body against his. A passion takes over me, one I thought died the second I saw the photo of Jamie with Tara, but here it is, burning every inch of my skin. The ground beneath me feels like it's shaking and I tumble backwards, falling onto the bed with Jamie's body on top of mine, falling for him like I did all those years ago.

His lover.

His victim.

Jamie's hands make their way down my body, tracing my curves, touching me in places he knows I like to be touched. He fumbles with the zip of my jeans. My brain roars in protest but I don't ask him to stop. I don't want him to, even though I know in doing so I've lost a part of my soul to this moment.

Suddenly, somewhere beneath our bodies, the mechanical ringing of Jamie's phone blares. The jolt of sound serves as the slap across the face I need, and I pull away.

"You should answer that," I say, pressing my fingers to my lips.

Jamie groans but searches the bed for his phone, locating it underneath my shoulder. He turns the screen to show me Anne's name, then accepts the call. "Hi, Mum."

As Jamie talks to Anne, I hold the mattress for support. Shame scalds me. How could I let those lips touch mine, those hands wander my body so freely?

I bite back a shudder, only registering reality again when Jamie hangs up the phone.

"Mum's setting off for me now, but I do believe we were in the middle of something…"

He slinks over to me, but I stand before his lips can secure themselves on mine. "We've no time. We need to check you've got everything before you go."

Ignoring his protests, I reel off a list of items Jamie needs for an overnight stay and for the wedding. Jamie checks them off then, when there is nothing left to pack, he comes for me. I surrender to his embrace.

With my head resting on Jamie's chest, the atmosphere around me thickens until there's no air in the room. By the time the intercom buzzes to announce Anne's arrival, I'm ready to faint.

"I can't believe she's here already," Jamie groans. He pulls his overnight bag onto his shoulder, and together we walk to the front door. "Text me bits about your day, okay? I'll miss our chats."

"You're being soppy," I say, punching his arm, but Jamie catches my fist.

"I mean it, Cass, I'll miss you. I love you. I love you so much."

His words tighten around my neck. "I love you too."

After one more kiss, Jamie walks away. He steps into the lift, waving goodbye. The doors close. I watch the illuminated numbers on the panel above decline until he reaches the ground floor, and then he is gone.

Numb, I disappear back into the apartment and sink onto the bed. Our bed. The bed I've slept in while hating him. The bed I've slept in while loving him.

A sob bursts from me. I press my hands to my lips to stifle it. I don't have time to break down, not when there's so much to do before I leave for my mum's.

Hauling myself to my feet, I head into the bathroom and splash my face with cold water. I do everything I can to avoid catching sight of my pinched reflection in the mirror, then I hear it – a buzzing.

The burner phone. I almost forgot about it, almost forgot life before that kiss.

Locating the phone, I find two missed calls and a text waiting.

I don't know what you think you're doing sending that shit to my home but mark my words – you are NOT having my child. I will kick that baby out of you if I have to

I sink onto the lid of the toilet, sitting before my legs give out on me.

The threat may be written via text, but I believe it. I believe every word. I've read Jamie's website. I saw the flash of rage that night at his parents' house. There's a side to him, a side I am coaxing out. What that means for me, I don't know, but I pray I'm strong enough to withstand its fury when the time comes.

41.

My horror at Jamie's message fuels me into action. Grabbing a binbag, I stash Tara's love story cards inside then get to stuffing the envelopes with my own version. I seal each one, no going back, and tuck a spare into my handbag.

While I'm packing an overnight bag to take to my mum's, the intercom rings.

"Delivery for Mr Patrick."

I buzz the deliveryman into the building and open the front door in anticipation of his arrival. A few moments later, he steps out of the lift carrying two large boxes. Even though I'm the one who placed the colossal order, my jaw still drops at the size of them.

"Wow!"

"Tell me about it, and there's still another one in the van," the man huffs, dropping the boxes in the hallway where they land with a dull thud.

Playing innocent, I message Jamie.

Some parcels have arrived for you. Hope they're gifts for me ;) xx

After pushing the boxes into the living room, I move onto the next phase of my plan. Opening the Abby Dunne email, I compose a message to Meadow Park, Craven Primary, and every other school I can think of. I explain that I know of multiple parents who have been encouraged to send explicit photos to a teacher named Jamie Patrick. I write that Mr

Patrick is abusing his position of power and any school employing him is failing their duty of care to both students and parents.

I schedule the email to send an hour after the wedding starts, and in doing so hammer the final nail into the coffin of Jamie's demise. His reputation, his career, and his financial stability have all been ruined thanks to me. The best part is, only Jamie will ever know who was behind it all. It's brilliant. I'm half tempted to pour a glass of wine to celebrate but my phone ringing drags me from revelling in this moment.

"Everything alright, Cass?" Mum asks when I accept the call. "I thought we were dropping off the last decorations at the venue this afternoon?"

"Sorry, I got tied up at the apartment. I'll be with you in half an hour."

I hang up and grab the things I need for the weekend. Between wedding stuff and everything for an overnight stay at Mum's, it takes me two trips to the car to pack it all, but I don't mind. Being rushed off my feet ensures I don't have time to think of how I'm leaving this apartment engaged, but when I return, I'll be alone.

After dumping Tara's love story cards at the tip, I drive to Mum's. As soon as I'm parked, she runs up the driveway and wrenches my car door open. "You're getting married tomorrow!"

"Am I? I'd forgotten all about that," I grin.

"Cheeky," Mum says. "Anyway, I've picked up your dress like you asked and we've cleared out the spare bedroom so your bridesmaids have space to get ready. Is there anything else you need before we set off?"

"You couldn't help me bring some of this in, could you?" I ask, gesturing to the mound of bags in the back of the car. "The stuff on the left is for the house. Everything on the right is to take to the venue."

Mum calls Colin to help and between us we carry everything inside. The scent of home greets me when I enter, and my chest pulls tight. So many memories are wrapped up in that smell, a mix of vanilla candles, Mum's perfume, and her favourite cleaning products. A reminder of childhood when life was uncomplicated, and I looked at the world and only saw the good.

Colin whistling interrupts my sadness. "Look at all this stuff! Are you planning to move back in without telling us?"

"Well, you might've said no if I'd asked first," I joke. "I'll put my overnight bag upstairs then we can go to the venue, okay?"

Mum nods and I head to the bedroom that was once mine. Even though an exercise bike and yoga equipment now stand in the corner, this room is still an extension of my soul. My personality touches everything, from the patterned bedding to the artsy posters lining the walls.

Then I spot it. Hung outside the wardrobe and encased in a garment bag - my wedding dress.

I walk towards the ominous white bag, ready to open the zip and torture myself with visions of what could have been, but a creak on the staircase stops me.

"Only me, Cass," Colin calls. "Your mum wants to know if you want a drink before you set off?"

His interruption shakes me from my melancholy thoughts, and I withdraw my outstretched hand. "No thanks, we don't have time."

Colin's footsteps grow softer as he retreats downstairs. When he's gone, I drag my gaze from my wedding dress and check the burner phone for the final time. Another vile rant of a message from Jamie greets me.

I would never touch you without a condom. You've probably been with everyone the country and are trying to pin it on me. Not. Happening. Tell me what you want then disappear. I'm through with your games

Knowing this will be the last message I'll send to Jamie, I make it count.

I want nothing but to watch you burn. Just wait, Jamie. The truth will come out. It always does. Enjoy your wedding, if you can

Slipping the phone into my handbag, I thunder downstairs. Mum's waiting at the front door, ready to go. "Have you got everything you need?"

I nod. "You don't mind if we make a quick stop on the way, do you? There's someone I need to see."

"It's your day, Cassie. I'm here to do whatever you need me to."

We leave the house and I drive to a florist a few streets away. Leaving Mum in the car, I go to pick up my order. "Collection for Cassie Edwards?"

The young woman serving disappears into the back of the store then returns a moment later to present me with a beautiful wildflower bouquet. "Do you want to write a card to go with the flowers?" she asks, holding out a pen.

I take it and select a generic card from a stand beside the counter. Inside, I write '*Thank you for everything*', a message I know will take on an entirely new meaning on the day of the wedding.

Before sliding back into the car, I hand Mum the flowers.

"Do you think you could show Colin these? You know, give him a shove in the right direction when it comes to romance," she jokes.

"Colin's romantic in his own way. Besides, they're not coming home with us. They're for Tara to say thank you for all her help with the wedding."

"What a lovely gesture! You're so kind, Cassie."

"Yes," I reply, starting the car once more. "Yes, I am."

Having taken Tara's address from the printing invoice she sent, I drive to her house. Envy taunts me as soon as we pull up outside. It's the kind of home Jamie and I were saving to buy. Big windows, a neat garden, a double garage – it's perfect.

"What a lovely house," Mum comments, rubbing salt in the wound.

Ignoring her, I grab the flowers from the backseat. "I'll be right back."

The walk from my car to Tara's front door is only a few metres but it feels like scaling a mountain. I ring the doorbell, listening as footsteps draw closer, then the door opens and unveils Nico. He blinks at the unexpected sight of me. "Cassie, what a surprise!"

He looks so casual with his shower-damp hair and grubby white t-shirt that for a moment I can't find the words to say to him, this man whose life I will soon shatter.

"Cassie?"

"Sorry, I was miles away! Is Tara home? I'm just dropping off some flowers to say thank you for everything she's done for the wedding."

"That's so kind, but I'm afraid she's out with her mum today. Her consultation went well, so Tara's taken her for afternoon tea to celebrate."

"Her consultation?"

"Tara's mum has kidney failure, didn't she tell you?"

The world around me tips off centre.

Kidney failure? Tara's mum has kidney failure?

The flowers suddenly feel like a deadweight in my arms, and I'm overwhelmed by the urge to run back to my car and drive away.

"We're hoping it won't be too long until she has a transplant, so fingers crossed! Shall I ask Tara to call you when she's back?" Nico asks, prompting me back to life.

"Oh, don't worry about it. If you could just give her these, that would be great," I reply, pushing the flowers into Nico's arms.

He takes them then leans on the doorframe, his expression soft. "You know, you've been a great friend at a time Tara needed one. Instead of focusing on her mum all the time, she's been having fun with you. She's really enjoyed making those cards. I can't wait to see them! I really can't thank you enough for being such a good distraction for her."

I nod, my throat too clogged with emotion to speak.

A beat of silence rings out. Nico wavers, clearly wondering if it's appropriate to say goodbye, but I jump in first. "Do you mind if I use your bathroom before I leave?"

"Sure, it's just upstairs," Nico says, waving me inside.

I take the stairs two at a time. The faster I am, the less time there is to think about what I am doing.

I wait until I hear Nico disappear into the kitchen. As soon as he's out of earshot, I tiptoe around, opening doors and peering inside the different rooms. Behind the third door, I find the master bedroom. Blushing as if I've walked in on Tara and Nico having sex, I back away and turn my attention to the last unopened door. Nerves ripple through me as I push it open to reveal a home office.

Tara's laptop bag is easy to locate. Dumped on the floor by the desk, the same place all teachers toss their laptops at the start of the school holidays. Peeling the front pocket open, I drop the burner phone inside alongside the spare love story card.

Then I close the bag and walk away.

Before heading back downstairs, I flush the toilet. "Thanks so much for letting me use the bathroom," I call out when I reach the front door.

Nico replies from the kitchen. "No problem. I'll see you tomorrow!"

"You will," I smile, then with a wave I leave Tara's dream home and all the evidence needed to tear her world apart behind me.

42.

The constant calls and messages from the venue's wedding coordinator, Hanadi, were worth it because everything looks incredible. Stunning floral arrangements stand tall and proud in the centre of the tables. Jars of candles line the aisle ready to be lit before the ceremony tomorrow.

"It's incredible," I breathe.

Mum and Hanadi beam, an expression I try mirroring but fall short of pulling off.

Hanadi leads us through the venue and explains the finishing touches that will be completed in the next hour. I try to listen, but the only thing I'm able to focus on is my devastation at the pointlessness of it all. I almost want to tell the staff to stop working so hard because no one will get to enjoy that cupcake tower or sign our guestbook tomorrow anyway.

Walking around rooms that are even more perfect than I could have imagined kills me. I want more than anything to sit at that table, laughing at speeches and eating delicious food. I want a photographer to catch mine and Jamie's jubilant moments, to hand my mum a tissue as she weeps with pride, to thank everyone for making us feel so special. I want that day. I want that future.

But as I pass Hanadi the bags containing the story cards, I know that the only way the day can go is the way I've orchestrated it to.

"The envelopes need placing on the chairs in the ceremony room. One per guest, and everyone needs to be told only to open them when instructed," I say.

"They're very specific instructions, Cass," Mum jokes.

"I know, but these cards are a surprise. Jamie's friend Tara made them for us. Neither of us have seen the final product," I lie.

"I love that idea!" Hanadi smiles. "Don't worry, I'll set them up exactly as you've said."

With the cards now out of my hands, we leave the white and blush pink scene of my dreams behind.

"I can't believe how amazing everything looks," Mum gushes on the drive home. "You've done so well, Cass. Now all that's left to do is enjoy the ride!"

I struggle to muster the enthusiasm to respond. I'm still flat when we arrive back at Mum's house. I trail down the driveway, wondering if I can spend the rest of the day in bed if I fake a headache. Only when Mum opens the front door, a shriek escapes that silences any thoughts of spending the day in isolation.

"Surprise!"

I take in the sight of Laney, Lily, and Alisha stood in the kitchen. "What are you doing here?!"

"Your mum thought it might be nice for you to have a sleepover with your bridesmaids. You know, one last celebration before the big day," Alisha says.

"Mum," I say, choking on my emotions and turning to her. "You're the best."

"She is. Now let's pop some Prosecco and have some fun!" Laney cheers.

We spend the rest of the day curled under blankets watching films. Colin stays out of the way so we can have a 'girls' night', only appearing every now and then to top up our drinks or bring us food.

My evening is blissful until it's interrupted by a message from Jamie. I force myself to read what he has to say.

Having fun? You've no idea how much I miss you! Wish we could run away and get married on our own tomorrow... xx

Stuffing a handful of popcorn in my mouth, I reply like a good bride-to-be.

I miss you too! I'm having a night with my friends, it's so cute! How's your night going? And LOL at running away... no chance! Not after this wedding has cost so much xx

There's a pause as I wait for Jamie to reply. Lily skips through the opening credits of the next film, accidentally fast-forwarding too far.

"Go back, go back!" Alisha cries.

I'm laughing when my phone lights up again, but my laughter soon fades when I read Jamie's response.

Worth a try. We can elope to renew our vows! Your night sounds perfect. Mum's fussing as per so I've gone out for a bit. Don't worry – no hangover, I promise!xx

I re-read Jamie's message, double-checking he really does think it's okay to go out the night before he's due to get married. When the words on the screen don't miraculously change, I turn to my friends. "I'm going to make a quick call. Pause it for me, okay?"

Running to my bedroom, I dial Anne's number.

"Hello, mother of the groom speaking!"

"Hi Anne, I'm wondering if you know where Jamie's gone? We're having a girls' night here so I thought he could take Colin out with him but he's not picking up the phone."

I sense Anne frown. "Hasn't he gone to see the venue with you?"

I sink onto the bed. "The venue?"

"Yes, dear. He told me he's going to do the final check of the décor. I must say, it's brave of you to let Jamie be the one to say if it looks perfect or not," Anne jokes.

"I think we've both got a little confused. I went to see the venue earlier with Mum."

"That makes sense. I thought you wouldn't let him have final approval! Oh well, at least you've both seen it now. I don't think Jamie's going anywhere after though. He's coming back for one last homecooked meal."

"That's fine, I just thought I'd ask before Colin endures another rom-com."

"Tell Colin I'm sorry he's outnumbered, and I shall see you tomorrow."

"See you tomorrow," I reply. I hang up and double over, resting my head on my knees. Another lie from Jamie, another night where I have no idea where he is or who he is with.

As a ripple of laughter rings out downstairs, I peel my body into a sitting position and blow a long, steady stream of air out of my mouth. "It's nearly over," I whisper. This time tomorrow, it will be done. Jamie will be ruined, and I will be triumphant.

I just hope that triumph is enough to heal this hurt.

<u>43.</u>

With my best friends on air mattresses on the floor beside me, I sleep surprisingly well for a woman who's about to throw the last few years of her life away. If anything, I'm a little dismayed when my alarm blares at half past seven and demands I wake up.

"Someone's getting married today!" Alisha, a typical early bird, trills.

"Someone needs another hour or ten of sleep," Laney groans.

I snort with laughter and stretch, savouring one last lingering moment of peace. Sunlight peeps through the curtains, a kiss from fate all brides pray for. I smile at the irony. I got the weather, but not the wedding.

"Your phone was going off all night, you know," Laney grumbles, pulling her duvet over her head. "Do you not know how to put it on 'do not disturb'?"

"Laney, you are so grumpy on a morning," Lily laughs. "Cass was probably just getting loads of well wishes for today."

"Maybe," I say, reaching for my phone. Sure enough, notifications fill the screen. Most are good luck messages but then I spot one from Debbie.

Whatever you've done, it's not too late to back out x

My stomach churns. I delete the message without replying then join my bridesmaids as they pile downstairs in their pyjamas. We find Mum in the kitchen pulling croissants out of the oven. "Morning, girls! Coffee is brewed and there's fruit laid out on the table."

"Cassie, please let your mum adopt me," Lily says wistfully.

As soon as we eat, the house comes alive with the buzz of excitement. The fever pitch reaches dizzying heights with the arrival of the photographer, makeup artists and hairdresser.

I've never experienced getting ready as part of a bridal party before, but it's intense. It's a blur of foundation, stressful energy, compliments, and heat. Mum opens the patio doors to cool everyone down, but the sheer number of bodies in the room makes it impossible to not be damp with sweat.

When everyone else's styling is complete, the hairdresser and makeup artist go to work on me. Nerves radiate from me as my transformation into 'the bride' begins. My fingers can't keep still. They toy with the hem of my nightgown, twisting it into a knot. I try imagining what normal brides feel like on the morning of their wedding, but I can't put myself in the position of a normal bride. I haven't been one of them for a month now.

"You're all done," the makeup artist says, stepping back to admire her handiwork.

"Already?"

"You've been in the chair for almost an hour," she smiles, handing me a mirror.

When I see my reflection, I almost can't believe it's me I'm looking at. My hair is half up, half down, styled in a way that looks effortless yet would be impossible for me to recreate. My eye bags have been eradicated, my lips are glossy and full, eagerly awaiting the moment they get to kiss their groom.

"Cass," Mum breathes. "You're beautiful."

"Steady on, Mum, I've not got my dress on yet," I joke, turning my back on her to shield myself from her unedited joy.

Thankfully, my wobbling emotions are interrupted by my bridesmaids filing into the room, dressed to perfection.

"You look sensational!" I cry.

"I know, right?" Laney jokes.

Alana, the photographer, snaps away, documenting the moment without instructing anyone to pose or look a certain way. We specifically chose her because of her natural approach but now she's here she seems intrusive, like she's going to expose that none of this is real.

I angle my shoulders away from Alana's lens as Alisha stretches her hand out to me. "Come on, Cass. It's your turn now!"

With a gulp, I take her hand. Mum follows and together we ascend the stairs to my bedroom, the excitable chatter from Lily and Laney the soundtrack to our departure.

The walls of my old bedroom seem to close in on us as we pile into the room. I don't look when Alisha unzips the garment bag, or when I step into my dress. The luscious fabric brushes against my skin, but I do my best to ignore it and everything it stands for.

When Mum has almost finished lacing up the back of my dress, Alana is allowed into the room. I keep my head low, shielding my face from her, but every click of the camera reminds me that the worst time in my life is being documented.

"Beautiful," Alisha whispers as my bridal look nears completion.

Eventually, they finish fastening my dress.

"Oh Cassie," Mum weeps. "You're perfect! Your dad would be so proud."

My throat constricts at the mention of my dad. I can't help but wonder if he would be proud of what I'm about to do, a tortuous path I'm saved from walking down by Alisha resting her hands on my shoulders.

"You, my friend, make one hell of a bride. Look at yourself. See how beautiful you are," she instructs.

Instinct begs me to say no, but sense overrides it. I take two purposeful steps forward, aligning myself with my full-length mirror, ready to see myself as a vision in white.

My eyes lock with my reflection and in that instant, something inside me dies.

Women are conditioned to not compliment themselves for fear of appearing arrogant but right now I know it – I am beautiful.

A beautiful liar.

As I dissolve into tears, Alisha and Mum rush to my side.

"Don't! You'll ruin your makeup!" Alisha commands, cupping my head and fanning her hand in my face.

"Alisha's right, love. You look far too nice to spoil it by crying!"

"Plus - no offence, Cass - you're an ugly crier," Alisha jokes, nudging my hip. I choke on a half laugh, half sob. "Emotions under control?"

"Emotions under control," I confirm.

"Good, because Jamie gave us something to give to you when you were in your dress, but you can only have it if you promise not to cry."

"What is it?" I ask.

"A surprise," Mum says, winking at me. She exits the room then comes back a moment later with a small package wrapped in pink paper. I take it from her. I don't want to open it, don't want to see what loving lie Jamie thought to gift me on our wedding day, but there's too much excitement in the air for me not to.

Alana clicks away as I pull the delicate wrapping away to reveal a box with a golden heart embossed on it. I lift the lid and inside find a chain with a locket attached.

"It's for your bouquet," Mum informs me. "Open it up."

I follow her instructions. The clasp on the locket is fiddly, especially with my shaking hands, but I manage to unlock it. Inside, on the righthand side, my favourite photo my dad greets me.

"It's so he can walk you down the aisle," Mum whispers.

I nod, unable to find the words to reply. I take in my dad's long nose and kind smile and wish for something I've not allowed myself to wish for in a long time – that he could be here.

My chin wobbles as I look to the other side of the locket. It's a photo of me and Jamie, the first one we ever took together. We look so young, so innocent, so unaware of the people we were destined to become.

"Do you like it?" Mum asks.

"I love it," I lie.

"Great! Now come on, let's go downstairs, take some photos, and get you married!"

Gulping, I take Mum's hand and walk away from the safety of my childhood bedroom and the mirror's poignant reminder of the bride I could have been.

44.

With my bridesmaids ahead of us in a separate vintage car, Mum and I travel together, holding hands and making menial small talk.

"How are you feeling?" Mum asks.

"Nervous."

Mum squeezes my hand. "You have someone waiting for you who worships the ground you walk on. What's there to be nervous for?"

My soul bleeds at her words. I rest my head on her shoulder and watch the world go by out of the window.

It feels like we arrive at the venue in seconds, even though the journey is well over half an hour. I pull a compact mirror out of my clutch bag and check my appearance. My makeup is immaculate, but all colour has drained from my face underneath the mask of cosmetics.

"Stop worrying. You look beautiful," Mum says as she slides out of the car.

I snap the mirror shut and drop it into the bag. It clangs against my apartment keys, then I leave the bag on the backseat and shuffle towards the door. The layers of my dress coil around my limbs, and I fight to move freely. "Who knew getting out of a car would be such a struggle."

"Tell me about it," Mum huffs, reaching to help me. "I don't think Alana's going to get a flattering photo of this."

We laugh at how ridiculous we must look, the silliness of the moment breaking some of my tension, until finally I'm outside and bathed in glorious sunshine. I take a second to admire the stately home I fell in love with all those months ago before following my giddy bridesmaids inside. We walk down the chestnut wood panelled hallways, my arm entwined with Mum's.

When we reach the doorway of the ceremony room, Hanadi greets us. "Are we a little nervous?" she asks, taking my hands and giving them a kind squeeze. "Everything's going to be okay. This is where you are meant to be."

Her words wake something in my core, and I return her smile.

Hanadi arranges us into a neat formation, with Laney to enter first, then Lily and Alisha and finally, me and Mum. "All good?" she asks.

"All good," we echo.

With one last smile, Hanadi slips into the ceremony room to tell everyone we are ready, and just like that, it's time to go.

"Is now a bad time to say I need a wee?" Laney hisses when the nerves clattering in the air get too much to bear. "Cass, do you mind if I waddle down the aisle?"

Fate chooses that moment for the music I am to walk down the aisle to kick in. A gentle instrumental version of our song.

Our song.

A sound escapes my lips, half hiccup, half sob.

As the staff open the heavy double doors for us to walk through, my bridal party turn to me. They look so unnaturally uniform thanks to their wedding makeover it's like being stared at by a swarm of robots.

A bead of sweat trickles down my back. The exit is right behind me. All I'd have to do is run. People wouldn't stop me, not if I told them what I was running from.

But then I see him.

Standing at the front of the room, tall and proud before his audience. His smile wide, his shoulders back, the whiff of confidence he exudes practically knocking me to my feet.

As the congregation turns for their first glimpse of the bride, I remember

263

Tara is somewhere in the crowd. A woman who lied to my face. A woman I welcomed into my life for a reason.

I pull my shoulders back, my target in sight. "Laney, as long as you don't trip over your dress, I don't care how you walk down the aisle."

My joke breaks the tension like the snap of an elastic band.

Turning back around, Laney takes her first steps down the aisle. Lily and Alisha set off next. I watch them go, then Mum wraps her hand around mine. "Are you ready?"

"I'm ready," I reply, then hand in hand, we set off towards the man I'm about to destroy.

45.

I fix my smile and make brief eye contact with our guests as I walk down the aisle. My cousin Noah, Shari and her girlfriend Tia, Jamie's cousin Lisa and her husband Graeme. I try to find Tara in the crowd. I want to see her one last time before everything happens, but there are too many people to search through, too many smiles I must return.

I nod at Mum's neighbours and Jamie's aunt Fiona as I continue my journey, inching towards my fate. When I'm almost at the front of the room, I look at Jamie.

Like a magnet, I feel myself being pulled towards him. He looks so handsome in his sharp suit, ecstasy etched into his every pore. A single tear escapes his right eye. He wipes it away, half self-conscious, half so happy he doesn't care who sees him cry. He acts his adoration so well that for a moment my insides swell with joy and I fall for it myself.

"Wow," he mouths when I reach him. He holds out his hand, a hand that is steady, no sign of nerves anywhere on his person.

With one last lingering look at my mum, I take it. We stand together at the end of the aisle, side by side, with me the only one aware of what will happen next.

A hush descends as our celebrant Anthony begins, his booming voice carrying to all four corners of the room. "We are gathered here on this joyous day to celebrate the union between Jamie Daniel Patrick and Cassandra Edwards. Judging by the love I feel from you all today, I know this is going to be a blessed marriage."

I brave glancing at Jamie. He tightens his grip on my hand and beams at me like I'm the most beautiful thing he's ever seen. I return his smile and start to count down the minutes until I can break free of him forever.

"Love is a special bond between two people. A solemn promise, an intimate connection, the very cornerstone of life itself," Anthony proclaims. I let his words wash over me and remind myself to breathe, just breathe.

The room is so silent you could hear a pin drop. Everyone listens intently, celebrating our love while we stand at the front of the room, the pinnacle of their hopes and dreams. Hopes and dreams that will soon shatter.

Adrenaline rushes through me at the thought but I don't have time to focus on the lightheaded sensation because before I know it, Anthony says the words I've been waiting for.

"I'd like to invite you to open the envelope left for you by Jamie and Cassandra. An envelope containing their love story in their own words, I believe."

Behind me, the sound of rustling paper rings out. I turn to Jamie. Our eyes connect. I hold his gaze, barely blinking. I don't want to miss the moment he's struck by the horror of realisation. I want to devour his pain, every bitter millisecond, savouring it like a meal at a fancy restaurant.

My body clenches as Anthony clears his throat, then he reads loud for all to hear. "Today is a day of joy, but each and every day Jamie and Cassie have been together could be described this way."

I blink and twist my head towards Anthony.

"It's common knowledge that soulmates are a rare thing, but in each other Jamie and Cassie have found theirs."

My eyebrows furrow.

That's not right. Those aren't the words I had printed.

This isn't how it's meant to go.

My nostrils flare, my mind racing with questions I don't have the answers to. I glance at Jamie only to find he's already watching me. He has been the whole time.

Then he winks, and suddenly I know.

He knew.

He knew all along.

46.

My heart drums in my throat as Anthony continues to read words that describe a love that doesn't exist between me and Jamie. Words he wasn't meant to be reading, words that change everything.

Every instinct I have tells me to flee, but Jamie's grip on my hand tightens, squeezing so hard I almost yelp. I try pull away, try flexing my fingers, but he's got me.

He's got me right where he wants me.

My eyes plead with Anthony to stop but he's too busy reciting Jamie's falsehoods to notice. He reaches the end of his script with a satisfied smile, then he tucks the story card back into the envelope. He straightens up to address the room and I realise what's coming next before he even says the words.

My brain roars, my heart thunders, and all I can think is that I need someone, anyone, to rescue me.

"And now, everyone's favourite part – the vows."

A bead of sweat trickles down the back of my neck.

This can't be it. This can't be happening. I cannot say those words.

Jamie pulls me so I'm facing him then he squeezes my hand so hard my bones crunch. That one moment, that one gesture, is all I need to know he will never let me go if I don't do something.

I do the only thing I can think to – I crumble to the floor as if I've fainted.

Gasps rings out around the room.

"Cassie!"

"Cass!"

In seconds, hands are on me, voices instructing me to sit up, shouts demanding to give me space so I can breathe. Then the loudest of them all cuts through the crowd.

"Move, move! I'm a pharmacist!" I hear her shoes against the tiled floor, then Gill's bony hands grip my shoulders. "Cassie, sit up. You're making a scene."

Slowly, I open my eyes and a sea of concerned faces appear in my field of vision. Central to them all is Jamie. There's an amused smirk on his face despite the sympathetic act he's trying to project.

"She's too warm in this dress," Gill says. "I knew she would be as soon as I saw it. Too many layers, too much fabric, and on a hot day like this too. Honestly, fashion these days! Did you eat this morning?"

Mum answers for me. "Yes, she did."

"Probably not enough. You girls and your diets," Gill scolds. She grips my hands. "Come on, up you get."

I do as I'm told because following Gill's commands is easier than trying to process how the hell everything went so wrong.

When I'm stood, Jamie clamps his hand around my waist. "Are you okay?"

"Of course she's okay," Gill dismisses. "She just needs to sit down and have some water."

"There's a backroom. Follow me," Hanadi says, bustling onto the scene and clearing a path for me.

Jamie steers me towards the room. My legs protest, but he's too strong for them to put up much of a fight. My bridal party follow us, but Gill shoos them away. "She doesn't need everyone fussing around her. Just get everyone back in their seats."

"Jeez, mum," Alisha sighs, but she obeys orders.

"Take Cassie through there and I'll grab her some water," Hanadi says, opening a side door for us. Gill and Jamie lead me to a chair in the small,

269

sparsely furnished room.

"Brides never think of the heat when they get these big dresses, do they?" Gill says, fluffing my dress up and exposing the bottom of my legs. I move my hand to cover myself, but Gill waves me away. "Oh, don't be shy Cassie, it's nothing we've both not seen before."

I catch Jamie's eye and he winks, a smug gesture that fries every nerve in my body.

"I hope fainting isn't an omen for this marriage. So many end in divorce these days, did you know that? All those years, wasted."

I flinch at Gill's words, then Hanadi enters the room carrying a glass of water. "Here you go. Ice cold."

"Thank you," I croak. I take the glass and try to drink but my hands are shaking so much I spill on my dress.

"Here, let me help," Jamie offers.

Before I can protest, he rests his hand on the glass and tips it towards my mouth. He thrusts it too hard, sending too much water down my throat. I choke and push his arm away, spluttering water down myself.

"Oops," Jamie says before turning to Gill and Hanadi. "Could you give us a second? I want to check Cass is okay."

Gill and Hanadi nod. I lurch to beg them to stay, but as Jamie rests his hand on the back of my neck, I'm silenced. I watch the door swing shut behind them, and then I'm alone with Jamie.

For a moment, the only sound is the faint hum of conversation coming from the ceremony room, but then Jamie lets out a hiss of air. "You really thought you were going to get away with it, didn't you? You thought you could stand there and embarrass me, and I wouldn't have a clue what you were up to."

"I don't know what you're talking about." I try to project confidence, but my voice comes out scratchy and weak.

Jamie pinches tighter on the back of my neck. "Come on, Cass. I'm not stupid. I'm not like you."

I move to turn away, but he grabs my chin and forces me to face him. My blood freezes at the emptiness behind his eyes.

"I've known you found out about me from the start. Didn't you think I'd notice you flinching every time my phone lit up with a notification or that strange texts were suddenly being sent to me? Didn't you think I'd find it odd you were creating a surprise keepsake I wasn't allowed to know anything about when you've harped on about every detail of this wedding for months?"

"I told you, I don't know what you're talking about."

"Why are you denying it, Cass? It's over. Look around you. Look at what happened to your pathetic plan. Surely you can give me enough credit to admit I'd know when you were lying."

"You'd know all about lying, wouldn't you?" I fire.

My anger makes Jamie happy. "That's the Cass I was hoping to see today. I knew she'd come out to play. I can predict your every action, you see. I know you, Cass, inside and out."

"We don't know each other at all."

Jamie snorts. "Your laptop password is Paris457. Your phone passcode is 123789. You aim to leave work at half past four every day. You have the same best friends you've had since school. I know you, Cass. You can't keep shit from me. You can't do shit to me. I've been there for every fake account you set up, every card you doctored then ordered. Did you think I wasn't onto it all? Cass, I've been accessing your life our entire relationship. I've read every text you've ever sent, seen every email you've ever received."

My mouth dries. "What?"

"Oh, don't be so dramatic. A little surveillance between partners is no big deal," Jamie shrugs.

"No big deal? Jamie, you've violated my privacy!"

"Well, it's a good job I did, isn't it? If I'd not found that Abby Dunne email on your laptop, who knows what could have happened today. I'd have never been able to create my own cards. Beautiful design, by the way. Real classy."

The walls close in on me. I hunt for air in this oppressive room but then Jamie crouches before me and I dare not even move to breathe.

"It's over, Cass. I've burned every one of your cards. I've deleted every stupid text you sent me. Your little revenge plot? It's finished. I've won. You made it easy because you're so easy," Jamie whispers, brushing a strand of hair from my face. I move away but he grips my chin, pinching the flesh tight. "You genuinely thought you could mess with me and come out and top." Then he laughs and lets me go.

Reeling, I turn away and curl into my devastation.

Jamie stands up and stretches, flexing his neck. "So, what's it going to be?"

"What do you mean?"

"You've fainted. You've bought yourself some time, but now what? Are you going to go out there any tell everyone what I've done and admit you tried to stitch me up? Are you going to go out there and marry me?"

I recoil at the suggestion.

"Well, what happens next?"

Truthfully, I don't know. I never imagined I'd be in this situation. Never imagined Jamie snooping on me or creating his own cards to swap with mine.

I can't tell people I know about Jamie's cheating. They'll ask why I went through with the wedding, then what do I say? I did it so I could rack up debt on his credit cards? So I could harass him and pin the blame on someone else? So I could humiliate him in front of everyone he knows and loves? Listing it makes it all sound so dirty. Listing it makes me sound no better than him.

But what's my other choice - saying 'I do'? I would rather die.

As I drown in desperation, Jamie laughs, cruel and vindictive. "You don't know what to do, do you?" My silence is the only answer he needs.

He crouches before me once more, his head tilted, his eyes mocking. "There's no Abby Dunne to hide behind now. No fake account, no cards. Just you, me, and the truth. So, what next?"

My chin wobbles. "They'll find out about you eventually."

"I wouldn't bet on it. I've kept it hidden for so many years now. Besides, that's a worry for another day. Right here, right now, you've a choice to make, and I can't wait to see how this plays out. The ball's in your court, Cassie. What's your next move?"

My eyes gloss with tears as my brain works in overdrive, searching for answers but finding none.

"I... I..."

"What was that? I didn't hear you," Jamie says, cupping his ear and grinning.

I'm about to respond when an almighty roar comes from the ceremony room, one so fury filled my organs flinch at the sound.

My head whips around. "What was that?" I ask, but it's clear from his dumbfounded expression that Jamie is as clueless as I am.

47.

With Jamie distracted, I push past him and run to the door. Opening it, I unveil a scene that can only be described as carnage. The love that was in the air has shattered. Everyone is on their feet, shouting, pointing, holding people back as they fight to find an outlet for their anger.

I sense Jamie behind me, his body too close for comfort, but I'm too awestruck by the riot before me to cower from him.

Amidst the arguing, Colin spies Jamie. "You bastard!" he roars, his thick fingers outstretched, ready to wrap around Jamie's throat. Two of Jamie's uncles hold him back, but it's a struggle for them to do so.

I stumble into the ceremony room. The tsunami of pain in the air smashes into me, making me sway on my already unsteady feet. "What's going on?" I ask but my voice disappears in the uproar.

Everywhere I look, all I see is devastation – Anne weeping into her hands, my mum in the arms of her best friend Anita, Lily and Alisha tripping over their dresses to get to me, Laney frozen, her face twisted in horror.

"What's going on?" I call out again, louder this time.

It's as if people only just remember my existence. My naïve words send a ripple of agony through the crowd, their cloud of anger parting and a gush of sympathy filling the gap.

Alisha reaches me first, gripping my hand so tight her knuckles protrude through her skin. "An email's been sent to everyone. Cass, Jamie's… Jamie's cheating on you."

Jamie hears those words and takes a step backwards to flee, but he doesn't get the chance to because Martin grabs him. "What have you done? What have you done?!"

Jamie's mouth opens and closes but no explanation leaves his lips. I could watch him fluster forever but another hand coils itself around mine and pulls me away from him. My legs fall over themselves as they move through the crowd, steered by Lily holding one hand, Alisha holding the other. They charge towards the raging crowd and then Simon appears, pushing people back so my friends can help me escape.

"Move, let them through!" he bellows.

Some people part, some stay frozen to the spot, but guided by Simon, Alisha and Lily find a way through. In this moment, being dragged away from the chaos, I've never loved my friends more.

"What's happened?" I ask as we dash through the venue and out into the sunlight.

Alisha stops and tightens her grip on my hand. "One of Jamie's cousins checked their email while we were waiting for you to come back out. There was a message. It's… it's not good, Cass."

I'm about to ask more but the sound of pandemonium approaching from behind nudges me onwards.

"I want to go home."

I don't need to say more. My friends pull me to the car I'd arrived in, now parked around the side of the building. The driver jumps when he sees me and stubs out the cigarette he was smoking. "Are you ready for your photos already?" he asks but his face falls when he picks up on the hysteria I'm running from.

"He… he was cheating on me," I confess.

As soon as the words leave my mouth, the driver springs into action. He goes to start the car while Alisha and Lily stuff me into the backseat. Over their shoulder, I see that some of the guests have spilled outside to find me, their sympathy as potent as chloroform. My friends notice them too. They push the material of the dress harder, cramming me into the car like their life depends on it.

"You're in. Do you want us to come with you?" Lily asks.

"No, not yet. Give me an hour alone. I need to be alone right now."

Alisha nods and closes the car door. "I love you," she mouths through the window, then the car bursts into life. We speed away from the venue, the tyres crunching on the gravel driveway until the sea of people desperate to console me are no longer in sight.

"Are you wanting to go back to the house I picked you up from?" the driver asks a few minutes into the drive.

I shake my head and check the bag I left in the car. My keys are in there, as planned, even though nothing else about this day went like it was supposed to. Beside my keys sits my phone. I snatch it up and open my email but find no 'Jamie is cheating' message waiting for me.

The driver coughs. "Sorry, sweetheart, but I need to know where we're going."

I tell the driver the address of my apartment. After that, he doesn't speak to me. He glances at me in the rear-view mirror like he wants to, but whenever he psyches himself up, he thinks better of it.

The silence suits me fine. After all, what is there to say?

I pull hair slides from my hair until the elaborate style I paid so much for is ruined and my hair tumbles around my shoulders. Then I have nothing to do but sit with my thoughts.

I don't understand. I don't know how I ended up here. That should worry me but I'm too tired to care.

Exhaustion wasn't part of the plan. Emptiness wasn't either, but that's all that consumes me. There has been no tidal wave of elation, no euphoria at Jamie's destruction. If anything, all I'm left with is the same feeling of nothingness that's plagued me for weeks.

I turn my attention to the window, the world on the other side of it moving as it had been thirty minutes earlier, and interrupt the stagnant silence. "Do you think everything happens for a reason?"

The driver sits with my question for a moment. "I think... I think sometimes bad things happen to good people. There's no reason for it or no way to make sense of it, but they happen. That's just the luck of the draw."

"What are you meant to do when bad things happen to you for no reason?"

"I guess you carry on living and hope things get better."

I nod, even though nothing about the driver's answer makes me want to agree with him. He makes it sound so simple, no big deal, but all I see is a mountain before me, one I'm not sure I have the energy to climb.

I turn back to the window and stare blankly ahead until the car slows to a stop outside my apartment.

I gather my dress to get out of the car but before I leave, the driver stops me. "Look, sweetheart, I'm not going to tell you things will be perfect and that this won't hurt tomorrow, but you'll get through this. Take care, okay?"

Nodding, I climb out of the vehicle and duck inside before he sees my tears.

Home has never felt so unlike home before. Tiptoeing through my apartment is like walking through a museum. Eerie, mute objects lay there, illustrating a multitude of memories now lost forever. The bed that's a little rumpled from last being slept in, the washing basket half full of clothes we need to clean, fingerprints left behind by the ghosts of who we were. Even the air smells stale, the apartment's way of acknowledging the love that once lived here is now dead.

I check my phone again. Forty-seven missed calls and countless messages are queued and waiting for acknowledgement. I drop it to the floor and stand in the living room, swaying in the abyss of nothingness until I can't take it anymore. With no idea what else to do, I pour myself a glass of wine. The first one slips down easily, so I pour myself another, then another.

Hazy from alcohol, I strut into the living room. Wine sloshes over the side of my glass and onto the carpet, the liquid seeping into the fibres. I should care, but what is there to care about anymore? I tip my wineglass over more, the puddle at my feet growing.

A burst of laughter escapes from me. The sound ricochets into the silence.

Out of the corner of my eye, I catch sight of the boxes of Jamie's new clothes. My body moves instinctively. I rip them open, an animal tearing apart a carcass. Grabbing a pair of scissors, I go to work destroying every item in there until Jamie will only be laughed at should he ever try to return the contents. Next, I move to his existing wardrobe, cutting the crotch out of every pair of trousers and chopping holes in his shirts.

Jamie's clothes lay in a pile of maimed rags on the floor, but I still don't feel that elusive sense of triumph I've been chasing.

Stumbling for more wine, I glug another glass then head back to the living room. Acidic remnants glisten on my lips as I look around. The obnoxious sofa we bought thinking it would last for years, the idiotic, smiling photographs encased in carefully selected frames. The promise of a future surrounds me, a future that never existed, and I want it gone.

I pick up the nearest photograph – a shot of us on the grass at Jamie's cousin's wedding last spring – and hurl at the wall. The frame splinters and glass shatters to the floor.

The two of us distorted behind fragments of broken glass seems so apt I can't help but smile. I reach for another photo. This one was taken at a Christmas market, hot chocolates in our hands and happiness oozing from every pore. Again, I launch it at the wall, and it breaks into a thousand pieces.

I spin around to find another photo, something else to break, something else to hurt, but the sight of a pale, traumatised person in the doorway stops me in my tracks.

I go to speak but they get there first.

"It was you, wasn't it?"

48.

Jamie and I stand, stuck in a frozen stand off for what feels like an eternity, until he finds his voice once more. "It was you," he repeats. "You sent that email."

"No -"

Jamie takes a step forward, his nostrils flaring. "Don't lie to me, Cass. You've been out to get me for weeks. Who else could it be?"

"I don't know, Jamie. Read it and see who it's from."

"It wasn't sent to me!" Jamie shouts. The anger in his voice is so powerful it could crack the walls, but it barely registers in my tipsy state.

"If I'd sent the email, I'd be laughing in your face right now. I wish I sent it, but I didn't."

"I don't believe you."

"That's not my problem." I go to walk away, but Jamie grabs my arm. "What did you write? What did it say?"

I wriggle to pull free, but Jamie holds strong. "How should I know? I've not seen it."

"You're lying!" Jamie snarls, a speck of spit flying from his mouth and landing on my cheek.

My heart flutters as it finally dawns on me how enraged he is. "If I was planning to send a message to everyone, don't you think you'd have found out? You were hacking my email, even the Abby Dunne one, remember?"

Jamie blinks, my logic too truthful to fight off. "Then who did you tell?"

"Do you seriously think I told anyone about this?!" I cry. "I didn't want anyone to know you'd betrayed me! I wanted to destroy you."

"Well, you've done that alright."

"Jamie, I didn't send the email!"

Jamie hisses then lets me go. My arm stings, angry red marks left behind where his fingers were. I want to rub my skin and check it's okay, but I don't want to give Jamie the satisfaction of knowing he's hurt me.

He paces the room, raking his hand through his hair, before spinning on his heel to face me. "If it wasn't you, then who the fuck was it?!"

I shrug. "You've a long list of exes. It could be any of them."

"Very funny, Cass."

"It is amusing if you think about it. Half an hour ago you were bragging about how you wouldn't get caught, and now everyone knows about you, even your mum and dad."

Jamie's nostrils twitch. "Don't."

"What, you were fine to lie and cheat, but you didn't want anyone to know about it?"

Jamie's hands coil into fists. "I said don't! Do you have any idea how upset my parents are? I've just been humiliated in front of my family and friends –"

His words explode inside me. "That's what you're focusing on, your embarrassment? The fact that your parents know you aren't their little angel anymore?"

"You shouldn't have hurt them like that."

"I didn't hurt them - you did! You chose to have an affair with Tara –"

Jamie blinks. "Tara?"

"I know about the two of you. I saw a photo of you both kissing."

Jamie's eyebrows knit together. "I don't know what you saw or what you think you saw, Cass, but I never had an affair with Tara."

An awful tingling makes its way from my head to my toes. "You're lying."

"I'm not."

"But... but the photo... I saw it."

"Well, whatever you saw, it's not what it looks like. About a month ago, I asked for Tara's help with finding a new job and tried to kiss her, but she pushed me off. There was no affair. There was barely even a kiss."

Jamie's words ring in my ears. I shake my head to dislodge them from my brain, but they hold tight.

"You can shake your head all you like but it's true. Tara wouldn't have anything to do with me. That's not to say I didn't try, but she always said no."

"You're lying," I whisper.

"Do you know something, Cass? For once I'm not."

My legs give way. I lean against the wall for support, my shot nerves brewing with the wine in my stomach.

The sound of Jamie's laughter twists inside me. "Wait, were you going to say the cards were from Tara? Is that why you asked her to help with the wedding? Was I supposed to think she was the person texting me too?"

My pained silence is enough of an answer.

"This is brilliant, Cass! And there I was, thinking you were going to blame the mysterious Abby Dunne for everything. Never once did I think of Tara! I thought you'd only asked for her help so you could get close to her and find out what she knew. I didn't realise you were trying to frame her because you thought we were having an affair! Wow, you got it so wrong, didn't you?" Jamie laughs again, but his laughter subsides as he studies me. "Did you do something else to Tara?"

I don't speak, don't tell him about the incriminating card and burner phone that are planted in her house right now, even though they're all I can think of.

"You did, didn't you? This is amazing! What did you do, Cass? How badly have you messed up?"

I look at him and all I can think of is wiping that arrogant expression off his face. "What did I do? I destroyed you, Jamie. You're done, in every sense of the word."

Jamie scoffs. "You didn't do shit, Cass. You couldn't even get who I was dating right, so I doubt whatever else you think you've pulled off will have worked."

"Open your eyes! You can't lie your way out of this. Everyone knows about you now."

"They'll forgive me."

"You're crazy if you think that! You're always going to be the lying, cheating scumbag who lost a good woman."

"And you're the woman who couldn't keep her man," Jamie fires back.

"Jamie, I don't want to keep you. I never have. I just wanted to ruin you. I might not have sent that email, but your mountain of debt is all on me."

Jamie's eyes narrow. "What debt?"

"You spent so much time focusing on me, you never thought to pay more attention to yourself, did you? Maybe you should check your bank statements before the end of the month, although I imagine looking at them won't be pretty."

Jamie's jaw goes slack. "What have you done?"

"Your credit cards? The ones I know nothing about? You booked a honeymoon on them, aren't you sweet? It was a bit much to buy yourself all new clothes for it, but what can I expect from someone who's secretly such a big spender?"

"You... you took my credit cards?"

I nod. "And I didn't use Abby Dunne or anyone else for the transactions. I used you. Your tablet, your email, your cards."

"That's illegal! That's identity fraud!"

"You'd know all about identity fraud, wouldn't you, Todd Goldman? Really, of all the names in the world, that's the one you pick?"

Jamie speaks through gritted teeth. "All I did was tell a few bimbos a fake name, but you've committed a crime. I'll get high fives at the pub, but you'll be in prison."

I stick my jaw out. "Prove it."

"What?"

"Prove it was me. I dare you to try."

The air between us crackles as our loathing intensifies. Jamie waits for me to crumble but I won't, not this time.

A beat of silence rings out, the world moving in slow motion as we glare at each other, and I wonder what's going to happen next.

I don't have long to ponder my question.

Suddenly, Jamie roars and lunges forward.

Whatever I was expecting him to do, it wasn't hurl the full weight of his impressive frame on me. He throws me hard against the wall. My head cracks against it, the sound ringing in my ears. A gasp is caught in my throat, one that stays trapped there as Jamie wraps his thick hands around my neck.

"You bitch!" he bellows.

My nails scratch his skin, clawing at his fingers, his wrists, anything that might set me free, but he holds strong, slamming me against the wall so forcefully my bones rattle.

Jamie has never been violent towards me before, but the person I'm looking at isn't Jamie. His face is a contortion of hatred, a half melted, waxwork version of the man I knew. His hands coil tighter, the hunger to crush the life from me consuming Jamie's every move. I gasp for air but find none.

Then I spot the clock on the wall behind him. Ten to three. Ten to three and the world around me is dimming, the edges of my vision fading into grey.

As Jamie's hands compress tighter around my throat, I don't think of revenge or winning, only one clear, screaming thing – I am going to die at the hands of this man.

49.

Because it's the only thing I can think to do, I raise my knee and ram it into Jamie's crotch. The layers of my dress muffle the impact, but Jamie's momentarily shocked by my aggression.

A moment is all I need. Moving my hands from trying to peel his fingers from my throat, I press my thumbs into his eyeballs. Jamie roars and jerks his head backwards. As he does, my freshly manicured nails scour his cheeks.

He screams and staggers away from me, but I barely hear his bellows. I fall to my knees, gasping for air, my throat throbbing as if Jamie's hands are still wrapped around it.

"You've cut my face!"

"You strangled me!" I protest, but my voice barely comes out as a rasp.

Jamie slams his way towards the kitchen. He splashes water onto his bleeding cheeks, then holds onto the edge of the sink like he's gripping the edge of a cliff. His shoulders heave up and down as he tries to regulate his breathing.

Water drips from Jamie's chin, the noise rhythmical against the metal basin. I watch him on tenterhooks, ready to run should he come for me again, only his unpredictable rage seems to have dissipated. In its place is something else, something equally terrifying.

"You're all the same, you know," Jamie spits, his tone icier than I've ever heard it before. "You women, you're all the same. You play it so cool, so coy, so full of bullshit. You say, 'I want a man who listens, who brings me flowers, who believes in *equality'*." Jamie hisses the word. "It's all lies. What you want is a man who makes you beg for it, who walks into a bar and could knock out anyone who looks at you the wrong way."

"Jamie, what are you talking about?"

He spins to face me, livid once more. "Are you seriously telling me you'd have looked at me twice if I didn't have these muscles, this confidence?"

"I fell in love with you because of who you were, or who I thought you were anyway!" I cry, tears springing to my eyes because, as much as it pains me to admit I once loved the twisted hulk of a man before me, it's true.

Jamie shakes his head. "That's what you fell in love with, but that's not what you *noticed*. That's never what anyone notices. Laura McDermott didn't notice how many times I stayed after school to listen to her problems. The girls at university didn't care if you were the one who got them back to their room safely when they were too drunk. They wanted the guy buying all the drinks, the larger than life, biggest mouth in the room."

"Jamie," I breathe. "You haven't been to university in over ten years. What has it got to do with anything?"

"As always, Cass, you're missing the point," Jamie says through gritted teeth. "Tell me the name of a celebrity crush people have who is anything but tall and in shape. Tell me the last time someone said, 'he listens, it's so sexy'. That's not what you want! You women, you go out in your little dresses, making eyes at anyone who looks like they could bankroll your shopping habit, and all the while normal men are supposed to be grateful for any scrap of attention they get."

"Do you hear yourself? Do you hear how insane you sound?"

"You don't get it, do you? For years I listened to you women go on and on about how there were no nice guys in the world, how all men were horrible, how men only wanted one thing. I was a shoulder to cry on. I gave advice, I sympathised, and do you know what? It got me nowhere. Nowhere but the friendzone. So, I snapped, Cassie. I snapped and I became that guy. And guess what? I've never had as much pussy in my life."

If I wasn't already leaning against the wall, I'd have fallen to the floor at Jamie's words. "You're telling me you cheated because a few girls rejected you when you were younger?"

"Women, they systematically reject you –"

"God forbid women thinking they can pick who they want to be with," I snap.

Jamie glares at me. "I wouldn't expect you to understand, Cassie. You don't exactly have the brain capacity."

"If I don't have the brain capacity then why did you want to marry me?!" The question bursts from me, the one I've wanted to know the answer to all along.

Jamie comes close, so close I can see the fresh blood from his scratches glistening. My body tenses at his proximity, a response that only amuses him.

"You were sweet. You kept doing stuff for me. You were so grateful whenever I did anything nice in return. It was like living with a puppy. You never asked any questions, just ran when I clicked my fingers. You made it so easy, Cassie. I could do whatever I wanted as long as I came home in time for dinner."

I shake my head, but Jamie nods.

"Do you want to know why I did this? Why I got away with it for so long? It was because I could, Cassie. Because I could."

My brain reels from the poison in Jamie's admission. I fight to retain my composure, struggling to hold on so much so I only notice him drawing even closer when his face is inches away from mine.

"It's a shame it went like this. You would have made the perfect wife. So forgiving, so eager, so grateful. Plus, you've got great tits." Jamie's glinting eyes drop to my chest. I raise my hand to cover myself, and Jamie laughs. "What, can't I say that anymore?"

He reaches for my cheek, but I push his hand away. "Don't touch me," I whisper.

Laughing louder, Jamie breezes past me. I don't follow. I need a moment to catch my breath while his callousness rings in my ears.

By the time I build up the courage to move, Jamie is stood in the centre of the living room with his cut-up clothes in his hands. "I'm disappointed at this. This is a little stereotypical, Cass."

"Everyone has to think I took some sort of revenge," I shrug, my voice hoarse.

"And this is what you chose to do," Jamie says with a mocking tut, dropping the rags that were once his clothes. "I'll out you for what you've done, you know. You'll be arrested before you know it. That's the thing with you women – you think you can do it the same as men, but you never can. There's always a flaw or something you did wrong. Probably while you were bitching about your best friend or getting your nails done."

Feigning a confidence I don't feel, I take a step forward. "Good luck with that."

Jamie's eyes twinkle. "You know, if you'd have shown me this Cass from the start, I might have really loved you."

"And if you'd have shown me who you really were, I'd have done what everyone did before and reject you."

Jamie scoffs, then with one last withering look at me, he walks away. When he reaches the front door, he turns back to face me. "I really hope you didn't go after Tara in your little plan. I mean it when I say nothing happened there."

My face must give away the truth because Jamie can't fight his smile.

"Oh Cass, imagine if the only person you've ruined today is her." With one final laugh, Jamie leaves the apartment, and my knees give way with the slam of the door.

50.

True to her word, Alisha comes to the apartment with my mum, Laney, and Lily an hour after I fled the wedding. Their questions when they see the bruises forming on my neck hit like arrows.

"What happened?!"

"Did he do this to you?"

I don't answer them, not when I have questions of my own. "What was in the email? Will someone show it to me?"

Everyone bristles at the mention of the email.

"Cass, you don't need to read it right now. There are more important things to worry about," Mum soothes. She reaches for me, but I shake her off.

"Please –" I begin, but Alisha's hand on my arm silences me.

"We can talk about the email later, but we need to get you sorted first. Your mum is going to call the police. Laney and Lily are going to remove all traces of him from this apartment, and I'm going to get you out of that dress. Okay?"

There's something about having someone as calm as Alisha take control of a situation that's impossible to resist. I nod at her instructions. Lily gets to work straight away, but Laney hovers, her vision fixed on my injured neck.

"Laney?" Alisha snaps her fingers in front of Laney's face.

Laney jumps, her cheeks flooding with colour. "Sorry," she flusters before dashing away. I stare after my friend, wishing more than anything she hadn't just looked at me like I was a stranger.

Alisha takes my hand and I let her lead me to my bedroom. She strips me from my wedding dress. Neither of us comment on how she'd been with me that morning to help me into it, but I know it's on her mind.

As soon as the dress is off, Alisha bundles it in her arms, screwing it up small as if making it disappear would fix everything. "I've laid some fresh pyjamas out for you. Change into them. You'll feel better when you do."

She goes to leave the room, but before she can I call her name. "Please, Alisha. Please let me read it."

Alisha pauses but she hands over her phone. "We're here when you need us, okay?"

I nod and watch her go, then turn my attention to the glowing screen before me.

You deserve to know the truth about Jamie Patrick. Serial liar, serial cheat. I could go on, but I think it's best he tells you his story in his own words. So here it is, a link to Jamie's website. Jamie Patrick aka 'The Good Bad Guy's Guide'

I almost laugh at the simple brilliance of it all. Sharing Jamie's website, his life in his own words, more implicating than any poetic story card could be.

Then I read the email address of the sender.

Tara.

Tara sent this.

I hold Alisha's phone to my chest. Of course it was her. The wedding information pack I gave her that day at the apartment had everyone's contact details in it.

She saved me.

I want nothing more than to run to Tara, fall at her feet and thank her. Without the cards, I had nothing. Without her, I'd have been forced to admit I knew Jamie was cheating. Then, when word of his debt got out and Jamie insisted he wasn't to blame for it, everyone would have looked to me. I'd have been arrested. I'd have a criminal record. I'd never be able to teach again.

Then it hits me – the card I left in Tara's house. The phone. The evidence I planted so I could destroy her too.

I leap to my feet and throw on the nearest clothes I can find, frantically pulling them over my exhausted limbs. I'm wrestling a t-shirt over my head when Alisha enters the bedroom.

"What are you doing?"

"I need to go somewhere."

"Cass, the police are on their way." Ignoring her, I reach for a pair of shoes. "Cass, stop!"

"What's going on?" Mum asks, bustling into the room. She takes one look at my frantic state and softens. "Cassie, sit down."

"I don't want to sit! I need to go!" I protest, trying to push my way out of the room, but Mum grabs my face, staring into my eyes like she's looking into my soul.

"He's gone, Cass. He's done something terrible, and it's over. I need you to hear that. I need you to process it."

I jerk my head to free myself from Mum's grip, but she doesn't let me go. She holds me steady, her eyes boring into mine until a chasm opens in the centre my chest and raw, new agony spills from it.

I think of Tara and the evidence I need to remove from her house before it's too late but then I think of Jamie. His poisonous words, the hateful way he looked at me, and his grip around my neck. I think of the last few years of my life, every moment of happiness, every lie, and I can't help it - I fall into my mum's arms and shed the tears I should have cried when I first saw that photo.

Sometime later - it could be five minutes or five hours, I'm too distressed to tell - the police show up. Two women, one younger than me, one older. One wearing a wedding ring, one not.

We sit in the living room while I recite the pain of my day, minus the parts where I am anything but the innocent party. My replies are robotic, clipped, and vague. Jamie cheated, I didn't know, he came to the apartment and attacked me.

When I can no longer speak to answer the officers' questions, Mum and my friends fill in the blanks for me. They tell anecdotes that were once viewed as charming but now, in light of the truth, sound controlling.

The sympathy from the officers is overwhelming. They take photos of my injuries and tell me they will be in contact soon. Mum walks them back to their squad car, whispering about counselling when she thinks she's out of earshot, then it's just me, my friends, and a gulf of pain. The trauma of the day is etched into everyone's face. Laney especially looks stricken, so much so I almost ask if she needs to lie down.

"I know this is a stupid question, but how are you holding up?" Lily asks, handing me a cup of tea.

"I'm okay. Better than Laney, by the look of it," I joke but she crumbles at my words and presses her hands over her face.

"Cass, please don't hate me but I need to tell you something," she says. Her voice comes out reedy and thin, then I remember her frozen horror at the wedding, and I know. I just know.

51.

"When?" I ask.

"When what?" Lily repeats, looking from Laney to me and back again, but Laney doesn't respond. Lily takes in her traumatised expression then steps backwards. "No. No, you wouldn't do that to Cass."

Laney flinches. "It was only a kiss."

"What?!"

Alisha holds her hand up to stop Lily's shouts, to stop this moment, but it's happening. I keep my gaze on Laney, waiting for the story to unravel.

Laney sits beside me on the sofa. "It was right at the start of your relationship. Remember I wasn't there the night you met? Remember how I was on holiday when you brought Jamie to Alisha's to meet everyone properly?"

I close my eyes, trying to not remember those bittersweet memories.

"It was about a week after that. I'd gone to a party. A friend of a friend, you know how it is when you tag along. I got wasted. Wasted, Cass, I mean it. I don't think I've ever been as drunk."

"Is that meant to make her feel better?" Lily hisses.

"Lily," Alisha interjects.

Lily looks incredulous. "You're telling *me* off?"

I wrap my arms around myself, unable to stand the sound of my best friends arguing or the tension in this room.

"I was showing off, trying to fit in, you know how I get. Then Jamie walked in. He was so confident and charming. We got chatting, then…

then it just happened."

A groan escapes me, one I don't remember commanding my mouth to make.

"You've got to remember, at this point I had no idea who he was. He was some guy I met, not even worth mentioning. I didn't know he was your Jamie! I couldn't even remember his name the next day. I left the house thinking I'd never see him again, then three weeks later you shared your first photo as a couple. When I saw it, I felt sick."

I want a moment to digest this news but Lily leaps in. "And you didn't think to tell Cass you'd kissed her new boyfriend?"

"Of course I thought about it! I thought about it all the time, but I was so scared. Then time went on and it felt like I'd left it too late to speak up. Besides, Cass was so happy. I didn't want to ruin that. Cass, you were so happy," Laney says, her bottom lip quivering.

I can't look at her, can't listen to her remind me of how happy I once was.

"This is insane, Laney. You don't kiss your friend's boyfriend," Lily cries.

"I didn't know who he was!"

"You should have said something as soon as you found out!"

"Lily," Alisha warns, but Lily turns to her, outraged.

"Why are you saying my name? Why not hers? She let Cass waste years of her life with that man!"

"Lily!" Alisha snaps, nodding in my direction.

Lily takes one look at my face and pales. "Cass, I didn't mean…"

I shake my head, cutting her off. A heavy silence weighs down on us until Laney breaks it.

"I thought about telling you, I really did, but the longer it went on, the less sense it made to. The first time I met Jamie, he introduced himself as if we'd never met. I started to wonder if maybe I'd got it wrong? Maybe it wasn't him I kissed that night?"

Tears fall from Laney's eyes and land on the sofa, leaving little marks in their place. I stare at them, transfixed.

"I promise I spoke to him about it. He said it was the start of your relationship and you weren't exclusive then -"

"That's a lie," I cut in.

"I know that now, Cass. I knew that a few months after the kiss too, but it was too late. I'd already decided not to tell you. The longer I left it, the worse it looked if I did say something. I couldn't exactly say, 'happy one year anniversary. By the way, I think I kissed your boyfriend eleven months ago', could I?"

"You should have said something," Alisha says.

"And risked losing my friend?"

"Well, you've lost three of them now," Lily states.

The bluntness of her words makes me flinch. I look around the room at Lily's furious stance and Alisha's disappointed one. My chest compresses at the thought of something else in my life being broken, another thing lost to Jamie Patrick.

"Cass, I know you must hate me right now but when Jamie talked about that night, it made sense not to tell you. He made it sound like nothing happened, like you were both still dating other people. I know I should have said something, but I... I..."

I finish her sentence for her. "You made a mistake."

Laney nods and dissolves into shaking sobs. Lily turns away, but I can't do it. I can't watch Laney break. I reach out and wrap my arms around her. Her body judders as she cries on my shoulder, her tears coming from the pit of her soul.

As I hold Laney, I wonder what would have happened if she'd told me the truth all those years ago. Would I have left Jamie as soon as I found out? Would I be in a wedding dress today, about to marry someone else? Would I be single, happy, and free?

And the biggest question of all - would I have believed Laney, or would Jamie have twisted the truth so I saw the world through his eyes, the way he had so many times throughout our relationship?

I pull out of the hug and clasp Laney's hands. "Jamie was clever. He fooled everyone. In your situation, I'm not sure I'd have done any differently."

"Do you mean that?" Laney asks, her chin still wobbly.

"I mean it, I promise."

At that moment the front door closes, marking Mum's return. She enters the living room to find a thick tension clogging the atmosphere. "What's happened?"

"Nothing," I reply.

"Cass," Mum begins, but Alisha shakes her head and Mum stops. She studies me, assessing my needs in the way only a parent can. "You look exhausted, sweetheart. Maybe we should let you get some rest?"

"Maybe," I nod, even though sleep is the last thing on my mind.

"Why don't you go to bed? We'll stay and –"

"No. Please, come back first thing tomorrow if you want, but tonight I want some time alone."

"Being alone is the last thing you need," Alisha says.

"I'll be fine."

"Cass, I'm spending the night with you, end of discussion," Mum states.

I take in her earnest expression and know whatever I say will be pointless. "Fine, but will you get my stuff from yours first? All my things are still there."

"We'll stay with you while your mum does that," Alisha offers.

I shake my head. "I love you all, but I need half an hour alone. Please." Everyone hesitates, but Mum nods.

"We're coming around first thing tomorrow," Lily warns, wagging her finger at me.

I give assurance I'll be fine and say goodbye, then everyone leaves. The silence after their departure screams louder than their collective voices. Part of me breathes in the peace, the rest is on the verge of begging them to come back.

I pad through the apartment, marvelling at the difference my friends have made. It's like I'm in someone else's home. The cut-up clothes are long gone, the walls now bare, all traces of my previous life nowhere to be found.

Sinking wearily onto the sofa, I find my phone and open the photo Debbie sent me.

It's a photo of Jamie and Tara kissing, there's no doubt about that, but when I look at it again without the cloud of anger, it's Jamie's hands on Tara, Jamie leading the kiss. Sure, I can't see her push him away, but maybe if Debbie would have taken the photo a second later, that's what it would have shown.

What's on the screen is a snapshot of a moment without context. I mean, how many times have we seen photos of celebrities blinking at the exact second the camera shutter closes, ones that are then splashed across the front pages of newspapers to make them appear drunk? Or photos of ourselves when we're having the best time, only the way our expressions are caught makes it look anything but?

They say a picture is worth a thousand words, but within those thousand words are multiple different stories, each one open to interpretation. Yes, this is a photo of a kiss, but I didn't stop to question what that kiss meant before I walked down the path of vengeance, ready to ruin someone who then went on to save me.

Now it's my turn to save her.

Dropping my phone, I race from my apartment to my car. I break every speed limit on the way to Tara's house, but it doesn't feel like I'm driving fast enough. One minute could be the difference between Nico finding the phone and Nico being blissfully unaware, Tara's future obliterated or Tara's future intact.

I press my foot on the accelerator harder, take corners sharper, until I screech to a halt outside their house. A light is on downstairs. I can't tell if I'm relieved or not to know that they are home, milling about while the planted evidence waits patiently to be discovered.

I run to the front door and bang on it repeatedly. I'm making a scene, I know, but there's too much at stake to worry about the neighbours. When the door opens, I've no idea what I'll say, no idea what I'll do, but it doesn't matter. What matters is fixing my mistake.

Blood pounds in my ears as footsteps draw closer from inside the house. I fix a smile on my face, only when the front door opens and a tear-stained Tara stares back at me, I know it's too late.

52.

For a split second I think Tara's going to close the door on me, but instead she sighs. "What are you doing here, Cassie?"

"I came to thank you… to thank you for stopping my wedding."

Tara's lips twitch. "I didn't stop your wedding."

My eyebrows furrow. "But the email was from you?"

"It might have been from my address, but I didn't send it."

"Then… then who did?"

"Nico, right before he walked out of this door and told me he was never coming back."

It takes a moment for Tara's words to hit me, but when they do, they slam into my ribs.

"Genius move, giving me the contact details of all your guests. Nico got his message to everyone so easily, thanks to you."

"Tara –"

"Don't," she sniffs. "I don't want to hear it."

Tara turns and walks through the house, leaving the front door open. I'm not sure if she wants me to follow or not. I hover, then enter the house, closing the door behind me. I find Tara in the kitchen making a cup of tea. She doesn't react to my presence. She stirs her drink, swirling the milky liquid around, her spoon clinking against the side of her mug.

"I didn't know whether to go to the wedding or not. I didn't think I could sit through watching you marry Jamie, but I didn't know if I should tell you what I knew. I'd been asking myself that question ever since we met at the market. Nico said you deserved the truth. He said to write it in an email if I couldn't bring myself to say it to your face. He was a fan of writing. He used to write me letters when we were first dating. Cute, right?"

Tara takes the spoon out of her mug and shakes it. Tea splashes onto the counter but she doesn't wipe it away.

"I went to get a drink while I thought of how to word my message. Telling someone their fiancé is cheating on them is a big thing. You want to say it right, to let them know it's not their fault. Nico said he'd set my laptop up for me. By the time I'd gone back upstairs, he'd found the phone and the card."

My stomach plummets.

"You can cut the act now, Cassie. The card he knew I'd designed, the one I never showed him? The phone you planted in my house? The one full of messages to Jamie? Nico's smashed it I'm afraid, so I can't give it back to you, but not before he read the texts. Not before he saw what you wanted him to see."

I close my eyes as the weight of her words crushes my chest.

"You left it here when you dropped the flowers off. I know it was you. I saw the phone when we went out, remember?"

I open my mouth to explain, to say sorry, but nothing comes out.

Suddenly, Tara flies across the room and grabs me. Her fingers dig into my shoulders. They'll leave bruises, I can tell, but I don't shake her off.

"Speak!" Tara shouts. "I want to hear you say it! I want you to tell me that you did this. You rigged the card, you planted the phone, you ruined my relationship, my life!"

"Jamie -" I start, but Tara snarls.

"Don't you dare blame him! Jamie ruined your relationship, but you ruined mine."

"Tara, I saw a photo of you both kissing and -"

"A photo of us kissing? Cassie, Jamie came onto me! I'd had so much

300

to drink I could barely stand when he forced himself on me. I pushed him off as soon as I registered what happened."

"I know that now," I admit.

"You know that now. Now everything is ruined." Tara runs her hands through her hair. "Do you have any idea what you've done?"

I hang my head, sinking into my shame.

"I told Nico the phone wasn't mine. I told him you must have planted it, but then he asked why you'd do that, and I had no choice. I had to... I had to tell him about the kiss."

My face scrunches. "Tara, I thought you were having an affair –"

"But we weren't!" Tara shrieks, the pitch of her voice cutting through me.

"I know that now but back then I saw the photo and that was it. Everything fell apart. Everything in my life turned out to be a lie. I'd have done anything to hurt Jamie back, and you seemed like the perfect person to blame it on. I thought I could save Nico from being with a cheat as well as save myself. I didn't stop to think –"

"You didn't think at all," Tara spits.

Her words hit like knives. "I'm so, so sorry."

"So? What does that mean? What does that *fix?*"

"I can go to Nico! I can admit -"

"He knows about the kiss, Cassie. Whatever you do, whatever you say, won't matter. It's over."

"But you said Jamie forced himself onto you! We can tell Nico that. We can..." I trail off as Tara shakes her head. She leans against the kitchen counter, exhausted.

"When Nico and I first got together, I kissed someone else. It was a silly, drunken mistake, but I didn't tell him. He found out a few weeks later through a mutual friend. We eventually moved past it, but it wasn't easy. Nico said if anything happened again, he'd be gone. Well, he's true to his word."

"But what if he knows you didn't want the kiss? If we say Jamie came onto you -"

"Do you think I didn't tell him that? It didn't matter! I still kissed another man. I met Jamie alone, I went for drinks, I put myself in that situation."

"Tara, this is *not* your fault."

Tara's lips flick at the irony of me being the one to convince her she isn't guilty. "Nico doesn't see it that way. I told you he sees things in black and white. He said, 'A kiss is a kiss'. Besides, I didn't tell him when it happened. I kept another secret." A raw sadness gleams in Tara's eyes. "But it was *my* secret to keep. My burden to carry, not yours to drag from me. Nico will never trust me again."

"I could try fix it," I protest but Tara shakes her head.

"Don't you get it? It's done. Nico told the world who Jamie was then walked away. He's not coming back."

"Maybe –"

"It's done, Cassie," Tara interjects, her tone firm, her tone final.

Her words crucify me. I can't look at her, can't take in the ugliness of what I've done.

"I don't understand why you didn't *ask* me. All those times we met you never said a word. I thought about telling you so many times, but I was scared if Jamie found out what I'd done then he'd tell Nico about the kiss. I didn't want to ruin my relationship or be the one to hurt you with the truth. I mean, would you want to be the person who told someone that not only was their fiancé a cheat, but that he wrote about it for fun on the internet?"

I flinch at her words. "So you knew… you knew everything?"

Tara grimaces, her expression more telling than any other response could be.

"Who was the teacher Jamie was having the affair with?" I ask.

"Tracey, Tracey Mead."

I close my eyes. Mrs Mead, the woman in Patricia's prediction. Tracey, the T Jamie was messaging that I never stopped to think might not be Tara.

"Tracey and Jamie... they weren't discreet. They got an official warning after a student caught them kissing, but it didn't stop them. They were caught again, this time by a cleaner and doing more than kissing."

I can almost picture it, Jamie enjoying the thrill of a classroom hook-up, knowing he had me waiting at home for him when he was done.

"Why didn't anyone tell me what was going on?" I ask, my voice breaking. "You all let me carry on living my life like everything was okay."

This time, it's Tara's turn to twist with anguish. "How do you tell someone that, Cassie? How do you drop that bombshell? Besides, we were told to keep quiet. Two employees acting like that was embarrassing enough for the school without everyone gossiping about it. Only a few people know all the details."

"And none of you thought I should know them too."

"It was such a scandal, Cassie. I thought you'd find out eventually. I thought Jamie would have to tell you when he lost his job."

"He didn't tell me anything."

"I know that now. I found out when I went to help him find another job."

I shake my head. "Why did you meet him? After everything he'd done, why go?"

Tara clenches her jaw in a futile attempt to stop herself from crying. "I thought I was being kind. We made a good team when we worked together. You could have even called us friends. I thought he'd realised his mistake with Tracey and was trying to make it right. You know, start afresh with a new job or something. Then he told me about his website – he thought I already knew. I was disgusted. I walked out of the bar, but he came after me. He grabbed me, then... then he kissed me."

I imagine it so vividly – Jamie reaching for Tara before she slipped away, one final, desperate attempt to assert his dominance.

"The day we met at the market, I should have said something. I should have spoken up, but Nico didn't know about the kiss. I kept quiet because I was scared, and now? Now I've lost everything."

"I don't know what to say," I croak.

"What is there to say? You got your wish. I'm as ruined as Jamie."

"I'm –"

"Don't. I don't want to hear you say you're sorry. I don't want to hear anything from you. There's nothing left to say other than I'll keep your little secret. I won't tell anyone what you tried to do or that you knew Jamie was cheating – what's the point? Nico's gone. He won't come back. There's no need for anyone else getting hurt in all this."

I should be relieved, but Tara keeping quiet about everything somehow makes what I've done to her feel even worse. "Look, maybe we can –"

"There's no 'maybe' anything. It's over, Cassie. In a moment you're going to leave this house and I'm going to walk away knowing that for the rest of your life, you will carry the guilt of what you have done to me." Drying her tears on her sleeve, Tara lifts her gaze to meet mine. "You can go now."

"Tara –"

"I said you can go," she repeats, her tone final.

My chin wobbles, but I nod.

After taking one last look at Tara, I walk away, the knowledge that there is nothing I can do to fix this weighing down on me. I am trapped in these lies, as is Tara, as is Jamie. Jamie might have started our twisted tale, but I finished it. We are the liar, the victim and the guilty, a trio forever bound in this deceit.

<u>The Next *Beginning*.</u>

"You look incredible… what a bride!"

This time, the train is made from the most delicate lace I've ever seen. A subtle touch of sparkle glimmers here and there. Off the shoulder, fitted and flowing, it's the dress of a beautiful bride alright.

"Alisha, you look amazing," I whisper, clutching my champagne to my chest.

"I love it. It's even better than I remembered," Alisha admits.

We whoop and holler in agreement as Alisha twists to study the back of her dress in the mirror. She catches my eye in the reflection and we share a smile. I know she'd been nervous to invite me today, but she had no need to be. Simon proposing to Alisha one month after my wedding disaster was one of the things that got me through the darkness. It was a much-needed reminder that true love exists, and that happy endings are real.

Our tender moment is interrupted by an alarm ringing. Lily grimaces and holds up her phone. "I'm sorry, I've got to get going. I'm meeting Justin at his parents' place tonight."

"Dinner with the parents, three holidays in a year – you'll be next!" I joke. Lily flushes but she can't hide her happiness.

The one good thing to come from my disaster of a wedding was Lily meeting Justin. Before rescuing me, Lily threw her bouquet at Jamie's cousins who were trying to stop people getting to the front of the room to attack Jamie. In return, that meant stopping my friends from getting to me. When Lily ran out of flowers, Justin pulled some from the decorations and supplied them to Lily to launch. The rest, as they say, is history.

"Another wedding I can be the drunk bridesmaid at," Laney cheers, winking at Lily. The pair giggle and peace flows through me. Despite an initial rocky few months, Lily and Laney's friendship is back to where it was. Lily's heart is too big to not forgive, and Laney lights up a room too much to not have her in your life.

"You'd best get going too, hadn't you, Cass?" Alisha asks.

"Yes!" Lily gasps, grabbing my arm. "The big date!"

I groan. "Please don't call it that."

"I'm sorry, I'm just excited for you."

"Me too," Alisha says. "Russell Harrington... a nice, solid name."

"Not the name of a serial cheat?" I joke. Lily bats my arm and I sigh. "I'm excited too but I want to be careful."

Everyone nods, knowing all too well why I need to protect my fragile heart.

"Well, wherever you go tonight, make sure there's no TV there. I've heard *he* stars heavily in tonight's episode," Laney warns.

"Honestly, the fact that he made it onto TV..." Alisha says with a shudder.

I nod along with Alisha's revulsion, but if my wedding has shown me anything, it's that nothing in life surprises me anymore.

For some reason, one of Jamie's cousins thought it would be a wonderful idea to film our wedding showdown and share it on the internet. It turns out, a stranger's heartbreak makes for perfect viral footage and, thanks to some error on fate's behalf, Jamie's received minor fame as a 'celebrity' bad boy.

With a teaching career out of the question after the revelations of Jamie's true nature came out, he had to find another source of income. Selling his story to a national newspaper of how he was pushed to cheat due to the modern woman not fulfilling a man's needs resulted in Jamie insulting every woman alive, but his charm and good looks ensured there were plenty out there willing to try and 'change' him. On top of that, he became a hero among the kind of men who shake their head and mutter 'feminists' whenever women talk about sexual assault or the gender pay gap.

The press asked me for an interview too, but I declined. I didn't want to be a part of the spectacle more than I already was. I wrote a two-sentence statement claiming no knowledge of what Jamie had been up to and removed myself from the situation as best I could. Thankfully, my lack of engagement coupled with the fact that the victim is nowhere near as interesting as the salacious villain ensured I was left in relative peace.

As soon as Jamie's version of events hit the papers, so did stories from his other victims.

The depths of Jamie's treacherousness sank lower than previously thought. Even though 'The Good Bad Guy's Guide' had only existed for eighteen months, Jamie had lived this double life for almost six years. Todd Goldman was one of three aliases he'd used over that period, and the damage he'd caused in that time was colossal.

He'd caused an irreparable family rift by dating a woman then having a one-night stand with her older sister. Two neighbours only found out they were both dating Jamie when he gifted them identical necklaces with identical notes. It transpired that Jamie met one of the women in the lift after spending the night with the other and liked the convenience of having them both in the same building.

Worst of all, one woman even had a four-year-old son she swore was Jamie's. She claimed that when she'd tried to speak to him about it, he threatened the life of her child. It was enough to scare her away from pursuing a paternity test, but not enough to scare the public away from giving Jamie the gift of fame. Apparently, these days misogyny sells, and Jamie capitalised on that.

Of course, being famous for being a vile pig doesn't come without its drawbacks. Jamie gets heckled wherever he goes. At a nightclub appearance he did, someone threw a bottle at him. It resulted in Jamie needing five stiches in his temple. I've heard rumours of his car windows being smashed more, bars and restaurants refusing to serve him and so much more.

But still, somehow the TV gigs keep rolling in. After a stint on Celebrity Love Hunt, Jamie met ex-WAG Carmella D'Fonte. The pair currently star on Celebrity Secrets, a reality show that mixes counselling with dating. I've never watched it, but I pick up on enough to know Jamie is doing what he does best – lying, being caught out and somehow walking away on top.

"No TV," I confirm, grabbing my handbag and ordering a taxi. After saying our goodbyes, I walk out of the bridal shop with Lily.

"You will be okay tonight, won't you?" Lily asks as we walk towards our respective rides.

"I'll be fine. I've not forgotten how to date."

"And you've not closed up down there?" Lily says, nodding towards my crotch.

I laugh and shove Lily. "No!"

"I told Alisha a vibrator was a good gift," Lily giggles, then she reaches for my hand. "I can't tell you how proud of you I am. Putting yourself out there again is huge."

I gloss over Lily's kindness, her words reminding me that I have little to be proud of.

"I hope you have the best time. Text me when you're on your way home and tell me everything!"

"Sure, but I can't imagine there will be much to tell."

Lily wags her finger at me. "You never know."

I wave goodbye and climb into my taxi. A middle-aged man with ruddy pink cheeks greets me from the driver's seat and we set off towards the city.

As we pass high-rise buildings and trendy bars, my apprehension grows. To distract myself, I check my phone. I find a queue of messages waiting, including one from Alison wishing me luck on my date.

One of the only good things to come from the aftermath of the wedding was my continued closeness with the Patricks. The day after everything imploded, they showed up at my front door. I invited them inside. Together we mourned the man we thought we knew, and now I'm closer to Jamie's family than ever.

The same can't be said for Jamie. Alison was so horrified by what her brother did, she cut him off immediately. "I don't want someone like that anywhere near my sons," she said.

Martin was a close second. He met with Jamie once, but he couldn't marry up the son he thought he had with the man behind that website. He buried himself in work for the first few months, only coming up for air when Alison announced she was pregnant with her third child.

"A new beginning," he said tearfully when we met to celebrate the good news.

But not all new beginnings created in the time after Jamie's revelations were good ones. Anne was hit hard by what happened. Some of her closest friends, friends she'd had most of her life, withdrew from her as if she were tainted. They froze her out of the group, ignoring her calls and making plans without inviting her.

She held it together well, but one day I went around to pick up a book and found her sobbing in the living room. She showed me a photo of her former friends enjoying an afternoon tea without her. "I was with Penny the day she went into labour with Owen. I held May's hand through the loss of her husband. But now? Now it's like I don't exist."

Losing her friends wasn't the only major change in Anne's life. She gave up her beloved job at the library, a choice that was more forced upon her than one she wanted to make. The whispers and stares from visitors had been torturous enough for her, but the final straw was when a group of local mums requested that she no longer oversaw the children's reading program. *'Who knows what she'll be teaching our children'*, their letter to the head of the library had said.

Anne now spends most of her days alone, losing herself in the fictional worlds she had spent so many years of her life sharing with others.

Whenever I meet Alison, a good chunk of our conversation centres around our worries about Anne. "I can't believe the way people have turned on mum. It's like they blame her for how Jamie turned out."

"People always want someone to blame," I always reply, knowing all too well how much a person needs someone to place their anger upon. "It's easier than admitting that some people are just bad people or that something needs to change in the world."

"But the way they've all turned on her! Mum was nothing short of a brilliant mum, a brilliant friend, a brilliant librarian, but now? Now her whole life is about the vile things he did. How is that fair?"

"It's not."

The conversation circles our anger and the desire to shake people into realising the cruelty of their actions, then ends with the same question – how will Jamie feel about what's happened to Anne?

"It will be killing him," is my response, because that's the truth. Whatever Jamie did, whoever he was, he loved his family. Seeing the shadow Anne has become will break his heart more than anything, and he will see it because Anne meets him once a month for a coffee. It's a visit Martin confessed does more damage than good.

"I think she's trying to understand where it all went wrong and how he grew up to be this person. We thought we'd raised him right," Martin said, his voice catching as he neared the end of his sentence.

Jamie's actions broke his parents, and in return his relationship with his family is severed forever. While Jamie might have fame, I know he'd give it all up for a third Thursday dinner with his family.

After replying to Alison, I open my next message.

Looking forward to finally meeting you x

A smile takes over my face. My date with Russell is another consequence of the fallout of my wedding. I left my last job as soon as I could. Some of the staff were wedding guests and their sympathetic glances in the staffroom made me shudder.

Then there was Debbie. Debbie who never said to anyone I'd known about Jamie all along but who always looked at me with sad, silent judgement.

Being in such close proximity to what I'd done was suffocating so I moved schools. New job, new start, new Cassie – or so I hoped.

Once my new teaching assistant found out about my past, she offered to set me up with her friend Russell. "Tall, handsome, successful and, most importantly, not a psycho."

After a lot of convincing, I agreed to let her pass on my number. A few weeks of playful, consistent, and lengthy texts later, we've finally agreed to meet.

Butterflies flutter in my stomach but I remind myself that whatever happens tonight is fine. Really, truly fine. If I've learned anything, it's that I don't need to be someone's plus one to be happy.

Not that I can ever be fully happy. Not after what I did.

Jamie could never get anyone to take his claims that I'd got him into more debt seriously. With so many lies behind him, the police weren't inclined to take his word on face value.

Still, they investigated. They took his tablet, something Jamie admitted I didn't know the passcode for, and found all credit card purchases were made on there. Combine that with Jamie's existing debt, his penchant for extravagant gifts for his mistresses, the 'Todd Goldman' selfies in designer stores and the fact Jamie lied to borrow money, all signs pointed to Jamie blaming me to exonerate himself.

As luck would have it, Jamie insisting the police took his tablet only served to put him in even hotter water. On it they found evidence of Jamie threatening to leak the nudes of his conquests when things between them soured. While he never actually shared the photos, he still toyed with his victims with such cruelty one officer told me she thought Jamie was a 'raging psychopath'.

The police were quick with their verdict - Jamie was a pathological liar with expensive taste, a nasty streak, and a history of getting into debt. I was labelled 'innocent' and left alone.

Not only could Jamie not pin his debt on me, but he could also never prove I'd known he was cheating.

Nico had destroyed the burner phone and the story card. The Abby Dunne email and social media profile were deactivated, with everyone she contacted too relieved they had a lucky escape from Jamie's lies for them to care that they didn't know who she was. When I left my job, I handed in my work laptop. It was wiped, ready for the next teacher to use, any searches I made gone forever.

On top of that, the day after the wedding Alisha showed up at my apartment with a new phone so I didn't have to go through the pain of deleting the history of my relationship. We threw my old one away, and with it any social media trail or internet history that could lead back to me.

So as loudly as Jamie protested that I'd known all along, he was the only one saying it. Debbie never spoke out because she gave her word that she wouldn't. Even Tara kept silent, although her reason for doing so was because she knew her silence would cause me more pain than her shouting.

Tara. Just thinking of her name twists my chest.

I tried fixing things for her. I showed up at Nico's work and asked to speak to him. His face drained of colour when he saw me, but he agreed to a coffee, even if only to prove he didn't want to hear me out.

"What is there to say? Tara kissed another man. It's over."

"You know what he was like, Nico."

"She knew what he was like and still went to meet him. Why would she put us at risk like that?"

"I don't know but you can't walk away from your relationship because of Jamie."

Nico's eyes flashed with fire. "You don't get to tell me what to do, Cassie. If it weren't for me, you'd have been stuck. I saved you from marrying a cheat, and you saved me from wasting more time with one. We're even. We've both walked away the winners."

"We don't look like winners to me."

At this, Nico drained his coffee and rose to his feet. "Leave it, Cassie, okay? I won't tell anyone what you did if you stop hounding me about Tara. What's done is done. I'm never going back. Move on. I have."

Defeated, I slumped in my seat and watched him walk away. Tara's indiscretion at the start of their relationship plagued Nico too much to let go. Thanks to the confession I forced from her, there was no going back for them.

As habit whenever my thoughts stray to the past, I hit social media and check on Tara.

She packed up her life and went travelling soon after everything happened. She's currently in Thailand and dating an Australian called Lachlan. She seems happy, but I know there will always be the thought of what might have been if not for me.

That thought keeps me up at night too.

Swallowing my shame, I go to lock my phone, but as I do another text comes through.

I think we have a mutual acquaintance

It's from a number I don't recognise. I respond, *'I think you may have the wrong number'* then lock my phone.

Glancing out of the window, I see we're close to the city. I gulp, my nerves eating me alive and asking if I'm doing the right thing. Am I ready to date again? Am I even someone who *should* date?

My counsellor, Dr Roberts, tells me these anxieties are to be expected from someone who's experienced what I have. My trauma fosters these kinds of thoughts. It's normal.

Of course, Dr Roberts doesn't know the full story. I tell her what I tell everyone else, the version where I'm the victim not the perpetrator.

But that's what I am – a perpetrator. A horrible person who did a horrible thing, and one who can't find a way to fix it.

The city lights blur as I gnaw my lip, biting so hard I draw blood. I'd been so pigheaded, so sure they both had to pay. In the end, they paid for actions only one of them committed.

As the taxi pulls to a stop, I sniff back my emotions. I can't be the girl who cries on a first date. I may be out of practice, but even I know that.

I walk towards The Bar, the newest hipster spot on Greek Street, with my head held high. My stomach flips when I see Russell waiting for me outside. "You made it!" he cheers, a dimple appearing in his right cheek. "I was beginning to worry you'd back out."

"I'm not that late, am I?"

"I'm just exceptionally early. Good manners, you see. The perfect gentleman."

I think of the last time I thought someone was a gentleman and how wrong I was, but as Russell holds his arm out for me to take, I silence those doubts. I link his arm and together we step into The Bar.

Loud chatter and raucous laughter fills the air. After the serenity of the bridal shop, it's almost too much, but I push myself to smile.

"I'll get us a drink. What do you want?" Russell shouts in my ear.

"Gin and tonic, please."

Russell slips into the crowd, weaving his way towards the bar. I watch him go, then scan the room for a place to sit. My eyes linger on couples with intertwined hands, but I force them to move on until I spot an empty table. I sit at it and try not to stare at the other people on dates, but I can't help it. Everywhere I look I see the potential for love, and for heartbreak.

Inside my handbag, my phone buzzes. Russell's still waiting for our drinks, so I check it. I find another message from the unknown number. I open it and nearly throw up on the table.

A screenshot of Abby Dunne's Facebook profile stares back at me, the photos I'd used of Ethan and Joel filling the screen. Photos I'd only have access to if I knew Alison. Photos of children that aren't mine, saved and used as if they were.

A bead of sweat trickles down the back of my neck. This doesn't make sense. I deleted Abby Dunne's profile almost as quickly as I created it. Only Jamie knew it was me behind it. It needs to be that way. If Jamie can link me to Abby Dunne, he can prove I knew about him. He can prove I lied.

"You okay?"

I barely hear Russell speak, barely acknowledge his existence as he takes a seat opposite me.

"Cassie?" he says but I don't look up, not now another message has been sent my way. I open it and all the air in the room disappears.

It's a photo of two people I recognise. Two people I prayed I'd never see together.

Jamie and Patricia Campbell, arm in arm, smiling at the camera. Jamie and Patricia, united by the knowledge of the truth about me, the power to destroy me now in Jamie's hands.

And just like that, the bottom of my world falls away.

**Acknowledgements**

Now that 'How to Destroy Your Husband' is finished, there are so many people I'd like to thank. It's true what they say – second book anxiety is a thing. Publishing a debut is terrifying, but with a second book people have expectations… how scary is that?! Thankfully I have supportive people around me who were on hand to help whenever I doubted myself.

First, I'd like to thank the team at Kingsley Publishers, in particular Cindy and Matt. Your limitless patience and belief in my writing means more than you will ever know. I'm so happy to be working with you, and so proud to be a Kingsley author!

Throughout my author journey, I've been lucky enough to meet many incredible people. I want to start by saying thank you first and foremost to the readers. The incredible, incredible readers. Readers who took the chance on a debut. Readers who passed my book onto their friends. Readers who have reached out with their thoughts, opinions, and well-wishes – THANK YOU!

Then there are my fellow authors. The people who have taken me under their wing and shared inspiring words of wisdom (a special shoutout to Elle Croft for hosting my book launch and for always being so kind, as well as a writer I look up to).

Thank you to the amazing book clubs around the world who invited me to attend their meetups and engaged with my writing in a way I could only ever dream of.

To the incredible bloggers and reviewers who have championed my writing at every opportunity – thank you, thank you, thank you. You're all amazing! A huge shout out to everyone at The Fiction Café, as well as Emma B Books, Dan, Lesley, Justin, Kathy, Nancy, and Sam, to name just a few.

And then there's bookstagram, aka the best place on the internet. I've met far too many incredible people on there to call you all out individually, but please know that your messages and friendship mean the world to me. Thank you for making my TBR pile grow at a rate I can't keep up with, and for always being on hand when I want to procrastinate. Seriously, I adore every single one of you.

Then to my 'IRL people'. So many of you have inspired the characters and friendships in this book. For letting me steal some of your personality traits, I thank you.

Now for a few special mentions. Katie – you believed in this story first. Laura, Charlie, Sanch, and Emily – your insights into the many drafts of this book were invaluable. Brigid - your kind words after reading the first chapter saved me on a day I was about to give up.

A huge thank you to everyone who has been on hand with a glass of wine, a FaceTime, and/or a distraction – Robyn, Aidan, Rachel, Beth, Sunaina, Amber, and everyone else I could add to that list. A special thank you to my oldest friend, Lily – the postcard you wrote me sits on my desk and keeps me going.

An extra special thank you to Amy and Grace for being the best friends a girl could wish for. Can't wait to share a bottle of wine (and maybe a few shots of tequila…) with you both again soon!

While I'm mentioning Grace, I'd like to shout out Steve Greenwell – I told you I'd put your name in my next book! One day I'll make you a character, I just need to learn to write jokes as hilarious as yours before then.

I best write this next bit quickly before I start crying at my computer, but a million and one thank yous to my family in the UK, who I miss every day.

To my uncle Mick and auntie Lesley, who surround me with laughter and love whenever we meet. I'll get the first round in next time I see you.

Victoria, aka the smartest person I know. I'm so proud of everything you've achieved, and grateful that you make time to swap Stranger Things theories with me when you're so busy.

To James and Lauren, who I love and appreciate more than I'm able to express. Thanks for always being there, and for being a constant source of style inspiration. I'm serious, forget Tara and Nico's house - your home is the DREAM.

To Mum and Dad – thank you, thank you, thank you. You've supported every one of my dreams, even the ones that have taken me far away from home. Grateful doesn't cover it. Love you, always.

Poppy – I wish I could explain how much you mean to me. As I write this, you've just turned one (how are you one already?!). You are the most amazing niece, and you bring so much joy to everyone's life. I'm counting down the days until I next get to give you a cuddle!

And finally, because I'm definitely too teary to continue writing acknowledgements for much longer, to Jack. Jack who has read multiple drafts of this book and listened to me ramble on about my ideas while I pace the kitchen too many times to count. You are blessed with the patience of a saint. For that, and so many other things, I love you.

Special note – the name of the character 'Lily' was chosen by a reader as part of a social media giveaway I hosted. Jade Adams selected the name as it is the name of her daughter. Thanks so much for taking part in the giveaway, Jade, and for selecting such a beautiful name for me to use!

Author Bio

Jess Kitching is the bestselling Author of *The Girl She Was Before*, which was nominated for a Sisters in Crime Davitt Award.

A proud advocate for anti-bullying, sexual assault survivors and beauty diversity, Jess uses her spare time to discuss and raise awareness of these issues.

Originally from the north of England, she currently lives in Sydney with her fiancé.

Connect with Jess on social media

Instagram: @jesskitchingwrites

Twitter: @kitching_jess

Facebook: Jess Kitching Writes

Or her special readers group on Facebook:

'Official Jess Kitching Reader Community'

The
Girl She Was
Before

A crime thriller with a brilliant twist you won't see coming!

Powerful, packed full of gruelling details that will linger with you long after the book has finished.

Nat lives a picture-perfect life, but it wasn't always this way. A victim of horrific bullying when she was a teenager, Nat will do anything to keep distance between the girl she was before and the woman she is now.

But when her best friend is murdered and people begin to point their finger at her, Nat's new life quickly unravels.

To Nat, it's no surprise the crime happened at the same time as the return of her biggest tormentor, Chrissy Summers. A woman with a violent streak who destroyed lives when she was younger and isn't afraid to do it again.

Face to face with the past she so firmly keeps behind her, Nat's sanity wavers as her determination to reveal Chrissy as the monster she knows her as rises to dangerous heights.

The question is, can Nat prove Chrissy is a killer, or will Chrissy get to Nat and her family before she has the chance?

The Girl
She Was
Before

By Jess Kitching

KINGSLEY
PUBLISHERS

"Can you believe they didn't show? I wore my good bra for nothing," the passenger grumbles, flicking her hairspray-crunchy curls forward and tying them in a messy bun on top of her head. "Honestly, Hallie, why do we bother with dating?"

With her eyes still fixed on the dark road ahead, Hallie takes a break from gnawing her lower lip to reply. "It's fun, apparently."

"Yeah, well, clearly anyone who says that doesn't have friends getting hitched left, right and centre and the onset of wrinkles to keep at bay." The passenger snorts at her own joke, but she's the only one laughing. She turns to her friend, only now noticing how pale she is. "Are you okay?"

"What? Sorry, you know I hate driving at night. The idiot behind me won't back off, either," Hallie replies, flexing her clammy hands before tightening her grip on the steering wheel. As if on cue, the vehicle behind lurches forward, so close the two cars almost kiss.

"Fucking hell, what a dick! Just go faster," the passenger instructs.

"I don't know, Bree. I'm already over the limit as it is…"

"So what? No one comes down here. Not at this time, anyway."

Hallie bites her lip but does as she's told. She's usually the one who calls the shots in this friendship, but tiredness and agitation from being stood up seems to have given Bree a new sense of decisiveness. After a long day of teaching and a tedious staff meeting afterwards, never mind the dating no-shows, Hallie's only too happy to have someone else do her thinking for her. She presses her foot on the accelerator and the humming engine leaps into life.

The car behind mimics the movement, their engine snarling back in response.

"What the fuck is their problem?" Bree snaps, winding down her window and waving her arms at the encroaching vehicle.

That only seems to antagonise them more. Their engine roars into life, their glaring headlights blinding in the rear-view mirror.

"They're speeding up!" Bree shouts, but Hallie doesn't need Bree to tell her that. She can see the outline of the bigger vehicle homing in and dwarfing her car as if this is a game of cat and mouse that's got out of hand. Her speedometer climbs faster than she's comfortable driving, especially on somewhere like Carlton Road at night, but what can she do? They won't back off. They won't slow down. It's almost like they want her to drive faster.

With adrenaline coursing through her veins, Hallie glances in the rear-view mirror once more. Headlights shine so close they're dazzling. White spots dance in her eyes. She winces and turns the steering wheel ever so slightly, but at that speed the slightest movement is all it takes.

The wheels spin out of control as the car hurtles off the road towards the unknown.

There's a scream, the last thing either woman hears before the sickening crunch of metal rings out into the night. Then… nothing.

<u>Then.</u>

A painful growl escapes from underneath the girl's shirt. She raises her hand to muffle the sound, cupping the concave curve of her stomach protectively.

"You'll get there soon," she tells herself, thinking of the row of artificially lit vending machines that will greet her on arrival. Two bars of chocolate and a can of Coca-Cola, her breakfast for the last two weeks, paid for by stealthily siphoning money from her mum's savings jar.

The thought of the jar makes her already aching stomach spasm with anxiety. She reckons she has another four or five days' worth of funds in there, tops, and then it's back to life with no breakfast. Back to feeling lightheaded and nauseous from the moment her sleep crusted eyes open in the morning to the moment her weary head hits the pillow at night.

Worse than that, though, in four or five days her mum's pitiful life savings will be completely gone. She will have stolen it all.

An icicle of dread traces its way down her spine at the thought.

She is glad He doesn't know about the jar. If He knew she had been stealing money He could have used for beer, He would kill her. She wishes that were a dramatic statement, but it's not. Not with His temper.

Sometimes she is surprised she has made it this far in life.

Sometimes she wishes she hadn't made it this far at all.

Two minutes later than scheduled, the bus pulls to a stop in front of her. As the double doors hiss open, she silently repeats the mantra she has recited every morning for the past three years – 'another day closer to leaving'.

She's jostled aggressively as students push past her from all directions, desperate to sit with their friends, desperate to not be at the front with the losers, desperate to not be stuck next to her.

She lets them force her to the side without a fight. What's the point in trying to battle her way onto the bus first, anyway? There's nothing waiting for her on there. Nothing good, at least.

When the eager clamouring is finally over, she climbs aboard and flashes the driver a nervous smile. His nostrils flare as she approaches. His eyes bulge. He doesn't say anything, but he doesn't need to. She knows exactly what he is thinking. He's willing her to take a seat and be quick about it - he can't hide his disgust for much longer.

Head down, cheeks burning, the girl walks on.

She tried to wash her clothes last night, but there was no detergent left. There hadn't been for over two weeks. Her mum was too sick from her latest round of treatment to go out and get some, and since when did He do anything to help around the house?

She had put her ratty underwear and pungent uniform in the chipped bathroom sink and soaked them the best she could, but with no soap either it was hard to get them clean. Still, she had hoped the water would have an effect.

It had an effect alright, but one that made the smell ten times worse than before. Not only had the build-up of sweat clung to the fibres of her clothes mercilessly but washing them added a dampness that caught in the back of the throat.

Personally, she can't smell it anymore, but it's clear from the way people clamp their mouths shut and shuffle away as she walks past that everyone else can.

A part of her feels like apologising to them - I'm sorry for the smell. I'm sorry you have to sit near me. I'm sorry I exist – but would they even hear her if she did?

A dramatic cry comes from the back of the bus. "Oh my god! What is that smell?!"

The pit of the girl's stomach falls heavy as she takes a seat, far from them but not far enough to be out of their firing line.

"Seriously, I'm going to barf! What is it?!"

Chrissy Summers's voice rises loud and clear above the chorus of over-the-top gags. "What do you think it is? It's Fish Sticks!"

The beautiful girls at the back of the bus fall about laughing at their own cruel joke. The rest of the bus sniggers along. Their laughter hits the girl's chest like poisoned arrows.

"Fish Sticks! Fish Sticks, over here!"

She doesn't turn around. She made a vow to herself years ago – she will never respond to that name, even though it's the only one anyone ever calls her. She looks out of the window and does her best to ignore their taunts, the cruel name stinging like antiseptic in a papercut every time it's screeched in her direction.

"Fish Sticks, are you deaf as well as dumb? We're talking to you!" Amira Johal barks.

The girl forces herself to count the number of letterboxes the bus passes. Through the blur of her tears, she makes out letterbox five... then six... then -

Suddenly, something hits her hard on the back of the head.

A cold liquid runs down her neck, soaking into her shirt. For a moment, she panics it might be blood, but as a bottle of chocolate milk clatters to the floor and brown liquid pools at her feet, the girl realises what they have done. It's an injustice far more painful than cutting her could have ever been.

She will wear that chocolate-stained shirt until next Thursday when she finally comes home to washing powder. The smell of sour milk will mingle with her already toxic odour, growing increasingly stronger and more putrid with every day spent in the summer sun.

They will conveniently forget they had thrown the milkshake and will use the dark stain against her, not that they need more ammunition in the first place. They will call her shit stain and ask why she can't wipe her arse properly at fifteen. They will gag theatrically when she walks past, and every time they do, a part of her will die. Every time they do, she will feel smaller and more insignificant than she ever thought a person could possibly feel.

<u>Now.</u>

1

"The sky looks amazing," I comment, marvelling at the sun kissed world on the other side of my windscreen.

Sunaina glances up from replying to messages on my behalf and whistles. "Not a cloud in sight! It would be a great backdrop for content."

"I don't know. We've got to drop the goodie bags off with Joelle…"

"We'll still have time."

Sunaina's words hang between us while I weigh up my options. "Jay will be okay for a few more minutes, won't she?"

"She always is," Sunaina shrugs, putting my phone away and getting the camera ready.

I take the next right, pulling my four-wheel drive into the almost deserted carpark of Coral Bay Beach. At 2:50pm on a Wednesday, most people are either still at work or out on the school run. The timing of this spontaneous photoshoot couldn't be better if I tried.

We hop out of the car and I open the boot. A sports bag stuffed with a variety of outfits for all occasions greets me. My husband thinks I'm crazy for having a second wardrobe in the back of my car, but I like to be prepared for all eventualities. He doesn't understand that sometimes the lighting is just right and I can get four posts worth of content in one location… but only if I have clothes to change into.

"Should I wear something else?" I ask, plucking at my black, fitted trousers.

Sunaina eyes me analytically. "Roll your hems up and grab one of the hats. We can write a 'taking a moment for myself after my big meeting with the gallery' style of post."

I nod and reach for a wide brimmed hat, thanking the stars for the millionth time today alone that Sunaina came into my life just under a year ago.

At just twenty-one, Sunaina strikes me as someone who has the skills to take on the world, but for my own sake I hope she stays with me forever instead. She has expertly managed my life after things unexpectedly took off and I could no longer keep up with running a popular social media page, painting full time, and looking after a newborn by myself. Most days I trust her opinion more than I trust my own. After all, she got me from thirty thousand followers to well over eighty thousand – clearly, she knows how to style an impromptu photo shoot.

"Not that hat," Sunaina instructs with a shake of her head. "Go for a 'Dress to Impress' one. They've been nagging for another ad for a while now."

I rummage around in the back of the car and pull out a straw trilby.

Sunaina nods approvingly. "We should use the stats from this post to negotiate a raise. I know 'Dress to Impress' have been supporters from day one, but you can charge triple what they pay you now."

After making a mental note to call Suzanna at 'Dress to Impress', we step onto the beach. Warm sand spreads between my toes and instantly I am at peace.

"Stand there and look out to sea," Sunaina instructs. "And look cute!"

As I scan the shimmering horizon, the green-blue waves crashing onto the shore with a satisfying fizz, I realise how, even if someone offered me all the money in the world, I would never want to move away from here.

Coral Bay, with its picture-perfect ocean views and sunsets that need no filter, has always and will always be my home. Well over an hour away from the nearest city and so laid back the suits stay away, it's the perfect slice of chilled, coastal life. That's what my followers tell me, anyway.

My Instagram account, 'Finding the Good Life', started just over three years ago when I moved back to Coral Bay after falling out of love with city life. Storming around bars in short skirts with a patchy fake tan was fun when I was a student, but astronomically rising rent and the only romantic prospects being fleeting encounters with emotionally unavailable bankers lost their appeal soon after graduating. I stuck it out for a few years, but one day I decided I just couldn't do it anymore. City-girl life wasn't me, no matter how hard I tried to make the identity fit. I wanted the ocean on my doorstep, space to create and a life not bound by the ties of a 9 to 5.

So, Coral Bay beckoned me home.

To say I was nervous about coming back is an understatement. I once swore to myself I'd have to be dragged back to Coral Bay kicking and screaming, but I still pulled up in my battered Nissan with a pounding heart and a chest full of hope.

I rented a small house on the edge of town and set up a painting studio in the spare bedroom. I started posting photos of my artwork and the coastal life that inspired me online. To my surprise, the orders and followers were soon rolling in. Within my first year of dedicating myself to my passion, my canvases were stocked by Arlene Davies in one of the biggest contemporary galleries in the country, with pieces selling almost as soon as they were unveiled.

When musician Michelle Obanye shared a photo of one of my seascapes in her living room, everything kicked into overdrive. My prices quadrupled, my follower count skyrocketed, and my life changed forever.

Suddenly I didn't have to hide away. Doors opened to me that were once firmly shut. After years of being invisible, through self-preservation not choice, all of a sudden I was the one people wanted to talk to. I was the one they invited. I was popular, a sentence I never thought I'd say other than in my daydreams.

Pretty soon, I was real life friends with Hallie Patterson, Brianna 'Bree' Jackson, Bex (or Becca, as she likes to be known now) Harper, Amira Johal, and Melissa Curtis. Fifteen-year-old Nat would have never believed it to be possible, but it's true. They called upon me to join them, and I've never looked back.

These days, instead of hiding in the background and wanting to disappear, you'll find me at the head of the table for every cocktail fuelled girls' night. A place I've worked hard for and one I never want to lose.

The biggest surprise of my homecoming, though, was Lucas Redding. Voted most fanciable male at formal, captain of the football *and* cricket team and now my husband. Sometimes I find myself studying my wedding ring or counting the stretch marks left on my stomach from carrying our nine-month-old daughter Esme to remind myself that it's really true - *I* am married to *the* Lucas Redding.

Coral Bay called me home, alright. It called me home and made up for all its past mistakes, and for that I'll forever be grateful.

"Whatever you're thinking about – stop. You look kind of smug in these photos," Sunaina says, cutting into my disbelieving trip down memory lane.

"You mean smug isn't the vibe we're going for?" I joke, but there's nothing to laugh about. There isn't a day that goes by where I'm not beyond thankful for how my life U-Turned, or a moment I'm not terrified the tide will turn and drag me back to how things were before.

As I hold onto my hat to stop it from blowing away in a sudden gust of wind, Sunaina snaps away.

"That's the shot," she says, turning the camera to face me.

She's right – she's got it. She caught me mid laugh, free, easy, and light, the epitome of 'Finding the Good Life'.

With our spontaneous photo shoot now over, we drive towards Joelle Nichols's house. In the passenger seat, Sunaina edits the picture. I'm not one for blurring out wrinkles or redefining my waist, but a little upping of the contrast and fiddling with the brightness never hurt anyone, right?

I pull to a stop, smiling at Joelle's multicoloured windows and rainbow door. Joelle, my Coral Bay Arts Council co-chair, is the only other creative in town earning a full time living from her work. She makes beautiful ceramics and holds workshops in schools all around the country. Every three weeks we host classes for the local community to help them get in touch with their creative side. They're rewarding sessions, and the least I can do to thank the people of this town for never reminding me of the girl I used to be.

Hauling a mound of carrier bags from the backseat of my car, I make my way up Joelle's path, her overgrown, wildflower garden like something from a fairy tale.

"Nat! So good to see you," Joelle enthuses from the front porch. She pulls me into a bosomy hug, her bright red corkscrew curls tickling my cheek.

"I can't stay long – I've got to get back for Esme – but I thought I'd drop off the goodie bags you asked for while I was in the area."

Joelle takes the bags from me, her eyes dancing with delight. "The kids are going to love these – thank you so much! You really are a treasure."

"Oh, it's nothing," I blush, my chest swelling with pride. "I'd best be off, but I'll see you at the next meeting, okay?" Joelle nods and I wave goodbye as I hurry back to my car.

"Was she happy with the bags?" Sunaina asks, not once looking up from her laptop.

"She loved them."

"So she should – it took you weeks to source those materials."

"I know, but it's nice to do something for someone else," I shrug, but Sunaina's right. Joelle's little favour had turned into hours of painstaking research and reaching out to different suppliers. The effort is a small price to pay for belonging though and I'm happy to go the extra mile if it keeps me in Coral Bay's good books.

We set off towards the four-bedroom house with panoramic sea views I'm lucky enough to call home, all the while Sunaina works on perfecting our impromptu post.

"For the caption, how about 'after a busy day of meetings with gallery owners, the beach was calling. Never forget to make time for yourself, even if that time is spent trying to keep hold of your hat'?" Sunaina suggests.

"That's great. I've noticed my shorter captions get the most engagement."

"As do posts about Esme," Sunaina reminds me, her tone cool but her words hard.

I smile tightly. Lucas isn't keen on the idea of Esme being 'all over the internet like a meme', as he so eloquently puts it. I see his point, but I can't help wondering what my following would be if he let me share photos of her rather than just referencing her existence.

As we reach Maple Drive, I shelve the thought. "A conversation for another day," I tell myself.

We roll into the driveway just as Sunaina hits post. Unclipping my seatbelt, I slide out of the car. I can already feel the likes rolling in, but I ignore them and smile at the building in front of me instead.

I know in my bones I will never tire of this house. Whitewashed and hidden from the street by a luscious garden, it is my paradise within paradise.

"We're home!" I shout, dropping my handbag and walking into our recently renovated kitchen-diner where I find Jay prepping dinner. "Sorry we're a little late."

"Oh, it's no problem. I know how these gallery visits run over."

I beam at Jay, our exceptional and exceptionally understanding nanny. Jay joined us a little over six months ago and became part of the family overnight. She moved to Coral Bay after a bad breakup, one I don't ask about after she explained that the scar by her left eyebrow was a parting gift from her ex and not the result of a childhood accident. Jay's arrival in town was a well-timed kiss from fate, and life has been pretty perfect ever since.

On days like today when everything seems to align just right, I find myself thinking 'pinch me'. After 'pinch me' always comes 'please don't let this all be taken from me'.

The urge to grab everything and hold tight could consume me if I let it. Lucas says when your childhood was as rough as mine, life owes you a favour or two. That sentiment, however sweet, always sets off a spark of fear in me. I know better than most that life owes us nothing.

Blessings counted, I walk to Esme. "Hello, angel," I coo, scooping her up and showering her with sloppy kisses. She erupts into a fit of giggles so pure my heart soars. She is the spitting image of Lucas, apart from the springy curls she has inherited from me. They're going to be a nightmare to comb in a few years' time. I can already hear the tantrums.

I turn to Jay. "How has she been?"

"Good, as always."

Jay's report makes me glow and I plant another kiss on Esme's forehead. "Aren't you an angel?"

Just then, the front door clicks shut.

I glance at the clock above the fridge and frown. "You're home early," I call to Lucas, but my blood freezes when I see him – ashy faced, pale, traumatised. Questions pour out of me in a breathless stream. "What is it? What's wrong? What's happened?"

"There's been an accident," Lucas says, swallowing so hard I hear his gulp from the other side of the room. "Bree's in a coma and Hallie... Hallie's dead."

2

The room tilts off kilter for a moment. The white tiles seem too bright, too harsh. My vision clouds. "That's not funny Lucas," I say softly.

Lucas blinks. "Why would I joke about that?"

"Why would that be true?!"

In my arms, Esme starts to whimper. I open my mouth to tell her mummy didn't mean to shout, but I can't find the words.

Like an angel, Jay appears at my side. "Come here, cutie. Mummy's just had a nasty shock, okay?" Jay says, her tone children's entertainer high and grating, but it does the trick because Esme stops fussing.

I turn to Lucas and his features slip back into focus. The sadness covering them hits me like a barbed wire whip. "That can't be true," I whisper, but his crestfallen expression tells me it is. I go over the news in my mind – Hallie is dead, Bree is in a coma.

Hallie is dead, Bree is in a coma.

Then I break.

In seconds, I'm in Lucas's arms. He strokes my hair and tells me everything will be alright but, as I cry for my friends, his words couldn't seem further from the truth.

"Here, sit down," Sunaina instructs, pulling out a chair. Gratefully, I collapse into it. Lucas sits beside me, my hand small inside his.

"What happened?" I manage to ask.

"No one knows exactly. When Hallie didn't show up for work and no one could get hold of her, Tim called the police." Tim is the head of Coral Bay High where Lucas teaches PE and where Hallie works - worked - as an English teacher. "There was no one at home, so the police did a drive about. They found Hallie's car in a ditch off Carlton Road."

"Carlton Road?! That's miles away!"

"And in the middle of nowhere too, which is why they weren't found until the police went looking for them. It turns out they went on a double date to some sketchy bar in Whitehaven. Apparently, the guys didn't show – Hallie text Chloe and told her they'd been stood up. That's the last anyone heard from her. The theory is that Bree and Hallie stayed out. Hallie was drink driving. The police think she took a wrong turn and…"

"And?" I ask, even though I already know the answer.

"And they crashed, Nat. By the time the police got there, Hallie was already dead. Bree's alive, but it's not looking good." Lucas rubs his temples, exhaustion radiating from his every pore. "We had to break it to the kids this afternoon. No one can believe it. Everyone's devastated."

I stare at my hands and allow my tears to fall freely.

"I'm so sorry, Nat. I know they were good friends of yours," Jay says softly. Nodding, I flash her a wobbly smile.

"You never know, Bree might be okay," Sunaina offers, but she catches Lucas's eye and instantly regrets the glimmer of hope her words give me. Lucas doesn't need to say anything for me to know that even if Bree is alive, she is most definitely not going to be okay. I choke on a sob.

Lucas cradles me. "I'm sorry, babe. I know how close you three got."

I know he means well, but his words strike me as reductionist. How close we got? Those women were my *best* friends.

Hallie and Bree were the first people to really welcome me back to Coral Bay, even though they were probably last on the list of people I thought would be glad to see me again. When I bumped into them outside Coffee by The Sea, my heart was in my throat. Instantly, I recognised Hallie's upturned nose and Bree's electric blue eyes. Even with a few years, a few kilos and a few too many late nights between us, I could never forget what they looked like, but they did a double take when they saw me.

"Natalie Evans?!" they shrieked.

The first thing that shocked me about their response was that they knew my name. I'd only ever heard them refer to me as a derogatory slur. The second thing was how happy they were to see me.

"I can't believe it's you!" they cried, pulling me into warm, welcoming hugs.

Things only got better from there. We caught up briefly over a coffee, then two nights later we went out for cocktails. We spoke about the past, glossing over the parts of our shared history that weren't so pretty until eventually Hallie faced it head on.

"Can we take a moment to address the HUGE elephant in the room?" she interjected. "I was a bitch in school, Nat, and I'm so, so sorry. I teach at Coral Bay High now and I can't believe some of the shit I used to do, especially to you. If any of my pupils did that, I'd lock them in detention for the rest of the year. I am so embarrassed about who I once was. I was such a bitch."

Following her lead as always, Bree nodded in agreement. "We both were. We were kids, you know? We never really thought it through. We just followed Chrissy -"

Hallie had shaken her head adamantly at this. "Chrissy was the leader, but we made our own choices. We knew what we were doing was wrong and we did it anyway, and for that I'm so sorry."

"Me too," Bree added.

I remember sitting back in my chair and thinking, 'if only teenage Nat could see me now!'. Two of the most popular girls at Coral Bay High saying sorry to *me*. I used to apologise to them for walking past, for breathing, for simply existing, but there they were, wanting *me* to be nice to *them*... me!

A part of me wanted to laugh in their faces as they had done in mine so many times before, but at the sight of their earnest expressions and guilt-tinged cheeks, something inside me tugged. They wanted *my* approval. They cared what *I* thought. A world I'd only seen from the periphery suddenly opened up to me, a rainbow footpath leading the way to belonging in a way I could only ever dream of.

"Water under the bridge," I shrugged, raising my cocktail.

The three of us toasted each other and, just like that, the ugly past was laid to rest. We never mentioned it again, not even when I was introduced to the rest of the gang and Amira dug her old yearbook out one wine fuelled night. No one commented on my absence from their grinning, pouting group photos, but it hung heavily between us until Hallie squeezed me close and told me the past was the past, we were friends, and this was where I belonged.

She was a wonderful person like that. Her friendship quite literally changed my life. No call was ever too late, no favour too big, no conversation off limits. Hallie was so important to me that Lucas and I made her Esme's godmother, a move that reduced her to tears and a role she fulfilled with such love and care. She was the best friend I ever had, and now she is gone.

My pain sticks in my throat, choking and oppressive.

How can Hallie be *dead*? She was only twenty-nine. You don't die at twenty-nine. It's not the way things are supposed to go. You're supposed to be travelling the world, falling in love and building a life for yourself, not leaving it all behind.

And Bree in a coma? What will become of her?

My body shudders involuntarily.

As I spiral downward, my phone buzzes into life, the vibration loud against the dining table.

Sunaina glances at the screen. "It's Amira."

I flush and shake my head. "I can't talk to her, not yet."

Sunaina nods and lets the call ring out. When the phone finally stops ringing, her eyes widen. "Nat, you've got twenty-six missed calls and over fifty texts already."

A hand wraps itself around my throat. Of course I have that many notifications - Coral Bay is reaching out to soak in the misery of the moment with me. In a small town like this, sadness is communal, only I'm not ready to share my grief with anyone. How can I be expected to speak about what has happened when I can barely wrap my head around it myself?

"Can you take care of it for me? Please?"

Sunaina nods, slipping my phone into her pocket. A weight lifts from my shoulders, but my chest is still crushed from the blow of the news. I struggle for air in this grief filled atmosphere.

As if sensing my sadness, Jay reaches for my hand. "Why don't I put Esme in her playpen? Then I'll get you a glass of wine and we can talk for a bit?"

I smile a watery smile. "That would be nice."

"I'll stay too," Sunaina adds supportively.

"If it's a late one, you can sleep in a guest room if you want," Lucas offers.

"I will do – we don't all have the luxury of onsite accommodation!" Sunaina jokes, grinning at Jay.

Lucas and I built a guesthouse next to my painting studio in the garden a year ago. Little did we know how perfect this would be when Jay came into the picture. The onsite accommodation saved her from having to hunt for a place in Coral Bay's notoriously tricky rental market and gave us the benefit of having Jay on hand for Esme at short notice.

After a much-needed cuddle, Jay carries Esme away and Lucas brings me a large glass of wine. He sets two more bottles on the table. Teetotal Sunaina raises her eyebrows but doesn't comment.

The alcohol burns my throat as it makes its way down to my hollow stomach. "I just can't believe it. It feels like a bad dream."

"Me either. It really makes you think, doesn't it?" Sunaina says, taking a delicate sip of water, a sharp contrast to my desperate gulps of Shiraz.

"Life's so short. You never know what's going to happen next."

"It's just like when Blaine Rankin jumped off that building, do you remember?" Lucas asks.

A shiver runs down my spine as the memory of the first time I found out someone my own age had died floods back into my consciousness.

Blaine, the loudest mouth in school with the ultimate playboy reputation, jumped from the roof of his fifteen-storey apartment block in the city at the start of the year. It was a huge shock to everyone. With no suicide note left and no apparent motive, no one knew why Blaine had done it. He had a good job, a beautiful apartment, and a different girl on his arm every weekend – the life he always wanted. He became the poster boy for the idea that you never really know what's going on inside people's heads.

Even though they hadn't seen each other since they were eighteen, Lucas was shaken to the core by the death of someone who had once been so prominent in his life. For the first few weeks after Blaine's suicide, he held me tighter and told me he loved me more. He wore his hurt like it was a suit.

I guess it's my turn to wear the grief suit now.

I wipe my tears and finish my wine. Seconds later, Jay re-enters the kitchen with a baby monitor in her hand. "She's playing with pretty much every toy she owns, but she's okay."

"Thanks Jay. What would we do without you?"

"Struggle," Sunaina winks, and I laugh, an act that feels wrong given the circumstances.

"Someone could do with a top up," Jay says, nodding at me.

Lucas obliges, pouring wine until my glass nearly overflows. I don't stop him.

We sit and we drink. We talk about Hallie and Bree until the words become too painful to say out loud, the stories too raw to recite. It is then that Jay swoops in and tells us about Esme's day. Her stories are a welcome distraction, but the news of what happened to Hallie and Bree has soured the night. Every colour is now sepia. Hallie and Bree lit up a room; I guess it's only right the world would seem duller without them in it.

3

My hungover brain screams as soon as I open my eyes the following morning. I groan, the sound rattling around my head like a pinball machine. Heavy limbed, I fumble for my phone, but it's not on the bedside table. My heart lurches, visions of losing followers and missing deadlines bursting into my mind, until I remember I offloaded it to Sunaina last night.

Panic subsiding, I brave sitting up. My head swims. Blinking my pristine, white bedroom into focus, I look to the clock on the chest of drawers opposite the end of the bed.

"Shit!"

I shuffle to the bathroom and guzzle water from my scooped hands. My mouth is so fuzzed from alcohol I barely taste it. Catching sight of my reflection in the vanity unit, I grimace. Swollen, puffy eyes, skin streaked with mascara and patches of crusted foundation dotted around my face.

"Hot," I mutter, then a stab of guilt winds me. How can I be worried about what I look like when Hallie died yesterday?

Squirming eels of shame writhe around my stomach. I pinch the flesh of my thigh hard so it will bruise, a habit I haven't been able to break since my teenage years. When my guilt is less all-consuming, I let my skin go.

After quickly cleansing, I pad into the kitchen where I find Esme in her playpen and Lucas packing his lunch into his backpack. "You're up," he smiles. "I was going to leave you sleeping this morning."

"I've too much to do today to sleep."

Lucas pours me a cup of coffee then puts his backpack on. Seeing him ready to leave sends a jolt of panic through my body.

"Can you stay home today? Please?"

Lucas brushes a stray strand of hair from my face and cups my chin. "I wish, but I need to be in for the kids. They were just as cut up about Hallie as the staff."

My wobbling chin betrays me. "I don't want you to leave me," I confess.

"I know, babe, neither do I, but you won't be alone. You've got Jay and Sunaina with you, and I'll be back before you know it." Lucas gives me a coffee-tinged kiss then waves goodbye.

I watch him leave, a fizzing mixture of conflicting emotions brewing in my stomach. I know normality needs to restart, but I don't want it to. Without Hallie, life will never be the same again anyway.

Hallie. Just thinking of her name tears me apart.

Sighing, I kneel beside Esme's playpen, waving her favourite teddy in her face. She squawks and takes him from me, grasping the matted toy in her chubby arms.

Tears fill my eyes as my daughter stares at me expectantly, wanting more from me than I can give her today.

"What a bitch you are, Nat," I think scornfully. "Hallie would have given anything for a family, yet you're shying away from your daughter while she lies in a mortuary."

It's just not right.

I'm just not right.

Hallie never got to experience motherhood. It was all she ever wanted, but she never found the right person. The men she met were either already married, commitment-phobes or only with her for sex. Her useless picking ability became a running joke in our group, albeit a sad one.

"Laugh it up ladies, but one day my prince will come!" she would cry. "We will have lots of wild sex and make ridiculously cute babies – then who'll be laughing?!"

343

I smile at the memory, then deflate. If only that was how things had worked out for her.

Jay enters the kitchen and studies me. "Why don't you go for a run? I'll let Sunaina in when she gets here."

Temptation snaps at my heels, but I hesitate. "I don't know if I should…"

"Nat, take some time for yourself. You deserve it. Hell, you need it."

Deliberation over, I flash Jay a grateful smile and jog upstairs to change into my running gear. A few minutes later, I'm out the door.

There are many great running spots around Coral Bay, but my favourite is Hillman's Trek. Not only is it the quietest track, but it's also the most beautiful. In the right season, the path is framed by the most stunning array of brightly coloured wildflowers. The terrain is uphill and challenging halfway through, but once you get past that part you end up at the most stunning lookout that shows all Coral Bay beneath you like a miniature village. It's my favourite spot in the entire world.

My running philosophy is usually slow and steady, enjoy myself and take in the sights, but not today. Today I run to escape what I know. I turn up the volume of my workout playlist and plough down Maple Drive.

The buzz of activity throughout Coral Bay jars with my sombre mood. Everything is open, business as usual. The sky shines bright blue and birds flutter from tree to tree. Last night, the world felt like it was ending, but today life continues. People are still taking card payments and serving customers. People die, but the world keeps turning.

My heart hurts at the sight of it all.

Racing towards Hillman's Trek, I wave to the familiar faces who spot me. Everyone's features twist in sympathy as I dash past, but only Fiona, deli-owner and relentless gossip, tries to stop me for a chat.

"Can't stop – I've got to get back for Esme soon," I lie.

Finally, I reach the start of Hillman's Trek. My feet slap against the ground, dust clouds forming with every punching step. I'm sweating profusely before I reach the incline, but I don't slow down, not even with my heart pumping so hard I can't hear my music over the pounding in my ears.

The path bends before me, rising like a snake about to attack its prey. I push onwards, ignoring the screaming in my calves and straining in my lungs. I don't dare stop. If I stop, I'll fall apart.

Suddenly, I spot a lone figure doubled over in the distance. For a moment I wonder if it's a mirage, the sight of another person on Hillman's Trek so rare, but when I blink, they're still there.

It's a woman. Her clothes are last season's H&M, well-worn and covered in dust from the dry path. Her sports bra is shocking pink and too tight, as are her leggings. As I draw nearer, I discretely eye the bulk of flesh hanging over her waistband and the terrible box dye job on her straw-like, blonde hair.

I debate running past without interacting, but the woman hears my footsteps and straightens up. She turns to face me, and I stop dead in my tracks.

The only sound is that of my racing heart.

"Chrissy? Chrissy Summers?" Her name tumbles from my lips before my brain has time to register who I am addressing. When it does, it shrivels in fear.

The woman blinks, trying to locate me in her memories, but I know she will struggle. I don't look anything close to the person she would remember.

But then again, neither does she.

Chrissy Summers, head of the school, all-star, beautiful, popular, ringleader, bitch, nightmare inducing bully… none of those words seem right to describe her anymore. She looks old before her time, like she has been washed, wrung out and left on the side to airdry. Her wrinkles are deeply etched and savage. A poorly designed flower tattoo takes up most of her left arm and one of a badly executed butterfly spreads across her ribcage like an exploded fountain pen.

There is something incredibly sad about seeing her like this. I almost want to run back home at the sight of what has become of my biggest tormentor, the girl I used to loathe with every breath I took and envy with all my heart.

Most of all I want to run back home at the sight of her back in Coral Bay.

"It's me," I find myself stammering. "Natalie Evans."

Chrissy takes a moment to place me, my real name never the one she called me. When she does, her eyes bulge in shock, then embarrassment sweeps over her. She's thinking what I'm thinking – if people saw us now, they would imagine she was the loser and I was the popular one.

How wrong they would be.

"Natalie," she says, her voice still carrying with it the same harsh edge it always did. She straightens up to her full height, a good few inches taller than I am, perfect for leering over me. Something she had plenty of practise at. "Don't you look different."

"So do you," I add, then cringe. "Older. More grown up I mean, not older, sorry!"

"I guess we all change a little when we leave school," she shrugs, scrutinising me up and down.

Suddenly, I'm fifteen again, cowering in the girls' changing room and trying to get dressed without Chrissy teasing me, without being forced to notice her body, already so curvaceous and adult compared to my own.

In my head, I know I'm not fifteen anymore. I know my outfit costs at least four times as much as hers. I know my skin looks younger, my hair healthier… but still, I am cowering. Still, I am fifteen.

"You look well," she says in a way that makes it sound anything but a compliment.

"So do you."

Chrissy tilts her head. "You always were a terrible liar."

I open my mouth to protest, but I don't waste my time. Chrissy sees right through me. She always did. Those dark, cold eyes see through everything.

"Did you hear about Hallie and Bree?" I find myself asking.

Chrissy cocks her eyebrow. "No?"

"They were in a car accident the other day," I explain. "Hallie's dead."

Her eyes widen. "And Bree?"

"In a coma."

Chrissy blows air out of her mouth, thinking for a moment. I wait for her reaction but the one she gives is not one I expect. Her laughter hits first, cruel and menacing. "Fuck! Those two always were terrible drivers."

I take a step back like I've been slapped.

Chrissy eyes me with amusement. "What? It's not like you were friends."

"We were," I say defiantly, trying to ignore the fact that I'm shaking. "We have been for the last few years."

"You and them?" Chrissy asks, then laughs once more. "Fuck, things really did go downhill when I left!"

I fold in on myself, which only entertains Chrissy more. She looks up at the rest of the track before turning back to me. "Good luck with the run. There's a beautiful view at the top. I think you'll like it," she says before brushing past me and heading back towards Coral Bay.

I watch her go, amazed it's really her, amazed that, even after all this time and when so much about us both has changed, she can still cut me down to nothing without batting an eyelid.

Suddenly, Chrissy stops and turns around, a devilish smile dancing on her thin lips. My heart freezes, knowing all too well that whatever comes next is not going to be pleasant.

"You know, I lost my virginity up there," she says.

"Oh?" I reply, the only thing I can think to respond.

347

"To Lucas Redding. He's your husband now, right?"

My jaw drops.

Chrissy laughs and walks away before I have time to think of a comeback. I watch her disappear, the acidic pink of her neon sports bra burning my eyes. I think of all the things I should have hissed after her, choking on the snarling, bitter words stuck in my throat and blocking my airway. Words I'd never dare say, not to Chrissy Summers.

What I don't think of until much later, though, is how the hell Chrissy knew I was married to Lucas in the first place.

CPSIA information can be obtained
at www.ICGtesting.com
Printed in the USA
LVHW032232300922
729683LV00002B/3